N.J. COOPER
FACE OF THE DEVIL

SIMON &
SCHUSTER

London · New York · Sydney · Toronto

A CBS COMPANY

For Mary

Acknowledgements

As always, I have many friends and generous sources to thank for support and information. Among them are Allen Anscombe, Suzanne Baboneau, Hugh Carter, Stephanie Glencross, Isabelle Grey, Emma Lowth, Jane Gregory, Roland Johnson, and Florence Partridge. I have been much indebted to Norman Doidge's *The Brain That Changes Itself* and Richard Bentall's *Doctoring the Mind* for their insights into current work in neurology and psychology. This is, however, a novel and nothing in it should be taken as any kind of comment on their work.

Prologue

Day One: Wednesday Afternoon

A sudden swell threw Giles sideways. His elbow cracked against the wheel, and pain spiked up his arm like an electric shock.

The momentary agony made him sicker than anything since the markets had crashed around him in 2008 and he'd had to sink three bottles of fizz in twenty minutes to dull the horror. Clutching the funny bone with his other hand, he hoped his blood's warmth would stop the torture on its own this time. He couldn't risk getting drunk today with a tricky sail ahead of him.

Waiting for the pain to recede, he silently added his niece to the list of people he'd be happy to see dead at his feet. There'd been plenty of those over the last couple of years, but he'd never expected to include pretty Suzie until now. The little bitch was twenty-five minutes late and the weather was closing in. As he scowled up at the sky, he thought it looked like a cross between decaying lead and a massive goose turd.

Giles's cheek caught a blast of the freshening wind, as the sea heaved again. He was ready for it this time and rode the rocking deck well enough to avoid any more damage. Like him, the sea was getting angry.

He'd promised his sister he'd deliver her bloody daughter to Lymington by five and if Suzie didn't appear within ten more minutes they'd miss the tide. Which would also make him late for his mates, who'd be waiting for him a few miles east of the Hamble estuary half an hour later.

A thin, panting, rhythmic sound reached him through the creaking of the sheets and the groaning of the timbers of his magnificent old yawl. He leaned forwards against the wheel, enjoying the way the rounded end of one spoke massaged his solar plexus. The words of the rhythmic chant became clearer: 'Oh shit, oh fuck, oh shit, oh fuck, oh shit, oh fuck.'

'Suzie?' he shouted into the murk. 'That you?'

'Uncle Giles! I'm sorry.' The fifteen-year-old's high voice was breathless but much more chirpy than it should have been. 'I got held up. Don't be cross. I've been running as fast as I can.'

She emerged into the light at the foot of his gangway, all tangled blonde hair, bouncing tits and bee-stung lips. The little cow had been in bed with someone. You couldn't miss the signs. Her skin was glowing, even in this filthy light, and she had the smug look of every woman who's ever reduced a man to a heaving, grunting wreck of his former self. So that's why she was late. Making him hang about and risk missing a crucial rendezvous for an under-age fuck. Little tart.

He opened his mouth to tell her what he thought, then saw she was wearing heels: teetering, pointed, destructive heels.

'Kick off those fucking shoes before you come one step closer,' he yelled.

'Can't, Uncle Giles. 's too cold for bare feet. Let me on board. I need to ...' She broke off, and giggled. 'Come on, darling Giley-Wiley, let me on board. I'm cold and wet, and I need a pee.'

Giles saw she hadn't any tights under her stretchy pelmet of a skirt. Silly little cow. He stuffed his hand into his fat wallet and peeled ten twenties off the pile, before running down to meet her.

'I'm not having you on my deck in those fucking heels,' he said, shoving the money at her. 'Run back and buy some socks and deckies at Captain Joe's at the top of the quay. Run fast. If you make me miss the tide, I'll be really cross. And your mother will blame me till the end of time. She's never yet let me forget anything I've ever done.'

'Don't tell her it was me who was late, Uncle Giles.' All the giggles had gone from Suzie's breathless voice now. 'You can't. Promise you won't tell.'

Suzie wound her hands around his sore elbow, hanging on for dear life and completely ignoring the money. He caught a blast of Malibu on her breath. She wasn't going to be much good as crew today. He wondered who it was who'd got her drunk and shagged her, but she was beginning to sound a lot more sober now. He wasn't surprised. His sister might look fragile but her disapproval could fell most people at fifty paces.

'She'll kill me if she thinks I've ... Promise, Giley-Wiley? Please. I'll do anything for you if you promise. *Anything.*'

'We'll see,' he said, grinning to control his sudden fear of what she could make him do. 'Run fast enough, get some decent deckies, and behave yourself on the sail, and I might help you out. But I'm not promising anything. Go on. Fuck off.'

She slobbered a big, wet Malibu-scented kiss on his cheek and ran, disappearing into the gloom. Moments later he heard the sound of her tripping over her feet, then a high cascade of giggles. It was going to be a fun trip.

His elbow was better now, but that was the only thing going for him. He squinted up at the looming grey-green sky and knew that any safety-first, shore-hugging, weekend sailor would get on the phone to explain to both parties why he wasn't going to make it this afternoon, before dumping Suzie at the ferry terminal to make her own way home. But he wasn't one of them. He'd always been a risk-taker.

Suddenly Giles smiled and drew in a huge gulp of salt-laden, tarry air, feeling the old power and the pleasure it had always brought him. Of course he was a risk-taker! How else would he ever have made it so big in the City? Or ridden out the financial storms after the crash and more than doubled his income in retirement here on the Isle of Wight?

Even risk-takers needed to check on the weather sometimes though, so he nipped below to tap the barometer, revelling as he always did in the antique perfection of every plank of his beloved *Dasher*.

A series of pinging drops sounded, muffled by the thickness of what he always thought of as the deckhead insulation but still noisy enough to get through. Rain. Now he had to deal with that as well as a rising gale. Bloody Suzie. They could have been home and dry by now. If the temperature dropped again and the rain turned to snow, he'd be in real trouble. The weight of freezing snow on the sails added to the other odd imbalances in the old boat caused every sort of problem, even for an experienced winter sailor like him.

The cabin floor lurched under his feet as if to underline the danger. Giles looked at his chart table and the course he'd plotted so carefully, timing everything to the second.

Three twenty-two already. The light would soon be gone completely, and the tide with it. He was buggered if he was going to make this journey with the engine and the navigation lights. That would spoil everything.

He reached for his phone and made a quick call to one of the blokes from his investment syndicate, who would all soon be mustering at the tiny bay east of the Hamble estuary to divide the spoils of their latest coup, before cracking open the fizz to celebrate.

'Hah!' Giles laughed out loud as he put down the phone again, then ran up the companionway.

Where the hell was Suzie? It couldn't take seventeen minutes to go fifty yards and buy some deckies. Not if you were using cash.

Ten minutes later his rage was turning to something else, something much less familiar and distinctly uncomfortable. He was getting worried about the little cow. What was she up to now? She should have been safely back a good quarter of an hour ago. More.

Huddled in the shadows thrown by the big schooner tied up next to the *Dasher*, Billy watched big Mr Henty lock his cabin and stumble down the gangplank, shouting the girl's name in his posh voice. When he got nothing back but the screaming of the gulls and the creaking of the reefed sails, he speeded up and sprinted towards the shops at the end of the marina.

Billy waited till he was sure the old man had really gone, then he scuttled up on deck silently, like a vole. This was his chance because no one would be coming this way now.

The crappy lock on the cabin doors wasn't going to hold him back for a second, and he'd only have to be inside for moments. He knew where the food was and the stash of emergency cash hidden behind the galley stove in case Mr Henty ran aground and wanted to pay off any rescuers quick so they couldn't claim the boat for salvage.

He'd explained it all one day when the weather was rough and Billy'd asked what would happen if they needed help. Anyone towing you off a sandbank could make you sell the boat to pay them off if you didn't have the cash to give them there and then.

Billy wouldn't be able to spend any of the money on the Island itself. Too many CCTV cameras near all the shops. But he'd need dosh when he got to the mainland, and this was the best chance he had of getting his hands on some.

The food locker was nearly always full of tins and bottles. Billy's mouth watered at the thought. This wasn't thieving. Not really. Not like the old days. He would've asked to work for his food – and his passage across the Solent – today if things had been different.

Billy had waited so long for the *Dasher* to come back from wherever the old man had taken her that he wasn't going to blow it by asking for anything till Mr Henty had calmed down again.

The lock gave in to Billy's frozen fingers and he was in the warm cabin in seconds. The sudden heat hurt his hands and he knew they'd turn bright red any minute now and then they'd hurt even more.

What wouldn't he give to stow away, safely warm?

Billy shut off the thought at once. Stowing away was too risky, specially now. Mr Henty might look like he was on Billy's side against his crap parents, but you couldn't trust a grown-up. Not when they were cross like Mr Henty was today. Not when you were thirteen and on the run. Specially not when you'd seen everything Billy'd seen today.

He grabbed some tins of beans and sausages and spaghetti from the stock in the locker. His penknife had a tin-opener on it, so he didn't have to worry about getting at the food. When he'd shoved the tins in the backpack he had with him, on top of the stuff he didn't want to think about, he slipped his now-warmer hands in the gap behind the galley stove. Big enough for Mr Henty's fat fins, the narrow space was no problem for Billy. His fingers found the money and tugged it out.

The pile of fifties and twenties looked bigger than ever. It didn't even seem like real money when there was this much; more like a game. Billy didn't know if the old man had a record of the numbers, but, just in case, he pushed his finger and thumb into the middle of the pile and pulled out a big pinch of notes from where they wouldn't be missed, slapping the rest back into shape. He didn't even count what he'd got. Wasn't worth the risk of being found here.

As he turned to climb back on deck, he listened, pushing his head forward and upward to make sure there was no sound of the old man returning. His eye was caught by a patch of dark blue, and he waited long enough to see it was a sweater, soft

and thick. It couldn't be the old man's – too small for that –
but it would fit Billy. He'd need it if it got any colder. He took
it, stuffed it in the backpack and ran.

He didn't want to go anywhere near the alley at the top of
the marina but there was no other way into Cowes itself.

Voices, scared angry voices, came to him as he got near it.
One voice, sharp and female, came over clearer than all the
others.

'A foot. That's what I saw. A naked foot in a new blue deck
shoe with the price label still on it. That's why I looked. And
then there was all that blood. Blood everywhere. They ought
to do something. It's not right. All that blood for anyone to
see. And her face . . .'

Billy pushed his fingers in his ears and ran.

Chapter 1

Day One: Wednesday Afternoon

'So that's it, Karen,' said Max Pitton, Professor of Forensic Psychology at Southampton University, as he shoved his notes on their discussion of next term's responsibilities into the top drawer of his desk soon after half past five. 'Thanks. Now you can concentrate on your book. How's it going, by the way?'

Karen Taylor shivered a little, then decided she owed him honesty: 'It's sticky. The first bit, explaining the concept of cognitive dissonance, is fine, but now I'm stuck on chapter seven, where the self-help chunk begins.'

Max produced a great bellow of derisive laughter.

'Serve you right for trying to make money prostituting your profession,' he said. 'Self-help, my ar— my foot! You won't be having much of a Christmas break then, will you? Going away with Will?'

Holding the thick mass of files between her left elbow and her ribs, Karen fought to remember how much she liked him.

'I'm not sure where we'll be.' She pushed her free hand through her thick blonde hair and looked out of the high window at the grey sleety sky, not even wanting to think of her mother's increasingly shrill demands for a joint Christmas in the parental penthouse in London. 'Will and I are ... we're in discussion about whose flat's going to be best. Mine's bigger, but he thinks his is more comfortable. One more ...' Her voice faded and she didn't let her eyes meet those of her broad-shouldered boss.

Max and her boyfriend, Will, were old friends and she had always thought they might share a few too many of her confidences for comfort, especially now that Will was trying to make her say she'd marry him. She couldn't pretend she'd never thought of it herself, but they both had way too much emotional baggage for her to want it so soon.

'One more what?' There was another laugh somewhere in Max's deep, rattly voice. Karen glanced at him and saw that his dark eyes, which could look unforgiving when he was angry, were now full of friendliness.

'Oh, I don't know.'

Max's jowly face lost its affection in a familiar taunting expression.

'Are you ever going to do the decent thing and make an honest man of him?' he said. 'Or is it too much fun playing hard to get?'

In spite of the warmth of the cluttered office and the thick black cashmere polo-neck Karen was wearing over her skinny jeans, she shivered all over again.

'Don't, Max. I have enough of that from Will.'

'Relationships can't be static, you know. You'll either have to move on to the next stage or get out. What's stopping you?' Max picked up his fat, expensive fountain pen and examined a minute scratch on the barrel. After a moment, he looked up. Some of the kindness was back in his expression, as though he could see how hard the question was for her. 'You know I'm only asking because I care about you both.'

The assurance made her laugh out loud. Max, whose early training had taken place in the days when formal psychoanalytic theory had ruled nearly all branches of their profession, was incapable of ignoring the more Byzantine workings of anyone's mind. No question from him about her feelings or behaviour could be anything but loaded.

'If I knew I'd probably tell you,' Karen said, lying.

The heaviest bit of her own baggage was her difficult first marriage, which had ended with her husband's violent death a decade ago. Will's sometimes seemed to her to be unresolved infantile omnipotence, but she was never going to share that disloyal thought with a brilliant, manipulative man like Max.

'Only probably?' His eyebrows were raised into almost clown-like hoops above his popping eyes.

'What about you?' she said, determined to move them away from the tricky subject of her love life. 'Where are you going for Christmas?'

'Touché,' he said. 'We're more alike in our misanthropy than I ever realized in your early days as a lecturer here, Karen. In a mad moment, I committed myself to eating the wretched bird with my sister, her pompous husband, their screaming hordes of children and God knows how many hangers-on, but there's still plenty of time to find the perfect excuse to duck out of it.'

'You wouldn't.' Karen was sure. 'Not if she's expecting you and making her plans around you.'

'Want to bet?'

Karen nodded. She knew how much genuine warmth lay behind his acerbity and occasionally deliberate mischief-making. 'Ten quid?'

Max heaved a huge sigh, then said:

'OK. OK. So I probably won't dump her at the last minute – unless the weather's bad enough to give me an excuse. But I'd much rather sip some fabulous vintage alone in the company of my books and music and contemplate the heavenly peace of no longer having a wife to tick off my faults one by one.'

He came round the desk to kiss Karen's cheek. His skin was rough with the day's stubble, and he smelled of the strong coffee they'd just shared.

'Think about it, won't you?' he said as he drew back. His voice was more serious than usual. 'I want to be godfather to your first, and your biological clock's ticking fast.'

'Sod my biological clock,' Karen said.

'You won't think like that in a few years. What are you now? Thirty-six?'

Karen's phone rang, vibrating against her thigh. She could almost feel Will's presence, urging her to answer him.

'Pick it up,' Max said. 'And get out of here. I must be off and I need to lock up.'

Karen felt for the phone in her jeans pocket as she left his office. The number on the screen was strange.

'Karen Taylor,' she said into the phone as she walked down the long dull corridor to her own much smaller room.

'Karen? Great,' said a familiar Geordie accent. 'It's Charlie.'

'I recognized your voice.' She allowed her own to sound

dry. The last thing she needed now that Will was being so demanding was the complication of Charlie Trench, officially Detective Chief Inspector of Police, unofficially chief disturber of her peace.

His rough tough dark sexiness, powerful rages, equally powerful neediness, and great company, might not be the reasons why she couldn't yet bring herself to say 'yes' to Will's pleas for a wedding and a family. But they were still a problem.

Karen thought of one evening last summer, when she and Charlie had been working together on the same case and he had suddenly kissed her. She hadn't meant it to happen, and they'd never gone any further, but the memory of his hard muscles and the softness of his lips, and the way her nerve endings had jingled all over her body made him a dangerous proposition for a woman fighting her doubts about committing herself to the very different charms of Will Hawkins, neuro-surgeon and – most of the time – supreme manifestation of rationality and self-control.

'You've changed your number, Charlie,' she said, playing for time. 'Why?'

'Everything changed with my job.'

'I didn't know you'd moved. Are you back with the Met?'

He'd been pushed out of the London force a few years ago after a false allegation of assault had almost wrecked his career, and she was fairly sure his ultimate aim was to get back there and make his detractors admit just what they'd risked losing for ever when they'd shafted him.

'Nope,' he said. 'I'm with Major Crimes on the mainland now. Started a couple of weeks ago. Ironically, my first big case takes me right back to the Island. I'm there now and I need you.'

'Me?' Karen fought a scary upsurge of excitement at the thought of working with him again. But she had to be careful: last time his budget had run out. She couldn't afford to work for nothing now. 'Why?'

'Fifteen-year-old girl murdered,' he said in his usual staccato style. 'We've got the boy who did it. Covered in blood. Found at the scene: squatting in a corner between two buildings, only feet from the body, jabbering nonsense. Dozens of samples of what looks like her hair on him and his on her. The lab's bound to link them. But his denial's got just enough in it to make the CPS itchy. I need a shrink. Will you come?'

'Why me?' Karen was keeping her voice under much better control than her blood pressure, which felt as though it was rising with every second. 'Major Crimes must have dozens of specialist interviewers.'

'The boy's a psychotic schizophrenic off his meds. Highly vulnerable. Unless he's faking it. We've got to have a forensic psychologist in on the interview to stop any defence lawyer's garbage about unfair pressure – or worse – in court. You're one of the best I've seen, and I'd trust you to pick up on any acting.'

'Charlie ...' she began, but he didn't give her time to finish her protest.

'You've good professional standing,' he said, the words emerging like water from a boiling kettle, 'and you're already accredited to take part in murder investigations. I've got enough in the budget to pay you for once. *Will* you come?'

Karen thought of her flat and the emails and messages from Will that were likely to be waiting for her there. Or maybe there'd be nothing. Which would be worse. Maybe all she'd find at home would be silence and coldness. Too much of either would force her to face everything she preferred not to admit about why she dreaded letting anyone else have any rights over her, even a man she loved as much as Will.

Work was the answer. Deep professional engagement could always distract her from anything and everything else, and Will would accept it without question. After all, work was his god, too; and his refuge.

'When do you want me?' she said to Charlie down the phone. 'And where?'

'Thank fuck! Now. On the Island. We're setting up an incident room here in Cowes. At the nick in fact; the big unused room on the first floor. Get the first Red Jet you can. The clock's ticking and our boy's already off with the fairies and on suicide watch.'

'Then why are you questioning him at all? He can't be fit for interview.'

'There's off with the fairies and off with the fairies,' Charlie said impatiently. 'He's been classed as fit for interview with his appropriate adult – that's Dad – and the solicitor. They're happy for us to talk to him. So don't waste time arsing about asking questions. I'll meet you on Fountain Quay and brief you on the way. Hurry, Karen.'

She didn't bother to go home, merely dumping her files in her own office and scooping her old dark-blue parka off the back of the door, before locking up. Her bag had a little cash and plenty of credit and debit cards, BlackBerry, phone and aspirin, and she was already wearing thick-soled ankle boots. What more could she want?

A Red Jet was rocking on the rising sea, clearly on the point of departure. She waved from twenty yards away and began to run.

'You just made it,' said the bloke in charge. 'I shouldn't have waited, but it's nice to have a few passengers in this weather.'

Karen sank gratefully into one of the many empty seats for the fifteen-minute journey across the Solent.

Not until she'd got her breathing back into its normal easy rhythm did she notice quite how rough the waves were today. This sheltered patch of sea was usually like a child's bathwater, which was what made it so appealing for novice sailing lessons. But today the surface was more than lively. She felt lucky the hovercraft were still running. Ferries took much longer, and she wanted to get stuck in to Charlie's case fast.

A strange sensation of being off the leash, like a schoolchild bunking off, filled her mind as she sat by the rain-savaged window watching the swooping waves, thinking about the Island.

Unglamorous, deeply old-fashioned, rather shabby, it was her favourite place in the world. Not only had it been the scene of all the best moments in a chaotic childhood, it was also the setting for the holiday house she hoped would start to rise from the ruins of an ancient shack as soon as the planners cooperated and the weather improved in spring. With or without Will's encouragement. So far he was withholding his approval, and she occasionally wondered whether he was subconsciously using it to barter: you say you'll marry me and I'll show enthusiasm for your building project. If you don't, then I won't.

Charlie was waiting for her on the quay, just as he'd promised. Standing under a light in his usual winter gear of black jeans, black leather jacket, and grey flannel granddad shirt, he looked more than dangerous. Not the kind of man you'd want to meet on a dark night, she thought, checking off the familiar features with guilty pleasure: the round dark eyes, creased in the corners by deep frowns as much as smiles; the high, barely lined forehead under stiff spiky black hair; the sexy mouth; the hard chin.

When he smiled as she hurried across the wet concrete to join him, he revealed teeth that were white and even enough for any advertisement. They were also clenched, and the little muscles at either side of his jaw were pumping. She knew what that meant: he was worried, as well as excited by his big new investigation. His skin was tight and yellow enough to tell her he hadn't been getting his full share of sleep or food for some time.

'Karen,' he said, gripping her elbows so hard they hurt. 'Thanks for coming.'

'It sounded important. Do you know why the boy came off his meds? How old is he anyway?'

'Seventeen.' Charlie let her go and they swung round together to walk up towards the familiar old police station. He was only a couple of inches taller than her five feet nine inches and so she could easily match his impatient strides. 'His shrink doesn't agree with medicalizing distress, believes in something about excess cortisol triggering psychotic episodes, or something like that, and . . .'

'Not James Blazon?'

'Yeah.' Charlie looked suspicious. 'You know him?'

'A bit. Even if I didn't, I'd certainly know *of* him. He's a pretty big name, you know.'

'But you're not mates? You're not going to fudge your report out of . . . you know, professional loyalty, are you?'

'Have you ever known me fudge anything?' Karen allowed herself to sound offended, but Charlie didn't notice. 'I respect his ideas though.'

'Agree with them?'

When Charlie rapped out angry questions like that, Karen was always glad she wasn't a suspect in one of his cells.

'Not entirely. Although he has got a lot of evidence on his side, and he's had some good results with his own way of treating patients. Why isn't he helping interview your suspect? If he already knows the boy, he'd get much more out of him than a stranger like me ever could.'

As she spoke, Karen looked sideways and was interested to see the muscles pumping even faster under Charlie's sallow skin.

'What?' she said. 'What's the matter?'

'I did try to have Blazon in on all the sessions. Like you say, it's the obvious thing to do. But the boy's parents got me stopped.'

'What?' Karen was amazed. 'I mean, why? And how?'

'In his condition, he has to have one of them present when he's interviewed. We sent for them. They got straight on to their lawyers. Moved with the speed of light. And we had an order from on high: Doctor James Blazon is not to be allowed anywhere near the suspect.'

'But . . .' Karen began just as they reached the police station.

'Later, Karen.' Charlie put a hand in the small of her back and ushered her towards the security door between the public foyer, where some eager hands had already strung up sparkly Christmas decorations, and the reality of the small station behind. She heard her name called and whirled round to see James Blazon himself.

His face was grey and haggard. His blue eyes were half hidden behind tightly clenched lids, and his blond hair looked both wispy and unwashed. His expression was that of a man in physical pain.

'Karen?' He sounded amazed, then wary, 'It *is* Karen Taylor, isn't it?'

'Yes. Hang on a sec, Charlie.' She walked towards her colleague and reached out to shake his hand.

He flinched at her touch, then relaxed before gripping her hand between both of his.

'Karen, will you ...? I mean, can you ...? Sorry. Are you here officially? For Olly Matken?' he said, sounding more like a patient than an internationally known expert in the anti-psychiatry movement.

'I don't know the suspect's name.' She glanced over her shoulder at Charlie, who nodded. She turned back to James. 'Yup.'

'Then take care with him. Please.' James was still holding her hand between his. She was aware he was sweating, but she didn't try to pull away. She couldn't choke off any information he might give her. 'He's immensely vulnerable. You could ... I mean, they may already have done incalculable damage. He needs the gentlest possible handling at this point in his treatment. Now that he's beginning to respond, he's on a knife edge. Lost all his old defences and hasn't had time to figure out new ones.'

'I can imagine, James.' Karen made her voice soft. But she couldn't promise anything. From the little Charlie had said, it sounded as though the seventeen-year-old was guilty of murder. Kindness and care could go only so far. 'You have been told what they think he's done, haven't you?'

'Knifed a girl he grew up with,' Blazon said, letting go of her hands and staring at the floor. 'Not just cut her throat or anything, but slashed her all over. Cut after cut. Her body's almost exsanguinated. They say he's denying it, but ... I think ... If he was ...' His voice faltered and died. Then he visibly took a grip on his emotions and added more professionally, 'I'd be amazed if he's proved capable of anything like that.'

Karen thought if James became this deeply embroiled in all his patients' problems, he was going to need a lot of help himself, and soon. Such lack of boundaries would have affected his judgment, and it must be tearing him apart emotionally.

She ignored Charlie, who was now tugging at her other arm, to focus on her troubled colleague.

'James, why don't you think Olly would be capable of doing this?'

James's hurt eyes closed completely. He breathed with great care, then offered what sounded more like an expression of faith than anything else:

'Even when he's been in the grip of paranoid psychosis, Oliver Matken has never manifested any tendency towards violence whatsoever.' He opened his eyes again. 'Does that cover it?'

Chapter 2

Day One: Wednesday Late Afternoon

'I didn't hurt her. All I did was keep her from the devil. He was waiting for the minute my back was turned to have another go at her.' The boy sitting on the far side of the table from Karen spoke so calmly that his statement sounded shocking rather than straightforwardly delusional. No wonder Charlie wanted to know whether he was for real. He wouldn't be the first schizophrenic patient who believed his life was organized by supernatural forces, but she herself had never met any others who spoke so sensibly about the irrational.

Beside him were his father and their solicitor. Neither had said a word since Karen had been introduced into the interview. Richard Walby, the solicitor, was formally dressed in suit and tie and looked concerned but unshaken, while Philip Matken was in gardening gear, with mud and torn tufts of grass still sticking to his ribbed sweater and the knees of his thick khaki cargo pants. A Swiss army knife hung off one of his belt loops and a hank of green twine was falling out of his pocket. His face was that of a man at the extreme edge of endurance.

Apart from his exhaustion and suppressed anger, Philip looked almost exactly like his son, their faces square, with prominent chins, full lips, grey eyes and thick but well-shaped brows. What must it be like, Karen wondered, to watch a mirror image of yourself disappear into wild and dangerous mental disturbance?

'How did you protect her from the devil, Olly?' she asked, holding down her sympathy for both father and son. The only way she would get anywhere with this session would be to keep her own feelings right out of it.

'By straightening her out and pulling down her skirt and wiping off as much blood as I could. I used my sleeves and my fleece. Everything. Then I sat over her so he couldn't get at her again,' Olly said with an earnestness that made him sound like a boy scout, reporting on some fully sanctioned adventure.

'So, if you didn't hurt her – stab her,' Karen went on, with the same matter-of-fact air, 'who did?'

'The devil. I *told* you.' Olly had one of the clearest, most appealing voices she had ever heard. He sounded intelligent and aware, as though he believed he was making perfect sense.

'The devil?' she said, making a question out of her repetition.

'Yeah. That's right.' Olly was nodding, as though pleased that she was catching up at last.

He'd been cleaned up, and there was no trace of blood anywhere on his face, or in his hair, but Karen had been shown photographs of how he'd looked when they'd brought him in.

His short dark hair had been matted in clumps by the dark-purple dried blood, and smears had been rubbed all over his face. His blue jeans and loose, hooded grey sweatshirt had had great splashes all over them. Karen could imagine the stench.

Now he smelled of nothing but soap, like a child just out of his bath, and he was wearing a pristine white paper suit. He hadn't zipped it right up and, in the neckline, she could see faint marks of last summer's tan. The twin bumps of his collar bones and his bobbing Adam's apple made him look very vulnerable.

'I had to tidy her up when I saw her like that, with the blood pumping out of all those slices in her skin, and I had to stay with her to keep him off and make sure he didn't do anything else.' Olly smiled up at Karen, with a little pleading mixed in with the confidence in his expression. 'You can see how I had to stay, can't you, Doctor Taylor? She wasn't decent like that, or safe.'

'I can see exactly why you had to stay,' Karen said carefully, smiling back at him. 'What did the devil look like?'

Olly seemed surprised by the question.

'Like he always does. You know. When he makes you do things you don't want to do.'

Karen saw a tiny movement from his father and let her eyes shift sideways for a second. He met her gaze and she couldn't tell from the pleading expression whether what he wanted to say was 'make this stop' or 'let this be true and he'll be someone else's problem'. She watched him, but he didn't let his eyes drop and she recognized the grit that had kept him going this far.

'Suzie was scared of him,' Olly volunteered, making Karen look back at him. 'All the time. But she had to do the things he said. Like everyone does. So she was trying to run away.'

Now Karen had questions almost bursting out of her brain, and the answers she could imagine jostled them for space, but she couldn't let any of them out. Olly might sound as though he was telling her the devil was inside him, part of him, but she couldn't make that kind of assumption, and she mustn't lead him to say anything that might not be real. The tapes of this interview would form the basis for any prosecution – and defence – that might be heard in court.

'What did he make Suzie do?' Karen asked.

Olly looked puzzled. 'I don't know. It's private, like always. She never said.'

'Did you know her well?' Karen said, trying to find her way into the patterns of his mind. One of her few certainties was that even the most disturbed had their own particular logic, usually well hidden from outsiders.

'Yeah.' Olly smiled with real sweetness. 'Since we were little.'

'Were you in love with her?' Karen asked, looking away so he wouldn't feel crowded by her attention.

'Love? Of course not. I mean, she was OK. I liked her. Sometimes she got on my tits. Not often, but sometimes.' Now Olly sounded almost middle-aged, and weary. 'But she's safe now, so what's it matter?'

'What was making her unsafe today of all days?' Karen asked, with care.

'The devil. I *told* you. She was running away.'

'Running away from you?' She allowed herself one crucial suggestion.

'No. I told you: from the devil. She was running away from the devil.' Olly's voice had risen. 'Not *me*.'

'Does the devil talk to you, Olly?' Karen said, watching him but still not trying to force him to meet her gaze.

'Of course,' he whispered, flicking a glance over his shoulder.

'What does the devil say when he's talking to you?'

Olly looked at her and shook his head. His lips were clamped together, as though he was determined not to let out another word.

In the silence Karen became aware of all the noises outside. Doors banged, some people shouted, others talked normally. Bells rang. Computers beeped. Someone crashed a fist heavily on the door of a nearby room.

Suddenly Olly's whole body jerked and he pushed his right hand over his left shoulder, brushing madly like someone trying to get rid of a shower of dandruff.

'What does the devil tell you to do, Olly?' Karen said, keeping her voice very calm in the face of his growing panic.

He drew up his legs, balancing his feet on the edge of the chair and hugging his knees. Then he opened his mouth at last and produced an eerie keening sound, all on one note: a high, plaintive signal of extreme distress.

Beside him, his father looked ready to faint.

A moment later, Philip leaned sideways to mutter something to the solicitor, who was sitting with them to ensure fair play. He listened, paused, nodded and then turned to Charlie.

'Chief Inspector, my client needs a break. These questions and answers are merely going round and round the same points. Oliver has answered them in the same way both to you and now for the past half hour with Doctor Taylor. You are putting him under quite unnecessary pressure.'

Charlie turned to Karen, who took a moment to decide how far pushing the boy would get her, then she said: 'I think a break would be a good idea.'

Obediently Charlie organized a uniformed constable to take Olly back to his cell.

As soon as the interview room door had closed behind them, Philip dropped his handsome, greying head into his hands, sighing for longer than Karen would have thought he had breath in his lungs. At last the sound ended, and he pushed his garden-stained hands hard against his forehead then up over his scalp, forcing the hair to stand straight up.

'How long is this agony going on?' he asked at last in an ordinary voice.

'As long as it takes, I'm afraid,' Karen said, still concealing her sympathy as well as she could.

'What on earth do you think you're going to get out of him? If he thinks it was the devil who killed Suzie, he's not going to give you the confession you so obviously want. In any case, he's not fit to give a meaningful confession.' Philip looked at his solicitor, who pursed his lips, nodded, then shrugged in a strange set of gestures that Karen assumed were intended to suggest sympathy, uncertainty, and emotional support. 'You must see that.'

'We need to get a clearer picture of what happened, sir,' Charlie said. 'It's possible that Oliver is telling the truth, that he saw someone else kill Suzie. If so, we have to get every scrap of information so we can ...'

'Where's the knife?' Karen asked, having only just thought of it.

Charlie looked at her as though she'd pulled down his

jeans: furious, embarrassed; almost agitated. Philip sighed again.

'That's what this is about, isn't it? You can't find the weapon, and you know our barrister will get Olly off because of that, so you want to force a confession out of him. Christ! If *I* knew where the knife was, I'd tell you. And save us all from this hellish pantomime.'

'You would?' Karen said, fighting the knowledge that she'd seriously pissed off Charlie.

He could be the most entertaining man she knew, and the best flirt ever, but he had a hair-trigger temper and enough dark matter in his mind to make him a scary adversary.

'I bloody would,' Philip said. 'You've no idea what we've been through, how we've tried to get help for Olly, how we've tried to find someone – anyone – who can tell us what to do for him. If he did this, if he killed that poor child, then he can be put somewhere he'll be cared for by experts. He'll be safe and we'll be . . .' Philip stopped talking, and there was so much misery in his eyes that Karen's sympathy ratcheted up to almost unbearable levels. 'Oh, Christ! Don't tell his mother I said any of this.'

'Olly will be safe and you'll be free?' Karen suggested. With no possibility of a record of this question and answer session being needed in court, she didn't have to avoid leading questions.

'Right,' Philip said, gratitude fighting a whole lot of other emotions, the toughest of which looked like shame.

'You're not the first parent of a schizophrenic child to think like that,' Karen told him, with as much sympathy as truth. 'It's more than understandable. You must have a tough life, worrying all the time. And being afraid, too. Is Olly your only child?'

At her question, Philip's face hardened, as though he was summoning up just a little more of that fading endurance.

'Nope,' he said, keeping emotion out of his voice. 'We've an elder daughter, Caroline. Twenty. At university now. Bristol. Clever *and* artistic.' For a second he was almost smiling, then his face stiffened up again. 'And another boy, Matt. He's twelve. A mistake. We never meant to have any more, even though at that stage we didn't know how dangerous it could be.'

'When did you first notice Olly had a problem?' Karen asked, aware that she was making Charlie's impatience worse, but needing to know.

Philip looked away.

'His mother said something was wrong from quite early on. But, well ... I thought it was her imagination. For a long time. She's ... she's always been quite fragile, emotionally speaking.' His whole body stiffened and he sat up straighter, adding briskly, 'Unmistakable trouble started to show about three years ago, soon after Olly was fourteen. When he was sacked from his school – my old school – on the mainland. We had to send him to St Cuthbert's, here in Cowes. Only place that would take him.'

'I'm sorry,' Karen said. 'Has he ...?'

But Philip wasn't listening to her now that he'd been launched on his family's tragic history.

'I don't think my wife and I will be able to breathe properly until Matt's well past his next two birthdays,' he went on. 'They say it's genetic, don't they?'

Karen could feel how much Charlie wanted her to wind up this conversation, but she still needed more information.

'Some do,' she said. 'But none of the evidence is clear enough yet. If you have identical twins and one has schizophrenia there's a fifty per cent chance the other will develop it too. But it's only fifty per cent, so clearly there are other factors that have an effect on the genes involved. Cannabis, for one. Has Olly used that?'

Philip nodded, looking beaten. 'Skunk, unfortunately. That's why he was sacked from school. But how can you stop them trying it unless you keep them tethered at home for ever and watch them every moment of the day and night? What are you supposed to do? How can you ensure they don't wreck their . . . ?' His voice died.

'How long has Olly been treated by James Blazon?' Karen asked, not answering his question because there was no answer to give.

Philip's hands clenched into fists and he beat them against his thighs. 'Ten months. Olly was more or less stable under his old NHS regime. Doped up and not exactly functional, but more or less stable. Then my wife started talking about the miracles Blazon was achieving and she insisted we take Olly out of the system and send him privately to Blazon.'

Tears were welling in Philip's grey eyes, but he paid no attention to them, even when one slipped out to hang on the lower lashes of his right eye.

'She wanted him to be himself again and not a shaking zombie. It's true he did stop shaking when Blazon took him off his pills. But look what's happened now.'

'You think he killed Suzie, don't you?' Karen said.

Philip paid no attention to his solicitor, even when the man pulled at his sleeve. Instead he looked first at Karen and then directly at Charlie.

'How can I not?' he said at last, with sadness throbbing in his voice. 'Poor girl. And poor Jib and Simon. Oh, Christ! How are we going to face them now?'

Karen glanced at Charlie, who supplied a translation: 'Jib is Jennifer Gray, the dead girl's mother, and Simon's her husband. They live on the mainland, but have been holidaying over here all the girl's life.'

'Second husband,' said Philip. 'But he's been on the scene since Suzie was two. You'd never know she wasn't his. Adored her from day one. Thought she was the brightest and best. He'll want to kill us all now. Us and Giles.'

Karen looked round at Charlie again, who said, 'Later.' Then he turned to the solicitor to add, 'How long will your client need for his break?'

Richard Walby shrugged. 'Half an hour?'

'OK. We'll reconvene at seven. Karen!'

She followed Charlie out of the interview room and heard a babble of voices coming from most of the doors along the bleak corridor. His hand grabbed her wrist as he backed into one of the doors and dragged her into an empty office, snapping on the fluorescent strip lights. They flickered uncomfortably until they slowly built up into a single steady glow.

'Don't ever do that again,' Charlie said, leaning against the wall, with his arms crossed over his chest in a classic defensive pose.

I'm sorry.' Karen knew he was talking about her question about the missing knife. 'It just slipped out.'

'Well it fucking shouldn't. OK?' Charlie's bleak gaze warmed a little as he saw how worried she was. 'OK, then. So, do you think Olly killed her?'

'Probably. But that's not going to be much help. Even if he did, it'll be a psychiatric defence. He's clearly disturbed. A good barrister could probably get him off altogether – unless you find the weapon with his prints and DNA on it. Any other evidence of his DNA on Suzie, or hers on him, could be accounted for by his admitted rearranging of the body.'

Karen moved closer to him and laid a hand on Charlie's arm, feeling in its taut readiness what the pumping jaw muscles had already shown her: something about this case was really getting to him.

'You don't need *me* for this,' she said. 'You need a really good SOCO – CSI – whatever you call them now, to find you that weapon. Without it, you've got nothing. Even if Olly did give you a confession, it might not stand up to a determined lawyer.'

Charlie's lips bunched into a stubborn mass of whitening flesh as he fought frustration and anger and probably a lot else along with them.

'I've got the best CSI in the whole region going over that scene like a starving man in an empty grain store,' he said at last, his voice even more clipped and punchy than usual. 'Using the most powerful lights we've got. Naturally. We'll carry on in daylight tomorrow if we haven't found anything tonight, but the lights should be good enough to pick up anything that's there.'

'And presumably you'll be digging up the drains,' Karen said.

'Yeah. Right. And sewers, if we have to. We're already

doing house-to-house all round where they were found.'
Charlie looked at Karen and she saw in his eyes a desperation
that worried her. 'But if you were Olly wouldn't you run that
short distance to the marina and chuck the knife in the sea?'

'Probably. Unless I was beyond that kind of rational behaviour,' Karen said. 'If he was hallucinating and saw his devil, he
wouldn't have thought of anything as mundane as getting rid
of the knife. If he was merely delusional, he might; but then
again he might not. You can't tell.'

'So you don't think he's faking?'

'Absolutely not, Charlie. There's plenty of doubt about all
sorts of things to do with this killing, and Olly's condition, but
not that. I'd risk my professional reputation on it.'

He stared at her for a long, uncomfortable moment. 'You
may have to.'

Karen waited a little, thinking through the consequences,
then said carefully, 'So be it.'

A smile warmed her face as she thought of an old mentor
and the test he had used for serious mental illness.

'What?' Charlie said. 'What's so fucking funny?'

'I was thinking of the sabre-toothed-tiger test.'

'You what?'

'Someone with a personality disorder noticing a tiger
behind him will run like hell. A schizophrenic noticing a tiger
behind him stays where he is, still convinced it's the voices
from the dead telly that are his biggest threat.' Karen paused
for a second. 'I've always found it works. And from the way
Olly was talking just now, it fits him well enough. It's the devil
worrying him, not the girl's death.'

'Great. So where do we go from here?' Charlie was

unusually tentative, which made her want to help more than ever. His mixture of ferocity and overt need aroused a protectiveness in her that Will's certainty never touched.

'After his break, we start again, and I try to get him to give us a physical description of his devil.' Karen tried to will confidence into him. 'That should give us a clearer idea of whether there could – just possibly – have been another real individual involved, instead of a hallucination or delusion.'

'And if not?' Charlie said. 'What then?'

'Then we break for the night, and pray your CSI finds a weapon. How much longer have you got before you have to charge Olly or let him go?'

'We picked him up at ten to four, the first questions didn't start till he'd been processed and his father got here. I arrived at five ten, and the first interview started five minutes later. Five eighteen, if you want to be precise.'

'So you've got ages,' Karen said, wondering why he'd sounded quite so urgent when he'd phoned her. 'Sixty-something hours if a magistrate extends the time. Listen, Charlie, I think if we don't get anywhere with my questions about the physical appearance of the devil, you and I should go and eat something, get home, get some sleep and reconvene if and when the CSI comes up with a knife.'

'OK,' he said, 'but . . .'

Karen heard a familiar woman's voice from outside the door and held up her hand to quieten Charlie.

'Isn't that Eve Clarke?' she said, remembering the difficult sergeant, whose passionate but unwanted determination to protect Charlie from the rest of the world had made her almost impossible to deal with in any civilized way.

He nodded. Karen listened more carefully, wondering with a kind of shamefaced satisfaction just how Eve was filling her life now that Charlie's job had moved him to the mainland.

'Of course it's not your fault, sir,' Eve was saying out in the corridor. Her voice was far softer than usual. She sounded as though she really meant to be comforting. 'You mustn't blame yourself.'

'How can I not?' asked the plummiest of male voices. 'If I'd gone to buy her shoes for her, or even gone with her to buy them, she wouldn't be dead now. It *is* my fucking fault. And nothing you or anyone else can ever say will make it any better.'

'The uncle,' Charlie said in a low voice. 'Giles Henty. I'll fill you in as we eat. Let's just let them get clear of the passage.'

Glad he'd accepted her advice, Karen turned back to him, ready to ask another question, but a bellow from further away distracted them. It was followed by a confusion of shouted curses. Over it all, Karen heard the plummy man yell, 'You irresponsible, dangerous fuck! Encouraging that psychopathic boy to leave off his pills so he kills the first girl he sees. We've all trusted you for months, you bastard. Now this! If I had my way, you'd be in court on a charge of inciting murder. You ...'

Karen moved towards the door. 'Come on, Charlie! Shouldn't you do something? There's a fight going on out there.'

'The desk sergeant can handle it. Leave it to him. It's what he's there for. And Eve can make a note of anything useful either bloke says.'

As they waited, Karen wasn't surprised the uncle had switched from anxiety about his own part in Suzie's death to accusing James Blazon. There was nothing like guilt for making you want to blame someone else.

Outside, the shouts gradually diminished. Doors banged. High heels clattered on the hard floor outside. At last Charlie moved. Opening the door, he looked out.

'Ah, Eve. Come on in, and tell us what that was about.'

'Us?' she repeated in the same resentful, nasal accent that had once been all-too familiar to Karen. 'Oh, it's you. I didn't know Charlie had involved you in this.'

Eve flexed her narrow nostrils, as though Karen smelled of rotting rubbish, which seemed unfair. She was pretty sure no one would catch anything but a faint whiff of CKOne from her skin or clothes.

'I brought her in to talk to the boy,' Charlie said. 'What *was* that all about?'

'The uncle, Giles Henty, was giving me a statement – everything he remembers about this afternoon. And a DNA sample for elimination purposes. He gave me everything I asked, like a lamb really. It's what you wanted, isn't it?'

Charlie nodded. Karen hid a smile. Not even Charlie was immune to the urge to placate Eve in her unjustified aggression. She looked thinner than ever today in a tight skirt suit made of thin stuff in a khaki colour that gave her skin a muddy look. As usual she was showing off her tiny ankles with high heels, which had the unfortunate effect of keeping the muscles in her calves permanently bunched.

'Not surprisingly,' Eve went on, unaware of Karen's critical assessment of her clothes, 'Mr Henty blames himself for sending the victim off in the dusk to buy something more suitable to wear on deck than her stilettos. But he wasn't to know there was a killer waiting for her. He caught sight of Matken's psychiatrist in the foyer and let fly. I can't say I blame him. These shrinks always ...'

She coughed, looked Karen in the eye and clearly decided to leave her intended insult hanging, unsaid but obvious.

'Did he actually hit James?' Karen asked, curious about the violence she'd heard in the uncle's voice. After all, according to the account Charlie had given her, the uncle had been very close to where the girl's body was found, and not all that long after she'd been killed. In any search for other suspects, he'd have to be on the list of targets.

Eve glared at her, then turned to face Charlie. 'We managed to stop any actual contact between the two men, and I made the psychologist wait until Mr Henty had driven away, but of course I can't say what will happen off our premises.'

'No, right, Eve. Thanks,' Charlie said, giving her another unnecessarily pacific smile. 'There's not a lot more any of us can do tonight until the CSI reports. We've taken statements from everyone in the party that found the body. Doctor Taylor wants one more interview with Olly. After that we'll let the doctor in again, then get him bedded down for the night.'

'Fine,' she said, ignoring Karen. 'There is one thing you should know.'

'Like?'

'Mr Henty said he was sure Suzie had been making love before she came to his boat,' Eve explained. 'He's never heard of a boyfriend, so we should—'

'Find out more,' Charlie said, interrupting as though he couldn't bear to wait for her to finish the sentence. 'Yeah. The PM will be done first thing in the morning, and we'll know then if he was right. In the meantime, I'll get a call in to her parents.'

'Right,' Eve said. She moved closer to him, turning her back on Karen and added, 'When you've finished with Matken tonight, d'you want to eat? I've got some lasagne ready to go.'

'No thanks,' he said, without a pause or the slightest tact. 'I'll be going back to the mainland with Karen. You know how to find me if anything turns up.'

As Eve moved away from him and scowled, the sight of her face made Karen think of all the mythical creatures that could turn an enemy to stone with a single glance. Charlie noticed it too, and did his clumsy best to make things better.

'Didn't you say you were busy yourselves over here?'

Eve bit her lower lip. 'Yeah. We've got a thirteen-year-old boy gone missing. Clearly run away, but the parents won't believe it. They're talking about abduction and worse. Since the news got out about Suzie's body, they've been on the phone non-stop. She was only two years older in real terms, but ...'

'But nearly a decade in experience and emotional development,' Karen suggested in her friendliest manner. 'A rich fifteen-year-old girl, already having sex, is a world away from most thirteen-year-old boys. Who is he?'

'Name's Billy Jenkins.'

Charlie groaned, but there was a light in his eyes that intrigued Karen.

'I can see why you're not so worried, Eve,' he said. 'If anyone of that age can look after himself, it's Billy.'

'Who is he?' Karen asked, throwing a brief smile in Eve's direction, in the vain hope of easing her dislike. 'Can you fill me in?'

'We must've pulled him in a dozen times while I was here,' Charlie said for her. 'Thieving, damage to cars, causing trouble, harassing tourists for money, breaking windows with his football. No evidence because he knows every CCTV camera in the area and how to get about without being caught on them. A right little tearaway. But nothing cruel about him, no torturing animals or scaring old women. A real boy.'

'That's the one,' Eve said. 'He's the eldest child – of three – of a long-standing Island couple, Karen. Mum does seasonal work in one of the hotels. Dad was made redundant when the wind-turbine factory closed. Hasn't got another job. He's find-ing it tough on benefit. Lots of family friction. My view is Billy got bored with all the shouting and took himself off for some private fun. He'll be back home as soon as he's cold and hungry enough.'

'Still,' Karen said, glancing out of the window into the darkness and listening to the wind buffeting the building and rattling the glass. 'It's not a night for anyone to be living rough, least of all a child. Just before Christmas, too. Did he take anything with him?'

'All the money in Mum's purse,' Eve said with exaggerated patience, as though Karen was the biggest waste of time. 'A few clothes. Easily portable food. Two favourite books: Harry Potter and Terry Pratchett. His second-hand iPod, and his school backpack: dark-blue nylon with a Nike-tick logo.'

Eve paused, which allowed Karen to say, 'If he took all that, he was obviously running away. I think you're right not to be worrying about abduction, Eve.'

'I'm glad to hear it.' Eve's voice was sharp with a sarcasm she would never use with Charlie. She pressed both hands to her hip bones, then slid them down her thighs, as though to smooth some of the creases in her tight skirt, or perhaps to show off how much thinner she was than Karen. 'But we still have to find him. I must get on. Charlie, see me before you go, won't you?'

'If I can, Eve. Thanks.' He looked down at his plain steel watch. 'Come on, Karen, we must get back for the next session with Olly. He's had his half hour alone with his devil. That should've softened him up.'

Chapter 3

Day One: Wednesday Evening

An hour and a half later, Karen was sitting in her favourite Southampton restaurant with Charlie in the seat usually occupied by Max.

Mario's Pasta House was their local in the Old Town, and she and Max had eaten here more times than she could count. She'd been half afraid she might see him here tonight and had wondered how – or if – she would explain Charlie's presence, but luckily there was no sign of Max today.

'Gooda evenin', Dotoressa,' said Mario, coming up to make infinitesimal and unnecessary adjustments to the position of the Christmas Dinner Special Menu on the thick pink table-cloth. 'Is the *professore* comin' tonight?'

'No, I don't think so,' Karen said. 'And my guest has never been here before, so he will probably need an ordinary menu.'

'*Subito*.' Mario flourished a small plum-coloured leatherette booklet with his restaurant's name in flowing golden letters embossed on the front. 'But for you, Dotoressa, spaghetti puttanesca, isn' it?'

Charlie's eyes sparkled at Karen over the top of the menu. She was relieved to see he could enjoy Mario's hammy performance even with the disappointment of Olly's refusal to give them anything useful about his devil in their second interview.

'I'll have the lamb in red wine and rosemary,' Charlie said, snapping the menu shut and handing it back. 'It sounds great. Thanks. Drink, Karen?'

'I usually have the house red, but if you'd rather have a beer . . .' she began.

'House red's fine. We'll have a carafe. Great. Thanks.'

As soon as Mario had sped off, Charlie laughed out loud. 'Oh, Karen, I'd never have pictured a cool classy blonde like you in a place like this. Or eating something like spaghetti puttanesca. You do know why it's called that, don't you?'

'I know of two possible reasons,' she said, not feeling at all cool. 'I prefer the one that says it was the favourite cheap food of the Neapolitan whores, so I think we might just leave it there.'

Charlie's shoulders shook as the laughter overtook him. 'I'll bet you do.'

'Besides,' she said, with dignity, 'it's stuffed with umami.'

'What the hell's oo-marmie? Sounds like something from *Little Women*.'

Charlie's breadth of childhood reading had always intrigued Karen, but never more than now. Who would have believed a man like him would know anything about Louisa May Alcott's girlie classic?

'It's the word the Japanese use for the fifth taste, after bitter, salt, sweet and sour,' she said, looking at Charlie with severity mixed in with her own suppressed laughter. 'Found in dozens of their ingredients *and* tomatoes, anchovies, Parmesan, etc. All the puttanesca ingredients.'

He leaned back in his chair, stretching out his legs, as though they'd been cramped in too small a space for too long. His leather jacket creaked against the wood of the chair. The muscles in his jaw were still.

'It's good to be with a mate, doing ordinary things,' he said at last, dropping the teasing note from his voice.

'Most new jobs are tough till one's been in them a while,' Karen said, with a kinder smile. 'No allies to rely on and too many private languages to learn. Fragile egos to circumvent, too.'

'It's not so much those,' Charlie said, scratching one ear lobe, 'as the pace of life. On the Island the snails are the quickest things around.'

Karen knew him well enough to be sure the change of pace was only a displacement for whatever was at the root of his anxieties.

'What's happened to the flat you were buying in Cowes?' she asked, feeling her way.

'Let it,' he said, with a shrug that was clearly supposed to express lack of angst. 'Fairish rent, given it's winter now. Should be enough to wash its own face; pay the mortgage and the agents' fees, I mean. But if interest rates go up like they say they will, I'll be in shit creek, so I'm only renting here for the moment till I know where I am, and if I'm going to be staying here in Scumpton.'

'Whereabouts is your place?' Karen asked, suppressing a shudder at the thought of those likely to rise interest rates. She had huge debts of her own, which she had no idea how she'd ever pay off – unless her book became a bestseller, which didn't seem very likely the way it was going so far. 'And when did you start calling the city *Scumpton?*'

He gave her the address and all the warm cosiness that had been building between them was sucked into a cold black hole in her mind. His rented flat was about four minutes' walk from her own loft apartment only three streets from where they were sitting.

'I have seen you once or twice,' he admitted, looking round for Mario. 'Where's that wine?'

Karen waited until their glasses had been filled with the slightly bitter, cherry-flavoured Chianti that Mario shipped in bulk from his home town. She'd once asked him why he didn't serve food from the same locality and he'd shrugged and explained that when he'd first opened up, no one in England wanted Tuscan dishes, and he'd gone for the anglicized Neapolitan style that had always worked for his rivals.

'Why didn't you come and say hello, Charlie?' she asked, when Mario had gone again.

He grinned. 'You had Will with you, didn't you?'

Her phone rang, and she knew it was Will himself calling. She glanced at Charlie, whose face had reverted to its earlier tension. He shrugged and waved towards the phone, with a gesture that said: pick it up.

'I won't be long,' Karen said.

She left the table, thinking of the moment earlier on, when Charlie's call had dragged her away from Max. One day she might learn to keep her phone well and truly switched off. But how could she until she'd sorted out what she was going to do with her life?

'Hi, Will,' she said, having seen his number on the screen. 'I'm in Mario's. Where're you?'

'At your flat,' he said, his voice carrying nothing she could hear beyond a careful avoidance of irritation. 'With a surprise dinner I'd thought we might share to celebrate your end of term and my successful removal of a glioma this morning. I suppose I should've phoned to check you'd be up for it. Have you got Max with you? He didn't say anything about eating with you when we spoke this afternoon.'

'No,' Karen said, part of her mind urging her to lie, the other part yelling at her that if she lied to Will, she would lose something very important. 'Charlie Trench. I've been over on the Island, interviewing a schizophrenic murder suspect for him. We've just ordered our main courses. Would your food wait for tomorrow? Could you come and join us here?'

'Can't you ditch him? If he's in the middle of a murder case, shouldn't he be working through the night and eating at his desk?' Will's voice was sharp with the disapproval that Karen sometimes felt was his default mode. 'I thought they didn't let up till they'd got their killer these days.'

'I'm not sure I can ditch him at this point,' Karen said, answering the only important question. 'Why not turn off the cooker, put the fresh stuff in the fridge and join us? I'll get Mario to grill you a steak. It'll be done medium rare by the time you get here.'

Will didn't answer. She waited, hoping he'd give in. When he didn't, she tried again.

'Come on. Please. I can't abandon Charlie now that we've ordered. We're only here for half an hour or so – a brief refuelling before he goes back to work. Please, Will.'

'All right,' he said stiffly, after a long pause. 'I'll come for a steak. And order me some spinach, will you?'

'Great,' Karen said, before shoving her phone in her pocket and going back to Charlie to explain herself – and Will.

'I know he seems like a control freak,' she said, 'assuming I'll be there and available to eat his surprise food, but . . .'

Charlie shrugged and sucked down some more Chianti. 'If he presses your buttons, that's up to you. I like to give women surprises myself. And I like to know they're at home, waiting for me when I have a minute to spare. Don't give him too hard a time.'

To her great relief the men behaved impeccably. Charlie got to his feet as soon as Will's slight fair figure appeared in the doorway, and they wrung each other's hands with almost as much manly bonding as Ben Hur and Messala showed in the film, when they clanked their great arm rings and hugged each other before their more important loyalties dragged them apart.

Charlie then tactfully sat down again and poured wine into the third glass for Will, leaving him to kiss Karen and answer her questions about the operation that had gone so well this morning.

'It's a pity you brain surgeons can't do anything about schizophrenia,' Charlie said when they took their chairs at last and Mario came bustling forward with the food.

'There's a lot of experimental work under way now,' Will said, 'and interesting exploration of the effects of deep-brain stimulation, but the horrors of early attempts to cure mental illness with surgery are too vivid for anyone in my world to be knife-happy.'

He shot a quick, reminiscent smile at Karen and she felt as though he'd taken her hand under the table. The first time they'd met, as Max's guests in this very restaurant, she had savaged him for the excesses of his 1950s predecessors, whose clumsy attempts to separate bits of the brain or create 'therapeutic lesions' had resulted in terrible cognitive damage to their patients.

In a way it was a timely reminder. Karen had lost her temper completely that night and shouted all kinds of insults at Will. He'd weathered everything she'd said and done, answered her reasonable points reasonably and fought her on the others. Then they'd left Max alone, gone to a favourite bar and on home to her flat, where they'd made love with a freedom she'd never felt until then. She had given Will rights – emotional rights – over herself that night, so why was she still so twitchy about the much less important ones he wanted now?

'As I understand it,' he was saying to Charlie, 'there's still no general agreement about what schizophrenia is, or how it's caused.'

'Is that right, Karen?' Charlie asked, putting down his fork. 'I thought ... I mean, everyone's been talking about our suspect as though he passed some kind of test and was admitted to the ranks of fully qualified schizophrenics three years ago.'

'It's definitely right. Schizophrenia isn't one single illness; it's a collection of, well, you could call them syndromes, I suppose. Or symptoms. No one knows what causes it, beyond a probable genetic link, perhaps triggered by an auto-immune response to early infection, or infection in utero, diet, stress, insecure attachment, victimization. Any number of things.'

'And cannabis,' Charlie said, with a typical police officer's liking for something concrete amid all the variables. 'That's what you said today.'

'Yes, that is pretty well established,' Karen said. 'Adds something like a forty per cent increase in risk in susceptible individuals.'

'Another reason to blame all the posh gits who play around with drugs and don't come to much harm themselves, assume there's no problem for anyone else either and encourage the whole filthy fucking trade.' Charlie swallowed some more wine, then added, 'I'd like to string up the whole lot of them.'

Will's spare, square-jawed face had taken on an expression of respect he didn't often show, and Karen leaned against his shoulder to express her appreciation.

'I couldn't agree more,' Will said, reaching for his own glass. He raised it, as though in a toast, then took a small sip, before lowering the glass and staring straight at Charlie. 'It's lucky our own drug of choice doesn't carry all that illegal baggage, isn't it?'

Karen withdrew her shoulder, hating the idea that he'd faked the respect she thought she'd seen. Surprisingly, Charlie didn't seem bothered.

'That's the point, though, isn't it?' he said. 'Alcohol's legal, so it doesn't put you in touch with the scrotes destroying whole communities.'

'We're shifting ground here,' Will said. 'If you're talking health risks, alcohol probably does more damage to most brains and bodies than drugs. If you're talking about the crimes associated with the trade, then that's a whole different matter.'

Charlie checked his watch in the familiar gesture and swallowed down the last of his sliced lamb in red-wine sauce. 'I must get on. Got the PM first thing tomorrow, then interviews with the girls' parents. Karen, can you help me with those?'

She felt Will stiffen at her side.

'Why do you want a psychologist for them?' she asked Charlie, playing for time.

'Because the state of the body may tell you about the killer's motives and because you'll get more out of the parents than I will. I want your take on the relationships. We may think we know who did it, but in a case like this we've got to explore every avenue. Stepfathers of sexually active teenage girls . . .' Charlie let the sentence fade away without finishing it.

Karen knew the last few words could only have been something like 'are natural suspects'.

'Fine,' she said, partly because she'd hated the way Will had mocked Charlie, and partly because she was genuinely curious about Olly's devil, as well as interested in the case. 'Where shall I meet you?'

'I'll pick you up outside your building at 8.30. OK?'

'Yup.' Karen didn't look at Will. She wasn't going to ask his permission to do her own work. In any case, on the rare weekdays when he stayed at her flat he was always gone by seven.

Charlie pulled his battered wallet out of the back pocket of his jeans and hurried over to Mario.

'He shouldn't pay,' Will said, waving to Mario over Charlie's head. 'This is our bill.'

The Italian looked from one to the other, listened to something Charlie said, then sent Will an apologetic smile before escorting Charlie to the credit-card reader.

He raised his hand and grinned at them both from the restaurant door and disappeared.

'He *is* a good bloke,' Will said, as though he'd been weighing up the evidence on both sides. 'And I can see he's really up against it with this case, so you don't have to look daggers at me, Karen. I don't grudge him your help for one second.'

A smile forced its way through her irritation. 'I thought you were being a bit superior. That was all. On the ground-shifting allegations about drugs and drink.'

Will's face twitched, and a little colour seeped up towards his perfect cheekbones. 'God no! I realized I was sitting here pontificating about the damage done to society by drug dealers and about to swill down a whole lot of mind-altering, brain-damaging, poisonous liquid myself. I wasn't getting at him. I just felt like the world's biggest and most pompous fool.'

As Karen asked herself how you couldn't love a man so ready to say that kind of thing about himself, he grabbed her thigh with a friendly squeeze and said, 'Now, shall we go home for pudding?'

'Why not?' she said. 'What is it?'

He faced her, his head on one side as though trying to work out a route through a complicated map.

'Surprise,' he said at last and got up to lead the way out.

Control freak, she thought ungratefully.

'But it should be light enough to be fully digested before you face the challenge of tomorrow's post-mortem,' Will added. 'It'll be your first, won't it? I hope you'll be able to cope.'

Chapter 4

Day Two: Thursday Morning

The brown-haired devil opened his cruel mouth to confess and issued a loud continuous trilling, which turned into the alarm clock's morning greeting. Karen flung out an arm to silence the clock, then rolled over and buried her face in the pillow, trying to catch the tail of the dream that was disappearing from her mind. It had something really important in it. She was sure of that much. But she couldn't get hold of it. The devil was gone and all the information with it.

A second later, fully awake, she knew her brain had been sending false messages. She also knew she must have been on the point of waking when the alarm went. Deep-sleep dreams didn't leave these vivid pictures. Lifting herself on to her side again, she smiled at Will, who was lying watching her.

'Hi,' she said, working hard to get her eyes to focus. 'Sleep well?'

'Perfectly.' He raised a hand to push some of the hair out of her eyes and turned the gesture into a caress. 'It's only seven thirty. You don't have to get up quite yet, do you?'

The thought that he must have the day off or he wouldn't
still be here was chased by the idea that he'd made no protest
when she'd agreed to meet Charlie and go off to the post-
mortem with him today. Will let his stroking hand move from
her head to her neck and then inside the unromantic tartan
pyjama jacket she was wearing against the cold. Her nipple
hardened under his fingers.

She rang her tongue around her mouth, wishing the night's
exhalations hadn't made her teeth feel so furry. Will preferred
making love in the morning when they'd both slept off their
work-induced stresses, but she always wanted a shower and a
vigorous teeth-cleaning session first. Even so, she smiled. He'd
been so generous about not insisting that she spend his free
day with him that she owed him this, at least.

He moved closer.

Billy woke and felt his neck, which was stiff and sore again.
His only pillow was his rolled-up backpack and it wasn't
enough.

Even from here he could see the knife, all bloody in the
plastic bag he'd picked up off the street for it on the way back
from the *Dasher*. He'd have to do something with it today, but
he still didn't know what. The best thing could be to drop it in
the sea, but if he did that from the marina, it might get caught
by one of the boats or its ropes. Or it might get washed back
up. And he might not even get as far as the marina. Someone
could stop him on his way between here and there. If they
searched him and found the knife . . .

Maybe he should've done it yesterday – dropped it over the
side when he was on board the *Dasher* – but he'd just wanted

to get his food and money and be out of there fast, before someone got to him and started asking questions he couldn't answer, and made him go home to his mum and dad. Where he never wanted to be again.

He shivered. In spite of the blue sweater he'd nicked, he was cold as well as scared, like he'd never been scared before. The sweater was too big for him, and it had blood off the knife drying on it, but it felt good. It was the only soft thing he had now. His eyes flickered as he looked round the empty room. Maybe there was somewhere here he could put the knife so no one would find it and start asking questions he couldn't answer.

Sounds came through the wall from the restaurant next door. Sleeping all night was wrong. He should've used the darkness to get out and hide the knife before the cooks came to work. If they heard him moving about now ...

He rolled out from the sleeping bag he'd brought from home and crawled silently all over the floor, feeling for a loose board. There was usually one somewhere in an old room like this.

Half an hour later, Karen was standing under the boiling shower, while Will made the coffee. She kept her head out of the heavy stream of water. There was no time to dry her hair properly. Not that it mattered: she didn't think anyone would expect her to tart herself up for a post-mortem; and Suzie Gray's parents had much more important things to think about than how a visiting psychologist looked.

Reluctantly Karen turned off the jets, wrapped her towel round her dripping body and padded out to Will, leaving damp footmarks all over the floor. She would never have done that in his flat, but in her own she still felt free to live life as *she* wanted it.

'Shower's all yours,' she said, stroking his cheek.

'I'll wait. I've got all morning.'

'Will, I'm sorry I'm not going to be here. If I'd known you'd have the day off, I could have ...'

'Don't worry.' He was smiling easily, not in the tight way he had when he was trying to contain some impolitic emotion. 'I should have warned you I was coming.'

Karen felt her forehead contract, trying to understand what he was doing, and failing completely. After last night's unscheduled appearance and his recent demands for a formal commitment to a life of domesticity and babies, this morning's calm and affection were so unexpected that she felt seriously unsettled.

'In any case,' he went on, pouring out the coffee, 'with the police wanting your expertise you'd have to go. I take it they are paying you this time?'

'Yes.'

'There you go. A fee. Professional kudos. You need both.'

'What will you do all day?'

'I thought I might have a crack at my Christmas shopping. Shall I cook tonight?' Will's voice was as easy as his smile, and Karen felt more and more uncomfortable.

He'd never been any sort of bully, but he had been so sure of his place in the world and in her life that he'd never hesitated to tell her what to do. This kind of submissiveness was wholly out of character.

'I think I can rescue last night's menu,' he went on. 'Then

I'll leave at seven tomorrow and go back to work. How's that?'

'Great. I mean, terrific. Thanks. I'll be back as soon as I can.'

'OK. You'd better get dressed though. You've only got eight minutes left.'

Karen grabbed a mug of black coffee and took it back to her bedroom with her, taking great slurps in between putting on a well-cut pair of black trousers that showed off her long lean thighs, a clean black polo-neck sweater, and a soft camel jacket. She used enough eye make-up to add drama to her button-like face, which she'd always thought far too small for anyone of her height, and added a quick spritz of CKOne. To give herself an air of authority she bundled up her shiny blonde hair in a loose chignon.

When she kissed Will on the way, he laid his head briefly on her shoulder. He was only a couple of inches taller, so he didn't have to stoop far.

'I loved this morning, Karen,' he said. 'You're ... you're amazing.'

He straightened up, saying with a much more familiar confidence: 'Don't let the PM get to you. Dead bodies can't feel. It may look alarming – or disgusting – but if you focus on what it can tell you, there's nothing there to fear. OK?'

'Thanks, Will.'

She left him by the open door of her flat, still wearing his pyjamas and with his long, bony feet bare. Another change of habit; in the old days he would never have been caught in even a semi-public area like this without his clothes or shoes. He waved as she turned to smile at him, before shutting the door. She pushed the button to call the lift.

Nothing happened. None of the familiar wheezing, whining sounds came up the shaft. One of the tenants in a flat lower down the building must have been blocking the doors open, as they so often and so irritatingly did. Karen couldn't wait for more than a minute before running down the stairs, to emerge on to the pavement just as Charlie drew up in a smooth-looking dark-grey car that was new to her: an Audi. He must have acquired it along with his new responsibilities and extra pay.

'Will didn't make trouble for you then?' he said as she settled in the front passenger seat.

'No.'

'You sound surprised,' Charlie added, shooting a quick sideways glance.

'He's suddenly got all sweet and cooperative and it's freaking me out a bit.'

Charlie laughed. 'Enjoy it while it lasts.'

'How long till we get there, Charlie?' Karen asked, not wanting to share too much of her dealings with Will.

'Seven or eight minutes before we get to the mortuary. They usually do Island victims at St Mary's in Newport and mainland ones in Winchester, but there's a big backlog in both places, and we can't wait, so we've had the body brought here.'

'What can I expect from the post-mortem?' Karen hoped she could remain professional. 'Will I actually be there, smelling the smells, or . . .?'

'You'll be behind a full-length glass screen. You can see and hear, but you won't smell a thing. You'll be fine. And there are plenty of seats, if you come over queer. Here we are.'

He parked in a marked space outside a nondescript grey building, showed his warrant card at the desk and signed them both in, before leading the way to a sinister-looking door.

Giles looked down at his wife and wondered if she was faking. In the old days he wouldn't have been surprised to see her still out of it at half eight, but since Blazon had taken her off the sleeping pills as well as the anti-depressants, she'd been a lot less dozy.

She was still gorgeous, Giles had to admit, even though she was pushing thirty-eight now. With her red-gold hair spread out over the pillow, and her little tits making pointy hillocks in her nightie, she looked like some pre-Raphaelite angel.

Had Bloody Blazon seen her like this? Were they shagging? Was that why she was so cheerful these days, even though she'd chucked all her pills down the bog?

She certainly came home from her sessions with the shrink in a glow. But if she was screwing him, would she still open her legs for her husband? Which she did. With ever-increasing enthusiasm as she cheered up generally. It was Lucy's new zest for sex that had made Giles talk up Bloody Blazon all round the Island, so maybe he was twice guilty of getting Suzie killed.

Oh, Christ, Suzie!

Sometimes he could block out all thoughts of her death for minutes at a time. Then they'd come rushing back: how he'd gone thundering up the marina and heard the bloody passers-by screaming; how he'd looked down at Suzie's ripped and torn body, lying in the fucking psychopath's lap. If the passers-by hadn't held him off, he'd have strangled the boy there and then.

Don't think about it, Giles ordered himself in silence. But it was hard. Because it was his fault.

If he hadn't told everyone how good Blazon was with loonies, the Matkens probably wouldn't have sent their psychopathic son there. And if they hadn't, he'd still have been a shaking zombie stuffed with pills, instead of strong enough and mad enough to kill Suzie. But even that wouldn't have mattered if Giles hadn't sent her to get some deckies on her own, so she ...

Lucy's eyeballs moved suddenly beneath the lids, making Giles feel even more chunderous. It was like watching a corpse suddenly come to life. Then the lids flicked up. For a second she stared up at him, her pupils dilating like someone on a bad trip, terrified and hallucinating.

Giles didn't think she had been faking sleep. She wasn't a good enough actress for that. Her eyes were soon smiling as her tongue slid out from between her lips and she shifted her legs about under the duvet, stretching them. Then she smiled up at him with her lips as well and pushed her arms out from under the duvet, holding them up towards him, like a child wanting to be picked up.

'Morning, darling,' she said, blinking and moving her mouth as though there was some cud there to chew.

'Morning, Lucy. Got to go, I'm 'fraid. You be all right today?'

'Of course.' She blinked again, twice, still not bothering to raise her head from the pillow.

'What've you got on?' he asked, showing interest like Bloody Blazon had advised all those months ago when he first took her on and demanded an excruciating hour with Giles as the price of his commitment.

Lucy rubbed her eyes and smiled again.

'Nothing much. I want to sort out the last few arrangements for the shoot, and I thought I might make the puddings and freeze them. I don't want to be in too much of a rush on Saturday. And I need some new boots, so if I can't find any in Cowes, I might nip over to the mainland this afternoon. You?'

'I'm going over to see Jib,' he said shortly.

Lucy covered her eyes and muttered, 'I'm sorry. I ... You know, Giles, I'd kind of forgotten. It's awful. Something as bad as Suzie being killed like that ... You kind of bury it because it's too horrible to think about and you concentrate on your new boots and a shooting lunch instead.'

'Yah. I know.'

'Listen, Giles, do you think we should cancel the shoot?' Lucy was frowning, as if the idea was a bit too much for her to deal with so soon after waking. 'Kind of out of respect?'

'Jib says not,' he grunted. 'I phoned first thing to say I was putting if off. But she says she doesn't want that. Says it wouldn't help Suzie, so there's no point cancelling.'

'But Simon won't come, will he?'

'Apparently. Frankly, I think Jib wants him out of the house. Says he's ... in need of distraction, I think were her words.' Giles had a sudden very clear image of Suzie gazing up at him adoringly, pouting those bee-stung lips, and he gagged.

'You didn't actually have to see her dead, did you, Giles?' Lucy whispered, reading his mind and sharing the moment, as she sometimes did. It disconcerted Giles every time. Worried him, too, given what a loose cannon she could be.

'Thank Christ, no,' he said, pretending to be all bluff confidence and good humour again. Blazon would've been proud of him, the way he'd learned how to talk to her in words that didn't set off her neuroses. 'Look, you have a nice lie-in, Lucy. Get your strength up. It's going to be a tiring weekend. I should be back by mid-afternoon, probably.'

'Are you taking the boat?' She was frowning again, as though her little brain was working very hard to think her way through the practicalities of his day.

'Thought I might.' He was pleased at how casual he sounded. 'It's decent enough weather to manage without a crew today. I'm not sure when I'll be back because I'm going to meet up with some of the investment club after Jib.'

Her frown deepened, twisting her dyed eyebrows into wiggly lines like old-fashioned shorthand.

'Some of them are looking at offering start-up capital for a new venture,' Giles explained kindly. 'Doesn't sound too exciting, but I wouldn't want to risk screwing up one of our investments because I couldn't be bothered to go to the meeting.'

Lucy's frown disappeared completely as she beamed up at him, and then rolled over on her side, snuggling her body into the soft mattress. 'They were saying at bridge the other day that you're an absolute wizard when it comes to putting your money in the right places.'

She glanced back up at him over her thin, milk-white shoulder with its sexy dusting of golden freckles. For a moment he wondered whether to postpone his trip across the Solent for long enough to get back to bed and give her a good seeing-to.

'In fact Jessica was saying her Greg wants to ask you what he should do,' Lucy went on. 'With the money he's just inherited from his aunt, I mean.'

'I'm not a bloody IFA, dishing out investment advice,' Giles said shortly, his brief excitement dying. He saw Lucy wince at his tone. As her eyes filled up with tears, he quickly grinned at her and added, 'But I suppose it's flattering to be wanted.'

'Absolutely, darling.' She smiled again, but this time he was sure she was faking because her eyes were cold and somehow distant. She hid them from him by pushing the side of her face deeper into the pillow, so he only just heard her final comments, 'I hope it goes well today with the club. See you later.'

Giles looked at the slight hump of her body under the duvet and hoped he could safely leave her to her own devices. On the way out of the house he saw her bag on the hall table. Knowing she was still in bed, he flicked it open and pulled out her pink Smythson diary to see:

11.15 James Blazon.

'Fucker,' he muttered under his breath.

But at least the session would cheer her up. Giles wouldn't have to spend the journey home wondering if he was going to find her drunk in the company of some dangerous stranger, or snoring in bed with a half-eaten bottle of pills by her side. It wouldn't be the first time, but she hadn't done either since she'd been under Blazon's control. That was worth a fair bit, Giles had to admit. Like her enthusiasm for sex, which meant he got all he wanted at home and didn't have to through all those hoops ... Not that any of it was enough to make up for the way Blazon had caused Suzie's death and made Giles feel so guilty. Nothing would ever make up for that.

Inside the viewing gallery at the mortuary, Karen was surprised to see the familiar figure of DS Annie Colvin, whom she'd encountered as a suspect and then a witness in the last case she'd worked on with Charlie. This morning, Annie looked about a million times better than she had then, with her straight dark hair freshly washed and neatly cut, and a fullness about her rosy cheeks that suggested she was eating more and smoking and drinking a lot less than she had after her bloke had been killed.

'Hi!' Karen said. 'I didn't expect to find you here.'

'Nor me, Karen.' Annie grinned. 'Charlie likes to keep his fans well apart.'

'Are you with Major Crimes too, then?' Karen said.

'I got in first.' Annie slapped Charlie on the arm. 'I'm still hoping our boy will do me credit.'

He paid no attention, concentrating on flicking the intercom switch and making contact with the pathologist.

'OK, Frank,' he said, 'we're all here, so you can get going. Thanks for waiting.'

The white-coated pathologist raised a hand in acknowledgement, pulled the hanging microphone nearer his mouth, and picked up his scalpel.

'No problem, Charlie. By the way, am I looking for anything in particular?'

'Sexual activity, consensual or not. Otherwise, the usual. Anything you can give me on the type of weapon that made the cuts, force needed, type of blows, any peripheral damage that could identify the type of attacker. Like I say: the usual.'

'This is the body of a young female in good health,' Frank said into the microphone as he pushed the scalpel into Suzie's dead flesh.

Karen looked down at the corpse, surprised at how normal

it looked and how pretty the face still was. No wonder Suzie had had a boyfriend. Looking like this now, she must have been devastating in life. Could Olly's devil have been the boyfriend? Had Olly felt some kind of ownership over his childhood friend and been jealous of a rival, someone who'd had sex with her, taken her away from him? Was it as simple as that?

Frank's scalpel moved easily down the body. After watching lots of fictional autopsies on screen, Karen knew more or less what to expect. Her only bad moment came when the pathologist peeled back Suzie's lovely face, as though it was a rubber mask, and with it the hanks of long blonde hair. They made a golden puddle at the end of the table, with the face crumpled up between them and what was left. This was a reddish mass with bulbous, staring white eyeballs. Karen's stomach heaved, but she successfully fought the impulse to vomit.

Frank's voice was mixed with the mechanical whine of the saw he was using to open up the skull, so that he could extract the brain itself. Karen's mind switched involuntarily from thoughts of what might have happened between Olly and the girl to what Will must experience every time he worked on one of his patients.

His parting reminder that dead bodies do not feel gave Karen some clues to the mental discipline he must need, knowing how much damage a careless scalpel could do. She had seen Will cope with the death of a patient, but she hadn't yet ever heard him talk of making a mistake. What must it be like to operate in the full knowledge of what could happen if your knife slipped, damaging one part of the brain in your attempts to heal another?

Something like it must have happened to him, Karen thought. No one ever made a serious career of any kind without mistakes. It must be hard enough for any surgeon, knowing how easy it would be to nick some nerve or organ during a routine operation, but, Will, working on the brain, could change his patients' personalities, make them unable to live alone, destroy their ability to speak or see or think. She tried to imagine living with that kind of responsibility – and failed utterly. His occasional tetchiness, his frequent control-freakery, seemed wholly understandable in the context.

Looking down through the plate glass, she saw Frank carrying Suzie's brain in his cupped hand as he took it to the scales. The organ looked like a wrinkled greyish vegetable, a squishy but unpeeled celeriac, perhaps, Karen thought, her own mind sending her off on many different paths. When they came to dissect and analyse the brain, probably after about a week in formalin to stiffen it, would they see any signs of the fear Suzie must have felt when she first saw the knife coming towards her? Or the pain she'd endured?

What exactly *had* she felt?

The most merciful effect would have been such a dramatic flood of adrenaline triggered by terror that she hadn't registered the physical sensations of the knife slicing through her skin and muscles and nerves, just as Frank's scalpel was doing now. And that wasn't likely to leave any physical evidence behind.

A sudden thought made Karen swing round to face Charlie and tug on his sleeve.

'You said you'd had Olly examined by the doctor,' she said. 'Did he take blood and urine for drug testing?'

'He took mouth swabs for DNA. Blood and urine aren't routine, even in cases of serious violence. So, no. Why?'

'Could be worth doing even now,' she said. 'Cannabis stays in the body for weeks; so do plenty of other substances. Can you get it done now?'

'A cut, two point four centimetres at the point of entry, penetrated the left ventricle of the heart,' Frank was saying into the mike.

'That must be the one that killed her,' Charlie said to Annie. 'I hope it was the first, poor little thing. What would finding cannabis in Olly's blood tell us?'

Karen looked at him and saw an old stubbornness filling his eyes like a physical barrier against her. She bent her head a little to make herself seem submissive.

'Any information has to help. If cannabis is part of the reason for his schizophrenia, then maybe ingesting a lot more yesterday could have triggered unusual violence. It's worth checking up, I'd have thought.'

Charlie didn't answer her, but he swung round to face Annie. 'Will you get on to the doctor and organize blood and urine?'

'Sure thing,' Annie said, pulling out her phone and turning away. Karen realized that dealing with Annie was going to be completely different from trying to make Eve cooperate with any suggestion she made.

They waited while Frank and his assistant worked their way through the body, snipping, cutting, weighing, assessing and reporting. He found a lot of alcohol in Suzie's stomach, but announced that her liver was healthy and showed no signs of damage.

'So I should hope,' Karen said to Charlie. 'She was only fifteen.'

When it was all over and the assistant was piling the unwanted organs and ribs back into the body cavity, before pulling the face and hair back down towards the neck and sewing everything up, Frank looked up at the window.

'Sexual activity a short time before death. No sign of any sexual trauma, neither cuts nor bruises. I'd have said wholly consensual. None of the knife cuts are anywhere near the vaginal area or even concentrated around the breasts, so no sexual motive for the attack. We've taken samples for DNA.'

'Two separate blokes then?' Charlie said.

'I'd have said so. Though the attacker with the knife needn't have been a bloke. Could easily have been female. No evidence either way. With a sharp knife you wouldn't need much force for any of these cuts, and the edges of the wounds are clean enough to show it was a *very* sharp knife.'

Charlie turned to Karen. 'That shuts off one line of enquiry then. Good. Now, have you got any questions for Frank? If not, we'd better head out to talk to the parents. Annie, you go straight back to the Island and keep things going there. Do what you can to hurry up the blood-spatter analysis. That's the most urgent.'

'Apart from finding the weapon. OK. See you over there later. Bye, Karen. Good to be working with you.' Annie sounded as though she meant it.

'Likewise,' Karen said. When Annie had gone, she turned to Charlie. 'So your CSI still hasn't found the knife?'

'Nope.'

'Any blood trails from the site of the body towards the sea?'

'Nope,' Charlie said again. 'Not obvious-to-the-naked-eye ones, anyway.'

'Then I don't see how it could have been Olly.' Karen was frowning hard enough to make her head ache. She deliberately released her muscles. 'There was so much blood on him, he couldn't have taken the knife anywhere without leaving traces.'

'Which is why we're spending money on a full blood-spatter analysis.' Charlie rubbed both his eyes, as though he could feel grit in them. 'The whole thing's probably a waste of time and money. If the boy's as mad as you think, even if he did it he won't remember enough to tell us. Or will he, when this— what d'you call it? Florid. That's it. When this florid episode's well and truly over?'

'Probably not,' Karen said, not bothering to correct his use of the word 'mad'. They both knew what he meant. 'That's the terrifying thing about schizophrenia: if you have it, you can't work out what's real and what's hallucination – or delusion. We'll just have to find some other way of confirming whether Olly's devil is a product of his mind or a real person. I'll have to talk to James Blazon about him. Is that allowed?'

'Can't see why not. Unless you start trying to smuggle him into any sessions you have with Olly.'

'I won't do that.'

'Great. Now for the parents.' Charlie was scowling again.

'What's the problem?'

He shivered. 'I hate this bit. I hate it when they loved their kids and are all torn up by what's been done to them – or what they've done.'

'I know. And she was only fifteen. They must . . .'

'But I hate it even more,' Charlie said, interrupting as though Karen hadn't said a word, 'when they're like Olly's Dad. Did you see how he couldn't wait to have his son sent down? His own son! I'd like to watch that bastard's face when we tell him Olly's innocent.'

Karen heard the passion that deepened Charlie's voice, and she remembered everything Annie had once told her about the way Charlie had had to protect his mother throughout his childhood; how his father had once broken both Charlie's arms when he was trying to defend her from a beating. He had been eight at the time.

'Charlie,' Karen said softly. 'Charlie, don't pin your hopes to Olly's innocence. I know you haven't got the knife yet, but you have to face facts: he almost certainly did kill her.'

'I won't believe that till I have to,' he said, looking as though he hated her. 'Come on. No time to waste if we want to get there before the Family Liaison Officer. Which I do. I don't want them feeling comforted – or comfortable.'

'But why . . . ?'

'If they're comfortable they're less likely to let unguarded words slip out,' Charlie said, scowling. 'And it's only unguarded words that ever tell you anything. Hurry up.'

Chapter 5

Day Two: Thursday 10.15 a.m.

Suzie had grown up in a long, low, white Hampshire farmhouse, surrounded by deliberately wild gardens that charmed Karen in today's frosty glitter, even though most of the plants and shrubs were now no more than bare sticks. One big clump of ornamental grasses looked like the tail feathers of an exotic ice bird.

The front door opened and she saw a slender woman of more or less her own age, dressed in grey jeans and a long cream-coloured Arran sweater.

'Mrs Gray?' Charlie said.

The woman nodded, then leaned against the door jamb, as though she hadn't the strength to stay upright. She crossed her arms over her stomach, hugging herself, and the expression on her face made Karen look away. It wasn't fair, she felt, to watch so much mental agony.

Charlie told the woman who they were, and showed her his warrant card. She stood aside, ushering them indoors without a word. In the dark hall a slightly older man was waiting beside an ancient oak coffer, on which a pile of Christmas cards lay beside a muddle of red string. Had they already been strung up, only to be taken down out of respect for Suzie?

The man's face showed little, but when Karen shook his hand, she felt its icy coldness, and when he spoke his throat clicked with almost every tightly held word. A powerful peppermint smell surrounded him, as though he'd been scrubbing his teeth only seconds before their arrival.

'You'd better come in,' he said. 'There's coffee if you'd like. I think the kettle's boiled. If . . .'

'Some coffee would be great,' Karen said. 'Can I come and help carry something?'

He didn't answer, just turned and stumbled towards the far end of the hall. His wife opened the nearest door and ushered them into a light, pretty sitting room. Its walls were painted in a soft coral that was picked up in the rose-and-trellis pattern of the chintz curtains. Books were heaped on all the tables, a puddle of cream-coloured knitting lay with the needles sticking out of it on the dark-green sofa, and a pair of outdoor shoes had been kicked off beside one of the deep, soft armchairs. A modest flat-screen television stood on a table to one side of the fireplace, and an old-fashioned stereo tower on the other. This was obviously the room the family used most of the time, and it spoke to Karen of a relaxed and confident stability.

'You'll want to know,' Charlie said as soon as they were sitting down, 'that the post-mortem evidence suggests Suzie's boyfriend was not her killer.'

Jennifer sagged back against the sofa cushions. 'But she had had sex just before . . . last night on the phone, you said she'd had sex just before she died,' she said, her voice breaking.

'Yes.' Charlie kept all comment out of his voice. 'But not violent sex. She didn't have to suffer that.'

'Not much comfort,' said her stepfather, coming in to the room with a tray of mugs and a cafetière of coffee.

Karen was disappointed to see it, much preferring the cleaner taste of filter coffee. When this lot was poured she found it thin and flavourless, as though Simon had used too little coffee and then pushed down the plunger far too soon.

'Suzie's a child still,' he said when he'd served everybody else and poured his own half-mug's worth and added nearly a quarter of a pint of cold milk.

Not a sensuous man, Karen decided, watching him drink the tepid brew with apparent pleasure, in spite of the strong residue of peppermint toothpaste that must have been filling his mouth.

'Was a child, I mean,' he went on, looking from her to his wife and back again. 'How ...? Why didn't we know she was seeing someone?'

Neither Charlie nor Karen could answer that, and Jennifer had turned away and was staring at the small fire sputtering in the elegant white-stone fireplace.

A roaring engine from outside made Karen turn to look out of the window. She saw the long nose of a dark-blue Jaguar XK coupé appearing between the hedges that lined the short drive. The car pulled up just short of the front door and a big, fit-looking man with a loose shock of dark-blond hair levered himself out of the bucket seat and came to hammer on the front door.

'Giles,' said Simon, sounding resigned. 'In his mainland car, too, which means he's sailed over. We'll have to let him in. I'll go.'

Suzie's uncle led the way back into the sitting room with the same arrogance and bounce his driving had shown. He pulled his sister up from the sofa, flung his arms around her body and held her against his chest.

Karen watched Simon looking at the pair of them with disapproval, before returning silently to his chair. He hitched up his pristine grey-flannel trousers and crossed his legs, as though prepared to wait until his brother-in-law had finished a familiar but tedious performance.

'Jib, darling, I'm so sorry,' Giles said in an even richer voice than the one Karen had heard him use to Eve yesterday in the Cowes police station. 'If I could go back . . .'

'Don't,' she said urgently. '"If onlys" make it worse. It's not your fault, Giles. How could you know what she was doing? It's me. I should've asked more questions when she said she was going to have lunch with Selina and her grandmother. I mean, it's such an unlikely thing in the middle of winter. I don't know why I didn't check. I rang them last night and they hadn't heard a word from her. She'd made it all up. They didn't know she was even going to the Island.' Her voice failed and she let her head lie on her brother's chest, her red, swollen eyes leaking yet more tears. 'I don't even know who the boy she was seeing was.'

She pulled back and stood upright, fishing in her sleeve for a handkerchief. 'You said you talked before you sent her off to buy the shoes, Giles: did she tell you anything then? Give you any idea who it was?'

'None. They'd . . . Jibby, darling, the only thing is – the only good thing I'm clinging to is that she was happy. She really was.'

Karen and Charlie exchanged glances. This fitted with the post-mortem evidence.

'Giggly and triumphant and glowing,' Giles went on. 'Whoever he was, he'd been giving her a high old time. Whatever you think about what she was up to, she'd loved it. There was nothing sad or frightened about her. She was pleased as Punch. I'm hanging on to that, old girl. You should too. She'd had a *good* time.'

'It's not much consolation.' Simon's voice was harsh and it made Jennifer pull right away from her brother and return to her sagging perch on the sofa. Her husband waited until she was settled, then went on, 'Giles, you need to know: this is DCI Trench and Doctor Taylor, a psychologist.'

'Not another bloody shrink!' He rounded on Karen and she braced herself at the sight of the hostility in his brown eyes. 'Are you here to apologize for what your profession has done?'

'No, I'm not,' Karen said when he paused, clearly wanting an answer.

'If that boy Oliver had been taking the drugs the NHS had prescribed for him, Suzie would still be alive. You ...'

'Giles, don't.' Jennifer was whimpering. 'Please. Oh, please. It's not *her* fault. She's working with the police.'

'Doing what, may I ask?'

'They haven't had time to say.' Simon offered Karen an apologetic smile, and she thought that if she were Jennifer she'd go for his slightly dour good manners over Giles's flamboyant affection and aggressive temper any time.

'Karen?' Charlie said, putting her in charge of the questions, which seemed rather unfair. She pulled herself together and directed the first at Jennifer, more or less ignoring Giles.

'We need to know about the relationship between Suzie and Oliver Matken,' Karen said. 'I gather they more or less grew up together.'

'That's right.' Simon had taken it on himself to answer for Jennifer, which interested Karen in itself. 'We – well, my wife and Giles – have known the Matkens for years. And when Jib married me thirteen years ago and moved over here with Suzie, we went on holidaying on the Island. Giles was generous enough to let us share his house there. We saw a lot of the Matkens every summer.'

He paused for a moment and Giles, who looked as though he hated playing second to anyone, rushed in.

'Sharing the house was easy. It was only a holiday place for us then and more than a bit rundown. Now I'm retired, we've restored it, and we're there more or less full time, but in those days it was only the odd weekend, Cowes week, and ten days here and there, when I could get away.'

'Get away from what?' Charlie asked, taking part at last.

'The City. I was a market maker. Made my pile and retired early.' Giles laughed with a self-satisfied sound that set Karen's teeth on edge. 'Lucky for me. Avoided all the horrors of the crunch and the ludicrous campaigns against bankers' bonuses that've screwed up all my younger rivals' lives.'

'Why were you involved with Suzie's trip to the Island?' Charlie asked, looking puzzled. 'Had she been to see you as well as her boyfriend?'

'I'd agreed to sail her back,' he said, nodding his head towards his sister. 'Jib knew I was planning to take the boat out yesterday afternoon – winter sailing's one of my passions – and would be more or less passing her front door, so she asked if I'd bring Suzie with me. I was glad to. Of course. Thought she might crew for me. Helps in that sort of weather.'

'But she was late, I think you said in your statement. That right?' Charlie said. Then, as Giles opened his mouth to answer, Charlie held up his hand to stop him and said to Karen, 'Why don't you take Mrs Gray upstairs and get her to show you Suzie's room? See what you can see up there. I'll carry on down here. OK?'

Karen obediently got to her feet and waited for Suzie's mother to summon up the energy to join her. Karen knew Charlie hoped that, once away from the two men, Jennifer would talk more freely.

As soon as they were upstairs, hearing nothing from the others but a general buzz of indistinct sounds, Jennifer said, 'I'm sorry about Giles. He doesn't realize how he comes over. But he's the kindest man. You wouldn't believe.'

'Oh, I would,' Karen said with a smile. 'I know how generosity and sensitivity can come in the most surprising packages.'

Pushing open a white-painted door, Jennifer showed Karen into a typical teenage girl's bedroom, more or less carpeted with discarded clothes. Soft toys and a glittery fake Christmas tree showed its owner had still been a child, but there were also make-up and scent bottles on the dressing table. A hairdryer lay on the floor beside a full-length cheval mirror, and a neat bright-pink laptop sat open on a purpose-built computer table, while a pile of magazines filled the shelf below it.

Karen caught sight of several titles she had long disliked
with their emphasis on 'keeping your boyfriend happy' and
not being scared of anal sex 'if that's what he wants', or
enduring savage pubic waxing to fit in with the ideal the internet's pornography had taken into nearly every teenage boy's
life. Unnecessary waxing was one thing, but painful sex that
could never be enjoyable to anyone without a prostate was
something else. Karen was no prude but the idea of
encouraging very young girls to indulge in a sexual activity
that could be physically dangerous as well as uncomfortable
made her angry. But it wasn't going to help Jennifer for her to
say anything about it now.

'DCI Trench will need the computer,' Karen said instead.
'There may be evidence there of who she was seeing. Did she
tweet?'

Jennifer offered a short sad laugh. 'That's far too middle-
aged. But she did everything else: Facebook, Bebo, MySpace ...
All of it.'

She turned away and began to tidy the muddle of brushes,
hairbands, scrunchies and soft toys on the dressing table. A
bellow from downstairs sounded much more clearly than the
rest of the talk.

'Don't be so fucking disgusting,' yelled Giles.

Karen caught Jennifer's eye and murmured, 'You did say
sensitive, didn't you?'

'Maybe it's the wrong word. He's kinder than kind. We
wouldn't ... I mean he's helped us all Suzie's life, paid her
school fees, paid for her riding, paid off our mortgage when
Simon had to take a salary cut. All that sort of thing. We
wouldn't ... I mean, we couldn't afford to live here like this

without Giles.' She put a shaking hand over her eyes, then added, 'Not that we'll need nearly so much now. Suzie's pony will have to go, and there won't be any school fees, and ...' Jennifer bowed her head, gasping. 'Oh God! It's just going to be me and Simon now. What am I going to do without her?'

Karen could see the other woman wasn't more than year or two her senior, and yet here she was, contemplating starting a family with Will. But she could hardly say: don't worry about the murder of your daughter. You're still young enough to have plenty more children. As though that would make the loss of Suzie any easier to bear.

Karen waited until Jennifer had recovered a little control and mopped her eyes with a Kleenex pulled from a box by the bed.

'Did you really not know about Suzie's boyfriend?' Karen said then.

Jennifer's expression changed from horror to something a little more calculating.

'You did, didn't you?' Karen said gently.

'Not for certain.' Jennifer picked up a small round bottle without a stopper and released a wave of sickly floral scent.

Karen had a vivid mental picture of the beautiful girl getting ready for a party, followed instantly by another, just as vivid, of the moment when her face was pulled away from the flesh beneath, as if it had been no more than a rubber glove. Karen had to sit down on the end of the bed. Jennifer, unaware, felt around among the litter on the dressing table until she found a ground glass ball and stuck it in the bottle, shutting off the smell. Karen breathed more easily.

'But there was something?' she suggested.

'There was. I didn't ... I didn't want to alert Simon because he'd have come over all rule-making and alarmist. And he'd have disapproved so much. But what can you do? We couldn't lock her in. That's why I asked Giles to bring her back yesterday. I knew ... I mean he has enough natural authority for Suzie not to flout him. And I thought ... I was sure if she knew he was waiting, she would ... well, behave.'

'So, who was the boyfriend?' Karen kept her voice soothing. 'There aren't that many people she'd have known on the Island outside the holiday seasons. You must have some idea.'

Jennifer started to make her daughter's bed. Karen stood up and helped her shake out the duvet and bash the pillows into shape.

'In my day I'd have had his love letters in my pillow case,' Jennifer said, pushing her dead daughter's pillows back into place. 'But they don't write now. It's all texting and phoning, so there's no evidence. Suzie always deleted her texts from him before anyone else had a chance to look at her phone.'

'Texts from whom?' Karen was glad Charlie had sent her up here. She didn't think they'd have got this far in a group session.

'There was a boy last summer,' Jennifer said with difficulty. 'A bit older than the gang Suzie always played with. Already working in one of the hotels. I think that's why she didn't want ... didn't want us to know about him. Partly. Simon's ... You wouldn't think it to look at him, but Simon's a bit of a snob. More, in a way, than Giles, and ...' Jennifer glanced at Karen, looking as though she hoped Karen wouldn't force her to explain.

She didn't need to explain anything. Karen knew exactly what she'd meant. Giles's snobbery was so obvious that anyone who could outdo him in class prejudice must be extraordinary.

'Have you got a name?' Karen asked. This should have been Charlie's job, but it was the obvious question to ask.

'Jerry. Jerry Eagles. He's the junior barman at the Star hotel in Ryde. It's a kind of boutique hotel, much more stylish than most of the places over there. We'd go sometimes for Sunday brunch. He was very taken with her in the summer, and I could see she liked it. She's always been a bit of a flirt, but this was more.'

Jennifer fired up the computer, clicked on 'My Pictures', selected one file and opened it. A photograph bloomed on the screen, showing a vital version of the girl Karen had seen in the mortuary. In the picture, she was sitting on a sandy beach somewhere, with two other girls of her own age and a bunch of boys. The girls were all wearing the skimpiest of bikinis and the boys, speedos or surfer shorts. One, standing apart from the others and gazing at Sophie with adoration and a certain watchful proprietorial air, had a smouldering cigarette in his hand.

'That's him,' Jennifer said, resting her forefinger on his face. 'That's Jerry.'

'Great,' Karen said, making a note on her BlackBerry, and wondering whether his seeming apartness was just a chance effect of the photograph or whether he really had been spurned by the rest of the group.

He looked a few years older than them, and also different in some indefinable way. It could have been nothing more than the cigarette and the way he was squinting through the smoke, Karen told herself, determined not to read into the photograph stuff that wasn't there. She put her finger on the unmistakable face of Olly Matken.

'Oliver,' Karen said. 'What do you know of him?'

Now it was Jennifer's turn to plump down on the bed. She gazed pleadingly up at Karen, then let her eyelids drop.

'He was such a sweet little boy,' she said with sadness, 'imaginative, always dancing and chatty, always happy. Then something went wrong. He got odder and odder. Withdrawn and – what do they call it? Affectless? Something like that. What Phil and Ange have been through ... I can't bear to think, but if Olly did this ...' Her voice cracked like splitting ice. Then with a huge physical effort she made herself talk again: 'He shouldn't have been allowed to live out in the open. He should've been sent somewhere safe. Locked in. It's not fair ... Even if he didn't kill Suzie, it shouldn't have been allowed.'

'How did Suzie take his oddness?' Karen said, wishing she'd been able to record this impromptu interview. She hoped she'd remember all the crucial undertones. 'Was she scared of him?'

Jennifer's eyes grew rounder as she thought, obviously looking back into the past. 'I don't think she was ever frightened. Actually, she seemed to take his weirdness in her stride. She was always so ... so cheerful. I mean, if you take Giles's optimism and ... and bounciness and put them into a fifteen-year-old girl's brain and body, you'd see Suzie.' Tears slipped unnoticed down her face. 'She was very like him. All the good things about him I mean. They both took after my father. No,

Suzie never let Olly worry her. When he was going off on one, she'd just giggle and move away to give him room.'

'And did you ever see him offer her violence? Even verbal violence?'

Jennifer's eyes poured with tears again, as she slowly shook her head from side to side. At last she felt the dampness on her skin and dragged the screwed-up handkerchief out of her sleeve again to mop her face and blow her nose. Stuffing the cotton square back, damp and snotty, in her sleeve, she added, 'Never. Never. Never. He was the gentlest soul. And always so protective of her.'

I was just keeping her from the devil, Karen quoted to herself in silence.

Who *was* Olly's devil?

'Then did you ever see them with anyone who did scare her, or try to threaten her?' she asked aloud.

'No.' Jennifer sighed. 'Don't you think if I had I would have told DCI Trench on the phone last night? Nobody would ever want to hurt Suzie. She was such fun. *Everybody* loved her.'

Somebody didn't. Karen couldn't put that thought into words either.

Chapter 6

'Jerry Eagles?' Charlie said to the slight, dark-haired young man who was polishing the bar at the Star.

'Yeah. That's me,' he said with a wide, professional smile. He bunched up the cloth he'd been using and put it away somewhere below the bar, before washing his hands at a hidden sink. 'What can I get you both?'

Charlie dealt with the formalities again, while Karen searched Jerry's good-looking face for evidence of his real feelings. He was recognizably the same young man as the tousle-headed swimmer with the cigarette in the photograph on Suzie's computer, but here at work, in his chic long black apron with the barely discernible outline of a star woven into the fabric over his chest, he didn't have any of the outsider's watchfulness that had been so obvious in the photograph.

'I believe you knew Suzie Gray.' Charlie's voice was official and devoid of emotion.

'Knew?' the young barman said. 'What d'you mean "knew"? Of course I know her. She's my girlfriend.'

And that answers that, Karen thought, exchanging glances with Charlie.

'You haven't heard then,' Charlie said with barely modified coolness. 'It's been all over the news. She died yesterday afternoon.'

Jerry held his breath as he slammed both hands on to the bar, gripping its edge so that he wouldn't fall over.

'How?' he whispered, his dark eyes swivelling from side to side and his breaths short and gasping. 'How did she die?'

'You need to sit down,' Karen said firmly and loudly enough to penetrate his threatening faintness. 'Have you got a chair back there?'

'Stool,' he muttered. 'There's always a stool.' But he made no move to get it, just stood, swaying and panting, with his colour coming and going and sweat pouring out of his skin.

Karen pushed her way through a door next to the bar and found herself on his side of it. She grabbed a tall stool from under the sink, dragged it forwards and made him sit down.

'Put your head between your knees. Go on. Get some blood back into your brain. Come on, Jerry, bend down.'

She kept a firm hand on his back until she could feel his breathing return to something like normal. Then she let him sit up straight again, went to the sink to fill a glass with water and brought it back, nodding to Charlie to continue.

'She was on her way to her uncle's yacht,' he said, keeping a close eye on Jerry's face. 'Someone stabbed her. Can you tell me where you were between three fifteen and four o'clock yesterday afternoon?'

Jerry looked round the empty room. 'I was here. On duty.'

'What time did your shift start?' Charlie said.

'Three thirty.' Jerry looked away. 'After the lunch rush was over. We take it in turns. That's when Mike knocked off. Then we both did the evening.'

'Had you and Suzie been together here?' Charlie sounded bored.

Jerry shook his head. 'I've got a room – a flat I share – in the town. My flatmates work office hours so we were ... We had it to ourselves. When it was time, I drove her to the top of the marina at Cowes, West Cowes; then I had to leave her.'

'So you could get back in time for your shift?' Now there was something more in Charlie's voice than bored officialdom. Karen heard contempt and dislike, neither of which seemed justified. Or fair.

'I get fined if I'm late. Could lose the job, too. It wouldn't be the first time, you see. And if I lost it, I'd be lucky to get another. There's not much work on the Island. Not since the wind-turbine factory shut.' Jerry's eyes were red and damp. Karen thought he was concentrating on Charlie's questions as a way of keeping his grief and shock under control. 'Suzie didn't always understand about how my time's different from hers. She isn't ... I mean, being on time never bothered her.'

'This the first time you'd slept with an underage girl?' Charlie suggested with more aggression than Karen thought necessary.

Jerry frowned. 'That's not right,' he said. 'She had her birthday last month. I gave her a silver locket. Like a heart. We couldn't ... When she was over in the summer we couldn't have sex. She was still fifteen, then. She wanted to, but I wouldn't. We had to wait till her birthday.'

'You bother about that, do you?' Charlie said. 'Lad like you, with his pick of all the teenage tourists. Why would you care if she was underage or not?'

'It's not like that. I love ... loved Suzie. I wanted ... I mean it wasn't just a shag. It was never that. She was my girlfriend. I wanted it to go on, and if ... It had to be legal for that. I said we had to wait till her birthday. It was October the fifteenth, so that's when we, like, started.'

'She was lying to you,' Charlie's smile made him look like a wolf, hunting. 'Her birthday's in April. She wouldn't have been sixteen till then. Forget that. Here we have a girl who's just had sex with you and you love so much you want it to go on for ever, and you throw her out of your car in the rain to find her own way to her uncle's boat so you won't lose a pound or two being late for work?' He looked at Karen, nodding, and said with heavy sarcasm. 'I can go along with that, can't you, Doctor Taylor? My kind of love.'

'You're getting it all wrong.' Jerry sounded exasperated but not guilty. 'I couldn't take her any closer to the boat because her family weren't supposed to know about her and me, *specially* not her uncle. Not yet. She was going to soften them up slowly. That's why she made me leave her there in the High Street, by the shops. It's what *she* wanted.'

'Her uncle said she was drunk,' Charlie said. 'That right?'

Jerry nodded, looking sick. 'I didn't mean ... I didn't know she had such a weak head. She said she wanted Malibu and just kept pouring it down. Even when I had a shower ... I came back and there she was swigging again.' He sounded disapproving himself.

'What did you see after you dropped her?' Charlie asked.

Jerry wiped his eyes with the back of his hand, then wiped that on the glass cloth lying on his bar.

'Nothing.'

'Total blank was it through your windscreen?' Charlie was still taunting him.

'Of course not. There were a few people walking about in coats and scarves. Not many. It's like a desert this time of year. Gets a bit better near Christmas, when the lights go up and everybody has candles in the windows, but you won't see the crowds again till the summer.' Jerry frowned again, obviously trying to remember through his shock and misery. 'It was beginning to get dark, you know. There were gulls. A dog. Looked like a stray. Mongrel kind of thing. And there was this grey car parked near Captain Joe's when I did my U-turn and left.'

'What kind of car?'

Jerry shrugged. 'Nothing interesting. Fiesta, I think. I didn't look. Small hatchback anyway.'

'What about the driver?' Charlie was obviously determined to cover all bases.

'Didn't see. The car was parked. Cold day so its windows were all condensation, and that. And I was ...' Jerry's voice faltered. Then he looked at Karen and smiled a little, as though pleading to be understood: 'I was thinking about Suzie. About what it had been like; when I was going to see her again.'

'Did you have specific plans?' Karen asked.

'Yeah.' Jerry leaned across the bar towards her. 'She didn't think she'd be able to make an excuse to come back to the Island any day soon, so I was going to go over on Saturday morning, when I'm free, and she was going to take her horse out. She drew me a map of where I was to be at half eleven exactly. I promised.'

'Can I see the map?' Charlie put out a hand, palm upwards, and shook it with menace.

Jerry got off his stool and disappeared for five minutes. When he came back he was holding an A5 piece of paper, torn from a notebook. But he didn't offer it to them.

'You will give it back, won't you?' he said, holding it close to his chest. 'I don't want . . . It's the last thing she gave me.'

'You'll get it back,' Charlie said, wagging his hand again.

Karen looked over his shoulder to see a spirited sketch map, with trees and hedges and footpaths marked as clearly as the main roads. Beside a small copse, Suzie had drawn a cluster of little hearts, like a flight of butterflies, and coloured them with a pink felt-tip, adding an arrow and a large X.

'I was to take a rug,' Jerry said sadly, 'and we were going to make love under the trees, however cold it was. She promised. She'd tie up her horse and put his rug on him, and we could have half an hour. No more or she'd be late for lunch and they'd start asking questions.'

'What about a bottle of Malibu? She ask for that again too?'

Trust Charlie, Karen thought, to spoil Jerry's last romantic memory. She could see there was nothing to be gained from that direction, so instead she asked Jerry if Suzie had ever talked about Oliver Matken.

'Not yesterday,' he said, turning his back on Charlie with enough determination to make the gesture into an insult. 'But before. Sometimes. We saw him in the summer, at the beach and stuff. I thought he was weird, but she only said he was OK. Not a problem.'

'She'd never been frightened of him, then?' Charlie said.

Jerry's face changed into a mask of shock, his eyes narrowing and his nostrils flaring. 'Did *he* kill her?'

'We don't know,' Karen said, while Charlie chipped in from the background, 'If he did, would that surprise you?'

Jerry's hands were fists now, tight and stringy, and he banged them both down on the bar hard enough to raise instant bruises.

'I'll fucking *kill* him.'

'What now?' Charlie said as they left the hotel. 'Shall I drop you back at Fountain Quay, or have you got time to get some scran?'

'Scran?' Karen had never heard the word before.

'Food, dafty,' Charlie said, his Newcastle accent stronger than usual as he failed to hide his impatience. 'We're not far from the Goose Inn.'

At the name of his favourite pub on the Island, run single-handedly by a beautiful woman, who had always seemed to Karen to occupy too crucial a part of his life, she shook her head.

'I'd better get back to Will,' she said. 'He's got the day off. Will you be talking to Olly again today?'

'Depends what the others have got out of him.' Charlie looked as though he didn't relish the prospect. 'Why?'

'Someone must ask him more about the devil and about the devil's knife: what it looked like; whether he himself touched it; what the devil did with it, or made him do.'

'It's under control.' Charlie's voice was crisp and his accent much less pronounced now that he was talking work again. He opened the passenger door of his grey Audi. 'Being dealt with. Come on. Hop in. I'll take you back.'

'I don't seem to have done much for you today. I hope it was worth my hourly rate,' Karen said, pushing the steel end of her seatbelt into its slot.

'We got to Eagle, thanks to you.'

Charlie drove with absent-minded precision, taking the main road through Wootton and on into East Cowes and across the Medina river.

'He must have stopped about here,' he said, pulling up in the High Street.

They could see Captain Joe's, the sailing outfitters, where Giles said he'd sent his niece to get some proper deck shoes.

'He kissed her, didn't he?' Charlie said, leaning towards Karen, as though to re-enact the scene. Her finger ends tingled and she found herself swaying towards him, until they both remembered they were at work.

He stopped before he touched Karen, breathing hard. After a moment, he straightened up and pointed to the alleyway that ran along the side of Captain Joe's, where Suzie's body had been found. They had a good view of it, just as anyone in the alleyway would have had a good view of them.

'Maybe he didn't leave right away, like he claims,' Charlie added. 'Maybe he didn't trust her and waited to see what she'd do. To start with it looks great: she runs off towards the *Dasher*. But he waits to make sure. Then he sees her running back. This time he knows she's not coming to him.'

Karen thought of Jerry's announcement that Suzie was his

girlfriend, as though that would answer any question about her or himself. Had she felt quite as committed as he?

'What if Olly was there in the alleyway?' Charlie said. 'By chance or because he knew Suzie would be coming that way when she went to Giles's boat and he wanted to see her? What if Olly emerged from the alley when she came running back to buy her shoes, and Eagle thought she was running *to* Olly?'

Charlie jerked his head round so that he was looking straight at Karen instead of through the windscreen at the spot where Suzie had died.

'What if Eagle didn't like that? There she was, *his* girlfriend, only half an hour or so out of his bed, and running to someone else? What if he had a knife and went after Suzie with it? How would he be thinking in that scenario, Karen?'

She wrinkled her nose, not believing Jerry would fit into this scheme of Charlie's. 'I don't think my speculating is going to do you much good here. You need the knife. That'll give you real answers.'

'Your experience is what I'm paying you for,' he said shortly. 'Your expert opinion. Come on. Give it to me. How does the psychology work here?'

Karen shrugged.

'A certain kind of man could think "if she's not mine, she's not going to be anybody's". That's true enough,' she said. 'Women have been killed like that fairly often.'

'So what about it? Is Eagle Olly's devil?'

Karen sat watching Charlie, her head on one side, trying to work out what was pushing his buttons now.

'If he were, that would explain why you haven't found the

knife,' she said. 'And it's a plausible motive for the murder of a girlfriend. But ...'

Charlie put his hands on her square shoulders and pulled her round to face him. 'Listen, Karen, don't you think it's odd that Eagle claimed he didn't know she was dead? It's all over the local paper, with her pic and everything.'

'People his age don't read papers. You must know that,' Karen said, a little amusement fighting with her impulse to defend Jerry. In fact she felt sorry for him, lied to by what seemed to her to be a manipulative girl, who'd been using him for nothing more than fun and a secret advantage over her parents and uncle. Jerry had been serious about her. He'd believed everything she'd said to him, poor innocent bloke.

'Been all over the radio this morning, too,' Charlie said with a snap. 'Don't you think someone who'd read the story would've talked to him? Phoned, texted, emailed. Even if they were keeping the relationship secret, I'll bet his friends knew. I'm going back to the nick to talk to Olly again, maybe show him a photo of Eagle. Then we'll see. You go on back to Scumpton. You've got responsibilities of your own.'

That was true, but Karen didn't want to leave Jerry unprotected. Not with Charlie in this mood.

'I could see you didn't like Jerry,' she said. 'But what makes you want him to be the killer?'

Charlie let her go and hunched down into the driver's seat.

'Not just the fact that you sympathize with Olly for having a father who wants him in gaol?' she suggested, wanting to avoid saying anything specific about Charlie's relationship with his own violent father. In some moods he could talk to her about the most painful bits of his past; in others he could not bear to have them mentioned.

'Don't be stupid,' he said now.

'Or because you don't like young blokes who have sex with under-age girls?' Karen had always found it fruitful to offer up every possible story in the hope of seeing one reach its target.

Charlie tightened his shoulder muscles even more so that he looked like a crouching boxer, which suggested at least a partial hit.

'Having got them rat-arsed,' he said in a voice like a knife. 'I don't like people who mess with other people's heads and then . . . and then mess with them. He screwed her every which way, and she was just a pony-mad bairn – however tasty she looked.'

'Right,' Karen said, keeping all expression out of her voice. 'I can see that. In which case, presumably you'll get your amazing CSI to check out Jerry's car for evidence of the knife – or any trace of Suzie's blood.'

'Of course.' Charlie looked at her as though she were absurd even to think she had to mention something so obvious.

The idea that he had ever tried to get her to leave Will seemed absurd. But he had, and more than once.

'Great,' she said, hating the hostility, but trying to sound detached. 'Well, I'll get back, but as soon as you need me, phone. And I'll try to talk to James Blazon once Will's gone back to Lewes tomorrow. OK?'

Charlie nodded. His shoulders were opening out a little, but he still looked dangerous.

'And he's another one.'

'I'm sorry?' Karen said.

'Blazon's another bastard who messes with people's minds. Look what he did to Olly.'

Ah, thought Karen. It's that. You don't want Olly to be guilty because, like everyone else, you blame his psychologist for the way he was. Presumably you'd like to see James Blazon on a charge of conspiracy to murder. Thank God that's not going to happen!

Even so, she wished Charlie luck as she got out of his car. Her sympathy for James was increasing. The ideas she'd had in the mortuary about the effect on Will of his responsibility for the safety of the brains on which he was operating spread to embrace James, too. She'd never wanted a clinical practice herself and now she knew why.

What had drawn her to psychology wasn't the generous urge to heal that both men must share, but the need to understand, to get to grips with *why*: why people behaved in ways that could lead only to their own ruin or unhappiness; why some wanted others to suffer; why others, less sadistic, still couldn't see how to avoid loading pain and misery on to those whose lives they shared, or didn't think it worth the bother of trying to avoid it.

And of course, lying beneath all the other questions must be the crucial one of why she had so mismanaged her first marriage that she'd come to spend most of her time wishing her husband dead. She wiped her hand on the back of her jeans.

'No wonder I feel at home with murderers,' she muttered as she made her way towards Fountain Quay. 'What would I do to Will, if I ever . . .?'

Chapter 7

Billy needed something to do or he'd go what his Dad's best mate from the navy called Harry-threaders.

He'd bought his iPod with him so he'd been OK for a bit. But now he was bored and it seemed like a year before it got dark each day. It was good he didn't have to listen to his parents yelling at each other and blaming him and telling him to wash his hands or lay the table or look after his crap sisters. But it was too quiet here. And there was nothing to do. Even his two best books had stopped being any good. He couldn't stop thinking about the swearing girl and what had happened with the knife ...

He couldn't go to his mates because someone would tell. And he was cold. All his food was cold and he hadn't had any hot chocolate since he left home. He tried to work out the date and thought it must be nearly a week since he'd run away. The plan to get across to the mainland didn't seem so good now. He didn't know what he'd do there. It would still be cold and boring.

Maybe he should go and ask Mr Henty for more work. If the old man was in a better mood today, maybe he'd give Billy the promised second trip in the *Dasher*, and a hot shower, too. If he wasn't on board, maybe Billy would just go ahead and have the shower anyway. It would warm him up. He knew how to pump up the water and get it hot because Mr Henty had showed him.

Billy had tried to wash at the basins in the public toilets, but you couldn't do much when you were expecting other people to come in any time. He'd got rid of all the blood, but the rest of him was getting itchy, just like his mum always said when he didn't want a shower at home.

He slid out from under his covers and pulled his clothes straight, before climbing out of the window on to the old fire escape in the dark. No one had clocked him yet, but he was always ready to run and hide if anyone saw him.

When he turned on to the quay at the marina, he saw there were lights on in the *Dasher*, and he speeded up, forgetting the blister he'd got from his wrunkled sock and the way the cold had made his legs and neck and back go stiff and sore. No one stopped him, and he ran up the *Dasher*'s gangway, only stopping for a minute to listen in case Mr Henty had someone else with him.

There was no sound of any talking, so Billy banged on the companionway doors.

'Who is it?' called Mr Henty.

Billy pushed open the doors and leaned into the cabin.

'It's me, Mr Henty. Billy. Can I come in?'

'Phwa! You stink. What the hell happened to you?'

Billy felt hot stupid tears on his face and nearly ran away.

But Mr Henty grabbed his fleece and pulled him down the steps into the cabin.

'Hey, there,' he said, sounding so kind the tears got worse. 'It's OK, mate. You're OK now. I'll get you home. What happened? Where've you been?'

Billy just shook his head and snivelled. 'C'n I do some more work for you?' he said. 'I need some money. And I need a shower. I'm cold. *Can* I work?'

Mr Henty rubbed his head so hard it hurt. 'Don't be silly,' he said. 'I'm taking you straight home. You'll be OK then.'

'I can't go back. I need ...' Suddenly he couldn't remember why he'd run away, or what he wanted, or why he'd come here.

'Why have you come to me, Billy?' Mr Henty said.

Billy looked up at him through the fog in his eyes. 'You're the only person who's ever give me work. And I need more now. I got to earn something. You got to let me do it again.'

'But I haven't any work for you. It was a one-off. And you're not supposed to talk about it. You're too young for that kind of thing.'

'My dad's going to be one of your beaters at the weekend,' Billy said, wheedling. 'Why can't I be one too? I'd work hard. You know I would. I always done exactly what you tell me.'

Mr Henty smiled suddenly, which made it all better, and told him not to be so silly.

'You're thirteen Billy-Boy. Too young. But if you go home now and promise to stay there and behave, I'll talk to my keeper and see if he can find you something to do on Saturday. But you have to go home first and behave yourself, as you always promised you would. Come on.'

'I won't. Can't.' He wiped his eyes on his sleeve and saw a trail of snot like snail's juice all up it. 'I worked for you before. Everyone knows I can do it. You *have* to let me.'

'Come on, mate. How about I drive you back to your parents? That'll be easier than walking up through the town, won't it now? Cheer up.'

Billy didn't know what had gone wrong with his eyes. He couldn't stop them crying. He pinched his legs but that didn't help. Mr Henty had him by the shoulder now and was pushing him up the quay towards where he always parked his car, near where the swearing girl had died.

Mr Henty didn't say anything else to Billy until they were outside his house. Then Mr Henty turned off his engine and clicked off the central locking, saying, 'You don't have to tell *me* where you've been, but you'd better think up a story pretty quick because your mum and dad are going to want to know. The police, too. And once they start asking questions . . .'

'Police?' Bill whispered, thinking of the girl, and of the money he'd stolen from the stash behind the galley stove, and everything else. 'I don't want to talk to the police. I won't.'

Mr Henty gave a hard-sounding laugh, even though nobody'd said anything funny. 'Your parents reported you missing. They've been worried sick about you, thinking you were hurt. I don't know what you've been doing and I don't need to know, but . . .'

His face changed and he leaned closer to Billy and peered at his sweater.

'Where did you get that jersey?' he said loudly.

Billy looked down at his front and saw he'd forgotten to zip his fleece right up. Poking out at the neck was the soft dark-blue sweater he'd taken from the *Dasher* yesterday. He covered it with his hands.

'What d'you mean? It's mine.'

Mr Henty's face went all mean and tight. Then he said, 'I've seen a jersey like that before and I know what they cost. Your father's living on the dole and whatever cash hand-outs he can scrounge from casual work for people like me. No way he's going to buy you hundred and fifty quid cashmere. Have you been up to your old tricks again? Thieving, Billy? Is that it? Is that why you won't say where you've been? Or is it worse? What are you going to say to the police?'

'Nothing. ''s mine. I was give it.'

'Who by?' Now Mr Henty was sounding suspicious as well as mean. 'Maybe I do need to know what's been going on all this time. Who've you been with to give you expensive presents, Billy? Who is he? She?'

Billy's face got all hot as he thought about everything he'd nicked from the *Dasher*. But he'd been questioned about this kind of thing often before and he knew what to do. He let his eyes look down at his knees and made his voice shake a bit and said, 'No one. I took the money from my mum's purse.' Something was wrong about that, Billy thought, and soon worked it out. He wasn't special needs; he could do maths. When he'd done this lot, he added, 'Little bit every week till I had enough to run away with. Then I spent it on the sweater. That's why I need some work. I spent all the money I took from my mum's bag so I can't afford the ferry.'

Mr Henty didn't say anything for a long time, then ruffled Billy's hair much too hard again.

'Let's hope she's so pleased to see you back she forgives

you. Come on. Time to face the music, Billy. Do you want me to come in with you?'

Billy shuddered. The thought of his mum trying to stop shouting at everybody and tidying up the house to make it all right for Mr Henty to be in made him feel hot and cold all over.

'I can do it.'

'OK. And if you really do want some work on Saturday, and your dad says it's OK, then get him to phone my keeper. We'll sort something, Billy. I promise. We'll be good friends and you'll earn your money. Don't worry any more.'

Karen waited for the lift. Running downstairs at the start of the day was one thing; walking up when you'd been dashing about for hours and had two heavy bags of groceries to carry was something else entirely. The lift came at last and pinged as the doors opened. She pressed the button for the top floor with her elbow and felt a spurt of such strong pleasure at the thought of Will waiting upstairs in her flat that all her doubts seemed idiotic.

As she put her key in the lock, rehearsing her account of the day's events into a set of stories to amuse him, she heard a woman's voice. After a second's puzzled crossness, she recognized it. Stella Atkins, a leading light of the university architecture department, was her best friend. She was going to oversee the works at Karen's holiday house on the Island if they ever got permission for it. Karen pushed open the door, calling Stella's name.

'Hiya!' Stella called in response from the sitting room.

Karen walked in and saw her sitting with Will. An open

bottle stood on the table between them, Mozart's saucily cheerful Horn Concerto in E flat was playing in the background, and delectable savoury scents wafted in from the kitchen. All the lamps were on, and none of the overhead halogen bulbs, so the light was golden instead of starkly white. Karen dumped the plastic bags on the floor by the door and prepared to join in.

'This is very cosy,' she said, kissing first Stella and then Will. 'I'll put this lot away and join you. That looks like a very alluring bottle. Which of you ...?'

'Me,' said Stella with a wicked grin on her round face. 'I want to wheedle a favour out of you, so I thought some nice claret might help.'

'And then I decided we should start it,' Will said cheerfully. 'To stop it looking like too much of a bribe. I'll get you a glass.'

'Great. Thanks.' Sensing some kind of danger, Karen turned from him to Stella, to ask, 'What favour?'

Stella smiled with her teeth tightly together and took in a big hissing breath, before relaxing her jaw enough to talk.

'Planning permission for your house has come through,' she said, 'with one or two provisos about extra fire-proofing of the timber structure. And ...'

'Then I should be buying *you* expensive wine,' Karen said, feeling even more wary. 'You've done all the work.'

Stella had taken on the exciting but not technically accomplished design an artist had produced for Karen's new house and turned it into working drawings precise enough to satisfy the planners.

'Yes, but ...' Stella licked her lips. All the relaxation and humour in her face had been taken over by embarrassment. 'I should have asked you this before, but I didn't think ... Oh, shit! How to start?'

'From the top, if I were you,' Will said from the open-plan kitchen.

'Yes, but ...'

'Oh, for goodness' sake, Stella!' Will was polishing a large wine glass for Karen. He sounded as though he was chastising one of his medical students.

Standing in my kitchen as if he owns it, Karen thought, forgetting how pleased she'd been only a moment ago at the thought of seeing him; polishing *my* glass with *my* cloth, and telling *my* friend what to do.

When he was satisfied that the glass was adequately shiny, he put away the cloth and half filled the glass and brought it to her.

'Here you are, Karen.'

Taking it, she couldn't bring herself to thank him. He didn't seem to notice.

'What Stella hasn't told you,' he went on, 'is that her agent has got her a commission from a very glamorous publisher to write up the whole project of your house from the original competition for its design to the moment you receive the keys from the builder. She's got the artist's permission and will be paying her some of the royalties, but she—'

'It's all right, Will. I can do this,' Stella said, interrupting at last. 'It's my job, too. Karen, darling, the only reason I didn't ask you first is that I never thought Jude, my agent, could get anywhere. But she has, and they're paying me a decent advance. I wondered if ... well, if you and I could do a sort of barter. I don't charge you any fees for the work I have done and will do on the house, and you . . .'

'Don't demand a share of the advance and royalties?' Karen said, amused but wishing Stella had discussed all this with her first, before sharing it with Will. On the other hand, the prospect of avoiding six per cent of the total building costs now was so attractive that the possibility of losing some potential royalties in the future didn't worry her one bit.

'Not exactly,' Stella said. 'I thought you might want to fight me for the right to write up the project, so . . . this is a kind of pre-emptive strike. Sort of thing.'

Karen felt more naturally affectionate. 'Honestly, Stella! I've got more than enough work on my own book to want to do this. And I haven't got your expertise in any case; the story will be far better written by you. So long as I get a right of veto and all identification of me and the house's address is kept right out of the book, that's fine.'

She shot a quick glance at Will and saw that his expression was blank, as though he was still keeping all his thoughts about the project to himself.

Stella, on the other hand, had subsided into her chair and was looking almost ill with relief. She drank some wine. Karen took a sip from her own glass, then looked more closely at the bottle's label.

'Wow!' she said. 'Haut Brion 1998? You *were* worried, weren't you? You must have blued your entire food budget for the month on this bottle. Stella, really you didn't have to.'

Karen swallowed some more of the delectable, voluptuous curranty wine and couldn't stop herself calculating the cost of the small mouthful at around a fiver. With bills and debts stacking up in front of her like an unconquerable mountain range, she couldn't help clenching her stomach as the wine hit. But Stella couldn't – and shouldn't – know how close Karen was to financial panic, so she smiled and raised her glass in a toast.

'It's a deal,' she said. 'Let's finish the wine and then eat. Is there enough for three, Will?'

'Of course,' he said, looking at her with the approval she'd been missing.

Karen wondered how long it would last.

Chapter 8

Day Three: Friday 12.45 p.m.

James Blazon had got back his usual ruddy colour. In a way that made his thinning blond hair seem even more inadequate than when he'd been looking grey with fatigue and anxiety in the police station two days ago.

Karen had arranged to meet him for lunch at a pub in Cowes to learn more about Olly. She hoped the encounter would banish the memories of yet another bruising discussion with Will about their future.

'What's scaring you?' he'd said, lying at her side after an unsuccessful attempt to make love at dawn.

'Nothing's scaring me,' she'd said, offended and a little sore.

'You'd be a fantastic mother, and it wouldn't get in the way of your job.' He'd stroked her hair, but his determination had made the gesture less affectionate than demanding, which hadn't helped her mood. 'Lots of mothers work these days. Most.'

'They always did,' Karen had said to the ceiling, remembering her own attempts to make her mother stop for long enough to notice that she was scared, or hungry, or had a cold sore on her upper lip, or wasn't getting on at school, or missed her Island grandmother so much she didn't know how she could carry on normal life in London.

Will hadn't noticed any of it. He'd pushed aside the duvet and strode off towards the shower, saying over his shoulder at the bedroom door:

'That's splitting hairs. You know it's different now. Everyone expects married women to work. You wouldn't be sacrificing anything.' He'd walked into the shower and Karen had rolled over and buried her face in the pillow. But he'd come right back to stand beside her. Even with her face stuffed in the pure linen pillow case, she'd known he was there: his clean, almost lemony, smell had been too familiar to ignore; and she'd heard the suppressed emotion in his breathing.

'And you could have a chance to put it all right. You could bring up our children as children should be brought up. Not as you were. You and your brother Aidan.'

Outrage had got her out of the pillow and turning back to face him.

'It's not fair to use my past like that,' she'd said.

'*Fair?*' Will had repeated. 'If we're talking about fairness, what's so fair about the way you want to have everything your way? *I* want a family and a proper settled life; not this adolescent, commuting kind of on–off relationship. Isn't it time you grew up?'

'What's up, Karen?' James asked in his normal, friendly voice, bringing her back into the present. 'You look very bleak. Gorgeous as ever, but very bleak.'

She shook her head and felt her hair fly across her small round face. How could he think she'd believe a ridiculous words like 'gorgeous'? Pushing back the loose hair, and trying to ignore the morning's physical memories, she said, 'Thanks. But don't worry. Nothing important. Personal stuff.'

The intense, yeasty, sweet and bitter scent of good fresh beer was all around her. It was nothing like the horrible stale blast she snorted walking past big student pubs in Southampton, and it made her thirsty.

'What can I get you to drink, James?' she said, hoping he wasn't going to want expensive single malt whisky or anything like that.

'This is on me.' He got to his feet, moving stiffly, as though he'd over-exercised and was aching. 'What would you like? They have a good range of real ales and some reasonably OK wine.'

'Then a glass of white wine, please. I'm not much of a beer drinker. Sauvignon Blanc in preference to anything with Chardonnay or Pinot Grigio in it.'

She stretched out her long legs, glad she had a job that usually allowed her to wear inexpensive jeans and boots instead of suits, tights and high heels. She loved clothes, but with her current financial crisis, she wouldn't be buying any more for a long time and had to keep the best for things like interviews.

'New World or French?' James asked.

'New Zealand if possible.' Karen felt herself relaxing a little. 'They do the gooseberry taste better than anyone else. I like it.'

'Me too,' James said.

But when he came back, he had a foaming tankard in his

hand. Seeing her surprise, he put down her glass of wine, took a sip of his beer, sighed with theatrical pleasure, and explained, 'I like wine, but I'm part of a beer-appreciation society. We're doing our single-handed bit to keep the Island pubs open as pubs and not as cafés or family destinations or bars. We want honest British pubs, where ...'

'Where a man can let his hair down and forget about women's stuff like pointless chit-chat about nothing that matters, and insisting on filling the sofa with cushions, besides nagging on about putting down the bog seat and taking out the rubbish on the right day?' Karen said with a smile to take away any sting in her teasing.

Her phone vibrated and she decided to let the caller leave a voicemail. She didn't want anything to get in the way of this encounter.

'More or less,' James agreed, but his voice was stiff and the expression on his face suggested she had not achieved the right frivolous note. 'I don't have any of that kind of complaint at home. But some of the others do. They like getting away from it. And why not?'

Karen wished she hadn't tried to bond with him by sharing a joke about his beer-loving mates. She tasted her wine, which was fine. No more than that, nothing like Stella's wonderful premier cru Bordeaux, but adequate.

'I'm glad you were prepared to meet,' she said, deciding to concentrate on work. It was usually safer, and her intentions couldn't be misinterpreted by even the most sensitive companion. 'I was afraid you might refuse to talk about Olly Matken.'

'There are things the investigation needs to know, and I can't get anyone to listen to me.' James's pleasant baritone was edged with frustration. 'When you phoned, it seemed like my best chance to make them pay attention.'

'Who've you talked to?' she asked, curious about why anyone involved in a murder investigation would refuse any offered information.

'I tried to get hold of the SIO: DCI Trench. The one you were with at the police station,' James said. 'But I'm always fobbed off with constables and civilian-support people. I'm not sure they even listen before dismissing everything I've said.'

'What do you need Cha— DCI Trench to know?' Karen asked, flicking open the lunch menu.

She hadn't wanted to eat any breakfast after the proto-row with Will and she was getting hungry.

James shifted on the bench, crossing his legs, then uncrossing them again. A big slurp of beer got stuck in his throat and for a second Karen thought he was going to have to spit it out. But he got it down at last. She filed the fact that his over-emotional engagement with Olly's predicament hadn't eased yet.

'Listen,' he said. 'This is going to sound as though I'm a candidate for the couch myself, but just because you're paranoid ...' He paused and she obligingly filled in the old joke:

'... it doesn't mean they're not out to get you.'

'That's right,' he said, looking less anxious. 'As I told you, Oliver never showed any inclination to violence. Not ever. I'd stake my life on his being in the lowest quartile for that kind of risk.'

'So?' Karen prompted when James had paused for too long.

'So, given that it is virtually certain – as I understand it –

that he did kill the victim, I believe someone else must have wound him up and sent him off to do it.'

Now it was Karen's turn to pause as she absorbed all the implications of what he'd said. She folded the menu again and laid it down, wanting to concentrate.

'Who?' she said at last. 'And why? Do you think Suzie had been threatening someone in some way?'

James got up from the small scarred oak table and walked towards the window, which offered a view of the icy-green sea and dead-white sky, marred only by the garish red-and-green Christmas lights draped over the doorway of one of the neighbouring houses. Gulls were fighting outside on the cracked old paving, and the usual sullen, sleety rain didn't seem to bother them as it fell on their feathers.

His shoulders were tight and held high up under his ears. Karen wondered how long she'd have to wait to learn exactly what he wanted the police to know. At last he came back to the table and sank his face into his tankard again. It was a battered pewter pot, which looked old enough to have been excavated from a Civil War midden.

'Why did you come to the Island in the first place?' Karen said, hoping to ease him into talking again. Without some help, he might never be able to break through his inner censorship. 'You haven't been here long, have you?'

Emerging from the tankard, he crumpled up his face in mockery of a thinking man. 'About three years. Give or take. It's silly in a way.' He sighed. 'I never meant to build up a practice here. I came for a kind of refuge while I did a bit of heavy research, without any clients at all.'

Now that he'd started to talk, Karen wasn't going to

prompt him any more, so she politely sipped her wine and waited until he was ready to get going again.

'We used to holiday here when I was a young child,' he said at last, 'and I had only good memories of the place. Then I read a travel piece in one of the Sundays about how polite everyone is here, how it's like a kind of 1950s throwback to civilized standards of behaviour and all that.' James reached for the menu and pushed it towards her, with a smile, adding, 'Talking of civilized standards of behaviour, I haven't asked what you'd like to eat. The steak and kidney's usually good.'

Karen looked down at the menu again and saw that the steak and kidney was a pudding rather than a pie. She could manage squidgy offal if it was cooked under crisp pastry, but not enclosed in a ball of damp suet.

'I'll have the fishcakes, I think.' She glanced at him and saw disapproval in his face. Too bad. 'I like to eat fish on an island, when I can.'

'It'll only be yesterday's leftovers pulverized in with whatever cold potatoes the kitchen had to spare.' James gestured through the window towards the quarrelling birds. 'More or less regurgitated gull's leavings.'

'Thanks, but that's what my students call "oversharing",' Karen said, making a face. 'I'll order at the bar. What're you having? The steak and kidney?'

James nodded. 'If you're sure. Thanks. That'd be great.'

When the barman was writing down her order, she took a quick look at her phone and saw she had a message from her mother. Handing her credit card to the man behind the bar, she put the phone to her ear and listened to the familiar over-enthusiastic voice, only slightly marred today with the hint of an uncharacteristic whine. 'Karen, you're avoiding me, and I won't have it. Aidan says you're in charge of this Christmas trip of his, so I need you to tell me when I can expect you both. Ring me.'

Karen clicked off the phone. It was true: she had been avoiding her mother's messages, but that was only because there wasn't anything to say yet. Aidan, who had lived in the States for most of the past twenty years, still hadn't confirmed the dates of his arrival and departure, so there was nothing she could give her mother. Hating being caught between the two of them, she returned to the table.

'You were saying,' Karen reminded him, 'before we got on to regurgitation . . .'

'Why I came to the Island,' he agreed. 'I'd had a bruising time at an international conference. In Zagreb of all places.'

Karen banished her family from her mind and dug around in her memory of the professional journals she had to read for work. 'I think I saw something about it. You were there as a figurehead for the anti-psychiatry movement, and some of the pills and shocks boys went for you. Wasn't that it?'

'That's right. Accusations came at me like bullets: irresponsibility, falsifying data, damaging patients and so on.' James sighed heavily, then drank some more. The beer had to be down to only a couple of inches at the bottom of his pewter pot by now.

'So I thought I'd show them all,' he went on. 'I'd stop seeing patients and come somewhere decent and kind and track down *all* the data from all over the world that confirmed my ideas, then write my stuff up, and go back out into the world like a conqueror.'

'What happened?' Karen was frowning. He couldn't have published something so important without someone at the university mentioning it, even if she herself had missed it.

'I got a bit distracted,' he admitted, with a secretive kind of smile. Then his face fell back into its habitual seriousness. 'There's a lot of distress on the Island. I started seeing patients again, remembered why I'd come into the profession in the first place, realized my book could take its time, and ... and here we are.'

'That all makes sense. But I don't see the relevance to DCI Trench's investigation – or Olly Matken.'

'Don't you? I'm still a hate figure to a large proportion of the psychiatrists of the western world. Not to speak of the drug pushers.'

Karen didn't need to put her question into words. Her face said it all. He shook his head even more impatiently.

'Not that sort of pusher. I'm talking about the big pharma companies. They've all got their pet antidepressants and antipsychotics to sell. They're even horning in on the neuro-plasticity theoreticians now. The last thing any of them want is to see incontrovertible evidence of psychotic patients recovering without poisoning themselves with "meds".' He banged down his now-empty tankard, making Karen jump.

'They've made it all so cosy with that pernicious little abbreviation,' he went on. '"Meds". Sounds so wholesome doesn't it? And yet their so-profitable pills just screw up many of the vulnerable, and add side effects like tardive dyskinesia to their other sufferings.'

The memory of Philip's despair was too clear in Karen's mind for her to accept James's loathing of pills without question.

'Pharmaceutical intervention is sometimes the only thing that stands between patients and disaster,' she said. 'And between their families and despair – or murder.'

The last word got through James's self-absorption, and he paused to give it due thought. Then he nodded so vigorously that his thin hair flew down over his red face, making him look like a figure of fun.

'I do know that,' he said, pushing it back. 'But it's no excuse for the way the drug companies market their products as "cures". Straightforward sedation would often have as good an effect. Better really because there'd be fewer side effects. You know what chlorpromazine does to some of the people who take it? And the non-responders, like Oliver, who get given higher and higher doses until they're right out of it?'

Karen knew all about the weight gain, skin problems, shaking and long-term cognitive damage that could be done by large quantities of many antipsychotic drugs. Even so, she didn't completely agree with James's views, but there seemed no point fighting the battle at this point, so she merely nodded.

'Nor does it let the government off the hook,' he went on, with bitter anger. 'They *have* to provide the money to house and treat the mentally ill in safety.'

'I agree,' said Karen, happy to be able to say something positive.

'I'm glad to hear it, but that's not the point. You're not here for me to convert to anti-psychiatry.'

'No,' Karen said. 'I'm here for you to tell me about Olly and about the people who . . .'

'Hate me,' he said with a smile full of self-awareness.

Karen thought of the division of people with paranoia into

'poor me' and 'bad me' categories. Was James a 'poor me' paranoiac, building up his shaky self-esteem by working in psychology and thereby finding a way to see everyone else as even more dysfunctional than he felt himself to be?

A shadow crossed the table. Karen looked up to see a man with loose dark curls falling over his lean tanned face, holding out two large white plates.

'You're not ranting on about global warming again, are you Jimbo?' he said, putting the plates down in front of them.

The two golden patties in front of Karen looked as far from seagulls' leavings as she could possibly imagine. A pool of cream-coloured tartare sauce, flecked with green and red, oozed over one side of the plate, while the other was filled with salad leaves glistening with olive oil.

As soon as the waiter had got James's approval of his suety pudding with its seasonal holly garnish and laid their cutlery in front of them, Karen started to eat. The fishcakes' flavour was as good as their presentation and she enjoyed every mouthful.

When she'd put down her knife and fork and finished her wine, she ran through her mental list of questions for James. But he started to speak first.

'Why did your eyes light up at the mention of global warming?' he asked.

Karen gave him top marks for perception. She hadn't thought she'd reacted at all. Maybe he wasn't quite as self-absorbed as he'd seemed.

'Are you a sceptic?' she asked, to get the ground rules agreed before they started.

'I am. Mainly because I look at the millions – billions – the government's spending on all their as-yet unproven stuff, while mental-health services are so direly under-funded. A fraction of their self-aggrandizing expenditure on carbon reduction and whatever would pay for dozens of local, well-staffed units for patients ... patients like Oliver. They'd be safe, their families would be released from the horror and responsibility. There'd be fewer victims. I ...' He shook his head. 'Clever, Karen: you deflected me. What *is* your interest in climate change?'

'I'm using it as a central example in my book on cognitive dissonance,' she said, planning to be brief, because it was a subject on which she could talk all day if given the chance, and she'd seen too many friends' eyes glazing over as she'd taken advantage of earlier opportunities. 'Much to my professor's fury, it's to be a popular book,' she added, 'so I need something everyone can see and understand.'

James put his head on one side and for the first time today looked at her with criticism in his eyes. She waited for the blow.

'Are you surprised your boss is unhappy about your writing pop psychology?' he said. 'How do you think it will it impact your academic career?'

Karen noted his use of the familiar counselling tactic of making the client see what you want to tell her by means of questions – always more easily received than instructions or criticism.

'It's like physics,' she said, having been through the same argument with Will and Max too many times to shy away from it now. 'There's nothing wrong with popularity, so long as you're honest. But forget that now. Tell me straight: who do you think wound up Olly to kill his victim? And why?'

James nodded. He hadn't yet finished his lunch. A dark brown smear of gravy marked the short space between his small lower lip and his receding chin. He put down his cutlery and faced her.

'There's a rep for one of the drug companies,' he said, reaching for his napkin and wiping his face, as though he'd felt the gravy smear, or perhaps correctly interpreted her staring at it. 'He covers Wilts, Hants and Dorset, and that includes the Island. In the old days – before I started work here – the Island gave him his biggest profits per hour of selling. Now, those have fallen through the floor. And a big part of his pay is commission based.'

'And he blames you?' Karen suggested.

'That's right. It's clear that discrediting me would give him the greatest satisfaction of all time. One of the best ways could be to show that one of the patients I've saved from over-medication went berserk without his antipsychotics. But I can't get the police to listen. You're obviously on good terms with them. Can *you* make them see sense?'

Karen shrugged. 'I can try. But I'd need a name.'

'Of course.' James stuffed his right hand in his pocket and brought out a neatly folded piece of paper. 'All the details are there. Name, phone numbers, email address, and an account of the time he banged on my front door during a consultation and harangued me. The patient was terrified, but she'll confirm the story if asked. Her name's here too.'

'OK. I'll do my best.' Karen took the piece of paper and slid it into the zipped pocket in her shoulder bag. 'Who else? Your enemies in the global-warming movement?'

'I don't have any.' James laughed. 'Don't know any of them.

Nor them me, if you see what I mean. The wasted-money thing is my own private concern. Publicly, it's just me and my beer-tasting mates collecting evidence of fudging, bad science, and downright lies from some of the warmist-alarmist groups. It's just a bit of fun.'

Not for the scientists themselves, Karen thought as she considered all the case studies she'd read in research for her book.

Cognitive dissonance, the quarrel within one person's mind between two incompatible beliefs, could make people do the most extraordinary things. The more they had invested in one – the more they'd suffered for it – the harder they had to fight against admitting the other might also have merit. One of the clearest examples she had ever seen had been a battered wife, who had endured appalling physical and emotional abuse from her husband rather than admit that the man she wanted to believe loved her in fact felt only hatred and disgust.

Karen looked across the table at James, who was staring at her with a puzzled expression in his round blue eyes. She smiled to reassure him.

'Say you're right about this bloke,' she said, tapping her bag to show James who she meant. 'Do you think he expected Olly to kill someone?'

'I don't believe it, Karen.' Charlie had great dark crescents under his eyes, making it look as though someone had hit him with a left and a right in quick succession. She didn't think he could have had any sleep last night. Had he even gone home?

'I can send someone to talk to this drug–sales bloke. But I can't see it myself.'

'I know what you mean,' she said in a quiet voice she hoped

would not wind him up any more. 'But I do think we should take seriously James's statement that Olly had never shown any sign of violence and that therefore, *if* he killed Suzie, there may have been some other ingredient we've missed so far. The least you should … I mean, the least you could sensibly do, would be to chase that up. Find out if it's true. If there's been any hint of an attack – physical attack – from Olly in the past, then you'll have an easier time making a case.'

Charlie turned away. Karen remembered the knife and asked if there'd been any sign of it. The slump of his back gave her the answer.

'Has he said anything more about it in interview?'

'Nope.' He turned back. 'You busy today?'

'Not particularly.' She had her Christmas shopping to do, but she didn't want even to try to buy something for Will after this morning. She'd have to wait until her anger had been taken over by all the stuff she felt for him when he wasn't pushing her too far: the love, the support, the trust that he would never hurt her – or she him. Only then could she find a present he would actually like. Or at least need.

She might even have to get presents for her parents too if Aidan decided he did want to spend some of his Christmas trip with them. What on earth could she buy the two people who had made it clear for as long as she'd lived with them that their only daughter was a dreary drag on their exciting lives? Shuddering a little, Karen banished her memories and concentrated on the issue in hand.

'Why?' she said.

'Can you take on the has-Olly-ever-been-violent-before questions?' Charlie said.

'Isn't that something for your team?'

'We can deal with actual events, but you can do all the behavioural crap. You know, asking about signs and habits that show he could ...' Charlie's voice died, then started up again, 'And you'll know how seriously to take the answers.'

He wheeled away, leaving her blinking and aware that she'd come to the incident room in the hope of having a spot of friendly flirting to take away the taste of the morning's rows. She caught sight of Annie talking into a phone. Annie saw her watching and gave a cheerful wave. Karen waved back. It didn't make her feel any better.

She wished she'd brought her car over to the Island, instead of taking the hovercraft as a foot passenger. If she'd had the car, she could have driven over to the patch of land at the north-western corner of the Island, where her new house was going to rise in the spring. Or she could have taken herself off to Freshwater for a reminiscent walk along the beach, or to the Needles, to regain her sense of Aidan as her beloved elder brother, rather than the now barely known stranger, who had lived in the States for so long.

It struck Karen suddenly that Aidan's planned appearance for Christmas had been producing a continuous low-level anxiety somewhere in her mind for weeks. Maybe that was why her response to Will's demands had been so aggressive.

What would it be like to have Aidan with her again? Would she be able to see him as the adored hero of her childhood? Or would he be the deserter, who had abandoned her to save himself and later on been so angry with her decision to marry at the age of eighteen that he'd stopped even answering her letters? Would she be able to love him again, or would all the buried resentment at what he'd done the last time she'd been contemplating a wedding make her hate him?

Wearily she took out her phone and rang her mother.

'Karen. At last! So when *are* you and Aidan going to arrive for Christmas?' Dilly's tone was so sharp she couldn't have sounded less welcoming if she'd yelled 'piss off'.

'Listen,' Karen said with as much politeness as she could find. 'I don't yet have his dates, so I can't say when he might be available to see you, and that's not down to me anyway. But I don't understand why you're assuming either of us would be coming to London for Christmas Day itself. I've already told you: I have plans to entertain here in Southampton.'

'Well, really! First you trick Aidan into pouring money into that pointless shack on the Pile of Shite, then you think you can keep him to yourself the first time he comes home from the States in nearly twenty years. Karen, you've always been selfish, but this is . . .'

Selfish! Karen felt as though outrage was strangling her. She couldn't hear anything but the roaring in her ears. Visions of Christmas after Christmas chased themselves past her internal eye. She and Aidan had yearned for the kind of family excitements their school friends enjoyed, only to be dumped year after year on semi-strangers or sent to the Island at the last minute because they were in the way. Their parents must sometimes have provided Christmas trees and tinsel, presents and plum pudding, but Karen couldn't remember any.

'Who owned the "pointless shack" in the first place?' she demanded, thinking of the way her mother had begged her to take it over in order to raise enough cash to save her own business.

Dilly produced one of her best cascades of laughter: 'Oh, darling, you can't shift your responsibilities on to me. I'd have sold it to someone else if I hadn't known of your bizarre devotion to the horrible place. I'd have got far more for it, too. You've had a real steal, you know, with what you paid me. Now, Christmas?'

'If Aidan has told you he's coming over for it this year,' Karen said, 'then you know as much as I do. When I hear more, I'll pass it on. In the meantime, I'm really busy at work just now. Bye.'

It's not as if Dilly's old and incapable, Karen told her swiftly rising conscience as she put away the phone. She's only sixty-five, still vigorously working and with whole armies of clients and friends and cellars-full of champagne. I am not going to play her games any longer. I'm *not*.

Chapter 9

Day Four: Saturday 8.30 a.m.

Giles was pleased with Lucy. She was really focusing on arrangements for the shoot and had organized a lunch that sounded damn good. He'd told her she could buy in whatever help she needed and, although she'd decided to do all the preparation and shopping herself, she'd booked a couple of nice girls from a private catering company to deal with all the last-minute stuff and be on hand for serving and washing-up.

He approved of the menu she'd chosen too. Much more sensible than the frilly ideas she'd had last time, full of salad and fruit and nonsense like that. This time they were to have game stew, cooked to the Wine Society's recipe, with baked spuds and green beans, followed by Eccles cakes and Wensleydale. Nice and simple; wholesome; and nothing fussy about it. Easy to transport to the old barn and easy to eat. Lucy had told him she wouldn't be walking with the guns, didn't like getting cold and wet. Fair enough, he'd said and meant it. She deserved a bit of slack these days. And the weather was freezing.

A year or so back, she'd been so twitchy and weepy that she'd hardly ever got out of bed. In those days you couldn't have trusted her to organize her own cup of tea, let alone a shooting lunch for ten. Now you could. Which was great. Especially since this was a bloody important shoot. For the first time since he'd left the City, Giles would be showing some of the most powerful of his old rivals just how good his life here was.

They might still enjoy the same success he'd once shared, but they were stuck on the treadmill, dealing with the sodding politicians groaning on about their bonuses, fighting for the few big clients left in the world and always facing the possibility of some disaster that could put them in court – and possibly even in prison. Whereas Giles was sitting pretty in a trophy house with a wife now nearly back to trophy status since she'd got her marbles back, a fantastic boat, plenty of dosh from investments known to the whole world to be absolutely brilliant and ... well, more or less everything a man could want.

Except for the things like Suzie's death and the police and nobody knowing who was telling the truth and who was stringing everyone along and what he ought to be doing about it all. Sometimes he felt as if that psychopathic boy had dug a hole in his head when he killed Suzie, then poured the resulting space full of molten lead. Boiling. Heavy. Painful. Stopping Giles thinking straight. Poisoning him.

And then one of his phones rang. This particular ring tone had become like a flea sucking at his blood. Knowing he had to answer, he pulled open the top drawer of his desk, felt for the phone and listened. He hoped it would be a wrong number. It wasn't.

Billy's dad looked him up and down, turned him round, then nodded.

'You'll do,' he said and for once he had a small grin on his face. 'Let's go.'

'Hang on a minute,' Billy's mum said, running down the stairs.

He could see she wanted to kiss him again and warn him not to get into trouble. His sisters were pointing at him from up on the landing and giggling, instead of making paper chains like they were supposed to 'cos their dad said he couldn't afford a proper tree or decorations this year.

'Now, Billy,' his mum said, smoothing down his hair. He'd spent ages getting it to stand up with the wax he'd nicked. 'Remember to do everything Mr Sprott tells you. And don't forget, shooting's . . .'

'Dangerous. I know, Mum.' Billy smiled up at her. He still didn't know why she hadn't been cross when he got home yesterday or tried to punish him or anything. She'd even said she'd wash his soft sweater. Herself. Not in the machine or anything. And she'd never doubted him when he said he'd been given it, like he'd been given the iPod.

Being home was better. Which was weird. So far she hadn't shouted at his dad when he was around either. Or made him look after his sisters. And his dad hadn't gone off on one. Not yet anyway. So it'd been worth running away. And he liked having hot food instead of eating out of those tins. His mum hadn't said she didn't believe his story of camping in a whole bunch of barns when he got lost outside Cowes. And she'd fought off the police for him too. No one had searched him or found the money he'd nicked. Or asked about where he'd been when the swearing girl had died, or who'd been in the car, or anything.

'All right,' she said now, bending down to kiss his forehead. 'Don't forget to say thank you to Mr Henty and make sure you don't make a nuisance of yourself today.'

Billy managed not to wipe the mark her lips must've made on his face till he and his dad were outside and climbing into the truck. But he gave it a good old rub then.

'Phew,' said his dad when the truck had turned round the first corner. He wound down his window and sucked in a big mouthful of the air outside. 'It's good to be out and free.'

He looked round at Billy.

'You really OK, son?'

'Course, Dad.'

'What did happen while you were ... when you were away?'

Billy hunched his shoulder. He couldn't tell anyone what really went on, so he wasn't going to say anything else.

'Did someone ... well, hurt you?' said his dad.

That was easy to answer. 'Course not.'

'So why did you stay away so long?'

Billy hunched his shoulders even more. 'Dunno,' he said.

'OK. We'll talk about that a bit later. How did you find Mr Henty? What were you doing when he said he'd bring you back?'

'I *told* you, Dad.' Now Billy was cross. 'I went to his boat to have a shower but he was there and he made me come home.'

'But why did you go *there*? What made you think you could break into his boat to get yourself clean?'

'I wasn't going to break in. I done some work for him once 'n' he showed me round his boat and said he'd take me for a sail one day. I see the shower then. And I remembered it when I was, like, cold and dirty.'

'But why were you there, at the marina, when you were camping around a whole lot of farms out in the country?'

'I don' wan' to talk about it.' Billy let himself sound snuffly, as if he was crying again, because that was the only thing that made all the grown-ups stop asking questions. It worked again this time, which was great. 'I got lost. I told you.'

The truck climbed up the road out of Cowes towards Mr Henty's place. When they got there, Billy could see the row of posh four-by-fours and the battered trucks and jeeps and old bangers of the other beaters. The minute his dad had parked their truck, Billy wriggled out of his seatbelt and slid down off the seat, and ran off to talk to Mr Sprott, the head keeper, without saying anything more to his dad.

'Hey, Billy-Boy!' It was Mr Henty's voice. Billy stopped dead and looked round. 'How're you doing?'

'I'm OK, Mr Henty,' Billy said, remembering how his mum would probably ask Mr Sprott how he'd behaved today. If he wanted more jobs off of Mr Henty, he'd better make himself look good. 'Thanks.'

'Cut along to Mr Sprott then. He'll tell you what he wants you to do. Hi, Dan, how's it going?' Mr Henty turned away to talk to Billy's dad. Billy knew they were going to talk about him so he got as far away from them as he could.

*

Karen was back on the Island, this time with her car, and she had Charlie beside her as she drove to talk to Olly's parents. Philip had asked that his wife be interviewed at home rather than in the police station because he was so worried about her state of mind and health. Charlie had phoned last night to ask Karen to go with him, saying, 'I can't trust myself with that bloke, so I want you there, checking his body language and all that crap. Oh, and bring your car. Mine's being serviced and I don't want to go in one with stripes and blue lights from the pool. I want him thinking I'm sensitive. If we go in yours . . .'

'You devious bugger,' Karen said, with affection.

'I'm not satisfied Blazon's on the level,' Charlie went on, as though he hadn't registered either the criticism or the warmth. 'So I want you to find out what you can about his methods with the boy.'

Since then Karen had spent some time at her computer, checking on James's public reputation, and found his description of the Zagreb conference to be exactly accurate. A lot of their colleagues clearly still hated him. The vitriol in some of the recent blogs she'd read still shocked her fourteen hours later.

One of the worst – and least technical – had simply said, 'Wankers like this one need a new arsehole torn in them. He's a dangerous fucker, getting off on other people's pain. No one should believe anything he says or let any other vulnerable clients anywhere near him.'

She wondered whether James had read the blogs and, if he had, whether he'd managed to see them as the excessive projections of inadequate and distressed individuals, or whether he'd taken them seriously, let them get to him. If he had, then they could explain why he was so twitchy about Olly's state of mind and crimes. Maybe all the aggression in the blogs had sensitized him, so that his reactions to any kind of criticism had become those of a man fighting for his life. She needed to talk to someone who knew him well enough to see him straight and not look at him through the prism of suspicion and anger.

'Charlie,' Karen said, as she signalled to turn right off the main road.

'Yup?'

'When you were living here, did you have a doctor? A GP?'

'I registered with one. Why?'

'Get on well with him? Her?' Karen said, concentrating on the bumpy surface of the side road. She didn't want to damage her tyres any more than necessary.

'I only went once – with a dodgy gut. Why?' Charlie said.

'It could be useful to get some idea of how the medics on the Island see James Blazon. I know how a lot of his fellow professionals think of him, but if he's getting generally good results . . .' Karen didn't have to finish her sentence.

Charlie was already getting out his phone. Karen listened in some amusement to the way he blandished his way through the obstructive receptionist who answered to the doctor herself. Karen smiled at the memory of how her brother had always called such women 'rejectionists'.

'DCI Trench,' Charlie said into the phone, 'investigating the murder of Suzie Gray, and . . .'

He broke off to listen. Karen could easily imagine the automatic expressions of shock and sympathy.

'I know. Yes. Very bad,' Charlie was saying. 'What I need is your take on Oliver Matken's psychologist, this Blazon character. You ever referred anyone to him?'

Charlie paused, muttering 'yeah' and 'great' and 'thanks' down the phone for a few minutes, at last completing the call with more decisive expressions of gratitude. Then he put the phone back in his pocket and turned his face towards Karen.

'She liked him. Great with depressed women. Not so hot with serious cases like paranoid schizophrenia. She thinks Blazon believed his own PR and got cocky. Came unstuck with Olly and caused Suzie's death.'

'So if James isn't paranoid himself and someone really is trying to screw his reputation, then it's working,' Karen said.

'Don't *you* think he was irresponsible?' Charlie sounded surprised rather than angry now.

'It's hard to say. I don't know enough yet. But James has definitely had success treating schizophrenics in the past with his own particular kind of therapy. He aims to get new neural pathways growing in their brains, to change the physical shape and therefore the . . .'

'Too much detail, Karen,' Charlie said sharply. 'I don't give a fuck about his ambition. All I need to know is what he made Olly do to Suzie.'

'Which we don't yet know. Where have you got to with the drugs rep?' Karen asked.

'Annie's taking that one on. She'll report when I get back. Here we are. There's the sign. Sharp left turn, Karen.'

She drove into a gravel semicircle in front of a big but ugly nineteenth-century house. Behind its red-brick solidity she caught glimpses of the tops of various specimen trees, including a monkey-puzzle and a vast cedar of Lebanon. Other smaller houses trailed down the hill towards the village. Several of them looked a lot more attractive than this gabled monster.

'What does he do – Philip, I mean?' Karen asked, looking around the well-kept place. 'He must make quite a lot.'

'Solicitor. Senior partner in a firm in Newport. Does wills, trusts, that sort of thing.'

'So why had he been gardening when he was being Olly's appropriate adult the other day?'

'No idea.' Charlie sounded bored. 'Maybe nobody wants wills or trusts at the moment. Maybe he's done so well he's going part-time. Who gives a fuck?'

Karen parked between a battered grey Ford Fiesta and a well-maintained Toyota Prius hybrid. Opening the car door, she heard a long series of clucking sounds.

'What's that noise?' she said, looking up at the cloudy sky.

'Shoot.' Charlie sounded casual, and slammed the passenger door shut without even looking for the source of the noise. He saw Karen had no idea what he was talking about and added, 'That's the pheasants going over. Any minute now you'll hear the pop-pop-pop of the guns. There you go.'

Karen felt sorry for the inhabitants of all the houses and cottages all round if they were often subjected to this slaughter.

'Don't look like that,' Charlie added with a short laugh. 'I hadn't put you down as a sentimental animal rights-ist.'

'I'm not. I just don't like the idea of braying bankers massacring defenceless birds. They don't even eat them, do they?'

'Some do. No need to feel so dowie about it.'

This time Karen didn't even have to ask for a translation because Charlie grinned and added a gloss at once, 'Dowie. Geordie for glum. More or less.'

'But don't they specially rear the birds,' Karen said, 'taking real care of the eggs and chicks, only to scare them up into the air when they're old enough and then kill them?' She grimaced, adding: 'For *fun*. Doesn't that bother you?'

'Next to what I feel about a fifteen-year-old girl stabbed to death?' Charlie shook his dark head. 'Nope. Let's go.'

The door knocker took the form of a well-polished brass hand with a frilled wrist band. It looked older and a lot more elegant than the house itself. Charlie rapped it hard on the door, which was opened a moment later by Philip himself. Dressed today in dark-blue cords and a grey sweater over a checked shirt, he looked more uncomfortable than he had in his gardening gear at the police station. At least he didn't have a knife hanging off his belt this time.

'Doctor Taylor,' he said, nodding politely at Karen. 'DCI Trench. Come on in. My wife's in here. Caroline's with her. I hope you don't want to see Matt. We sent him to friends for the day. He's upset enough about what's happened to Olly without having to face the police himself.'

Karen remembered that he'd talked of his daughter, saying she was away at university. She must be home for the long Christmas break.

'No problem, sir.' Charlie sounded crisp and more polite than usual.

'Good of you to come in a civilian car.' Philip's smile was forced. 'That'll help a bit with the neighbours. They haven't stopped poking around since they saw your search team here.'

'Have you been having a lot of trouble with them?' Karen asked, interested to hear about the search. Charlie hadn't said anything about it.

Philip leaned against the wall for a moment, closing his eyes. Then he produced another strained smile.

'Some have been great. Supportive. Kind. Worried, though, and coming round wanting to know and wanting to help and being ... But it's well meant. Unlike the stuff we're getting through the post and email.' Philip grimaced. 'The letters are anonymous.'

'Threatening?' Charlie said quickly.

Philip briefly shook his head. 'Aggressive and insulting, but not threatening or I'd have put you on to them right away. I've got them in a file at the office. Thought I'd wait till they stopped coming, then give you the whole lot in one go. They're on the lines of: aren't you ashamed of yourselves? Dreadful parents. Irresponsible letting someone that dangerous loose on the Island. Should have made him take his pills. Should have had him locked up. Unpleasant, but understandable. People are scared of what Olly will do next, who else will d— I mean, suffer at his hands.'

Karen hoped her smile expressed more sympathy than pity at the thought of Olly's future victims. Philip grimaced.

'Anyway, come on in and meet Angie and Caroline,' he added. 'And be ... gentle, won't you? It's been ... Angie's ...' He rubbed the heels of both hands against his face again in much the same way as he had when they first met him.

As they walked into the sitting room, Karen heard a sharp young voice say, 'Oh, come on, Mummy! You'll make yourself go mad again if you don't stop this. You *know* it's not your fault Olly was born with schizophrenic genes. Nor is it your fault that James Blazon wrecked the only treatment that ever worked. You were doing what you thought best. You were wrong, but it's not your fault. Or your responsibility. You've got to stop tearing yourself apart like this or we'll all suffer. Even more than we have to anyway.'

The message might have been encouraging, Karen thought, but the delivery was outrageous: hectoring, threatening – almost cruel. She wasn't surprised to see the older woman, who looked as if she couldn't be much more than forty-five, cringing on the sofa, while the younger one stood in front of her, small, neat, hard faced and wagging a finger.

She would have been pretty if she hadn't been frowning so ferociously. Her well-cut short dark hair, small high-cheekboned face and brilliant bright-blue eyes made her look like a pure-bred Siamese cat. Karen wondered if she knew it and had dressed accordingly. Both her skinny jeans and her short, very fitted cashmere sweater were the colour of a Siamese's fur, and her French Sole ballet shoes were the same sable colour as her hair and eyebrows.

Karen couldn't suppress a smile as she thought that all Caroline needed to complete the illusion was black make-up on her face.

'Don't talk to your mother like that,' Philip shouted, making Caroline flinch. 'And go and get some coffee for us all. A pot. And hot up some milk.'

Caroline looked as though he'd hit her, suddenly seeming much younger and far more gentle than she'd been with her mother. To Karen's surprise, she set off to do as he'd told her.

'Darling, these are the people I told you about. My wife, Angela. We'll do our best to answer your questions, but ...' His voice tailed off.

Angela got up off the sofa and knocked into a fruitwood

sofa table that seemed to be carrying a whole shop's worth of Christmas cards ready for signature.

'Sorry,' she said, leaving the gaily coloured heap to lie where it had fallen over the table and the dark-red carpet. She shook their hands and apologized for the state of her face, adding, 'I just can't ... it's impossible to ... to believe that Olly could have done anything like this to anyone. But to Suzie? *Why* would he hurt Suzie? They were friends. Had been friends for ever. She was no threat to him. She was never unkind to him.' Angela looked over her shoulder towards the door and added, 'Unlike nearly all the others.'

'Did he have hallucinations?' Karen asked quietly.

Angela nodded, trying to smile and failing. Karen saw exactly where Caroline had got her pretty cheekbones and dazzling eyes, but in her mother the eyes had already faded, and the cheekbones' sharpness was muffled by perimenopausal fat. She was also grey with fatigue, and her eyes were underlined by deep greenish-grey shadows, the colour of the sky just before a storm broke.

'Sometimes,' she said. 'But even then, he was only frightened by them. Not wound-up to hurt other people, I mean. He never did anything ...' She broke off, fighting the urge to cry.

Her upper lip lengthened and her nostrils spread, as her eyes narrowed into slits. She couldn't hold in the tears and turned aside to wipe her eyes on a man-sized linen handkerchief.

'I've talked to lots of other parents like us, and they've had awful things to say about what happened during crises,' she said, when she was once more in control. 'But Olly's never been like that. He's always hidden in corners, chittering like a terrified monkey, when he's been hallucinating.'

'Even when he's been smoking dope?' Charlie said, glancing across at Philip, whose expression was full of obstinate resistance. Charlie looked back at Angela. 'He does still sometimes smoke dope, doesn't he?'

'Not for a long time. It used to be skunk mostly. I got so used to the smell of it I always knew. Even when he was behaving normally.' Angela shuddered, looking sick. 'I hated it. More than you can imagine. That's why I'm so grateful to James Blazon. Somehow he got Olly to stop. I can't tell you ... But in the old days I'd smell it on his hair, and on his clothes whenever I could get them off him to wash them. Which wasn't often, you see. So I always knew. And it never made any difference. He was always frightened, whether he'd been smoking or not. Sometimes less when he'd been smoking. Not always, though.'

Karen thought of the moment when Olly had hunched up with his feet on his chair seat, keening, and recognized his mother's description of the frightened monkey.

'Did he ever take anything else?' Charlie asked, sounding so casual that Karen was instantly alert.

'What d'you mean?' Philip said, plumping down on the sofa beside his wife and taking her hand.

He was squeezing her fingers more tightly than simple comfort dictated, but Karen couldn't decide whether that was because he had no idea of what he was doing or because he was trying to warn his wife about something.

'Did he take other illegal drugs?' Charlie's voice was still polite but there was enough suppressed irritation in it to make Karen think he assumed Philip was being deliberately obtuse.

Philip's expression showed nothing but surprise, but Angela's was more suspicious.

'I'm not sure,' she said so slowly her voice was painful to hear.

'But maybe?' Charlie was carefully avoiding any hint of coercion in his body language.

'I did wonder.' Angela extracted her hand from her husband's grip. 'There was one day, early last autumn, when his mood was … kind of … well different.'

'More aggressive?' Still Charlie was holding on to most of his impatience. Karen admired him for it.

'Not aggressive exactly, but more jittery. More talkative. Much more talkative.'

Uh oh, Karen thought, wondering what the blood and urine tests had thrown up. 'Jittery and talkative' suggested cocaine to her. And if he'd taken it in the form of crack that could explain why a passive youth might have suddenly turned violent.

'Why are you asking this?' Philip demanded.

Charlie turned towards him, eyes serious and voice slowing down. 'At Doctor Taylor's suggestion, we did some blood and urine tests. The results are inconclusive.'

Bugger, Karen thought.

'There's no evidence of cannabis – or alcohol – which suggests you may be right that he'd given up. As I'm sure you know, cannabis traces stay in the blood for weeks. But there's other traces in the urine … could be cocaine.' Charlie waited for a reaction, but neither of the Matkens said anything. 'However, he told us he had a filling in his lower back molar a few days ago. We've checked with the dentist; he used lignocaine.'

Angela was nodding with vigour. 'That's right. About the filling, I mean. Olly had had terrible toothache and I made him go.' Her voice was rising in excitement. 'He said he had an injection. It must be that. I didn't know it was the same as coke.'

'Given that, we can't know for sure where the traces come from, so ...' Charlie said just as the door was pushed open and Caroline came in carrying a perfectly arranged tray of coffee and biscuits.

'Did *you* know Olly was on coke, too?' Philip said to her, without waiting for Charlie to finish his sentence.

Caroline's beautifully plucked and dyed eyebrows lifted. She bent to put the tray on a broad, kilim-covered ottoman in front of the sofa, and then straightened up to say coldly, 'I can't say it surprises me. That boy's such a mess, he'd take anything he could get his hands on.'

'Where did he get his drugs?' Karen asked, earning herself an angry stare from Charlie. But if he hadn't wanted her to ask questions, he shouldn't have brought her here.

Caroline shrugged one slender shoulder. '*I*'ve no idea. I've never moved in those circles. Someone once said Yarmouth's the best place round here, but I wouldn't know.'

'Surely you must have some idea, DCI Trench,' Philip said with a firmness that made it easy for Karen to see him as the senior partner in a law firm.

Charlie acknowledged Philip's point with a slight smile. 'We always monitor known dealers. No links to your son so far.'

'How is he?' Angela asked, leaning over her knees and looking up to plead with Charlie. 'When are you going to let him come home? He must be so frightened. I can't bear to think ... I don't suppose he'll ever get over this.'

'We've run out of time,' Charlie said. 'So we'll be releasing him this morning. You'll get a call.'

'Thank God,' said his mother, leaning back against the padded sofa and closing her eyes.

'But,' Charlie said, with pity in his eyes, 'we may need him again. Which is why I came today. I don't know what your plans for his treatment are now, but I don't want you sending him off the Island. Not yet.'

As Angela went white, Charlie gestured to Karen, quite obviously telling her to do something useful. But Philip got in first, pulling his wife into his arms, hiding her face against his broad shoulder, and saying over her head, 'You mean you're still hoping to find the weapon with his prints or DNA on it. Even though there's been no sign anywhere near where Suzie died?'

'Partly,' Charlie admitted. 'But there's other things too.'

'Such as?'

Charlie stared at Philip, as though trying to assess his reliability – or perhaps remembering how badly the man had wanted his son convicted.

'The blood-spatter analysis shows Olly was right there in the spot where the killer did it,' Charlie said at last, speaking as carefully as a doctor giving a terminal diagnosis. 'But there's evidence of a third person, who could've taken the knife off him.'

'Evidence?' Angela had fought her way out of her husband's protective embrace. She stood up and faced Charlie. 'I don't understand. They said the only camera that could have recorded anything in the alleyway wasn't working that night.

What evidence have you got?'

Charlie looked down at everyone's feet, then up again to meet her eyes. 'There are drops that must have fallen from the blade,' he said with a detached coolness designed to make the information less terrible for her, 'rather than spurted from a wound. They show the blade moved over her body and across some of the cobbles in the alley; then there's no more – as if the knife was wrapped up and taken away. There's a partial footprint, too. Blurred and the toe half of the shoe only. Smaller than Olly's. It looks like no more than a size five, and his feet were—'

'Size ten,' Angela said as her eyes poured with tears again. 'He always had huge feet, even when he was only tiny. Oh, God! I need some air.'

She rushed towards one of the two long sash windows, propped her knee on the chintz cushion and pushed up the heavy glass, inhaling the cold dampness as though it was some kind of restorative.

The change of temperature seemed to wake Philip out of a near trance. 'That's why you searched this place yesterday?' he said in a voice so clipped and quiet it was more threatening than any rant.

'Partly,' Charlie said again, just as the same sinister clucking sound pushed its way into the room.

Karen watched Philip's big dark eyes tighten. She looked away from him towards the others. All she could see of Angela was her back, heaving with the depth of her breathing. Caroline's pretty face, on the other hand, showed a mixture of contempt and fury as she shivered, crossing her arms over her body for warmth. For once the disdain did not seem to be directed at her mother, which intrigued Karen.

'Are you anti-shooting?' she asked in a friendly way, all ready to sympathize.

Caroline's small dark head shook so vigorously the silky hair flew this way and that like a flag in a high wind.

'No, but Daddy should have been there. He always goes shooting with the Hentys.' Her cold voice tightened. 'The bastards withdrew his invitation. It's not—'

'Shut up, darling,' Philip said. 'It's entirely understandable.'

'What happened?' Charlie asked.

Philip turned away, but only to fetch a single sheet of paper from the well-polished walnut bureau to the right of the fireplace. He handed it over. Karen caught a glimpse of sprawling black ink under a neat embossed address, but Charlie soon offered her the sheet. She read:

Dear Philip

In the awful circumstances of Suzie's death, it seems best if you don't join us on Saturday, don't you think?

As soon as everything's sorted out and Olly's back home – as I'm sure he will be – we can all get back to normal. But just now, I think it's best if you and Giles don't have too much to do with each other. We would have cancelled the shoot because of Suzie, but Jib and Simon said we must carry on.

Please give Angela my love. Oh, and Caroline too, of course.

Yours

Lucy

'Lucy?' Karen asked generally, looking from Charlie to the Matkens and back again.

'Giles Henty's wife,' Philip answered brusquely.

'She must be having a hell of a time,' Angela said quietly. She shut the window and came back to her old seat in the corner of the dark-red sofa, automatically plumping up its bright kilim-covered cushions.

'Why d'you say that?' Karen asked, noticing a new resentment on Caroline's face as she stared at her mother.

Angela lifted her tiny shoulders. 'Giles is ... Like so many very successful men, Giles believes the whole of life should go his way. When it doesn't ... when anything happens to spoil his picture of what he's due, well, he tends to be difficult. I think that's why ...'

'Why what?' Karen kept the delivery of her questions gentle, but she was determined to find out everything Angela wasn't yet managing to say.

'Why he found retirement so hard,' Angela went on. 'But he couldn't admit it, so it was poor Lucy who went under.'

She didn't look at either her husband or her daughter, so Karen did and was interested to see in Caroline's face even more contempt and a kind of resignation settling over her father's. Was this, perhaps, a backhanded way of explaining Angela's own recourse to James Blazon? Did she feel she had had to carry the whole family's emotional load for them? How much did they resent that?

'So who is this other person the spatter-analysis has thrown up?' Caroline said sharply, deflecting everyone's attention from her mother. 'Why aren't you charging *them*, Inspector?'

'We still have to find them.' Charlie smiled at her, but it didn't do anything to lessen her aggression.

'And just exactly how will you do that?' she asked.

Suddenly Karen glanced at Caroline's feet and regretfully assessed them at rather less than a size five. Hostility of this strength was often driven by guilt. It would have been very neat if Caroline had been the source of Olly's terror.

Somehow they had to get him to show them his devil's face.

'If you didn't do the blood tests in time to get a clear result on the drug testing,' Caroline went on even more spikily, 'and you can't even find a proper footprint in all that blood, how *do* you expect to ...?'

'It was raining that afternoon,' Charlie said with a dry legalistic voice that told Karen he had got well past the panic of the first hours of the investigation. 'We only got such a good spatter-analysis because the alley was sheltered. Whoever took the knife leaned over Suzie's body to get it from Olly.'

'What about the cameras?' Caroline snapped. 'Last time I was at the marina, there were CCTV cameras absolutely everywhere.'

'At the marina, yeah.' Charlie was showing amazing tolerance. 'And we have tapes that show everything our statements led us to expect. But, like your mother says, the only useful one wasn't working. There's a major upgrade to the cameras and monitoring due next year.'

'But ...'

'Caroline, stop it,' Angela said, with surprising confidence. 'They know what they're doing. Chief Inspector, what do you need from us now?'

Karen stopped listening as she tried to work out how the family's relationships operated. Caroline was so clearly a daddy's girl, and yet Philip was as tough on her as he had seemed with his son. Angela looked like her daughter's victim, yet she was clearly able to stand up to Caroline when she'd had enough. Karen concentrated again as she heard Charlie's voice saying the word 'suicide risk'.

'D'you think I don't know that?' Angela's voice turned into a wail that made Karen think again of Olly's keening. 'He's always been at risk of killing himself. What's different now?'

'No idea,' Charlie said, but the compassion in his voice was obvious to all of them. 'Our medic says it's a real possibility. I came to tell you.'

'And I suppose you want us to make sure your best suspect doesn't escape you by hanging himself.'

Karen gasped, just as Philip shouted his daughter's name. Caroline merely shrugged, then said, 'Why pretend? We all know what's going on here. They don't care about us. Why should we make it easy for them?'

Outside, back in her car, Karen turned on the ignition and put the car in gear, saying, 'Warning them about Olly's likely self-harm isn't the real reason why you came out here today – or why you wanted me, is it?'

Charlie laid a warm hand on hers as it lay on the gear lever. Now all his muscles were soft and easy. He was definitely feeling good again. Her own hand relaxed under his touch. She felt trusted and trusting. After a moment, Charlie tightened his grip, then let her go.

'I wanted you to see the family set-up and tell me if you think Olly's mother could've been the one who took the knife from him,' he said. 'Did you look at her feet?'

'No. I was concentrating on the sister's.' Karen tried to forget their moment of peace just now.

'Mum's are the right size. She's been his prime carer all along. In the past she's gone all over the Island to track him down when he's gone off on one. What if she followed him and found him – but too late to stop him killing Suzie – and did the only thing she could think of to protect him?'

'She did know the only camera overlooking the alleyway wasn't working,' Karen said slowly. 'She is very protective of him, too. And stronger than she looks. I can see where you're going with this. But presumably your search of the house didn't produce anything.'

Charlie shook his head, then said, 'Nothing important. An unregistered pay-as-you-go mobile that none of them could identify. The assumption is it must have been Olly's; maybe he had it to communicate with his dealer. The only number in the call records is another pay-as-you-go phone we can't identify. Otherwise we found bugger all that doesn't fit with a smug bunch of posh Islanders.'

His voice was so bitter that Karen leaned forwards so she could turn her head and look into his eyes.

'What?' he demanded.

She quickly thought up an important but untroubling question. 'Have you asked Olly who took the knife from him?'

'Yup.'

'And? Come on, Charlie. Tell me.'

'He said he didn't know what we were talking about. That he never had any knife. Then he said there wasn't anyone – and we know there was. Why would he protect the person who took the knife if it wasn't someone very important to him?'

Chapter 10

The windscreen was so steamy Karen could barely see out of it. She turned on the demister and opened her window, hearing the clucking sound of another batch of pheasant-victims flying overhead to meet death by lead pellet.

'Hang on, Karen. Pull over and clear the screen.' Charlie's voice offered no encouragement to question his orders. 'This lack of visibility is dangerous.'

Knowing he was right, but still disliking the way he'd talked to her, she drove into the nearest lay-by and parked behind a lorry.

Before she could reach for the scraper or sponge she kept in the glove box, Charlie had pulled a clean handkerchief out of his pocket and was rubbing down the windscreen in front of her.

'There you go,' he said at last. 'That won't smear and you won't kill us. On your way. I need to get back to the nick fast.'

'Fine.' She put the car in gear again, checked her mirrors,

signalled and manoeuvred the car out of the lay-by as slowly and carefully as though she were taking her driving test.

'OK, OK.' Charlie laughed, a little guiltily. 'I know you've been driving for nearly twenty years and blah, blah, blah. I still don't want to get killed because you miss a fucking great hazard in the middle of the road.'

Karen flashed a glance at him, as she put her foot harder down on the accelerator. The car responded and surged forwards. In her memory there had never been any traffic on this road, and none of the bends was savage.

'Like I say, I know you've been driving for decades.' Charlie sounded less amused now. 'But don't be stupid. You of all people know ...'

He broke off, and Karen remembered telling him exactly how her first husband had died. She was already braking gently enough to be safe. She took the next corner at a decorous thirty, then had to jam her foot down in a classic emergency stop. A bearded man was standing in the middle of the road, holding something heavy, as rain poured down over his head. The rain was hitting the car so hard that drops bounced right up from the bonnet, bringing steam with them.

Her tyres shrieked and skidded. The car was almost aquaplaning across the road. Karen didn't need to be told what to do. She turned into the skid and felt the car buck and slide until she longed for it to hit the bank. At least that would stop it.

Round they went, sliding sideways instead of simply circling. The soaking man in the road backed away, staggering under the weight of his burden. Karen kept the wheel at full lock and prayed. At last the tyres regained their traction and the car stopped. A hissing sound and the smell of burning rubber mixed in her mind with the pounding of her blood and the harsh scouring effect of adrenaline.

Not risking another glance at Charlie, who had behaved as the perfect passenger and neither shouted nor grabbed for the wheel, Karen wrenched open her door and ran towards the man in the road.

He was leaning hard against the high bank at the side of the road, his head grinding into the bare root of a tree that was growing precariously halfway up. Nettles and ivy were wrapped all round the rest of the bank, and water dripped off every leaf. About two feet away, a gap in the bank showed a five-barred gate, swinging open on its hinges. That must be how he'd reached the road. He shouted something Karen couldn't hear through the ringing in her ears.

She looked more closely. Then she wiped her eyes, not believing what she saw: a boy with a great hole in his neck, pouring blood, lying across the man's outstretched arms. The boy's body was floppy. His head hung down, stretching his throat, and his very straight brown hair was dragged into a sharp point that carried all the blood and rainwater, like a funnel. No more than two seconds could have passed since she'd got out of the car.

Her senses were working again. She heard Charlie's feet pounding behind her and the strange man sobbing, 'Hospital. For Christ's sake, take us to hospital. Please.'

'Come on,' Charlie said, taking his arm and urging him away from the bank. 'Get in. I'll drive, Karen. I don't know the hospital's number. Phone nine nine nine and get them to say we're on our way. Child. Shot. Breathing but bleeding out.

Make sure a team meets us at the A and E entrance to the hospital. Get in.'

Karen's wet hands slipped on her phone, but she didn't drop it. Charlie had taken the boy so that the man could get into the back seat. As soon as he was safely sitting there, Charlie fed the boy's body in over his knees, then folded up the handkerchief he'd used to wipe the windscreen and laid the pad over the boy's wound.

'Hold that there. Tight as you can.'

The man did as he said, then moved clumsily along the seat, so that Charlie could slam the door shut without crushing the boy's head. Karen saw blood soaking through the folded handkerchief. The boy's head bobbed and bounced against the seat.

She sat in front, concentrating on getting the three numbers pushed into the phone, wishing her hands weren't so clumsy. Charlie rammed the gear lever into first and roared back into the middle of the road. Karen realized she hadn't put on her seat belt and nearly dropped the phone as she tried to keep it wedged between her ear and shoulder while she stuffed the shiny metal end of the belt into its socket.

'Emergency,' said a bright voice in her ear. 'Which service do you want?'

Karen's voice was tight and hoarse as she gave the necessary information first to the general emergency call centre, then to the ambulance service, whose operator agreed to pass on the information to the hospital. When they'd repeated everything to make sure it was right, she shut off the phone and twisted round to look at the pair in the back. The boy's face was greyish white. His breathing was faint but unmistakable. He was still alive. But the wound had looked terrible before Charlie had covered it. There was nothing else they could do to slow the bleeding. You couldn't put a tourniquet around a neck.

'Now phone Annie for me,' Charlie said, before dictating the number.

This time Karen's fingers, a little warmer, worked better, and soon Annie's phone was ringing.

'Hold it to my ear,' Charlie said, then his voice sharpened. 'Annie. Me. Shooting accident at Folly Grange. Get Eve to give you a uniform and go with him out there. Take control. Secure the scene and start questioning the guns. I'll come asap. OK? Great.'

He let Karen take back the phone. She listened briefly, wondering whether Annie would be still there, asking for more information. But there was no one on the line. Karen switched the phone off and put it back in her pocket, before twisting round to see the bearded man, still panting on the back seat.

'Is he your son?' she asked because she had to say something and there were no reassurances anyone could give here. 'What's his name?'

'Billy,' said the man, looking like death himself. 'Can't you go any faster? He's ... *Please.*'

'Billy Jenkins?' Charlie said from the front, briefly glancing in the mirror. 'You're Dan, aren't you? I never recognized you behind that beard. I'm DCI Trench. We met when Billy's school was set on fire. Couple of years ago. What the hell happened?'

'I was beating at the Hentys' shoot,' he said, staring towards the mirror, as though looking for something he could recognize in the reflection of Charlie's eyes. 'Billy wanted to beat too, but the keeper said he was too small, so he was sent to help Mrs Henty and the cooks carry food and stuff for the lunch. He was well pissed-off. But he's a good lad, whatever they say, and he put up with it. I went off with the others. We had two drives. Then she – Mrs Henty – started screaming. Someone said it was Billy. I ran ... Panicked. Picked him up. One bloke said to leave him and wait. They'd ring the ambulance. I couldn't. Not with Billy bleeding so bad. Didn't want to leave him with that lot of wankers. Heard your engine. Thought you'd help.'

'What happened?' Karen said, thinking this disaster was another reason why killing birds for fun was so barbaric. 'Did he get in the way? Did a gun go off accidentally? Do they know whose it was?'

'That was no shotgun,' Charlie said grimly, keeping his foot flat on the accelerator. There was no thought of speed limits now. He slung the car round every corner, barely braking, never skidding once in spite of the layer of water that lay over the road. 'It's a rifle wound. Unmistakable.'

As they missed a turning lorry by inches, Karen was at last glad that she wasn't driving. They were in the middle of Newport now, heading for the hospital, pulling up at a red traffic light, which made Billy's father groan.

Moments later, Charlie screeched to a halt outside the emergency entrance.

'Go with them, Karen,' he ordered. 'I'll park your car and leave the keys in the exhaust pipe, then sort things out at the shoot end. Wait here. I'll come when I can. Or phone. Don't let them out of your sight. Call if there's a problem.'

A white-coated doctor and two nurses came rushing forward with a trolley.

Billy was whisked away and Karen was left with his father, blood all over his clothes, despair in his eyes. Water dripped off his beard, and he stood like a child, waiting to be told what to do.

'Look,' Karen said, 'we'd better go to reception and get Billy recorded in the system. They'll be able to help you get cleaned up there. I can buy you some tea or something.'

He looked dazed, not taking in anything she said.

'Tea?' she repeated, then added, knowing that a straight choice between alternatives was easier than any kind of open question, 'Or would you rather have coffee?'

His head wobbled in a kind of nod. 'Tea,' he whispered, putting up one hand to tug at his beard. Karen pulled at his elbow and he took one step, then another, and began to walk forwards of his own accord.

'Sugar?' Karen said, keeping pace with him and looking up at his face. 'How many?'

'Three.'

'Great,' she said, relieved to hear him making sense. 'Now, come to the desk with me, and we'll get Billy booked in. Come on.'

He topped her five foot nine by a good four inches, and his shoulders were broad, but she felt like a mother towing a toddler as she urged him towards the reception desk. It was staffed by a couple of harassed-looking women, who were fending off complaints and anxious enquiries with the same dogged politeness. Karen joined the queue and waited for nearly ten minutes before it was her turn to talk.

As soon as she had handed over responsibility to them, she went to find a hot drinks machine, slotted in the correct change and emerged with two cardboard cups of tea. She carried them to a pair of free seats in the front row and waited for Billy's father to join her.

'Who are you?' he said then, in the familiar Island accent with its long vowels, which always reminded her of her grandmother.

'Karen Taylor,' she said, with a professional smile. 'I'm a forensic psychologist, working with the police on the enquiry into Suzie Gray's death. I was driving DCI Trench just now when we nearly ran into you. I'm sorry if I frightened you then. What's your name?' She smiled again and offered him the sugared tea. 'I can't call you Mr Jenkins, can I?'

'I'm Dan.' He took the tea, holding the bendy cup across the top, squeezing the sides together. Drinking it like that needed an elbow crooked at mouth height, but he managed it, spilling only a little over his beard, to join the blood that clung to the coarse whiskers. He must have bent over his son to kiss him or try mouth-to-mouth resuscitation.

'Thanks,' he said, not looking at her. 'You know.'

'That's OK,' she said. 'I'm glad we made it. Tell me, didn't Billy go missing a few days ago?'

His father nodded, elbow up in the air again as he drank some more tea. 'Nearly a week he was gone.'

'When did you find him?' Karen asked. 'And where?'

Dan drained his tea, then dumped the damp cardboard cup on the floor by his feet. 'He came back on Thursday. Mr Henty brought him.'

'Back from where?' Karen was curious but she was keener

to keep him talking, and these questions were the only ones she could think of right now.

Dan wiped his hand over his beard, looked down at the red smears on his hand, and gagged.

'I got to get cleaned up,' he said, pushing himself up off the plastic chair.

Don't let him out of your sight, Charlie had said. But Karen could hardly go rushing into the gents with Dan. She compromised by promising to look after his things.

'Yeah, great.' Dan strode off, arousing curious and pitying stares from about half the waiting people. The others were too absorbed in themselves or their various electronic devices to bother with anyone else.

Karen sipped her own tea, wishing machines could be designed to produce drinks that tasted a little more like the real thing, and wondered if he would come back. Two women were talking behind her, discussing the wildness of a girl they both knew.

'And her gadding about the Island on her own never was safe,' said one. 'But now! With that poor mad boy on the loose again.'

'Not much "poor" about him,' said the other. 'He's a drug addict, isn't he? And a psychopath. No girl's going to be safe if they do let him out.'

'They have. I heard just now. No evidence.'

'No evidence?' The second woman's voice was almost a squeal. 'They found him holding that girl with her blood all over him. He won't stop killing, you know. They never do. Not those mad ones.'

'No knife,' said the other, more moderate voice. 'He didn't have a knife, so he couldn't have done it.'

'Don't you believe it. I'm not going out after dark until they've locked him up for good.'

Karen was about to turn round to ask them for their sources of information when she caught sight of Dan.

He looked cleaner but even more desperate. He took a detour to the reception desk. Karen blocked out the chatter behind her, watching one of the receptionists listen to him, then shake her head, then check something on the computer, then shake her head again. Slowly he walked back to Karen, as though he'd been defeated in a fight and had nowhere else to go.

'You were saying,' she said, when he'd settled at her side again, 'where Billy went.'

'He hoped Mr Henty would give him work.'

'Was that likely?' Karen asked. 'He's only thirteen, isn't he? What kind of work could he do?'

A faint smile made Dan look more human.

'Henty's a decent bloke. Billy thought he was a hero. I do odd bits and bobs for him, you see, and I had Billy with me once when I went to get my instructions. Henty was cleaning the boat, scrubbing the decks himself and he offered Billy a fiver to help him. Kept him out of mischief all morning and in the end paid him twenty-five quid; showed him all round the boat, too. Even took him for a sail. After that, whenever Billy was late home, we'd find him hanging about the marina, hoping for another go.'

'Did you look this time when he ran away?'

Dan looked at her with eyes that seemed full of every kind of pain. 'Of course. The first place we went when we found he'd gone. But the *Dasher* wasn't there. Henty'd taken her out.

At first we thought Billy might have stowed away, so we waited. Then when Henty was back we learned he hadn't ever seen Billy since he ran away.'

Pausing, Dan looked towards Karen, as though he expected her to help him, but she had nothing to offer. After a moment, he went on, 'When he got home, Billy said he had gone to the marina that first evening, but when he saw no sign of Henty or the *Dasher*, he started to walk out of town towards Henty's house. It's all of twelve miles. More maybe. He didn't make it, found a barn and made that his camp. He says no one hurt him and no one made him do anything. He liked camping out alone and stayed there till his food ran out, tried to snare a rabbit, failed, then panicked and tried the *Dasher* again, Thursday afternoon. Found her tied up at the marina.'

Karen waited, certain that Dan had more to say. But it took a long time. Two doctors emerged through the door to the treatment areas, looking for someone, before Dan had got himself under control. Each time, he half rose from his chair, but they weren't looking for him. At last, he turned to Karen again, looking for more help. This time, she did her best.

'Do you really think he was camping happily? It's not exactly the weather for it. He must have been very bored.'

Dan's eyes looked dead as the small glimmer of light left them. 'I don't think he was happy at all. But he wanted to be away from home ... from me.' He turned his head away and looked down at the black-and-white vinyl floor, muttering, 'It's my fault he went, you see.'

'Your fault?' Karen repeated, speaking very gently. 'Why? What happened?'

Dan glanced at her for an instant, then directed his gaze

over her head so that he couldn't meet her eyes. She thought she'd never seen a man so ashamed.

'He saw me hit his mum. I caught his eye just as my fist hit her face. I tried to pull back, but it happened so fast, I . . .'

He covered both his eyes with his hands, breathing heavily into his palms.

'It was the first time I ever hit her,' he said. 'The only time. You got to believe it. She'd been . . . We've been having rows. Billy hated it, tried to make us stop whenever we got going. We both swore at him, told him not to interfere.'

'Why?' Karen asked.

'God knows. We need the rows, I think. Life's been . . . Since I lost my job, life's been well tough. That night I'd gone to the pub. I only had a pint. Christ! Cooped up at home, I need to get out sometimes. You'd have thought I'd eaten one of the girls, the fuss she made.' His voice had hardened and lost all its shame and most of its aching hurt.

Karen could tell he felt justified in hitting out. She wondered how his wife would describe the same scene.

'Or at least gambled with the child benefit,' he went on, trying to sound funny and failing. 'So I . . . I hit her. Billy saw it, like I said, and ran off upstairs. I thought no more about it. I had enough to do sorting Sandra out. I . . . for a while I thought I'd broken her jaw.'

'When did you realize he'd actually run away?' Karen asked, understanding him, pitying him too, but not forgiving him. Nothing made it all right to hit a child or a partner. Ever.

'Not till next morning. I thought he was sulking. The girls were creating. Sandra was crying and holding her jaw. I thought I'd leave Billy to sort himself. Then when he wasn't there at breakfast ...' he looked pleadingly at Karen, as though he expected her to fill in the rest. It wasn't difficult, so she didn't even have to run the story by him, just went on with her questions.

'So how did you find out that Mr Henty hadn't seen him?'

'I phoned him right off. His wife said he was away, so I phoned his mobile. Switched to voicemail. When I did get him, he said he hadn't seen Billy. Henty said as soon as he was back he'd do anything we wanted to help look for Billy and promised to bring him straight round if he did appear.' Dan's colour turned a dusky red and he looked guilty all over again.

'What?' Karen said.

Dan's face turned an even deeper blood colour.

'I said he'd be doing me a favour if he dropped Billy in the Solent with concrete boots on,' he muttered into his damp beard. 'The trouble he caused us, you ... But I didn't mean it. And—'

'Mr Jenkins?' called a man. 'Dan Jenkins?'

They both looked towards the reception desk, where a tall, white-coated man was standing by one of the women, who was gesturing towards their chairs. The doctor walked towards them. Karen could tell from his lagging steps and determinedly fixed expression that the news was not good.

'Mr and Mrs Jenkins?' he said.

Dan must have known what was coming, too, because he got painfully to his feet.

'She's not my wife. I'm Dan Jenkins.'

'OK. Well, Mr Jenkins, Dan, we've operated and stopped the bleeding. Billy is now in ICU and he's being monitored. We're doing all we can, but ...'

'He's alive?' Dan said, reaching out to grab the doctor's forearm with both hands.

The doctor patted Dan's hands, then freed himself.

'The next twelve hours are critical. Do you want to come up and see him? He's not conscious, but you can take a look.'

Karen waited with Dan until Annie Colvin arrived to take over and to organize the safe storage of everything Billy had been wearing so she could take it for testing.

'Charlie's sorry,' Annie said very quietly to Karen when they'd moved a little way from where Dan sat with his head sunk between his fists. 'But he's got to deal with everyone at the shoot. Here're the keys to your car. He put the pay-and-display ticket in the windscreen.'

Karen frowned. 'Isn't dealing with the shoot a job for the Island force? I mean, aren't people like Eve going to think he's ...'

'No.' Annie looked as though she wanted to tell Karen where to put her questions, then thought better of it. 'The owner of the shoot – Henty – is the uncle of our knife victim. Now he's creating because his wife was nearly shot.'

'Billy Jenkins wasn't *nearly* shot. He had a bullet through the neck.' Outrage sharpened Karen's voice. 'Doesn't Henty care about ...?'

'I don't know.' Annie's interruption came with an unusual bite. She sounded almost as the end of her stock of patience. 'All I know is Billy was standing beside Lucy Henty's chair, leaning down to listen to something she said, when he took the bullet. The theory is it wasn't an accident, but a deliberate shot with her as the target.'

'Even so ...'

'Don't, Karen.' Now Annie just sounded tired. 'We're fighting enough people already. The blokes shooting today are ... well, influential. Charlie needs to stay on top of things there. He says if you want to go to the Goose Inn, he'll try to catch up with you there later. Even eat something maybe. But he can't say when it'll be.'

Karen thought about it, knowing how much she would enjoy a quiet meal with Charlie in his favourite pub, then shook her head.

'No point waiting. Tell him I'm going home. If he needs me, he can phone me there. OK?'

Annie nodded. It was clear that she was relieved.

Karen went to retrieve her car, noticing Charlie had paid for the maximum number of hours parking. Had he even expected to come back? Sighing, she turned her key in the ignition and set off.

Catching sight of the dashboard clock, she realized she had more than three and a half hours to waste before the ferry for which she'd booked an expensive space. She turned the car, deciding to have a quick look at the site of her new house, before using up the rest of the time gathering background information that might help her understand the psychology of everyone involved in Olly's drama.

Just short of Yarmouth, she headed right down an increasingly muddy lane to the place where her new house would be built.

Her grandmother's ramshackle old wooden chalet had been taken down now and the site cleared into an empty mud plane. The ground was so soft that the new wooden structure was to be build on a kind of raft instead of traditional foundations, so that it would float with the ground. Karen was still anxious about its stability, but Stella had commissioned the best consulting engineers and they – and the planning authorities – were convinced they'd got the design right.

Karen knew that as soon as the new house rose, the whole place would be transformed, but now it looked like an unhealed wound, a cruel scrape in the landscape, with all its raw nerve endings exposed. Ashamed of her sentimentality, she still wished they'd left the demolition until they'd been in a position to start rebuilding right away.

The site held nothing now of her grandmother's time here, or the atmosphere of security and fun she had built around her two grandchildren. All Karen's mental pictures of herself and Aidan as happy and safe had gone with the house.

Beyond the bare earth, where one day a new garden would grow, were the familiar creepy woods. The artist's original plan included cutting a great swathe through the undistinguished trees to create a view of the sea. But that turned out to be far too expensive and Karen had had to slash costs wherever she could to bring the project down to a price she and Aidan could afford.

So the trees still grew higgledy-piggledy, their branches meshed together at the top and wrapped about with stifling ivy at the bottom. Between their trunks were tangles of nettles and all sorts of ground-covering greenery. Depressed, wondering whether she would ever be able to open the place up to air and light, Karen turned her back on the trees and walked to the track that led down towards the sea itself. That, at least, would be unchanged.

Ten minutes later she was standing on the narrow line of big round grey pebbles, with the waves almost touching her boots, wishing she could remember the best episodes of her childhood here. The good ones seemed to be out of reach, but there was one, perhaps triggered by the sight of Billy, shot and possibly dying as he lay in his father's arms. Years ago, probably nearly thirty years ago, Aidan had almost suffocated himself with chemical fumes.

Karen couldn't now remember the purpose of the experiment he'd been conducting, but she thought it had been based on something he'd done at school. Something to do with ammonia. She remembered the horrible soaking-nappies, rotting-cheese smell of the fluid he'd poured out over a tray of some kind of powder. He'd told her to stand aside, making her feel too young and useless to be part of his important science, but his orders had saved her. As fumes had risen from the tray, he'd started to choke, then fallen back on the ground. His breathing had been terrifying, heavy with spasms and groans. As his throat muscles had worked and squeezed with his fight for breath, Karen had run for her grandmother.

Memory didn't go much further than that, but she was fairly sure the doctor had come out to the chalet. It must have been the doctor who had carried Aidan, as floppy as Billy had been, with his throat stretched and his head falling back like Billy's, and laid him on his bed.

Karen had sat for hours on the floor beside it, waiting for Aidan to wake and want her to do something for him. All Granny's persuasions had failed to make her move until her brother had been fit enough to leave his bed unaided.

Standing alone on the beach, Karen rubbed her damp eyes

and made herself laugh. Aidan's adoring acolyte. That's what she'd been. And he'd been the adventurer, the hero, doing all kinds of dangerous things because they excited him and because he'd felt immortal.

Was that how Billy had felt? Had he, like Aidan, believed he could do anything he wanted? What had his private impulses been as he'd run away from home? Had he just been escaping his parents' fight, as his father thought? Or had there been more to it? Where had Billy wanted to be? *Who* had he wanted to be?

Looking back to the sight of him bleeding in the back of the car, Karen decided that wherever he'd been, Billy had been eating. The terrible wound in his neck, that great tear in his skin and muscle that showed the red pulsing blood vessels had distracted her from everything else at the time. But there had been flesh on his cheeks and hands. He definitely hadn't been starved for a week.

Somehow she didn't believe in the barn-camping story, or the idea that the boy could have taken enough food from home to last until Thursday, when he'd failed to snare a rabbit. Karen was fairly sure he'd been near at least one shop where he'd been buying – or stealing – food.

If the story of his exhausting attempt to reach Henty's house had been real, Billy might have spent one night in a country barn, but he'd never have stayed for a whole week. Surely he'd have set out on the second leg of the journey the following day. Any reasonably fit thirteen-year-old could have walked twelve miles in two days, even if he hadn't managed it in one. The more she thought about it, the more Karen would bet that Billy had never actually left Cowes.

If he was as much in awe of Giles Henty as his father had hinted, then it was more likely that he'd found a refuge some-where near the boat, waiting for his chance to go on board.

Karen pulled her phone out of her pocket, then swore as she saw the warning icon telling her the battery was dead. She hadn't brought her charger with her, so even though there was an adaptor in the car, it wasn't going to be any use. And she hadn't got the BlackBerry either.

She turned back towards her car. One of her feet slipped between two big stones and her ankle turned sickeningly, fling-ing her forwards on to her hands and knees.

'Shit!' she shouted loud enough to startle a seagull, which screamed at her and shot into the air.

When the sharp pain became manageable, she pulled off the scarf she wore looped around her neck and turned it into a bandage. Tying it too tight might make the ankle swell even more than the original injury, but if she wanted to get back to the car and drive herself to Cowes, she would have to give the wobbly joint real support. She tugged the ends of the scarf as tight as she could and knotted them twice. Zipping her boot up over the improvised strapping was hard work, but she got it done and hobbled with extreme care over the last of the stones.

Giles couldn't understand why the black-haired Geordie cop didn't get the point. It should've been clear enough for even the thickest plod.

'First my niece is killed yards from my boat,' he said again, exaggerating the sound of patience in his voice, 'then my wife is nearly killed – and the son of one of my beaters *is* shot – on my land, during my shoot. Can't you see that someone's out to get me? Where was that fucking psychopath? Have you gone and let him out already?'

The cop sighed and looked stubborn as hell. 'Not in time for this, sir. Now, once again: we need to find the gun. It has to be a rifle, and ...'

'My dear man, no one brings a rifle to a pheasant shoot. Take my word for it.'

'I know that, sir.' The cop looked as if he wanted to swear at Giles, but he had the sense to keep a lid on it. 'I also know there's a rifle on your gun licence. Why?'

'Good God, man! I'd have thought it was obvious. I go stalking in Scotland. Stalking *deer*,' Giles added so the poor oik would be able to keep up. 'Can't shoot deer with a shotgun, you know. They're a little bigger than a pheasant.' Giles laughed, but not out of happiness or amusement.

'Right,' said the cop, apparently impervious to insult. 'We need it.'

'It's locked in the gun cupboard.' Giles's impatience turned to anger and the leaden sensation in his brain began to boil again. He had guests – important guests – to see to, and an understandably shaken wife. Good God almighty, she'd been nearly killed and had the boy's blood spurting all over her clothes. It was going to send her right back into the depths of madness. And this fool was wasting time with stupid questions?

'Good,' said the cop. 'We still need to see it.'

Now it was Giles's turn to sigh. He led the way into the house and saw Lucy, surrounded by a protective phalanx of the other wives, all holding what looked like bloody stiff drinks, while most of the men were out on the terrace, smoking his cigars. At least they looked happy enough. Lucy, who seemed to have got over the worst of her shock impressively fast, took a step towards him, but he shook his head and she retreated without saying a word.

If you didn't know her as well as Giles did, you'd think she wasn't bothered. But he could see the tightness in the lines around her mouth and the shadows in her eyes, and the woodenness of her expression. There'd be nightmares tonight and probably shrieking tears in the morning. Still, he'd cross that bridge when he came to it. They'd got to the gun cupboard now.

'Here.' Giles took out the key and unlocked the steel door. There were his spare shotguns and the rifle. 'All present and correct. All done according to the law and my licence.'

The cop took the rifle and opened it, handling it well, looking in fact as though he knew what he was doing. Which was a surprise.

'If that's been fired,' Giles said, 'I'll eat my hat.'

'No need,' Trench said. 'It hasn't. Who else round here has a rifle?'

'You must have records of all the licences.' Giles hadn't felt as frustrated as this for years. 'Do your job. Look them up.'

'The one they used today isn't likely to be licensed. Now is it?' Trench said, all sarky now. 'You ever hear of anyone who could have one?'

Giles shrugged. 'No. Although I seem to remember hearing my wife's psychologist talk about trying stalking while he was at university in Edinburgh. You could always ask him what he did with *his* rifle.'

The cop's dark face lit up, Giles was glad to see. That

would give Bloody Blazon something to think about, finding himself on the wrong end of a police investigation for once, instead of trying to make everyone believe that nothing was ever his fault. Suzie's death included.

'That it, Trench?' he said, moving away from the cop. 'I've got guests to see to.'

Karen's ankle was swelling badly when she drove past the police station in East Cowes, looking for somewhere to park. She found a space at last and manoeuvred the car into the gap between two four-by-fours. The lit window of a chemist distracted her and she made her way painfully across the road to consult with the pharmacist about the best painkillers and elasticated bandages.

With all the typical Islander's courtesy and gentleness, the young pharmacist chose the most suitable bandage herself, got it out of its cellophane and box, then knelt on the floor to help Karen remove her boot and scarf. She slipped the bandage over the swelling with a contraption like a lampshade frame, taking real care to make sure she didn't knock the ankle. Then she took Karen's money and carried it all over to the till.

Bringing back the change, she said, 'You shouldn't have any trouble, but if you're worried at all, talk to your GP. Don't take more of the painkillers than the maximum dose listed on the label. Will you be all right?'

'I should be. Thanks,' Karen said, pouring the change into her purse.

'Have you got far to go?' The pharmacist looked as though she had something she wanted to say but could not find the words.

'What's the problem?' Karen asked.

The pharmacist coughed, then looked over her shoulder towards the door. 'He's out again, you know. And it happened near here.'

'I'm sorry?'

'The murder. The boy who did it is out again. They say there isn't enough evidence to charge him, but we all know he did it. His parents are trying to keep him at home, but they can't lock him in, and you never ... You don't want to be on your own in the streets round here, specially not after dark. I could call you a cab.'

'It's OK.' Karen smiled at her. 'I'm only going across the road to the police station.'

'Well, take care. You don't know where he is. Hanging about, waiting. He could be anywhere.'

She helped Karen out of the chair and towards the door, then waved her off. Karen noticed without surprise that the ankle felt very much better than the change of bandage could have achieved on its own.

'Nothing like obvious care from someone else to make one feel better,' she muttered and pushed open the door of the police station. 'Best placebo there is.'

The desk sergeant didn't recognize her but showed signs of wanting to be helpful. Unfortunately neither Charlie nor Annie was in the incident room. The sergeant asked if anyone else could help or if Karen wanted to leave a message. She heard Eve's voice from the other side of the wall and decided to get out of the police station as fast as she could. She scribbled a note for Charlie, saying her phone was out but she was still on the Island.

'I'll call in again later,' she added. 'If I can. To see if he's back.'

'Right you are,' said the desk sergeant, with an impersonal smile. 'I'll tell him. But he hasn't much time. He's chasing a killer at the moment.'

Chapter 11

Day Four: Saturday Afternoon

Normally Karen would have left the car in its space and walked the half mile to the marina, but, with her ankle throbbing and making her feel vulnerable, she decided to drive. She didn't think she could possibly be at risk from Olly, whatever the pharmacist thought, but walking was still harder than usual. Taking the car was only sensible.

Once she'd reached the High Street, she saw it had been a mistake. All the obvious parking spaces were full, and she drove round and round, eventually finding a slot outside a school. She put some money into the pay-and-display machine and set the ticket up in the designated fashion on her dashboard.

Having locked the car, she looked at the big board that announced it as St Cuthbert's School for boys and girls between eleven and eighteen and wondered why she hadn't done the obvious thing and interviewed the head here. This was the place that had taken Olly in when he'd been expelled from his fee-paying public school on the mainland. Charlie had asked her to look into whether there had been any sign of violence from Olly in the past. This was one possible site of fights or exaggerated physical reaction to any kind of stress. But now, on a cold Saturday afternoon, there wasn't likely to be anyone here.

Still, it had to be worth a try. Karen rang the bell by the locked gate and waited. No one answered, and no lights showed. Back at the car, she fished her small dictating machine out of the pocket in the door and made a record of the head teacher's name – Margery Wilkinson – and the school's phone number, which were both given on the board.

The gulls criss-crossed the gloomy sky ahead of her, very white against the dark-grey clouds. The birds produced their usual alarming screams, and the sea scents filled her nostrils, banishing even the exhaust and petrol fumes from the cars all round. A burger stall announced itself with the sweet but acrid smell of frying onions and the throat-catching stench of burning animal fat. A few children shouted, and various adults were talking. The bell of a shop door rang as someone opened it, then rang again as it shut.

Karen turned her back on the town and made her way to the expensive-looking yachts tied up at the marina, while the rain dripped down on her head. The daylight had gone, but there were enough streetlamps to show her everything she needed. Most of the boats looked empty and well protected for winter, but a few had cabins glowing with artificial light. One or two even had Christmas tinsel twined around their masts.

She found the *Dasher* at last, and gasped. Sailing had never been one of her amusements, but she'd spent enough time on the Island to know what she was looking at. This was an old yawl, restored and beautifully kept, with all its planking gleaming, and the paintwork immaculate. The furled sails were red, which made her think of one of the *Swallows and Amazons* books she'd had as a child, with its account of a voyage in the *Goblin*, which had also had crimson sails. She put the likely cost of the *Dasher* at several hundred thousand pounds.

So much more interesting than the usual white fibre-glass modern boats, this one made her think much more warmly of Suzie's uncle than she had when he'd been so threatening in the police station. He obviously had taste.

Karen wasn't surprised Billy had been so excited by this boat that he'd hung around it whenever he could, hoping for another invitation to come on board. She looked around for CCTV cameras and noted that the nearest was at least ten yards away. The camera's likely sweep was approximately 120 degrees. It should record anyone arriving casually at the boat – or leaving.

But if you knew it was there, you probably could get to and fro without being caught. According to Charlie, Billy had had long experience of the CCTV all over the Island and was used to taking evasive action when stealing or causing trouble.

More and more she believed he could have been camping out somewhere near here, hoping for a sight of his hero.

There was no immediately obvious refuge, unless Billy had broken in to one of the other yachts. Several looked as though they hadn't been touched for months, but even for a fearless boy, it would surely have been too dangerous to risk being surprised by an owner. She walked slowly back up the marina, brushing the icy rain from her eyes and hair whenever she had to, until she reached the first of the buildings.

She saw Captain Joe's sailing equipment shop, where Suzie had bought her shoes, already bedecked with Christmas decorations and a magnificent tree. Beside it was the alleyway where Suzie had been stabbed. Someone had removed the police tent and all the tapes now, and the rain had washed away all traces of Suzie's blood.

If you didn't know she had died violently here, there'd be nothing to suggest it. Even so, Karen couldn't stop herself looking all round for lurking threats.

Beyond the place where Olly had been found with the dead girl in his lap, Karen could see an ancient wooden staircase, leading up to what looked like a small black door in the wall above.

She stepped carefully on to the cobbles, hoping she was avoiding the actual site of Suzie's death in just the way her grandmother had taught her to avoid flat-lying gravestones in churches and churchyards. The splintered steps were slick with rain, and she clung to the banister to stop herself slipping, wincing each time her wrenched ankle had to take her weight.

The door at the top was locked. She pushed and nothing happened. A large keyhole sat about halfway up. Karen crouched down to look through it. Nothing showed but blackness. She hobbled down to the street again, assessed the possibility of flats, occupied or not, above the various shops and saw lights on in one. She counted the doors along the street, guessed which belonged to the lit flat, and rang its bell.

Running feet pounded down some stairs, and a young

man's voice called, 'I'm coming. Don't go away. I've got the key. Hang on.'

Karen waited, hearing the crunch of keys turning, and then found herself face to face with a pleasant-looking young man who smiled at her from under his long straight fair fringe.

'Hi?' He looked puzzled. 'I thought you were my pizza. Can I help?'

'Pizza?' Karen couldn't help looking at her watch.

'So it's half past three,' he said with a cheerful smile. 'I'm a composer. I've been working. I'm hungry. I've got a mega-deal pepperoni and Coke on the way. Are you looking for me?'

'In a way,' Karen said, offering him one of her cards. 'I'm looking into the disappearance of a child, a boy, who I believe was squatting somewhere round here. I wondered if you . . .'

'A squatting child?' he said, frowning now. 'Why on earth? We had a murder just outside the other day, but no one's said anything about a child.'

'Were you here when the murder happened?' Karen asked and watched a dull pinkness steal into the young man's cheeks.

'Why are you asking?' The man looked at the card Karen had just given him. 'What's it got to do with the uni?'

'I'm working with the police on this case.'

'Oh, I see. OK. Well, like I told the uniformed woman earlier, I was working. I kind of heard a scream, but I, like, thought: why can't they shut up, those shrieky girls, and let a man concentrate? I thought it might be the couple who used to have noisy shags in the next-door flat back again. But it wasn't. And they haven't been here for a while anyway. It must have been . . .' His voice tailed off and he looked almost as shamefaced as Karen thought he should.

Even so she felt a little sorry for him. How would it be to know you might have saved someone from a horrible death if you hadn't been so self-absorbed? Unless it had been fear rather than self-absorption that had made him ignore the screams.

'Can you think of anywhere round here where someone might hide out?' Karen asked without much hope. He didn't seem to her to be interested in anything outside his own concerns.

He licked his lips, moving them up and down again and again, sucking at them as though they were sweets. At last he stopped.

'Lots of the flats are empty. They get let in the summer, but no one wants them now, except the couple wanting a shag-fest.' He looked at the floor. 'I think that's why no one else listened to the scream either. There wasn't anyone here to help her. Poor little ...'

Karen shook her head, wishing he'd let her in to his flat so she could get a better view of the buildings all round.

'A furnished flat would be a bit formal,' she said. 'I was thinking of somewhere empty and abandoned ... like a garden shed. That kind of thing.'

His eyes brightened, making him look as though he was glad to be able to help with something.

'There is one place,' he said. 'Could be what you're looking for. Maybe. On the other side of the road, above that Lebanese restaurant. Some Poles were living in it, but they got moved on. I don't know who owns it, if anyone does. But I used to hear them clumping down the fire escape, oh, it must be nearly a month ago, and I haven't seen anyone else. I'd talk to them sometimes. They liked the place, even though it was cramped for four of them, because it was always warm with the extractor from the restaurant's kitchen blowing all round. You could try there. But not through the front door. I don't think anyone's used that in years. The fire escape's the thing. Up at the back and in through a window. That's how they always got in and out.'

'I will. Thanks.' Karen gave him a smile. He'd deserved that much. 'How do I get to it?'

He jerked his chin across the road. 'It's the sister alley to the one where the girl was killed. Go in, past the restaurant's garbage bins. Paladin kind of things. And you'll see a crappy old fire escape. I don't think the window at the top'll be locked. It never was when the Poles were there.'

Karen thanked him again, and waited until he'd retreated and locked his own door. She heard a bolt being shoved home, as well as the locks clicking. She didn't imagine there would be working electrics in a place like the one he'd described and her useless attempt to look through the keyhole into total darkness just now was still making her feel stupid. She set off up the High Street until she came to a hardware shop.

In amongst bowls and baskets of glittery Christmas tat on special offer, they had plenty of torches and she bought a big one, encased in hard black rubber, and the batteries to go with it.

As she was leaving the shop, she noticed a series of plastic washing-up bowls containing piles of grubby marked-down items. One had knives and tin-openers, another a tangle of black-coated wires and many different plugs on the end with a hand-written note saying £5 on it. Phone chargers. She scuffled among them until she found one that matched her own and bought it, feeling instantly better and more in control. Now, as soon as she got back in her car, she could make contact again.

Taking the time to recharge the batteries seemed worth while and she took a detour to her parking space to set it up. Reassuringly, the red charging light glowed on the phone itself, and she knew it wouldn't take so much power from the car's battery that it would give her starting problems.

Back in the alleyway opposite Captain Joe's, she obediently made her way past the well-filled rubbish bins, stepping carefully around various unidentified lumps in the ground. Well away from any spectators, she retrieved the big torch from her shoulder bag and switched it on.

The light was useful as she picked her way up the rusty iron staircase, avoiding various scarily big holes in the metal, until she reached the top and a battered-looking window. There was no door to match the one on the other side of the street. The window was shut, but it hadn't been painted in years so there was every chance it would open. It gave way to a light push.

Karen looked over her shoulder but could see no one taking any notice of her at all. She shone the torch ahead of her and wanted to shout 'Bingo!'.

In front of her was a pathetic little encampment. A sheet of thickish foam, of the kind sold by camping shops to augment a sleeping bag, was stretched out against the wall, with a neatly folded but obviously ragged blanket beside it. Laid out on the floor by the mattress were an iPod, a small pile of change, two books, and a baked-bean tin with an old spoon stuck in it. Angling the light from higher up, she could see the tin was still half full.

She swung the light around the rest of the room and saw a broken-backed chair, an old packing case that could have been used as a table, bare dusty boards, with a few faint marks that could have been made by the Poles' beds, and – again piled neatly – an array of open tins and packets. And a small dark-blue backpack with the Nike-tick logo on it in white.

Charlie's CSI would have to comb through everything to pick up any evidence it might hold, so Karen didn't walk into the room. But this could easily be Billy's hideout.

The last inhabitant had definitely been a child. The top book's title was easy to read: *Harry Potter and the Half-Blood Prince*. Something about the spine of the other book, which was half-turned away and more or less covered by the Harry Potter, made her think of Terry Pratchett.

Looking at the evidence, Karen thought that if Billy had been here, he was worthy of respect. He was only thirteen, so if he had stuck it out here in this bleak place, trying to make a life for himself away from his warring parents for a whole week, keeping it tidy, feeding himself, reading and listening to music, he must have real guts. No wonder Charlie liked him.

Flicking the torch around the room, she could see nothing that looked like a window. Until she shone it in a much more systematic fashion, drawing sweeps of light up and down each wall. Halfway up one was an old shutter with a black iron latch on it. She took a moment to work out which way it faced, and was disappointed to realize it must open out over the buildings behind the restaurant.

For some minutes, she had been toying with the idea that Billy had watched Suzie's murder from up here. Then she saw a much likelier version of what could have happened: like the self-absorbed composer, Billy might have heard Suzie scream. What if, unlike the composer, he'd been brave and concerned enough to run down the iron staircase to find out who had made the noise?

Karen thought of the partial footprint, the size five partial footprint, and the person who had taken away the knife. Had Billy seen the same devil Olly had seen? Was that why someone had now aimed a rifle at him?

She had to get to her phone.

Climbing down a slippery, wet, broken iron staircase with a sprained ankle turned out to be a lot harder than going up. She clung to the rail and her hand kept slipping, always at the point where a broken tread caught her toe. The whole journey took nearly five minutes and her ankle was aching badly as she limped towards her car. On the way she heard carols being transmitted from a huge loudspeaker on top of a dirty white van. A man was shaking a collecting box with an aggressive air that seemed as out of place on the Island as it did with the words of the current carol: 'Unto us a child is born/King of all creation.' Karen blanked the bullying man and hobbled past him.

Ten minutes later, sitting in the car, she rehearsed what she had to say, trying for the shortest and most effective sentences she could. In the thick of this kind of investigation, Charlie would have no time to waste.

Seconds later, the phone beeped with the sound of a text. She didn't wait to read it, instead giving the phone a few more minutes on charge before ringing Charlie.

'Yes? Karen? What?'

'You need to get your CSI to an empty attic near the

marina. There's evidence there. I think it could be where Billy was living. And I think he could've been the one who took the knife from Olly; not Angela. Which means he could have been the real target of today's shooting. You'll need to measure his shoes with the footmark in the blood. And you need to talk to him about what he saw. I want to be there.'

'No point.' Charlie's voice had slowed, but none of the anger had gone. 'He's not conscious. His vocal cords were damaged as the bullet passed through his neck. He may not speak again.'

'He can still write his answers, Charlie.' Karen held on to her feelings about the child so they didn't colour her voice or water down her determination. 'When he's conscious, I mean. So you need to keep him guarded. If someone has tried to get rid of him, they'll try again.'

Chapter 12

When Karen had got her mind into some kind of order, her pity for Billy's father in one compartment, her own fury at the damage done to the ballsy child who'd lasted so long on his own into another, she unplugged the charging phone and checked the text. It was from Will.

Making herself breathe deeply, unlocking her suddenly tight jaw, she rang him back and waited with the phone at her ear for his voice.

'Are you OK?' he said at once.

'Yes. Why?'

'I was worried after yesterday morning. I ... I shouldn't have ... I mean, I shouldn't have nagged you about weddings and children. Just because I want them so much. It wasn't fair. I'm sorry.'

'Will,' she said, all her instincts telling her she should be with him, 'it's OK. I was ... I'm in a muddle about it all. But we'll talk. Next time I won't be so defensive. Are *you* OK?'

'I am now.' He produced a shaky little laugh. 'I'm all over

the place these days, all on tenterhooks – whatever they are. Are you on the Island?' Will's voice was studiedly casual.

'For the moment. I'll be on my way home pretty soon. Unless I get summoned for anything else, which isn't likely. But I'm booked on the six o'clock ferry.'

'Good. Will I see you at all this weekend?'

'I'd love it, Will,' she said, 'but . . .'

'It's all right,' he said, crisp and efficient again. 'I've been operating all day and I'm too tired to drive now, so I'll head your way first thing tomorrow morning, if that's OK.'

'That'll be wonderful,' Karen said, and meant it.

'See you then. I'll bring breakfast. Bye.'

He cut off the call before she could ask or say anything else. She sat, holding the phone, hoping Charlie wasn't going to want her tomorrow.

As a smile slowly relaxed her lips, she realized this would be the perfect moment to buy Will's Christmas present and got out of the car again to limp towards a jeweller's she remembered in the High Street from long ago, hoping it would still be open.

'Cufflinks,' she said to herself, ignoring the pain creeping up her calf. 'They must have cufflinks.'

They did. Trays and trays were laid out for her, glittering even more fiercely than all the decorations on the shops along the High Street. Antique cufflinks, 'second-hand', which were a lot less expensive than the only slightly older 'antiques', modern enamel, gold, silver, embellished with other people's crests, glittering vulgar coloured stones, anchors, boats, boars' heads: everything almost anyone could possibly want. But nothing she could imagine Will putting in any of his beautifully ironed shirts. His taste was far too austere for any of these.

'I was thinking of something a bit plainer,' she said to the stout jeweller.

'What were you thinking of spending?' he asked in return, putting her on a most uncomfortable spot.

'I don't know. Up to, well, say ...' Karen paused again and looked at some of the price tickets on the links she didn't like, then reminded herself that even if she named too big a price, she didn't have to buy anything he offered. 'I suppose up to about, well, five hundred pounds.'

'Ah. In that case, how about these?' He bent down to unlock a special case beneath the rest and brought out a small domed black-velvet box. Opening it, he revealed plain gold cuff links with the four bobbly bits exactly the size and shape of Smarties.

'That's them,' she said at once. There was no possibility that Will wouldn't like these. 'Could have been made for him. How much are they?'

The jeweller consulted the ticket and showed it to her, saying, 'Four hundred and ninety-five pounds. Engagement present, is it?' He glanced at her bare left hand.

Karen jammed it in her pocket. Then she forced herself to smile.

'That's the idea. I'm just not absolutely sure, yet, whether ...' She let her voice die, and watched an understanding smile on the jeweller's face.

'I can put them on one side for you,' he said. 'Until you know for sure. If you leave me your phone number, then if anyone else wants them, I can ...'

'That would be kind,' Karen said, wondering what on earth she was thinking, when her existing liabilities were already scaring her into sleeplessness several nights a month and she had no idea how she was going to settle her share of the builders' bill for the new house. Aidan was to pay half, but that still left far more than any junior academic could afford. If it hadn't been for her book, she could never have started the building project. But she wasn't going to get the next tranche of money until she delivered the finished text and she had a long way to go.

She wrote out her phone number and handed it to the jeweller.

Back in the flat, she poured herself a glass of wine, an ordinary Australian Shiraz of the kind she bought with her groceries, and phoned Stella for a chat before she settled down to have another crack at chapter seven.

'Hey!' Stella squealed as she answered the phone. 'Perfect! I was going to ring you because the Planning Department's come good at last. They're excited about the project and the main contractor wants to go over and check out the site soon. If the weather's good enough, they'll make a start digging for the raft before Christmas, with a view to getting it laid early next year and moving on to the above-ground work by March. How's that?'

'Fantastic,' Karen said, trying not to panic at the thought of having to pay a large chunk of the total cost so soon. 'How long after that before I can get possession?'

And pay the final bill, she added to herself in silence.

'They say August.' Stella's voice didn't sound as though she believed it.

'Great. Now, how's your book going?' Karen said, fending off a severe panic with pretended optimism. 'I'm nearly a third of the way into mine.'

'Smug cow,' Stella said cheerfully. 'I can't do more than the introductory bits because there's nothing to describe yet, except the competition and the struggles with Planning.'

'No wonder you want the work to start soon,' Karen said, tucking the phone between her ear and her shoulder as she hobbled into the kitchen and opened the fridge door, trying to decide what she wanted to eat. 'I hope you and Aidan are going to get on when he arrives.'

'So do I,' Stella said with surprising emphasis. 'You did say he likes the plans ...'

'He loves them, and he gave me carte blanche in any case. You don't have to worry about that.'

'Good. I—' Stella broke off, then giggled and said, 'I keep having this weird kind of Bridget Jones fantasy that he and I might ...'

'You and me both,' Karen admitted with a wicked smile neither Stella nor Aidan would ever see. 'It'd be brilliant, and give him a good reason to move back here permanently. Then I'd have both of you, and ...'

'Except that, knowing my luck with men, he'll take one look at my freckles and snub nose and faint in horror. Karen, I've got to go; it's the front door bell. Bye.'

Karen wondered whether Aidan might have the good taste to fancy her best friend and whether she should buy a Christmas tree yet. Would that tempt fate and ensure she didn't get to spend the day itself in her own flat?

She stared at the contents of the fridge, then decided

nothing would taste as good as saving money would feel, so she ignored the idea of eating. But she did take out a big bag of frozen peas to drape over her painful and still-swelling ankle.

Four hours later, the peas were back in the fridge for re-freezing and Karen was deep in one paragraph she could not get right. Written one way it sounded like an academic treatise, which would put off most of the readers she wanted; recast, it sounded like a bedtime story for four-year-olds. She thrust her hands up into her hair and let out a growling scream.

A few minutes later, her entry phone trilled. Had her frustrated bellow upset her neighbours? Planning a soothing apology, she reached out to take the intercom phone off its stand.

'Yes?' she said, projecting confidence and resistance in case it wasn't a neighbour but a mad stalker looking for lone women. Or a schizophrenic boy, off his meds and armed with a knife, certain he was being threatened by a devil.

'Karen?' Charlie's unmistakable voice was urgent. 'Can I come up?'

She looked at her laptop and the recalcitrant paragraph, pressed 'save' and said into the phone, 'Of course.'

When she'd logged off the computer, she extinguished the anglepoise lamp, shoved her chair under the desk and looked round to check for anything that needed removal. She wasn't the kind of woman to leave her underclothes hanging around, or dirty plates either, but she didn't want Charlie seeing her at any kind of disadvantage.

He banged on the door. Everything looked tidy, so she let him in. Once he'd kicked the door shut behind him, he marched straight ahead into the living room without a word. His swagger did not deceive her because she had seen his face: yellower than ever, with reddened eyes full of frustration, fury, and anxiety.

'Glass of wine?' she said, hoping to soothe him. 'A beer? Have you eaten?'

'Beer. I'm not hungry.'

She went into the kitchen, wincing a little from the ankle and aware the ice-cold pilsner Will liked would not be what Charlie meant by 'beer'. But it was all she had. She brought him a bottle, with the opener and a glass in case he wanted it.

'Now, what's happened?' she said.

He looked at the label, then at her, then back at the bottle. Opening it, he said, 'I've been told I'm over-complicating a simple case. In Major Crimes officers are expected to give value for money and not "start hares running and bust the budget for a fantasy". Fuckers!'

'Isn't that a straight management attempt to control costs?' Karen said, assessing Charlie's exaggerated reaction. 'It doesn't have to be personal.'

'Maybe not. Doesn't help, though.' He took a deep swallow of beer, wincing as the cold hit the back of his throat. He picked up the bottle to examine the label more closely, raised his eyebrows, then shrugged, as though he was too tired to complain.

'Can *I* help?' Karen asked, pouring herself a second glass of wine. It was clear she wasn't going to get any more time on her book tonight, so she might as well enjoy herself.

Charlie turned to look at her. 'Hope so. On the phone you said something about Billy and the knife.'

'Ah.' Karen tried not to sound too gratified. 'I didn't think you were listening. I had time to spare this afternoon, so I went looking around the marina for somewhere Billy might have hidden himself. I think I found it. I didn't search it or anything – didn't even cross the threshold; just pushed open the door – because I didn't want to screw up any evidence.'

She paused for an approving comment. Charlie didn't oblige, just drank again.

'The address is in my jacket pocket,' Karen went on. 'You should have the place searched by your amazing CSI.'

'You saying you think the knife's *there*?'

'Not necessarily,' she said. 'There isn't much in the room, no real furniture, but it has to be worth looking – at least for bloodstains. The spatter-analysis tells you someone took the knife, someone with smallish feet. Such a person has now been shot, perhaps to stop him giving any evidence about Olly's devil. Don't you think that makes it worth checking out – on its own? And his backpack was there. He could have put the knife in that. You should check for blood there too.'

Charlie got up from her dark-grey sofa and strode across the polished wooden floor towards the high plain windows that looked out across the Solent to the Island. Staring at the starlit view, he sucked up some more beer.

'That's not why Billy was shot.'

Karen grimaced at Charlie's back view. She didn't like his harsh voice one bit.

'Why then?'

'Accident.' He wheeled round, his hand still tightly

clutching the bottle. 'Think, Karen: why would anyone shoot a child in the neck if the plan was to kill him and therefore silence him?'

She didn't answer, concentrating instead on controlling her memories of the torn skin and muscle in the wound in Billy's neck, and the way the blood had quickened as his head jerked away from the handkerchief pad his father laid over it.

'If you were a sniper aiming to silence someone you'd go for a head shot at least.' Charlie sounded in pain now, rather than angry. 'More likely a body shot. He got in the way, Karen. You have to accept it.'

'I don't see why. You're theorizing. I'm theorizing. Neither of us can be sure either way. But say you are right, who d'you think *was* the intended victim?'

'That's what I want to fucking know!' Charlie came back to the sofa, perhaps soothed by her hints of support – or the beer. 'But I'm not allowed to find out.'

'What? Why not?'

'My boss thinks it was an accident. Some outsider wanting to gatecrash the shoot – or a protester wanting to shock the cosy rich while they slaughter little birdies.' Charlie produced a faint sound of amusement. 'Animal-lover like you, Karen. It's a problem for the Island cops, not an attempted murder for Major Crimes, in spite of what Henty says.'

'Which is what?'

Charlie blew out his frustration in a gust of beer-scented breath. 'That he has lots of enemies – every man working in high finance does – and that one of them has to be behind both Suzie's death and this latest shooting, which he thinks was an attempt on his wife.'

'And you want to buy into that because it makes Olly innocent of Suzie's murder,' Karen said. It was not a question, but Charlie nodded all the same.

'So what did your boss say?' Karen added.

'That Giles Henty is not half as rich as he pretends and "isn't likely to have that kind of enemy now, whatever might have happened when he was still working in the City".'

'But he's rolling in it.'

'That's what he wants you to think.' Charlie's leather jacket squeaked as he shrugged his big shoulders, suggesting he didn't care either way. 'According to my boss, who knows someone who knows, Henty was humiliated at being thrown out of his job in the credit-crunch. He was one of the first to go. So he's built up this image of himself as richer than Croesus on the Island. But all the talk of him being a brilliant investor is cock. His so-called investment club hardly buys and sells any shares, so he must be funding his grand lifestyle by raiding the profit he made on his London house when he cashed that in.'

'Makes sense, I suppose,' Karen said, thinking this could be yet another example of cognitive dissonance. How far might Giles go to keep up his picture of himself as a master of international finance? 'But if it's true, he's not going to be able to keep up appearances for long. That boat of his must have cost nearly a million quid. I was so impressed with it, I Googled antique yachts before I started work this evening and saw what kind of prices they go for. And think about his cars!'

'The house was in Chelsea,' Charlie said more moderately. He left the window and the view and collapsed on the sofa. 'Paultons Square. Henty bought it outright a decade ago with a fat bonus. He spent one point two million buying it and sold last year to a baby oligarch for three point five. Pocketful of change like that should last a while. And he got a good redundancy package on top.'

Karen thought about the extra work she was having to do to fund half the building of a modest two-bedroomed wooden bungalow in a muddy wood on the Island and fought off panic.

'It's another world, isn't it?' she said when she was sure none of the angst would leak into her voice.

Charlie didn't answer, saying instead, 'Christ, I'm tired.'

'You do look as though you haven't slept since the case started.'

He rubbed his bloodshot eyes. 'Hasn't been time for sleep. I've got to get this one right. First investigation with Major Crimes. First step on the road back. Unless they're right and I am complicating an open-and-shut case, in which case I'm fucked already.'

'Charlie,' she said, ready to offer comfort and encouragement, but he wasn't having any of it.

'The boss says they gave me this one because it's straightforward, the fuckers. "Use it to get up to speed on all the new systems put in place since you left the Met, Charlie".' He had put on a fake pompous, patronizing voice that was nothing like his own, then he sounded himself again, 'It's all follow routine now, acronyms everywhere you look, and officers allocated to specific tasks. No space for off-the-wall ideas.'

And no letting your subconscious register information and store it until you understand enough to make sense of it, Karen thought, resulting in the kind of thing snotty people deride as intuition, or a hunch. It's nothing of the kind: merely the crystallization of an apparently random range of facts and observations that have been swilling about at the back of your mind and suddenly emerge in a coherent whole.

'I'm ticking every fucking box there is and look where it's getting me.' Charlie sounded despairing. 'Fucking nowhere.'

He swung round on the sofa so that he was lying along its length with his head in her lap. He looked up at her, his round dark eyes with their reddened whites so openly needy that she found herself stroking the black hair away from his forehead. Most of the gel that usually kept it spiky and upright had worn off during the day and it felt very soft.

'I thought you weren't worried about getting back,' she said gently, touched that he trusted her enough to lie in her lap, excited by the sensation of his head heavy on her thighs, and worried about Will. 'You told me the only thing that bothered you was stepping up the pace because you'd slowed down so much on the Island.'

His eyelids closed. 'I lied,' he said. 'I want them grovelling. Begging me to work for them again.'

Karen thought of everyone who had dissed her over the years and knew exactly how he felt. In some ways he was more like her than anyone else she knew, but he gave himself a lot more latitude than she ever could. Which might have been why she enjoyed being with him so much.

'And I want Olly to be innocent,' he muttered, unaware of her thoughts. 'Unlike the rest of the Island, who can't wait to see him sent down for ever. They're shitting bricks over there now he's out of custody. Lots of chatter about who he's going to kill next. Consensus seems to be his mum. She doesn't believe it. Says no one needs to take special precautions against him. But she's the only one who thinks like that. I hope to God she's right.'

Moments later, his body changed a little, settled against her thighs. Karen heard his breathing slow. His head felt even heavier in her lap. His lips parted as his chin relaxed. She realized he was asleep.

Her second glass of Shiraz was close by and she'd barely touched it, so she reached for it now and sat sipping, while she waited for him to wake.

By the time the glass was empty, Charlie was still in deep sleep, and Karen had managed to stop thinking about him. But she had come to no more conclusions. It seemed to her that the empty squat she was sure had been Billy's refuge had to be searched with all the thoroughness possible; then someone had to cross-examine all the known drugs snouts on the Island in search of anyone who knew anything about Olly's buying cocaine; then, with or without that information, Olly must be brought back for more questioning about whoever had taken the knife from him. And then, once that identity had been established, they could talk again about his devil.

She wanted to believe in the devil as something outside Olly's own mind. All her questions to his family and his few friends had confirmed everything James had already told her: Olly had never been violent in the past, or shown any of the familiar behavioural tics that could warn of serious trouble to come. She still had to check with his teachers, but Island gossip would have picked up on any big brouhaha at school. Yet something had triggered his attack on Suzie.

Pins and needles were numbing her left thigh. If Charlie didn't move, she'd have to get out from under his head. In any case, he ought to be woken soon. He had to get back to his own flat tonight.

What if Will decided he wouldn't wait until tomorrow after all and drove over from Lewes tonight, only to find her sitting in the half dark with Charlie's head in her lap like this?

She laid her hand on Charlie's forehead and stroked his hair against his scalp. Her touch wasn't enough to reach him. He was so deeply asleep that he didn't even move. Shouting or shaking him seemed cruel, so she began to long for some outside noise to do it for her. Ironically everything was quiet for once. Most nights she was woken at least once by the sirens of police cars or ambulances and shouts from the drunks they were trying to control. But not tonight. Tonight everything conspired to keep Charlie asleep in her lap.

Somewhere in one of John Buchan's novels Aidan had told her to read long ago, there had been something about 'an old hunter's trick' of waking someone easily and soundlessly. She couldn't remember exactly but thought it had to do with pressing the neck just below the left ear. Letting her stroking hand slide down the side of Charlie's face, feeling his stubble against her palm, she found the spot and applied pressure.

His eyelids flickered upwards at once. Seeing her looking down intently at him, he smiled a long slow smile of recognition and peace. He looked a lot better than when he'd arrived.

'Hi, Karen,' he said.

'Charlie, you must go home. You're worn out.' Karen

extracted herself from under his head and stood beside the sofa, holding out a hand to help him up.

He managed the manoeuvre on his own, without help, and took her in his arms. She didn't struggle. What would be the point? In any case, she enjoyed feeling him against her and his hand on the back of her head and the warmth of his breath on her ear.

'Fancy a lowp, Karen?' he whispered into it.

His meaning was unmistakable in spite of the unfamiliar word. For a second she stood where she was, then she pulled back.

'You want it as much as I do,' Charlie said, blinking at her, still dealing with the after-effects of heavy sleep broken too soon. 'I can feel it.'

'Maybe,' she said, not prepared to lie. 'But I can't. Think what it would do to Will.'

Charlie turned away. 'He's such a tight-arse, I can't think why put yourself through all this to keep him happy.'

'He's not.' Karen sighed. 'Or not often. When he is there's every reason for it. His job carries unbelievable stress, and ...'

'And mine doesn't?'

'That's not what I'm saying. It's a different kind of stress,' Karen told him. 'I shouldn't have let you go to sleep here. Sorry. Go home now. We can talk next week about questioning Olly again. Once you've searched Billy's squat.'

Charlie walked automatically to the front door, then stopped and came back. 'He's a brain surgeon and I'm a cop still not yet off the skids. That it?'

'No.'

'He's blond and I'm dark?'

'Charlie, don't. Please.'

'Then what? What's he got that I haven't?'

'If I knew, I'd know what to do,' Karen said and found a way to smile. It was true.

'Does he know how stubborn you are? What you're capable of?' Charlie didn't wait for an answer, just slammed the door on the way out.

Karen picked up her wineglass again and refilled it. If Charlie had waited, she would have said, 'Yes; he does know. One night I told him all about how my husband died.'

Will definitely knew the worst about her, and it hadn't fazed him. The idea that she could have been responsible for her husband's death didn't stop Will loving her. So why did she keep running away from him in her mind, even though she knew she loved him back? Why couldn't she give in and agree to embark on the kind of family life he wanted?

Would it be *such* a prison? Even if it were, why would that matter? Being his wife, having children, wouldn't stop her doing the work she loved, or seeing her own friends. Her experience of family life was no great encouragement, of course. But that didn't mean she and Will couldn't do better than she and Peter had done, or her parents. Was it cowardice to keep on refusing to try?

Charlie had called him a tight-arse, and it wasn't hard to see what he meant. There was something unyielding about Will, some determination to bend the world to his idea of how it should be, that scared her. That and his patent disapproval of some of the things she thought too trivial to matter, or even that she actively enjoyed. Could she be happy living with someone who felt himself so superior to her and the rest of the human race that he dished out orders indiscriminately and criticized anything that broke his own private – and occasionally quite bizarre – rules? She certainly could not repress fundamental parts of her own character in order to placate him. That would be disaster.

Her best hope of happiness lay either in the security of the independence she already had or in an assurance that Will would not try to change her, that he'd respect the person she was, whether or not every aspect of her self fitted with his ideas of what other people should be. Was that too much to ask?

Could she ever actually ask it in a way that wouldn't damage the confidence he needed to open people's skulls and drive a scalpel into their brains? And if she didn't ask, what might her anger make her do to him?

Chapter 13

Day Six: Monday 8 a.m.

From the moment Will brought a breakfast tray into Karen's room on Sunday morning, she knew he was determined to make the day work. He had cooked her favourite, eggs Benedict, and he neither cross-questioned her about what she'd been doing so that he could tell her how she should have done it better, which was one of his worst habits, nor nagged her for the commitment that was so hard for her to make.

When she carried a large cup of delicate Kenyan peaberry coffee to her desk on Monday morning, she was still warmed by the pleasure of being able to enjoy Will's company without having to grit her teeth once. She sat, staring out across the Solent towards the Island and contemplating the possibility that her whole life could be like this if she said 'yes' to him. Tempted to phone him and do it now, she controlled herself. He would be operating, and this was not something to say to his voicemail.

Instead she tried to phone James Blazon on the landline number she'd found in one of the professional directories. It was unobtainable. Frowning in irritation, she opened her laptop, Googled him and found an email address. Hoping it was a current one, she quickly typed a message:

Hi, James. Would you have time to see me today?

She had no reason to suppose he kept his inbox open all day, but she assumed he'd be checking it pretty regularly at the moment. She would, if it had been her reputation at risk and one of her most vulnerable and dangerous patients was out of police custody and doing who-knew-what. While she waited, she sipped her coffee, enjoying every mouthful. The subtle fruity taste reminded her of the last time she'd seen Max, and it occurred to her that he might be able to help – if he would. His mind was one of the most incisive she'd met, and he had a wide web of contacts.

Max would definitely not be reading his emails every few minutes, but he did pick up his phone. She dialled his number.

'Karen,' he said. 'What's up now?'

'I wanted to ask your advice.'

'You know what it is. Settle your differences with Will, whatever the hell they are, and walk up the bloody aisle with him.'

'Max!' She felt as though she were shouting at a nagging student. 'That's not what I meant. It's a case I'm working on. Have you ever known a previously non-violent schizophrenic suddenly lash out and kill?'

'In my experience there have usually been prior incidents,' he said, sounding more interested. 'You know perfectly well that the clearest predictor of future violence is violence in the past. Animals in childhood, beetles, birds, cats, whatever. Then humans.'

'So what could trigger a first kill without any of that? Apart from alcohol and drugs.'

'Those are the two most obvious.' Max's gravelly voice was back to normal. 'Apart from them, I can't think of anything except a kind of random coincidence of some external event chiming so neatly with the patient's particular paranoid delusions that he lashes out.'

'That's what I thought. Thanks, Max. Oh, could a dentist's dose of lignocaine do it?'

'Doubt it. Not enough of the active ingredient. Sounds an interesting case,' he said, almost envious now.

'It is.' Karen thought of Billy and his father's agony of guilt. 'But full of pain for all concerned.'

'They always are. If this is specially interesting – if it throws up any new insights into the causes of violence, I mean – you could always write it up for the journals.' Max's voice had taken on a familiar mocking edge. 'That would do a lot more for your reputation than this self-help nonsense you're going in for.'

'It wouldn't pay as well.' Karen looked out over the old rusty cranes of the docks towards the trees at the north-western end of the Island. 'I need the money. And ...' She hesitated, which gave Max a disastrous opening.

'And if you were married to Will, you wouldn't have to worry for one second. It's not just what he earns, you know; he's rich.'

'Oh, shut up, Max.' Karen couldn't pretend that the idea of sharing her financial liabilities with Will hadn't occurred to her. 'Of all the reasons to get married, that's the worst. And I definitely won't do it for that. What I was going to say is that I'm only a third of the way through the first draft of my book now. *And* I haven't got a proper title yet.'

'So what are you doing chatting to me? Get writing, girl. Happy Christmas.'

'Max—' she started, but he'd cut the connection before she could ask if he had any knowledgeable contacts in the City, who might be able to tell her more about Giles.

Her email inbox showed two new messages. One from her mother read:

> You're being a cow, darling. I need to make Christmas plans. We've been invited to a client's in Verbier and I'll refuse if Aidan's coming. But I need to know by the end of tomorrow.

'So email *him*,' Karen said aloud. 'He's not my responsibility.' She couldn't imagine her mother passing up the chance of a free skiing holiday in Verbier for her, whatever she might do for Aidan.

There was nothing in her inbox from her brother himself. In fact there hadn't been any messages from him for more than ten days. Which was going to make answering her mother impossible. She typed a quick, unemotional explanation, then opened the only other email, which was from James.

> I'm free between 9 and 1. Or 3 and 4. Patients are cancelling because they've been led to think Oliver is a psychopathic serial killer and they're afraid he may be

hiding out here. Or you could come any time this evening.
My wife'll be out at her book group then.

Karen looked at the laptop, thought of the awful paragraph
in chapter seven she couldn't get right, and the punchy, selling
title she needed and couldn't force her mind to invent, remembered Charlie's exhaustion and the way Will would soon need
her and quickly typed:

I could be with you at 10. Address?

Once she'd written down all the details, she made a call to
St Cuthbert's School and talked to the head's secretary,
explaining who she was and what she wanted. She was given
an appointment for two fifteen, just after school lunch.

It's lucky, Karen thought, that schools have much longer
terms than universities or the head could be anywhere by now.
Her phone rang.

'Doctor Taylor?' A vaguely familiar voice, worried and
apologetic sounded as soon as Karen had answered. 'This is
Angela Matken. I'm so sorry to bother you. I got your
number from a friend who knows you at the university. I just
wondered ... I can't get the police to tell me anything, and
wherever I go now people either turn away or yell at me
about how dangerous Olly is. And how he should be locked
up. And how it's all my fault. I can't ... *Please* tell me what's
happening.'

'I can't give you any details of the police investigation,'
Karen said, with a lot of sympathy, 'because I don't know
them. But I'm doing my best. On my way, in fact, to talk to

James Blazon to see if I can't get something that will help show
what your son was really doing at the marina that day.'

'I wish ...' Angela's voice shrank and died. She said no
more; just cut off the call.

James lived at Brook, on what was known as the pretty side of
the Island, more or less directly opposite Karen's own dank
corner. He'd given her directions to his rented farmhouse,
which was quite a way from the village itself, perched on the
cliffs above the National Trust beach.

On this side of the Island, the shore was wide and sandy,
with cliffs rising up from it as neatly cut as though they were
blocks of white cheese – or modelling clay. They sloped
slightly inland and were topped with bright-green grass, nearly
as flat as a snooker table. Nothing could have been more different from the shallow muddy slopes that ran down to the
narrow pebbled beaches around her chalet.

Karen's route from the hovercraft stop in Cowes to Brook
took her across the Forest Road, which led towards her own
two acres of land and then on to Yarmouth. She was tempted
to make a detour into the town.

It couldn't be too hard to find someone who would tell her
who might sell a wrap or a line or even a rock or two. But it
would be much harder to learn which of the dealers had sold
to Olly. And the attempt could lead to all kinds of irritating
consequences. There was nothing Eve would like more than to
arrest Karen for buying drugs. Extricating herself from an
attempt to charge her could be embarrassing – and difficult –
for Charlie as well as herself. Will would hate it, too.

Feeling like a coward but hoping Charlie's team was

already on the case, Karen ignored the turning and drove on, cutting across the middle of the Island, past isolated farmhouses, tourist potteries, pubs and woods almost as dark, if not as muddy, as her own. Seeing St Mary's church on her left, she remembered the Lifeboat memorial there.

'The best of the best,' Granny had said to the five-year-old Karen, as they'd stood in the cold church, looking up at the tall stone plaque with its list of lives saved. 'The men who went out in the lifeboats to rescue those people didn't give up because they were tired or the weather was bad or they were scared. They went out in their boats, whatever they felt like, because it was their job. Remember them, Karen, every time you think life is too hard on you.'

Funny, she thought as she mentally saluted her grandmother, how vividly lost memories could resurface at odd moments.

She made her way through the village and on towards the Military Road. This ran along the south side of the Island and had some of the most spectacular views in the whole of the British Isles.

James had warned her to look out for a twisted dead tree on her right. He didn't know what species it was, but he'd said it was unmistakable. The lane to his house came immediately after the tree. Seeing it with plenty of time to spare, she could brake gently, then had to wait for a string of supermarket delivery vans coming in the opposite direction, followed by a muddied but stately-looking tractor with a digger attachment carried high above the cab and dripping filthy straw from its teeth. Karen felt her car quiver as the tractor passed on its colossal wheels, its weight so crushing it changed the air pressure between itself and her car, making it rock.

'What a monster,' she muttered, amazed that it was being driven by a slight young man, who looked little more than a child.

When the great machine had eventually lumbered away, clanging and dropping more gouts of muddy straw, there was no more traffic and she could whip across the other lane.

James's flint-and-brick farmhouse was only a few yards from the road. As Karen parked between a Toyota Corolla and a battered yellow Deux Chevaux, she envied him this view. Ahead was only sea, with nothing but birds and clouds and waves. Taking a direct line south, she thought, you wouldn't hit anything until you came to the coast of Normandy, somewhere between Cherbourg and Barfleur, some seventy miles away.

The air was superb, now the rain had stopped: clear and salty and as invigorating as an icy spritzer on a hot day.

'Karen! Hi.' James's voice made her turn reluctantly away from the sea.

He was standing under the small porch, an open door behind him, beckoning. Somehow here, on his own ground, with his hair blowing in the wind and wearing straightforward indigo jeans and paler-blue sweater under a padded Puffa absolutely right for the surroundings, he looked less peculiar than usual. Karen hardly even noticed his inadequate chin or the sparseness of his flying hair.

'Hi, James. Thanks for seeing me.'

'It'll help pass the time while I twiddle my thumbs, waiting for patients who never come.'

'Have you lost many over this?' she asked, with sympathy.

'A fair few,' he said, trying for a tone of casual resignation, 'but they don't worry me as much as the anonymous hate letters and the broken windows.' He pointed to the south-eastern corner of the house, where Karen saw a thick sheet of rough-edged chipboard nailed across one of the double window frames. 'My view of the Islanders as a source of endless kindness has been a bit dented.'

Karen approved of the understatement. 'Presumably even here there are people who'll grab any opportunity to legitimize an expression of their own frustration.'

'I try to think of it like that.' He smiled and looked better still. 'It makes me less angry than when I wonder if the drug companies are paying rent-a-mob to do it and scare me into recanting.'

'Is that likely?' she asked in a doubtful voice, remembering that Annie was supposed to be investigating the drugs rep James thought might be behind Suzie's death.

'God knows. Sometimes I think it is; then I think your idea's the right one. If so, I can more or less forgive the stone-throwers. My wife takes a tougher view. Now, she's busily cooking for her book group. They all take a contribution to the supper, and she's doing pudding today, so I won't take you into the kitchen. We can use my consulting room if you don't mind the windowless gloom, or take advantage of the weather and walk on the beach. Whichever you prefer.'

'Let's take the beach,' Karen said, hoping her ankle would stand up to it. Her careful treatment with the often re-frozen peas had removed most of the swelling, but the joint still hurt in some positions. 'I've got boots in the car.'

Clambering down the cliff was harder than she expected, the path being so steep and slippery. At one moment her weakened ankle bent sideways and she had to lean against the grassy side of the cutting in the cliff until the pain dwindled and the adrenaline rush eased. James loped on, unaware. Karen didn't want to complain and set off again as soon as she could. Eventually she reached the flat sand intact and together they set off westwards, towards the distant Needles.

'So,' James said, once they'd found a rhythm and were walking more or less in step, with the damp sand screeching beneath their soles. 'What can I tell you?'

'You're treating Mrs Henty, I gather,' Karen began.

'What's that got to do with the murder?' James's voice had moved from wariness to obstinacy.

'I'm not sure,' Karen said, hoping honesty would get better results than any kind of spin. 'But you've presumably heard how she barely avoided a bullet in the head on Saturday?'

'I have been told. Yes.' The polite but total obstructiveness in his voice warned Karen she was going to have to work hard to get anything useful out of him.

'I wondered,' she said, watching his face for any change of expression, 'whether you have any idea of who might have wanted to hurt her?'

His shoulders relaxed at once and he even laughed.

'None at all. But you don't believe she was a *target*, do you? Wasn't it an accident?'

'Probably. Did you find her easy to treat?'

'It's a fairly straightforward case. Karen, where are you going with this? I can't break patient confidentiality, you know.'

Karen offered him a sympathetic smile. He did not reciprocate. His protectiveness of his patient was entirely proper, but

Karen felt impatience juddering like a pneumatic drill in her mind.

'I suppose not,' she said, 'but I had been hoping you'd be able to tell me a bit about her dealings with her husband. Does she talk about him? Outside your consultations, I mean.'

James kept his mouth shut. His eyes looked stubborn.

'Giles has been so close to two violent attacks that he's an important witness,' Karen added with a directness she rarely allowed herself. 'In my capacity as psychological adviser to the police on the first and more serious of those attacks, I need all the background I can get to help them form an accurate picture of everything that happened. Otherwise I may lead them in the wrong direction and put innocent people at risk. I'm not asking for gossip.'

She hoped her pompous long-windedness would soothe James's anxieties and also make him as impatient as she was herself. It didn't work out quite as she'd intended.

'As I understand it,' he said, 'witnesses who found Suzie's body said Giles must've been on his boat when Suzie died, right at the other end of the marina, and he was nowhere near either his wife or the boy who was actually shot on Saturday.'

'Do you know where he was?'

'Not exactly. But it took nearly ten minutes, Lucy said, before they got hold of him to tell him what had happened.'

'You've seen her since Saturday, then?'

'She phoned yesterday and asked me to go over to their house,' James said in the voice of one being tormented by an itch he'd been told not to scratch but unable to resist. 'She'd had a bad night, nightmares, and early waking with panic. All the usual symptoms of incipient depression.'

'It's not really surprising,' Karen said, relieved to have got him talking. 'Even if she didn't think she was the intended victim, to have ...'

'A thirteen-year-old boy collapsing across her lap, shot and pouring blood, would affect anyone,' James agreed. 'I'm just thankful it happened before the cops had let Oliver go. He's already a hate figure for everyone on the Island, so if he'd been free he'd be ...' He let his voice dwindle to nothing and turned his face into the wind, as though it could clean out his mind.

'Right,' Karen said. 'So that I don't do harm when I talk to her, can you tell me what your original diagnosis was in her case?'

James stopped, with the sand creaking even louder beneath his rubber soles, and faced her again

'Reactive depression,' he said, no longer even trying to keep his professional secrets, 'caused chiefly by a mixture of under-used intelligence and the stress of trying to second-guess a difficult husband. It's fairly common in women who have chosen to take the subordinate role in marriage out of a desire for safety.'

'And how did you treat her? Given your views on medicating distress, I imagine ...'

'A technique I call mind re-ordering,' he said, with his voice settling into a confident lecturer's sonority. 'We work on visualization of roles, adapting expectations, managing conflict.' James smiled and his voice returned to normal. 'Nothing terribly technical, Karen: it's just a way of giving patients confidence and showing them that a modification of their own behaviour and speech patterns can completely change the way their partners treat them. My gut feeling is that with all this work being done now on neuroplasticity, the increased confidence may actually be building new neural pathways – which would explain the good results I've been getting. But I'm not in a position to organize fMRI scans with my patients here, so I've no proof.'

'That makes perfect sense,' she said, remembering the assessment of his work that Charlie's one-time doctor had offered. 'Did you use the same kind of technique with Olly?'

'Not entirely.' He swung round again and set off along the beach, bending forward into the wind. 'His illness is much more serious. But you know that.'

Karen followed, enjoying the way the buffeting gusts supported her weight. When James said no more, she applied a prod.

'I read a speculative paper you wrote in the late nineties,' she said, 'in which you suggested fear – continuing high-level fear – as one of the prime triggers for genetically based schizophrenia.'

'You do do your research,' he said, when she paused.

Karen hoped his comment was admiring rather than resentful, but she couldn't be sure.

'I find it helps.' She laughed a little to make herself seem like less of a threat and felt the coldness of the wind against her teeth, making them ache. 'Has your work with patients since then changed your mind?'

'I'm still certain fear is a crucial ingredient. Neuroscience is beginning to produce confirmatory results, too. The amygdala is involved in schizophrenia; so, perhaps, are cortisol and noradrenaline. The one is the seat of fear; the others, a response to it.' James paused, as though to make sure that Karen understood what he was telling her.

She smiled to encourage him, thinking that if he were one of her students she would advise less pompous language. But then she hadn't exactly stinted on over-formal phrasing herself. She'd often thought her colleagues used this kind of talk as a way of distancing themselves from the reality of their patients' experience, as well as making the irrational seem safer.

'And the development of neural pathways in the under-threes definitely has a bearing,' he went on. 'If a toddler is subjected to intense fear, his brain development is affected and it is likely that his subsequent responses to acute stress will be abnormal. Once his brain has been sensitized to fear, I mean.'

'So is it possible that a sudden frenzy of terror could have switched a previously non-violent schizophrenic into—' Karen was saying, when James interrupted with fury, 'I have already told you it is extremely unlikely that Oliver killed that girl. As I understand it, he's stated all along that he was trying to *protect* her from the killer, and that he was sitting with her in his lap for that reason and that reason alone.'

'So why did he have a knife?' Karen asked, with the most obvious question she assumed Charlie and his team must already have addressed. 'Doesn't that suggest premeditation – at least an intention to . . .'

'No. It suggests fear.' James frowned at her, as though finding it impossible to understand the byways of her mind. 'Haven't you ever come across adolescent boys who arm themselves with knives because they don't want to be at the mercy of . . . In any case, I don't think it's been proved that he *did* have a knife, has it?'

'Maybe not,' Karen said, remembering that Olly's father

had had a gardener's penknife hanging from the belt of his trousers. Perhaps the family were used to carrying knives of one sort or another. 'But the spatter-analysis suggests that he did and that someone took it from him.'

'That's not enough to *prove* anything.' Now James sounded insultingly patient. 'And Oliver has never been violent in the past.'

'What would have happened if he'd ingested a large amount of cocaine on the afternoon Suzie was killed?' Karen asked, changing tack.

James was arrested in his walk. 'Has *that* been established as true?'

'There's been a suggestion.'

He looked devastated, but he fought back. 'That could certainly explain a sudden frenzy of violence. But I'd be surprised if it is true here. Oliver never has taken cocaine, to my knowledge, and I can't see him doing it willingly now. In any case, I thought ... We'd been through ... I thought he'd worked out the sum and accepted it: drugs equals terror; no drugs equals less terror. Damn.'

Karen was surprised to see tears in James's eyes. But the wind was sharp. It could have been that making them water.

'I've heard it said that the person who scares most addicts more than anyone else, is their dealer. What if Olly's dealer had been trying to move him on from cannabis to the more expensive coke – or crack – and now forced him to take it?' Karen asked. 'Couldn't that combination bring on a frenzy of terror, and so lead to violence?'

The watering of James's eyes was worse now, but he didn't say anything.

She was just formulating her next question when she heard a woman's voice carried on the wind:

'James! James! Please listen. Oh, please. James!'

He was oblivious to the calls, so Karen prodded his arm and gestured behind them. Looking puzzled, James glanced over his shoulder.

'Ah.' He stopped and turned to face the newcomer, murmuring to Karen, 'This is Lucy Henty. I have to talk to her. I'll phone you so we can talk about Olly's dealer later. OK?'

'Of course,' Karen said, aware that he wanted her to disappear but far too curious about Giles's wife to do any such thing.

The newcomer was a couple of inches shorter than Karen and even more slender, but without any of the angular boniness that made DS Clarke look so odd. This woman was dressed in wide-legged navy trousers, a Breton striped sweater and a thick pea coat, with a scarlet scarf fluttering from her neck.

Granny would never have approved of scarlet with red hair, Karen thought. But it works.

'James, thank heavens you heard me,' the newcomer said in a high childish voice, broken by breathlessness. 'I thought you never would, and I knew I couldn't catch you up if you didn't stop. You need to come back to the house. Now.'

'Why? Has something happened to Georgina?' James was already running towards the precipitous path in the cliff.

'Who's Georgina?' Karen asked.

Lucy turned her head. 'His wife. Who are *you*?'

'Karen Taylor,' she said, holding out a hand. Lucy waited long enough to shake it politely, but she looked puzzled.

'I'm a colleague of James's,' Karen added. 'Another psychologist.'

'Ah, I see. Oh, that's OK. James, James.' She ran after him over the sand. 'It's not Georgie who needs you.'

This time her voice did reach him, and he stopped with one foot already on the horrible chalk path. As the two women hurried to catch up with him, he said crossly, 'Then who?'

'It's Giles,' said Lucy. 'James, you've got to help. He won't speak. He's just sitting at the breakfast table at home, not doing anything. I keep saying, "What's wrong?" But he won't answer. It's like what I've been reading about: catatonia, they call it. You must come, please.'

'You mean *your* house.' James took her by both forearms and looked as though he was about to shake her. 'You must have some idea what's wrong with him. I need to know before I ... before I go charging in.'

She sighed and leaned against the cliff's edge, as though she needed any support she could get to keep going.

'You know how we could never have children, Giles and me?'

'Yes.' James turned to Karen, as though he could make her leave with no more than a severe glare. She smiled blandly and waited to learn what she could.

'He always thought of Suzie as his daughter and so maybe he feels like this boy, this Billy, was kind of like his son. Now Suzie's dead and Billy's probably dying, and Giles ... he thinks it's all his fault.'

Karen watched her with interest. Something in the breathless outpouring of words didn't ring quite true.

'Giles must think ... He didn't sleep last night; he tried to eat this morning, but he couldn't. I can see he's desperate, but he won't talk to me. You're the only one who could help, James. He *needs* you.'

'But he hasn't asked for me, has he?' James sounded as though he was as sceptical about all this as Karen.

Lucy's freckles stood out like burns as her skin paled. 'Not as such. And you mustn't say I sent you. He'd be furious with me, if he thought I'd been ... well, talking about him. He hates that. Thinks it's treachery. But he needs you. You have to go to the house on your own, James, and say something. Anything. Something like you're looking for me. And then make him talk to you. He needs help, James. And he needs it *now*.'

This time it was she who reached out, grabbing his shoulders. And she did shake him.

'If you won't help, he'll kill himself. He said he'd take the boat out, and the way he said it, when I warned him about the weather and he told me to fuck off, I know that's what he's planning.'

Ah, thought Karen, so he's not completely catatonic. Perhaps Lucy didn't know what the word meant but thought it sounded dramatic.

'He'll throw himself over the side,' Lucy went on, sounding less childish now and therefore much more convincing. 'I'm sure of it. You must go, James. You must. You absolutely must.'

James looked at Karen over his patient's head. This time, his expression suggested a plea.

'All right, Lucy,' he said aloud. 'I'll go. But I want you to stay with Doctor Taylor here until I get back. OK? You can show her into my consulting room, and I'll be back as soon as I can. I don't want you running around the Island in this state. Promise?'

'All right, James,' she said, gazing up at him as if he were her hero for all time. 'I promise.'

'Karen?' he said.

She nodded her agreement. This opportunity to find out more about some of the crucial players in the drama was too convenient to ignore.

James set off up the path as quickly and easily as though he came down to the sea every day. As he went, he pulled out his phone. Even from twenty yards below him, Karen heard him.

'Georgie, darling? It's me. I've got to run to see a patient. Emergency. I'm sending Lucy Henty and Doctor Taylor to the house. They won't get in your way, but if you felt up to making them some coffee ...? Great, darling. That's really kind. Thanks. How are you feeling? Smashing. You are amazing. See you later.'

Karen and Lucy followed more carefully, with Lucy in the lead. On one particularly steep stretch of the path, the chalk pebbles skittered from under her shoes and Karen wondered what would happen to them both if she slipped. Karen paused for a while to make a bigger space in which Lucy could break any fall and avoid pushing them both down to the beach.

In fact Lucy was nearly as supple and quick as James, and Karen was left to toil up the last steep stretch alone, fighting to keep upright and ignore the pain in her ankle.

Back at the brick-and-flint farmhouse, Lucy led the way again, with far more confidence than she'd shown when talking to James. She called out to Georgie that they would be in his consulting room.

His wife came out of the kitchen, wiping floury hands on her apron.

'I wouldn't, if I were you. What with the broken windows being blocked up, it's miserable in there. Go into the drawing room and enjoy the view. I'll bring you coffee and biscuits in a minute.'

She smiled at Karen and held out her hand. 'We haven't met. I'm Georgie Blazon.'

Karen shook her hand, thinking of everything she'd read about how couples tended to choose each other because they shared a similar level of attractiveness. Georgie didn't fit that thesis.

Unlike her husband, she was dark-haired, very pretty, very pregnant. She looked as though she was not much less than Karen's age of thirty-six and seemed to be within a month of her due date. She also looked as though she were revelling in every moment. Her skin was radiant and her smile wide and generous.

'Thanks,' Karen said, smiling back. 'But you really don't need to do anything about coffee.'

'It'll be a pleasure.' Georgie's generosity flashed again as her lips widened once more. 'So, what sort of coffee? Lucy always has plain black, but I've got a machine, so you could have cappuccino, with properly tepid foam so you can drink the hot espresso through it.'

'Wow,' Karen said.

Georgie laughed a little, stroking her bump and picking up some of the flour she'd already wiped off her fingers. 'James told me you're a coffee fanatic.'

'I didn't know he knew,' Karen said. 'But cappuccino sounds great. Thank you.'

As Georgie went back to the kitchen, Karen followed Lucy into the drawing room, which didn't look as though the Blazons had done anything to it during their tenancy. The decoration was traditional and must have been chosen by someone at least two generations older than Georgie. The walls had been dragged in a pale grey and there were pink-and-grey striped curtains, a few gilt mirrors that pretended to be eighteenth century and some dreary landscapes hanging between them. Nothing wrong with any of it, Karen thought, but none of it imaginative or personal.

A faint smell of dusty roses hung in the air. She looked around for its source and noticed a large blue-and-white bowl filled with potpourri. She plunged in her hand and stirred, enjoying the much stronger scent she'd disturbed. The dried petals felt like fine suede against her cold fingers.

'How long have you been working with James?' Lucy asked from behind her.

Karen left the pot pourri and chose one of the wing-backed chairs near the white fireplace.

'I don't exactly work with him,' she said frankly, 'but I'm involved in the Olly Matken case. So I wondered if you could maybe tell me what you think happened between him and Suzie.'

Lucy shrank back against the well-padded arm of the sofa, crossing her legs. 'I don't know. I didn't see a lot of him, but Philip and Angela occasionally brought him to our big summer parties. I do know Suzie was always nice to Olly. He was more ... more kind of relaxed with her than with anybody else, I think.'

'Did he get jealous? If she was being nice to other people, perhaps,' Karen suggested.

'I don't know.' Lucy's beautifully shaped eyebrows were clenched tight over her small straight nose.

As the door opened, Karen got to her feet to take the heavy-looking wooden tray from Georgie. The delicious smell of coffee overtook all the faint rosy scent left in the air and on her own hand. 'That's so kind. But there are only two cups. Aren't you going to have any?'

Georgie said breezily that she had too much cooking to do to sit about and chat. Karen heard the unmistakable sound of a subtext and wondered if it was that she didn't want to make social conversation with one of her husband's patients.

'If James had been there, Olly never would have done it,' Lucy said, as soon as Georgie had gone. She was leaning over her crossed knees and staring at Karen. 'Even when everybody else couldn't control him, James could. Olly went berserk once. It was really embarrassing. One of our caterers told him he'd had too much to drink and he just went wild. His parents were hopeless and his sister yelled at him like a fishwife, and he screamed at her. Really screamed. It was awful. But James sorted it right away: you know, stopped the wildness *and* made Olly happy again. He's amazing, you know. That's why I wanted him for Giles now.'

'That's quite a reference,' Karen said, picking up her cappuccino. 'He's obviously been a real help to you.'

'Oh, he has.' Lucy's voice had warmed up a lot. She unwound her legs and got up to fetch her own coffee. 'I've always been able to tell him absolutely everything. And he's made me see so much.'

'Like what?' Karen tried the cappuccino and discovered it to be exactly as Georgie had described. The real thing. Her machine must be a Gaggia at least.

'Like how depression happens when people don't treat you like you want them to.' Lucy's voice was breathless all over again, but this time with enthusiasm. 'When they don't understand you, or they let you down, over and over again, and there's nothing you can do about it. So you just go back into depression because there's nowhere else to go. Or that's what you think. And, hard as it is, at least you know what to do when you're there. And people look after you. So till you're strong enough to do it for yourself, you kind of like it. Even though you hate it. If you see what I mean.'

'Has James said what the cure is?'

Lucy smiled a sad determined smile and straightened her back. 'Behaving like the person who deserves the better treatment; not the person you think they want you to be. I mean, you have to stop trying to change them and change yourself to be more like your real self. Then they change too.'

Karen thought back to Granny saying over and over again throughout her childhood, 'People take you at your own valuation.'

Folk sense, but without the twist James had put on it, and the transactional analysts too. People take you at the self-estimation you suggest by the way you behave and speak and interact with them.

Suddenly Karen had an idea for the title of her book: *Change and the World Changes with You*. There was the implicit subtitle, too: *Stay the Same and You Stay Alone*. It could work. Although a snappier version would still be better.

Change Yourself and Change the World? Maybe not. But there was something there. She'd have to give it more time later.

'Don't *you* believe that?' Lucy's voice, slightly plaintive, broke into Karen's thoughts. 'It's worked with us. Giles has even stopped seeing his girlfriend.'

'It certainly makes sense,' Karen said. 'And I'm glad it's worked for you. Can you tell me what happened on Saturday, when Billy was . . . hurt?'

Lucy shuddered and hunched back into the corner of the sofa, pulling up her legs so that her feet perched on the edge of the sofa, rather as Olly had sat when he'd been keening in the police station.

'I can't . . . Not till James has said . . . I need to talk to him again about it first.' Her pale-green eyes were filling with tears and she was shaking. Her voice was high and childish again. 'Don't make me say anything. Don't make me. Please.'

Karen took refuge in her coffee cup, thinking James's cure of Lucy's problems might not be as complete as either of them claimed, and wondering how much he enjoyed the power he clearly had over her. Rich and beautiful as she was, her dependence might do a lot to bolster a man so heavily criticized by powerful colleagues. And so weak?

As Karen emerged from the cup, she could feel a moustache of foam hardening on her upper lip.

And then someone screamed.

Chapter 14

Day Six: Monday 12 Noon

Before Karen could move, Lucy had her mobile out of her bag and was jamming three numbers into it.

'Stop!' Karen hissed, as loudly as she dared.

Lucy pressed the stop key obediently and looked up for more instructions. She definitely had a long way to go before she became a fully autonomous director of her own life.

'Don't call the police until we know what's happening.' Karen softened her order with a faint smile. 'Georgie could've been scared by a spider or a mouse.'

'Screams as hoarse as that are real.' Lucy sounded as though she knew what she was talking about. 'This is bad.'

Karen was on her feet and listening at the door. She heard shuffling sounds from the hall outside, and two sets of heavy breathing, and then a young male voice she recognized. Olly's. He sounded terrified. Was it he who'd screamed?

Straining to hear something specific in the general fuzz of noises, Karen made out some words in Olly's high, shaking voice, 'Where is he then? He's got to see it happen. He's got to see me kill the devil. That's the only way it's going to come right now. I've got to show James how I can kill the devil.'

'James is not here, Olly.' Georgie's voice was absolutely clear and astonishingly friendly. Karen recognized tremendous reserves of courage. 'Put down the knife. And tell me what you really want. Put down the knife. It's only a tiny knife, Olly. And you don't need it here. Put down the knife. No one will make you do anything you don't want. And no one will hurt you. Let go of my neck and put down the knife.'

'Where is he? You've got to take me to him. You've, like, got to. That way we can kill the devil, like she said. Where is he?'

Karen realized that Georgie had given her all the information she needed. Oliver Matken had grabbed her round the neck and was threatening her with a small knife. But almost any knife, however small, could kill. Karen knew of cases where a three-inch blade had been enough. She moved silently across the thick fitted carpet towards Lucy to whisper:

'I need to get behind them, so I'm going out of that window now. You stay here and, if they come in, talk very softly to Olly. D'you understand? Be kind and don't show any fear. When you see me behind them, make sure you keep talking to Olly so that he looks only at you. OK?'

Lucy was shivering and biting her lips but she nodded and made no protest, which was a relief.

'And if anything happens, I'll deal with him,' Karen said. 'I need you to look after Georgie. OK?'

As Lucy nodded once more, Karen kicked off her shoes and climbed on to the padded window seat. Opening the casement made the hinges squeak, but when she paused with her hand on the window frame, listening, she heard nothing, except Georgie's easy, safe-sounding voice, repeating her instruction to put down the knife, over and over again.

Karen swung her legs over the sill and dropped soundlessly on to the grass outside, flinching as her ankle protested. She carefully pushed the window shut behind her and ignored the front door. Unlocked though it was, it led straight into the hall-like passage between the kitchen and the sitting room. From the sound of voices, that's where Olly was holding Georgina. Karen's only hope of getting in without alerting Olly was to get in through a window in whatever room lay behind the kitchen.

She found a cloakroom, with a deep porcelain sink under the window. The window was divided into two parts, with the lower part fixed shut. The top lifted horizontally and was just big enough for her body. Balancing with one leg on the outside sill, she levered the other leg over the fixed lower half of the window and ducked her head so that she could get under the top of the frame. Her foot found first the taps, then empty space. She hoped her ankle would bear her weight when she did find a foothold. Swinging her leg from the knee, first left then right, she hoped to hit a draining board, but she couldn't feel anything. A quick squinting glance downwards told her the taps had been designed to be high enough to fill a bucket, and that the sink itself was very deep. Only the knowledge that there was a knife in the hands of a terrified and unpredictable boy forced Karen on.

As she shifted herself uncomfortably over the window bar, pushing aside the handle that was catching in her hair, she leaned carefully down and sideways, levering her pubic bone carefully over the obstruction until her torso was lying almost at right angles to her hips. Sliding a little further round, now she could feel the base of the sink with the toes of her left foot. She pushed herself further and felt a heart-stopping lurch as her foot slipped in the thin layer of water left in the bottom of the sink, sending pain shooting up from her ankle right up to her knee. Flinging out her free hand, she found the wall and pushed hard enough against it to regain most of her balance, fighting the waves of pain that made her feel sick.

Adrenaline was prickling all over her and her pumping heart was making the blood crash loudly in her ears as she twisted like a spring and forced herself upright again.

Terrified the noise would reach the psychotic boy outside in the hall, she paused before attempting the tricky manoeuvre of getting her other leg in over the fixed window. She could hear nothing beyond the sounds of her own body.

Now she made herself remember ballet lessons and how it had felt to balance on one foot, with the other leg high up behind her in an arabesque and pretend to pick something off the floor. Verbal memories of the movement brought back the balance she needed and made her limbs behave. The pain retreated.

The last movements were easy and she climbed silently over the edge of the big butler's sink and stood on the floor. At the door, she listened again and heard only Georgie's voice. Opening the cloakroom door, Karen saw the hall was empty and the sitting room door wide open. Olly must have pushed Georgie through it.

As soon as Karen had crossed the hall, moving silently in her socks and hoping her ankle would bear her weight again when it mattered, she saw Georgie's back and that of her attacker. He was standing on her right side, with his left hand clamped around her neck and his right out of sight. Karen couldn't see any sign of a knife, which suggested he must have it angled towards the child she was carrying, rather than her throat. In which case even the smallest blade could be disastrous.

The game of Grandmother's Footsteps had never appealed to Karen, and she'd always been the first to be spotted. But this time it was her only chance. She took a step forwards, thinking of the way the sand had squeaked under her shoes only half an hour ago.

This was better. Risking a look down at the floor, she noticed it was covered with a thick rush mat. Thank God! She looked again at her target, before taking another step, then another. Her ankle was doing OK so far. Now she was almost at the door jamb.

Through the sitting room door ahead of her, she could see Lucy, staring at Oliver, her eyes dilated in terror. One hand clasped her throat and the other was holding her phone. Karen moved forwards again and, in spite of her earlier warning, Lucy's eyes flicked towards her, over his head.

He caught the movement and turned at once, luckily whirling around to the right, away from Georgie. Karen saw nothing but the open penknife in his hand. The blade was bloody. Without thinking, she launched herself forwards, with her hands cupped as though to receive a present.

A sharp slicing sensation in her wrist was followed by the warmth of blood. She ignored it, taking his knife hand between both of hers, holding tight and twisting round to the right.

'Drop it, Olly,' she said quietly, hoping the cut in her wrist wasn't deep. 'Drop the knife.'

He gasped, but didn't let it fall. Karen twisted his hand further, knowing how much the torsion must be hurting him. His other hand left the back of Georgie's neck and plucked at Karen's wrist, but his nails weren't long enough to do any damage and he couldn't get a purchase on her fingers. She held on, still twisting.

He kicked out, accidentally catching Georgie across the shins. She stumbled and her own weight pulled her forwards on to the floor. Out of the corner of her eye, Karen could see that Georgie's back was heaving, but she couldn't look away from Olly's knife hand. Lucy would have to help Georgie, but she was too busy phoning to do anything.

'Police!' Lucy yelled into her phone. 'Police. We need the police now. He's got a knife.'

Karen, wishing Lucy hadn't done anything so inflammatory, twisted Olly's hand again. At last his fingers opened and the knife dropped to the floor, with a muffled thud.

She put both arms tightly round Olly before he could do anything else, and she felt his whole body trembling like a butterfly in a tornado.

'It's the devil,' he said, in a high voice that shook. 'She's hiding the devil inside her. We've got to cut it out. Cut out the devil. We've got to get the devil out. You mustn't stop me. The devil's hiding inside her. Cut him out. Cut him out. Then we'll all be safe.'

'You'll be safe without cutting anyone, Olly.' Karen knew she didn't sound nearly as kind and calm as Georgie had, but she did her best. 'You're safe with us.'

Lucy was talking into the phone again. Karen couldn't concentrate on her, but she hoped Lucy was cancelling the police. The last thing they needed now was any noisy rescue attempt with flashing blue lights and shouting, which could scare Olly into even more aggression.

Georgie was on her knees, shuffling towards the sofa, with one hand cradling her bump. When she reached the sofa, she turned so that she was sitting on the floor with her back to it. Splaying out her legs, she kept her right hand where the baby's head must be, and breathed heavily, as though her lungs had completely deflated when she fell and needed refilling. At last she nodded, turned her head sideways and upwards so she could meet Karen's eyes.

'He's kicked. He's OK.'

Karen found her tongue outside her mouth, licking her lower lip as she smiled and exhaled. Still clinging to Olly in a mixture of restraint and reassurance, she said, 'Everything's all right, Olly. There's no devil here. It's all all right now.'

Lucy was still talking into the phone, saying: 'Yes. Yes. Fine. Hang on a minute.' She raised her head and looked straight at Karen. 'DCI Trench wants to talk.'

'Could you bring the phone over here?' Karen said, talking now with the gentleness she would use to a frightened baby. She could feel Olly rigid and shaking against her and knew she mustn't let him go for a second.

Lucy walked towards her, staying a full arm's length away from the two of them and held out the phone towards Karen's face:

'Charlie?' Karen said, still quiet.

'Yeah. She said there's been a knife. But he hasn't got it now. Is that true?'

'Yes, to both parts.'

'You OK?'

'I'm fine.' From the crawling sensation on the inside her arm, she knew she was still bleeding, but it felt like an ooze not a spurt, so the damage couldn't be too bad. 'I have Olly here. James Blazon is away just now, with Giles probably; it would be good if you could get him back. OK?'

'Got it,' Charlie said, without asking a single other question. 'Be careful. Contain it, if you can. I'll be quick.'

Lucy took away the phone. Olly sagged, but Karen dared not let go of him. She hung on, but looked over his shoulder.

'Georgie?' she said. 'Georgie?'

The pregnant woman looked up at her again.

'Are you hurt? Do you think you'd be able to go upstairs?' Karen not only wanted to ensure Georgie's safety but also to get her out of the way so that Olly wouldn't see anything that might trigger the terrors of the devil he so feared.

Georgie nodded and set about heaving herself up, levering her back against the sofa until she had her bottom on it, then half turning to push herself up against the arm. As she waddled past Karen, she mouthed, 'Thank you.'

Karen nodded, watched Georgie quietly kick the Swiss army knife ahead of her, then waited until she heard the sitting room door close. Painfully slow steps sounded as Georgie climbed the stairs. A door closed, then came the creaking of the floor above the sitting room. Bed springs twanged. At last there were no more sounds.

Very carefully, speaking Olly's name and telling him that everything was all right, Karen eased her arms away from his shaking body. She put her hands on his shoulders and pushed him a little way away so that she might meet his eyes. He wouldn't look at her.

'There's a table over here, Olly,' she said, gently turning him and pointing. 'I want you to come and show me what the devil looks like. Can you do that? I need to see his face.'

He glanced at her for a second from under his long loose fringe, then hurriedly looked away again. After a long moment, he gave a tiny nod, which made the greasy hair swing like a curtain across his eyes.

'That's wonderful.' Karen kept her voice cheerful but still quiet. 'Lucy is going to find some paper for you, and I've got a pencil in my bag, so if you come with me now, we can walk together to the table and you can show me what he looks like so we can get him.'

'And kill him,' Olly said, as his voice shivered and ended in the single-note keening sound she'd heard before.

'We don't have to kill him,' Karen said, wishing she knew more about how to communicate with someone in the grip of a florid episode of psychosis. 'We're going to make him safe so he can't do any more damage. But we need to know what he looks like. Come on, Olly. Come to the table.'

Lucy was rootling in a mahogany bureau that stood on one side of the fireplace, and emerged holding a yellow lined pad, like the sort common in American lawyers' offices. She held it up for Karen's approval.

'That's great, Lucy. Come on, Olly. We've got some nice yellow paper for you to draw his face on.'

Karen knew that even if Charlie got hold of James immediately it would take them nearly half an hour to get here. And if James were in the middle of talking to Giles, he might have his phone on divert. She had to keep Olly contained until they got here.

He sat down at the table, his back stiff, and his hand gripping the pencil as if it were a miniature spear. Karen saw how sharp the point was and got ready to grab his arm if he turned it against himself. She sat beside him, not touching him any longer, but still talking, urging him to write his name at the top of the sheet, hoping in a blind kind of way that this memory of primary school might put him in the mood to cooperate. She admired her clinical colleagues even more than usual.

'Just your name, Olly,' she said. 'Just write your name.'

His keening had stopped, which gave her some encouragement, and she was impressed that Lucy had retreated in silence to the window seat. Her breathing was high and short enough to show how scared she was, but she'd got the point and was doing her best not to heighten the tension any further.

Olly sighed and relaxed his fist so the pencil dropped on to the table. Then he picked it up again and held it like a writing implement to scrawl his name at the top. Karen wanted to give him more instructions but didn't dare risk breaking whatever concentration he had achieved. For a long time, he sat with the sharp grey point of the pencil still lying on the tail of the y he'd written. Then he moved his hand. Karen braced herself, but he just wrote his name again. And again. And again.

She let him do it without interruption, only to watch him

turn the sheet over and make a differently shaped movement. This time it wasn't 'Olly' that formed on the yellow lined paper, but devil. The devil. Devil. The devil. Kill the devil. Kill the devil. Kill. Kill. Kill.

Chapter 15

Day Six: Monday 1.30 p.m.

Olly's eyes were wild as one paramedic held him down on the trolley and the other injected him with chlorpromazine.

'The liquid cosh,' Karen whispered to herself, as the terrified boy relaxed and flopped back onto the stretcher, his eyes rolling upwards in their sockets. She looked sideways at Charlie and saw him staring at the stretcher with a cold hostility that made her wince. It was so unlike him.

'Charlie?' she said. His head swivelled round towards her and he forced a small, bitter-looking smile.

'Has to be hospital now,' he said as they stood and watched the paramedics lift the trolley, collapse its legs and heave it into the back of the ambulance. 'He's too dangerous to be out any longer.'

One of the paramedics sat down on the bench opposite the patient, while the other jumped down and slammed the doors shut, before hurrying round to the front to drive to hospital.

And then more drugs, Karen thought, remembering all James's diatribes about the damage chlorpromazine and the rest of the antipsychotics could do to non-responders. They got no benefit from the drugs, except sedation, but suffered all the side effects.

'He had another knife,' Charlie said in answer to the frozen expression on her face. 'He's dangerous. I'd be irresponsible to let this go on. I had to get him sectioned. They're taking him to the adolescent secure unit for assessment – and treatment.'

'I know you had to do it. But I wish you'd got James over here to take charge first.' Karen brushed the plaster Georgie had found for her and stuck over the cut in her inner arm once it had been cleaned with antiseptic wipes.

Karen found a weird reassurance in the tightness she could feel in the grip between the plaster's glue and her skin. The bleeding had stopped now, and the cut was no more than a scrape about two inches long. It would heal soon. And she didn't have to worry about contamination from the blood she'd seen on the knife blade: it had come from a small cut in Georgie's neck, and she'd had all the standard blood tests at the start of her pregnancy.

'James understands Olly,' Karen added.

'I couldn't wait. Would've been irresponsible.' Charlie was angry. Karen hoped she wasn't his target. 'We will need to talk to his wife in due course.'

'She did brilliantly.' Karen began to relax herself and felt a singing sensation in her head as the tension seeped away. 'Come on.'

Charlie put one hand under her chin and turned her head to the light, staring into her eyes.

'Let me go, Charlie. This is work,' she said.

'You've just faced an armed killer. I wanted to see what it

had done to you. I need to know if you can carry on safely now.'

'Can you see anything?' she asked, meaning she was sure there would be nothing to see.

'No,' he said. 'You've shut me out again. You'll have to tell me: you OK to carry on?'

'I will be.' Karen kept her teeth from chattering but her body still trembled. It would be a long time before she stopped thinking of what could have happened here today. 'The person who needs help is Lucy. She had Billy's body falling across her knees on Saturday and now this. From everything she's said, she sounds a lot more emotionally fragile than I'll ever be. Come on, we must go indoors and see to her.'

The sound of a tinny wheezing engine made her turn her head and smile. James's car was bouncing towards them at its top speed.

He flung himself out, leaving the engine on and the door open, rushing towards them, shouting: 'Georgie? Georgie? Where is she? What's he done to her?'

'She's OK, James,' Karen said. 'She's upstairs, lying down. She controlled him really well, and he didn't hurt her, barring a small cut in her neck and the fall. She should probably be checked out, but she seems well in control.'

James ignored her and ran on into the house. Charlie put his hand into the car to switch off the engine and pull up the handbrake.

'You're right,' he said as he strolled back towards Karen. 'Someone's got to deal with Lucy. And I've got to get over to the Matkens and find out what happened to send Olly here with a knife like this. And what his mother's up to right now.

Can you take Lucy home? Doesn't look to me as if she should be driving, and, after all . . .' He looked speculatively at Karen, who obligingly finished his sentence for him, 'It would give me a chance to find out more about who could have wanted to shoot her – if someone did.'

'More important is why she came to get James away from his wife at this precise moment today,' Charlie said. 'I may be – what was it you called me the other day? – a devious bugger, but it all seems a tad too convenient. Here's a vulnerable pregnant woman unexpectedly alone just when a psychopath with a knife comes along.'

'He's psychotic, not psychopathic,' Karen said, irritated by Charlie's dangerous exaggeration. It seemed so unlikely in a man who had wanted Olly to be innocent.

'I don't think that's true any more,' Charlie said, sounding more punitive than she had ever heard him. 'See what you can find out from Lucy.'

'OK. And will you get them to do drugs tests on Olly again? The last lot were inconclusive because of his dentist. This time you might get something useful.'

'Tell James I've gone,' Charlie said, without answering. 'Catch up with you later. Maybe meet at the Goose, if there's time. Go there and wait. I'll phone when I know where I'll be.'

'Thanks a bunch,' she said.

Charlie didn't hear. He was already in his car and turning on to the main road before she'd thought of all the questions she still had to ask: had his CSI found anything in the empty squat she'd identified? Had Annie tracked down the drugs rep? Had Charlie's boss stopped harassing him?

*

Lucy didn't protest about being made to leave her expensive BMW outside James's house, which was surprising. Instead, she got into the passenger seat of Karen's bustling little Subaru Justy without a comment and merely offered directions to her house. Her voice was still high and breathless, which wasn't surprising. As Karen had said to Charlie, Lucy had been through a lot in the last few days.

'Tell me about your husband,' Karen said as they drove back through the village of Brock, passing the stone war memorial, which still had the Armistice Day poppy wreaths stacked up against it. They looked sad and untidy in their rain-beaten state. Soon, with luck, someone would swap them for something more Christmassy and cheer the whole place up.

'Why?' Lucy's question sounded frightened.

Karen turned her head for an instant to look at Lucy, whose thin freckled face was full of wariness.

'*Why* d'you want to know about him?' Lucy added. 'What's it to do with you?'

'Because it sounded this morning as though he was highly distressed,' Karen said, staring straight ahead at the empty road again. 'Does he often go silent on you like that?'

'Sometimes. In the old days it would mean he had a deal on that was scaring him, but there aren't any of those any more, so it hardly ever happens now, so I wanted ...' Lucy swallowed the rest of her explanation, quickly adding, 'It's the next right. Slow down or you'll miss it. The turning into the drive's quite sharp.'

Karen recognized the countryside here and knew they could only be a couple of miles from the Matkens' house. She wondered how Charlie was getting on there and whether he was managing to control his loathing of Philip as he probed their protective discretion for the truth of what had happened this morning. She also wondered how Philip would take the fact that his son was now in exactly the kind of secure professional care they had failed to get for him before he had started rampaging around the Island with a knife. In Philip's place, she would hardly know how to contain her fury. But that wasn't her concern now.

'Could your husband's silence be caused by anxiety?' she asked Lucy. 'I mean he must be worried sick about you after what happened at the shoot.'

Lucy gasped. 'I never thought ... I mean I heard him talking on the phone this morning before I got up and I thought ...'

'What did you think?' Karen asked when Lucy's silence had stretched out too far.

She shrugged her thin shoulders and her pretty freckled face scrunched up into a child's mask of distaste.

'He used to have a girlfriend. When I was ill. Before James saved me. When I got better Giles dumped her. But when his old spare phone rang this morning I thought he'd maybe started up with her again because I've been a bit wobbly recently. That's how they always set up their ... you know, assignations.'

'Who is she?' Karen asked, watching the thin shoulders shrug again.

'I don't know.' Lucy looked as though she would like to spit. 'And I don't care. Not really. But if you're right and he was worried about *me* ...' She hesitated again, then turned with a smile that held more yearning than Karen found quite comfortable.

'Giles did get our GP out to come and see me and give me some emergency happy pills yesterday,' Lucy went on, breathless now. 'I didn't tell James. He wouldn't like me taking them again. But I did feel awful after I was nearly shot like that. I mean, who wouldn't? So when Giles said – and the doctor – well, I just took them. Then more today. I do feel better. So maybe you're right and Giles was feeling awful too because of the shoot.' She sighed with satisfaction, clearly enjoying the idea that it could be she and not her rival who had so disturbed him.

'Oh, slow down, slow down. It's here. Just here. Stop,' she said, sounding excited. 'I hope he's still at home.'

Karen obediently braked, then turned to drive between two tall stone gateposts topped with gryphons and on to a well-maintained gravel sweep. The grand entrance warned her to expect something pretty imposing, but she was enchanted by the house itself. Built a hundred years or so before the Matkens', it was a grey stone country villa of the most elegant proportions. There were two main storeys beneath a balustraded roof. Karen counted seven windows along the upper floor, with three either side of the front door below. Climbers clung to the walls, so neatly clipped and shaped that they were attractive even in their leafless winter state.

'Come on,' Lucy said. 'Normally he'd be in his business room at this time of day, but I expect he's still in the dining room like he was when I went for James.'

Karen thought of another important question as she got out the car. 'Why did you go to fetch James in person? Why not just phone and stay to look after your husband?'

Lucy paused, with both hands on the car door.

'I didn't think he'd come if I didn't go and get him myself,' she said and slammed the car door so hard that Karen winced for the paintwork. 'Now I've got you instead, which is better than nothing, I suppose. You're a psychologist too. *You* can help Giles. Come on.'

Karen walked into the house and couldn't suppress a smile. The air smelled of a mixture of lavender and wood fires, with overtones of cedar. A tall Christmas tree, as yet undecorated, stood in the corner, with its roots still wrapped in damp sacking.

'Come *on*,' Lucy hissed. She was holding the well-polished brass handle of a door to the left of the big square hall, which was floored in great checks of black-and-white marble. As Karen reached her, she pushed the door open.

Karen's first impression was of nothing but the debris of a lavish breakfast. A basket of croissants, racks of toast, silver dishes of butter, jam and marmalade, a ten-inch high silver-plated egg-shaped container with a meths burner under it, ready for boiling eggs at the table, and matching flowered-porcelain coffee and hot-milk pots. Her second impression was that she had rarely seen a more luxuriously beautiful room, with its hand-painted wallpaper and ravishing antique furniture, all kept in a state of gleaming perfection. Every single thing in the place yelled one word at her: money.

Where had it come from?

'He's gone,' Lucy said, staring at Karen like an animal transfixed by oncoming headlights. 'He's gone. Where is he?'

Karen suppressed an irritable, how should I know? Aloud she said, 'You mentioned a business room. Could he be there?'

'Lucy? That you?' The loud male bellow was followed by a slamming door, then heavy footsteps coming towards them. Lucy fluttered one hand up over her eyes as she exhaled, visibly relaxing. Karen wondered what had frightened her so much. Had she really expected her husband to fling himself over the side of his remarkable yawl? Or was it the thought of the sacked girlfriend summoning him for an assignation that had sent fear racing through her?

Moments later, the man himself strode into the dining room.

'Where the hell did you go?' He glared at Karen, then pointed one accusing finger at her as he looked back at his wife. 'And why the hell did you bring this police shrink back with you? Haven't I had enough of them already? Your Bloody Blazon was here just now.'

'Was he?' Lucy was tightening up again under the interrogation and now sounded as babyish as ever, but it looked as though she was fighting to appear calm and confident. Karen didn't think she was a very good actress. 'Goodness! I wonder why. I mean, what did he want?'

'Christ knows. I wasn't going to let him in, was I?'

'Are you really all right now, Giles?' Lucy said, moving towards him.

'What the hell are you talking about? Of course I'm all right. Pissed off with you running away like that, leaving the breakfast things all over the table.' His face was reddening as he worked himself into a rage. 'Every time I phoned you, the bloody thing diverted to voicemail. Then I saw Blazon and I thought he was coming to tell me you'd ...' He hesitated, forced out an unconvincing laugh and added, 'You know, chucked yourself off the cliffs. But you clearly haven't. So what the hell have you been doing?'

'It's been awful, Giles,' Lucy said, with tears leaking out of her green eyes.

Karen watched with interest as Giles noticed them and made a visible effort to control himself. Perhaps he did love her. He patted her narrow shoulder and turned to Karen.

'What's been going on?' he demanded. 'Who's got her in this state? You?'

'I met your wife unexpectedly.' Karen recast her planned explanation to allow for the lies Lucy had already told. 'And asked her to help me when I found Oliver Matken threatening someone with a knife.'

'Good God! Again! Someone's got to do something about that psychopathic youth sooner than soon. String him up preferably. Did you get the police?'

'We did.' Now that her husband's aggression had switched to someone else, Lucy was no longer crying. Karen wondered just how often she used tears to control him. 'And nobody was hurt because Doctor Taylor did everything. She was brilliant, Giles. You wouldn't believe it. Olly came at her with the knife, too, but she just grabbed his hand and somehow made him drop it. You wouldn't believe it. She was *brilliant*.'

Karen felt her face heating as she blushed under his disbelieving stare.

'I was taught elementary self-defence once,' she said, suppressing memories of the terror of her husband's aggression that had sent her on the course. 'One of the things we learned was how to deal with a bladed weapon like that.'

Giles still looked unconvinced, so Karen found herself

telling him far more of the truth than she'd planned.

'I had no idea if it would work. But when he came at me with the knife held out – just like the instructor showed us all those years ago – instinct took over.' Karen held out her right arm with the two-inch plaster. 'I didn't come out of it quite unscathed.'

'You were bloody lucky to get away with a single cut,' he said, looking at her as though she was a real human being after all.

'And brave,' Lucy said, chipping in from the sidelines. 'She was *incredibly* brave, Giles.'

'Lucky,' he said again. 'This is why we need capital punishment. Violent psychopaths like Matken are never going to be ...'

'Oliver Matken is not a psychopath,' Karen said yet again, ready to provoke Giles because it was so important to make him see the truth. Him and Charlie and everyone else. 'He's a needy, terrified boy. We don't know yet whether he killed your niece, but if he did it's because something – or someone – wound up him so tight he exploded into aggression. He needs treatment.'

'Bloody bleeding-heart do-gooders. You need to have your faces rubbed in the shit of real life so you know what you're messing with. Like James Bloody Blazon.' Giles shook himself all over. 'I'll see him in the dock for conspiracy to murder, if it's the last thing I do.'

'It wasn't James's fault,' said Lucy, surprising Karen all over again. She hadn't expected anyone so fragile to have the guts to stand up to her bombastic husband. 'It *wasn't*. You mustn't start blaming James for Suzie's death. Karen's right: someone else made Olly into a killer. It wasn't James.'

'Like who?' Giles demanded, wheeling round to stand in front of Karen so close she could smell the boiled eggs he'd eaten for breakfast.

So much for not being able to eat – or talk.

'I don't know,' Karen said, taking several steps backwards. 'But there was a trigger of some kind. There's no doubt about that.'

She hadn't found anything that could help Charlie, but with Giles here, very much in charge, she wasn't going to get anything more from his wife.

'I'd better be off,' she said, looking round Giles towards Lucy. 'Don't ignore any signs of post-traumatic stress, will you? Flashbacks, nightmares, palpitations: anything like that, go and see your doctor.'

'Don't you worry, Doctor Taylor,' said Giles, recovering his temper and finding a way to smile politely at her. 'I'll have him out here pronto. And we won't be seeing any more of James Blazon. Ever. Either of us.'

Karen cast a quick look at Lucy and saw fury in her delicate face. Fury and hatred. She couldn't stop wondering which of them had been telling the most lies.

Chapter 16

Day Six: Monday 2 p.m.

Outside, Giles escorted Karen to her car, waited until she had deactivated the central locking and then opened the driver's door for her. Karen couldn't help searching his face for an explanation of this unexpected politeness.

He gave her a faint smile, as if reading her mind.

'I know, I know,' he said, 'but even if you are a police shrink, I hear you're going to be moving in down the road soon. I prefer to be on decent terms with my neighbours.'

'How . . .?' she began and he laughed at her.

'It's a small island, Doctor Taylor. You can't involve the planning department and one of our biggest contractors without arousing interest. Sounds as if your little house is going to be quite an improvement on the shack you inherited.'

'Thanks,' she said, uncomfortable with the idea that people like Giles knew all about her plans. 'But I'll never be able to be a full-time neighbour.'

'Pity that,' Giles said, sounding more than usually patronizing. 'But I suppose you do have to earn a living. And with blokes like Bloody Blazon already cleaning up on the Island there wouldn't be room for you to practise here too.'

'I'm not a therapist, so I'd never be competing with James. But I am based at the university in Southampton. I have to be there.' Karen didn't add that she knew she'd find living permanently on the Island unbearably constricting, however much she loved it. 'I'll be off now. Thank you.'

Giles shut the car door on her and sauntered back into his glorious house. Once he'd disappeared indoors, she checked her phone for messages. The first was a text from Stella.

Hi, builders wnt 2 start digging 2moro. Do U wnt 2 B there? 8.30 start.

All Karen's anxieties about the case and about how on earth she was going to pay the contractors were overtaken by excitement. Her own house, rising from that scar in the ground, built to her own specification to incorporate all that had been wonderful about her childhood with Aidan plus everything she'd learned since. She applied her thumbs to the tiny keys on her phone.

Wow. Yes. I'll b there. Kx

Then she pressed the speed dial for Will's phone and left a message for him, 'Hi. It's me. Stella says the builders want to begin digging the foundations on the Island tomorrow at 8.30 a.m. She's invited me there for the ceremonial breaking of the ground. Is there any chance you might be able to come too? Not if you're operating, obviously. But if not. It's ... I'd love it if you could come. Bye.'

With such a huge new distraction, she thought she'd better wind up everything with Charlie as soon as possible. She had just enough time to get to St Cuthbert's. After today's debacle, there wasn't really any need to find out whether Olly had ever shown behavioural traits that might suggest violent tendencies in the past, but the appointment was made and nothing called to her in Southampton except work on the book, so she might as well meet Ms Margery Wilkinson, as arranged.

Karen reached Cowes fifteen minutes later and found the same space empty and with enough room to park without neck-wrenching manoeuvres. She bought a ticket that would give her an hour, which seemed more than enough, and made her way into the big modern building.

The corridor was floored in the kind all-purpose blue vinyl she had last seen in a prison, and the walls were painted in much the same cream colour. The smell of the disinfectant cleaning fluid was the same, too. But there was none of the noise that filled every prison she had ever visited. With the lunch hour over and all the pupils back in their classrooms, there was enough peace to hear the traffic outside and the determined clack of the secretary's high heels as she led the way to the head's office. The walls were covered with paintings, presumably from the school's art classes, and photographs from year after year, showing massed ranks of pupils in their uniform, like in an old-fashioned grammar school.

Ms Wilkinson turned out to be about twenty years Karen's senior, solidly built and wearing a straightforward navy skirt suit. Her face, square and clear-skinned, looked the epitome of intelligent good sense. Karen's hopes rose. They shook hands.

'Now,' said the head in a brisk voice, 'you want to talk about Oliver Matken. In what respect?'

'I came to find out whether you had seen any evidence of violence in his time here.'

'Never.' Ms Wilkinson shook her head with such vigour that her very good haircut should have moved, but didn't. She must apply the spray with the power of a high-pressure jet washer, Karen thought. 'We had some difficult days when his terrors kept him hiding in cupboards and corners, chattering to himself and sometimes screaming at us. He could sound quite wild. But he never tried to hurt anyone else.'

'Right.' Karen smiled, trying to reach through the carapace of successful authority to the woman inside. 'So were you surprised when you heard what had happened?'

'Very.'

'Did you know the victim, Suzie Gray?'

Once more Ms Wilkinson shook her head, and the helmet of hair stayed in place.

Karen licked her lips, trying to think up tactful ways of putting her next question.

'We know Oliver had access to drugs,' she began. 'Various drugs. I gather his dealer has not yet been identified. Could he have bought them here?'

Ms Wilkinson straightened some papers in a matt aluminium tray to her right, then lined up the phone with them.

'We do everything we can to ensure the school is drug free. But it is impossible, short of minute-by-minute testing to be sure. I can be confident ...' She hesitated, then nodded as though agreeing with some private, internal voice. 'I can be confident that none of my pupils is dealing on the premises. Of course, they all congregate outside the school buildings, and they meet up with old pupils, too. The Island is small. Many of the families have known each other for generations. There's an excellent bus service here, so they can move around at will. When they get older, like Oliver, they have mopeds or cars. We can't police their out-of-school activities.'

'No,' Karen said, her interest quickening. 'I can see that. You talk of old pupils. Have you had particular problems with any of them?'

'It would, I believe, be invidious to mention any particular names. The b— young people involved may well have become clean by now.'

'Right.' This kind of diplomacy wasn't going to get them anywhere. 'I met a boy who must be in your catchment area,' Karen added: 'Billy Jenkins. Is he a pupil here?'

'He is.'

'He must be a bit of a handful if all I've heard is true.' Karen tried a smile and received an answering one from the head teacher.

'He has a bad reputation,' she said, 'but he's an appealing child. I've always found him reasonably easy to deal with, except for the truanting.'

'Any drugs?'

'Why do you ask?'

Because I'm sure he's involved somewhere, Karen thought, so there has to be some connection between him and Oliver. It can't just be that they were both here at this school. There are four years separating them and that's a lifetime in a place like this.

'I'm afraid I can't say. I'm working with the police on this investigation and so I am not free to pass on any information.'

'Very well: we did intercept a minute amount of cocaine in the form of a rock of crack,' said Ms Wilkinson, looking now as if she were sitting on a grid iron. 'We had it tested, although I was fairly sure I knew what it was. Billy said he'd found it in the gutter outside the school building, where he often found change dropped from the fathers' pockets. He told me he didn't know what it was.'

'Did you believe him?'

Ms Wilkinson folded her lips tight together, then relaxed them. 'More or less. He's young yet for something like that. In my last school, in inner-city Birmingham, a thirteen-year-old might well be dealing crack. Here? On the Island? It would have been unprecedented.'

A red light started winking on the phone. The head looked at it, then up again at Karen.

'As you see,' she said, pointing to the phone. 'I'm needed. I'm sorry I haven't been much help.'

'Oh, I don't know,' Karen said. 'You've confirmed that Olly was never violent here, and that there is a possibility that someone – not necessarily Billy – has been selling rocks of crack near, if not actually on, the school's premises, which would explain how Olly might have had access to it. That's helpful.'

Ms Wilkinson's face now looked thoroughly put out.

'But it's no more than I've already told DS Colvin,' she said, making Karen remember her brief to check out behavioural markers. There wasn't going to be time for that now, but she did have one question that had been nagging at her.

'When I was interviewing Oliver, I once asked him to draw me something, and he wouldn't. I've been wondering if he ...?'

'That's nothing to do with anything you said or did,' Mrs Wilkinson said, on her feet and looking even more impatient. 'He hates any form of art. We've had to let him sit out any art or craft lessons. If you'd asked him to write you a description of something he'd seen, that would have been fine. Words are Oliver's safest medium, not drawing. Now, I really have to go.'

Karen thanked her again, held out her hand and felt it shaken with all the vigour she would have expected.

'Good to meet you,' said Ms Wilkinson. 'Would you be able to find your own way out? As you see, we're very busy today.'

'That's fine,' Karen said and walked back out into the wide cream-coloured corridor, where the banks of old school photographs were hung. Her ankle was working better now and gave only the slightest twinge when she put all her weight on it.

She soon found the photographs taken during Olly's time, looked for him and then examined the faces around his in each of the three. Friends didn't always stand together in school photographs, but it was fairly likely. None of the faces meant anything. She looked down to the most junior pupils and wondered which one of them might be Billy Jenkins. Sitting cross-legged in the front row were dozens of cheeky-looking schoolboys, but none looked like the unconscious, bleeding victim she had had in her car.

Going back to the earliest pictures with Olly in them, she wished he showed something of the same zest for life the younger boys had. But he looked white-faced and scared as he stooped in the second row from the bottom, his arms crossed over his bent midriff. Defensive was the only word to describe his stance. What had made him so afraid? Who?

Another face registered in her peripheral vision, right at the end of the top row. She looked more closely, trying to work out where she'd seen it before. Dark hair, straight and flat, a narrow face with a determined chin, and watchful dark eyes. Where had she seen it?

Her small spurt of excitement died as she realized it was Jerry Eagles, Suzie's boyfriend, bartender at the Star in Ryde. But it was hardly surprising that he, too, had been a pupil here. Disheartened, Karen left the school and decided she needed cosseting.

She'd drive out to the Goose Inn and put all her thoughts into her laptop as she ate some of Peg's good food for a very late lunch. She could email the report to Charlie. If he deigned to join her that would be fine. If he didn't, it would be his loss. And if she finished writing up her notes about the case, she could get started on the next chapter of her book in the Goose Inn just as well as at home.

Peg, the landlady, looked as beautiful as ever when she smiled a distracted welcome. Karen could see she was engaged in some kind of accounts, or stock-taking, but she abandoned her paperwork to open a new, chilled bottle of Chilean Sauvignon Blanc and pour Karen a large glass.

'Would you like any food? I'm not cooking anything fresh today, but there's lots in the freezer I could microwave if you'd like,' Peg said.

Karen looked at the enormous glass of wine, then up again

to smile at Peg. 'I'd better have something. I've got the car with me. Whatever you've got. Chicken and olive pie. Rabbit pancake. Any of your usuals. Thanks.'

'Pancake then,' Peg said, turning to go through the swing door to the kitchen.

Karen took her wine to her favourite table in the bay window overlooking a small semi-circle of grass, where Peg's geese sat watching the inhabitants of the pub almost as intelligently as the people in the pub watched them. They were pure white, with orange beaks and bright eyes, and they turned their heads to follow every movement inside the pub. Sometimes Karen thought they looked like spectators at a tennis match, following the ball to and fro across the net. Today, with only a single person to monitor, they soon became bored and waddled off towards the low drinking trough in the corner.

Peg brought the pancake and a folded copy of the Isle of Wight *County Press*.

'You might like this while you're on your own. Is Charlie coming later?' she said, sounding to Karen's ear a little wistful. 'I know he's back on the Island, but I haven't seen him yet.'

'He's busy. But I know he's hoping to get here some time today. You must miss him since he moved to the mainland.' Karen smiled to show she wasn't trying to score points.

Peg laughed. 'My profit's certainly down. And these are hard times. I could do with a few more of what he always calls "thirsty coppers". Shout if you want anything.'

Karen nodded, picking up her fork. The pancake was as good as usual, in spite of its reheating in the microwave, and she polished it off in less than ten minutes. Wiping her fingers on the paper napkin Peg had supplied, Karen then pushed aside the newspaper and opened her laptop. She was so conditioned to it now that she always thought more concisely when she had her fingers on the keys, ready to make notes.

First she typed a list of all the questions she still had, which ranged from the straightforwardly factual – have the CSIs found anything in the squat? – to the much less easily answered kind: how serious *is* Oliver's condition and what triggered it, if he had a genetic predisposition? Could the same stress – or a variation of it – have driven him to violence now? Even if he hadn't killed Suzie, something had made him hold a knife to Georgie Blazon's body today and threaten to kill the foetus she carried.

'Do you want the WiFi?' Peg called from the bar. 'We've had it installed and it's all yours if you do.'

'That would be great,' Karen said, looking up from her screen.

'OK, well the code you need to enter is: 39-4B3Y-T2.'

Karen scribbled down the numbers and letters, read them over to check, then turned on the wireless switch at the side of her laptop, before double clicking on the email icon on her screen. Eight messages. Three should have been caught in the spam filter, one was from the editor of a psychology journal for which she wrote occasional articles, one was from Stella, giving more details of the contractors' apparently last-minute plan to start work tomorrow morning and her own intention to be there as the first clod was turned. The last email was from Will.

Got your message. Really glad you want me there. I've switched my list and taken on a colleague's weekend in lieu. I'll drive over to you tonight, but may not arrive till after eleven. Presumably we can go over first thing. Love, W

Karen felt her face stretch as she smiled. Good, she thought. Very good.

In a way, Aidan should have been there, too, but she still didn't know when he was due to fly in from Boston. Even so, he deserved be told that work was about to begin. Karen sent a quick message, ending:

And I can't wait for you to get here. Dillie is begging us to have Christmas with them, as she's probably told you. I must say I'd rather not. Will and I still haven't quite sorted out whose flat would be better for the actual turkey and plum-pudding feast, but I'm hanging out for mine. I've got the best views, and proximity to the Island for trips to check out progress at the site, even if he has the more magnificent kitchen. He's a better cook than me, too. We'll see. I hope all's well with you. Let me know your flight details when you can. Love, Karen

Karen hoped all would go well when she tried to mesh her old life with the new one. She and Aidan had a lot of catching-up to do and experience suggested that if she paid too much attention to him, Will would become terse and easily offended. It had happened in the past with other people, sometimes a friend of his rather than anyone to whom she owed loyalty, and she didn't think he had any idea he was behaving abnormally. But it did not make for a relaxed atmosphere.

Maybe she should try to entice Max to square their triangle. After all, he and Will were such old friends that they could entertain each other while she rebuilt her old affection for Aidan. But would it be fair on Max's sister, who had obviously made her Christmas plans round his entertainingly acerbic presence?

Karen's phone rang.

'Hi. Me,' said Charlie when she answered it. 'Where are you?'

'At the Goose. Have you finished with the Matkens?'

'For the moment.' There was a brief pause, as though Charlie was checking something. 'You eaten?'

'Just. But I can have coffee while you scoff something,' Karen said. 'And we can recap. Could be useful.'

'Be with you in about twelve minutes. Order me some scran.'

Karen switched off her phone and walked over to the bar.

'Hi,' she said as Peg lifted her head from her books. 'Charlie is coming, after all. Could you hot him up a pancake too? He'll be here in about ten minutes, he said.'

Peg's smile took on extra radiance at the news. Karen retreated to her screen and the list of questions she still had to ask other people, burying the one about why she minded the close friendship Peg and Charlie shared.

'That's easy enough,' Charlie said, shovelling food into his mouth as though he'd eaten as little as he'd slept since the investigation began. 'The suspect drugs rep hasn't been near the Island for something like six weeks. Olly's never heard of him. There's nothing on Olly's laptop or phone with any link to the rep or vice versa. Wild-goose chase.'

'OK.' Karen deleted that question from her list on the laptop. 'Now the shoe print in Suzie's blood in the alleyway: have you identified that? Was it Angela Matken's? Or the daughter's?'

'Billy's,' Charlie said when he'd swallowed an enormous mouthful of rabbit pancake. He reached for the pint Peg had drawn for him and washed the food down with a gulp of bitter. 'We got the shoe itself, with matching blood found at the base of the treads.'

'Any sign of Billy in the squat I found?' Karen added and watched a tide of beetroot colour wash up Charlie's yellow cheeks. 'Apart from the Nike backpack?'

He wiped his mouth on the back of his hand, drank some more, and put his heavy glass tankard on the table. Facing her, as though she was a judge, he said formally, 'That's why I made time to come here now to see you. Yes. The CSI found a loose floorboard, with a knife hidden underneath wrapped in plastic. Big Swiss army knife, like the one Olly had with him today. Again, the blood on the blade matches Suzie's. Which has made my boss listen to my pleas for more time on the case at last, and the investigation of Billy's shooting. My team's on it now. Thanks to you.'

'What've they found?' Karen asked, not wanting to sound as though she was crowing.

'Zilch so far. More or less. Angle of the bullet's taken us to where the sniper must've stood, about seven hundred metres away.'

'Isn't that rather a long shot?'

'Snipers can hit a target with a rifle up to a mile and a quarter away,' Charlie said in an irritated voice. 'The ground's all messed up by the dogs. No footprints. No witnesses. No rifle. Zilch, like I say. All licensed rifles on the Island have been checked and their owners questioned. All accounted for.'

'Bummer,' Karen said, with real sympathy, in spite of his impatience with her lack of knowledge of a rifle's range. 'What about the knife? Anything useful from that?'

'Gone off for DNA-testing. No results yet.'

'When will you get them?'

'Days probably. But the heat's off now Olly's on temporary section, poor little tyke. I've time to come back to you.' Charlie ate some more, then wiped his lips with the paper napkin. 'Not bad, Peg's pancakes.'

'What about Billy?' Karen said. 'Any sign of his being able to talk again? Now we know he really was there, and actually had his hands on the knife, we need to know ...'

'You don't have to tell me that. Or point out that it makes the shooting less easy to call. I can see why you think he could've been the target, not Lucy.'

'Great.'

'I called in at the hospital and they let me see him,' Charlie went on. 'Poor little bugger's just lying there, grey skin, tubes everywhere, still unconscious. His parents are on guard duty twenty-four hours a day; one goes home only when the other arrives, even though we've an officer there now. We haven't told the parents about the knife; they've got enough to worry about as it is.'

'OK. Next question: how did you get on with the Matkens this morning?' Karen asked, determined to suck every bit of information out of Charlie before he decided he had to rush back to his incident room.

'I didn't. Angela collapsed while I was there and had to be put to bed by the daughter. Philip said nothing happened this morning to provoke a knife attack on you or Georgina Blazon. Olly hadn't said a word about the devil when they saw him at breakfast. He seemed quiet.'

'What about the sister?' Karen said, with a vivid memory of the bullying tone Caroline had taken with her distraught mother. 'She's – what? – three or four years older than Olly. I know you hate his father, but it's not always a parent. With that kind of age gap, Caroline could have had a bigger effect on him if she thought he was her enemy.'

'A four-year-old girl? Come on, Karen. What could she have done?'

'You're an only child, aren't you?' she said, watching him with her head on one side.

'So?'

'So you never faced the hatred of the displaced god of the nursery, whose food supply, parental attention – even life – you threaten by your very existence.' Karen thought of all the case histories she'd read of the few children who'd committed murder. There had been roughly five a year from around the world for as long as records began. Olly was at least seven years older than most of those killers, but the link seemed clear to Karen. All the young murderers whose histories she had read had been atrociously abused or bullied, often by their older siblings.

'I think you should talk to Caroline,' she said. 'Find out what ...'

Charlie hunched one big shoulder and half turned away. 'Can't now. She's on her way to Innsbruck – left this morning to meet her boyfriend there for a few days' skiing. Last-minute package. Special offer. Back on Friday.'

Karen had had her shower before Will arrived that night and was lying in bed propped up on all four pillows, reading one of the most successful self-help books of the last decade, hoping that immersion in its particular style would help her find the right line between academic formality and the sweetly obvious tone of a child's first reading book. This guide to success in relationships wasn't bad – the advice given was fairly standard, even if the promises of happiness were overstated – but she kept finding her fingers itching for a correcting pencil.

Will's key grated in the lock and she quickly rearranged the pillows, beating out the creases in his, before lying back, waiting for the moment when he appeared in the doorway.

'Hi,' he said, kicking off his shoes even before he'd shut the door behind him.

Karen thought he looked as tired as Charlie, but for once there was no angst in Will's expression and his voice sounded creamy, as it only ever did when he was happy. She stretched out her arms.

He bent to kiss her, before subsiding slowly on to the bed beside her. He felt thinner than ever when she touched him, and he smelled of petrol and dust from the road. She laid her hand on the back of his head, pulling him closer, and liked the sharpness of his chin as it dug into the soft flesh at the base of her neck.

*

'Hungry?' she said with tenderness as he rolled away from her last.

Will ran his tongue over his lower lip, smiling easily. 'Now you come to mention it, I think I am. Have you got any food? I dashed off in such a hurry I haven't brought anything for tomorrow morning.'

'I've only got the usual breakfast things: muesli, bread for toast, eggs, yoghurt. But we wouldn't have time for anything elaborate anyway,' she said, sliding out from under the duvet and pulling down the extra-long T-shirt she was wearing in place of a nightdress. 'We'll have to leave at about seven to be sure of being at the site on time. Now, I could whip you up a quick omelette if you'd like. Or you could just have some delicious cocoa – which might be more digestible at this time of night.'

His often-severe expression relaxed into one of his easiest smiles.

'Cocoa!' he said. 'I haven't had that since I was a child. OK. Why not?'

'It's Green and Black's,' Karen said, 'so it should be much more luxurious than whatever you had in your youth. But I'd better make it sweetish to counteract the caffeine. I don't want you kept awake.'

'Nothing could do that,' he said, removing his sweater in the extraordinary way men had, pulling from the back of the neck instead of crossing their arms and lifting it up from the bottom like any normal person. 'In any case it's theobramine in cocoa, mostly, and that's not a stimulant. Hardly any caffeine at all.'

Karen had seen Aidan remove his clothes like that

throughout their childhood, and she had become accustomed to Granny shouting at him for risking all her careful knitting.

'What's the matter?' Will said, when his head was free again.

'Nothing.' She blew him a kiss and went off to brew the cocoa, wishing she had bought him the cufflinks for Christmas.

She still hadn't got a present for Aidan either. It was so long since they'd met, she couldn't decide what he might like. Maybe she should wait until she'd seen him again and then rush out at the last minute.

Chapter 17

Day Seven: Tuesday Dawn

Next morning the clouds had split apart before dawn. The sun rose while Karen and Will were on the ferry. Light shot up between the still-grey clouds to make the silvery-blue gaps between them shimmer. Emerging brightness caught the tops of all the waves and tempted the two of them out of the warm cabin to stand against the rail looking directly eastwards into the sun.

Gulls had woken from whatever kind of sleep they enjoyed and were swooping up into the sky and riding the air currents with an exuberance that made Karen think they shared her delight in the growing splendour.

For once she and Will had slept curled up together, with him lying behind her, his arms around her waist and his knees tucked into the backs of hers. She'd enjoyed the closeness and the warmth of his breath on her skin, and she'd slept as well as she ever did alone. That was a first.

His arm was heavy on her shoulders now.

'Worth it for this alone,' he said, jutting his chin towards the sun.

'Good. I'm hoping—' She broke off as her phone began to trill. It seemed mad to break the moment, but the sound had already changed things by itself. Will let her go and walked a couple of steps away to give her space.

'Go on,' he said, sounding resigned. 'Answer it.'

'Hi,' she said into the phone.

'It's Billy.' Charlie's voice was crisply alert. 'Come round and talking. But it's hard and painful. Docs don't know how long we'll get to question him. He's not making much sense. I need you. Where are you?'

'On the ferry, with Will. We're on our way to the site of my new house.'

Will waved to attract her attention. 'Charlie?' he said.

Karen nodded. Charlie's voice was still battering at her other ear.

'Could be the start of his recovery, according to the docs. Or our only chance. Drop into the hospital on your way to the site. Like I say, I need you.'

'Hang on,' she said and took the phone away from her face. 'Listen, Will,' she began and then outlined the situation, keeping to herself the growing feeling that if she could help Charlie with this case, which mattered so much to him, she would be able to sign off emotionally and concentrate entirely on Will. She knew now for certain that was what she wanted.

'Obviously you've got to go,' he said, even without that last explanation. 'I'm insured to drive your car. Why don't I drop you at the hospital, then go on to represent you at the site? As soon as you're through with the boy, you can make Charlie drive you out there or get a taxi. Either way, I'll wait for you.

Unless you want me to come and pick you up, in which case you can phone.'

'You are a prince among men,' she said.

He made a face like a child pretending to stick his fingers down his throat to make himself vomit. Karen laughed, before raising the phone again.

'Will's going to leave me at the hospital. We should be there ...' She broke off, looked towards the approaching shore of the Island and made a quick calculation. 'Shouldn't be more than twenty minutes.'

Charlie said no more. She shrugged and put the phone back. 'Sorry, Will.'

'It's work,' he said, as though there could be no arguing with that.

But the peace between them had gone and she started to worry about how he would react to the site, to the great wound in the landscape and the gloomy trees all around. Would he ever learn to see the place as she did? Could he come to love it in all its eccentric gloom?

Would *she* still love it when she'd got over whatever peculiar chain held her to the past? Had Will been right all along when he'd advised her to stick to the light and stylish life she'd made for herself on the mainland instead of delving backwards into the dark?

Now that she'd recognized the full charm of the south side of the Island, with its fresh winds and clean sand beaches with their sharply cut cliffs behind, would she want to spend time in the gloom of her own sodden two-acre plot? What was she doing mortgaging her future and whatever she might earn from her books and her work with the police to cling to a long-dead relationship she ought not to need any longer?

She shot a quick look at Will and was surprised to see him watching her with an impish glint in his grey eyes.

'You can always sell it,' he said, as though he had understood every word of her silent self-interrogation.

Such an easy, straightforward answer to all the doubts, she thought, leaning towards him to lay her warm lips on his wind-chilled cheek.

'You are clever,' she said, giving him words, too; words he clearly didn't need.

Billy was lying against the pillows, with one hand held between both his mother's. His skin looked like old cement, but the ventilator had been taken away. Drips were still attached to his arms, and a catheter snaked its way to a bag clipped to the side of his bed. In spite of it all, there was a faint smile on his lips, and they had a little colour in them.

'Hello, Billy,' Charlie said. 'Do you remember me?'

The small head nodded against the pillow and the smile dwindled fast.

'You're not in any trouble,' Charlie said quickly, but the fear in the boy's eyes showed Karen he didn't believe it.

'This is a friend of mine,' Charlie went on. 'She's called Karen, and she's not a police officer. But she does want to ask you a few questions. Is that all right?'

This time there was a longer pause before Billy swivelled his head on the pillow to inspect her, then nodded again.

'Can't talk,' he told her in a voice that was both faint and hoarse. His face contorted, too, as though forcing out the words hurt.

Karen laid her hand on his free arm and worked out how to ask the least number of questions so that he didn't have to speak more than was absolutely necessary.

'Billy,' she said, smiling and keeping her voice clear and very warm, 'I want to know about the day the girl was killed at the marina. When you heard the scream and ran to see what had happened, who was there, apart from the girl and Olly Matken?'

'Dunno.' His eyelids closed. The skin almost transparent. As his long black lashes lay across the deep shadows under his eyes, he looked almost like a waxwork. 'No one.'

'Who gave you the knife, Billy?'

'What?'

'The knife you wrapped in plastic and hid under the floor-boards,' Karen said gently, watching his eyelids fly up again and the faintest hint of pinkness seeping into his cheeks. 'We know all about it. And you're not in trouble. I just need to hear from you about the third person who was there when you took the knife.'

'Wasn't one.'

'So who did give you the knife?' Karen could feel Charlie's impatience, but she wasn't going to let it make her rush or push the boy too hard. And she wouldn't let herself look at Sandra, Billy's mother. Sympathy for her, questions for her, would all have to wait. 'You took it from someone, Billy. Who?'

He closed his eyes again, turned his head a little way away from her and tucked his chin into his neck, before stuffing his thumb into his mouth like a very small child. His mother reached out and pulled his hand away from his mouth.

'Billy.' The sound of her voice did make Karen look into her face because it was obvious she was crying. 'Billy, tell the lady. She can't help us if you don't.'

'Him,' Billy said, still not opening his eyes again. 'Olly. I heard the scream and went to see and he goes "take this". So I did.'

Karen looked at his mother. 'Do they know each other?'

The other woman shrugged, shook her head, then mouthed: 'A bit. From school.'

'Billy,' Karen said again, leaning over him. 'Billy, when you did first meet Oliver?"

'He's gone again. Lost consciousness,' said his mother, whirling away from the bed. 'Nurse! Nurse!'

Running feet brought two nurses to the bed. One felt for a pulse in Billy's wrist, the other shooed Karen and Charlie away from the bed, before whisking the curtains shut around it.

They stood beyond the flimsy patterned cotton, looking at each other. Karen thought Charlie was afraid.

'There won't be any more questions today,' said one of the nurses as she emerged through the curtains. She sounded severe. 'I'll have to ask you to leave the ward now.'

'Is he going to be all right?' Karen asked, seeing that Charlie was struck dumb.

'The doctor will have to see.' The nurse softened a little, adding, 'But it wasn't your questions that caused this. He's a very sick boy.'

Karen knew what it meant when medical staff said those words in that sad but emphatic tone.

*

Downstairs in the lobby, she made Charlie sit while she fetched him a cup of tea from the machine, remembering the way Billy's father had sat in this very space.

'You heard her,' Karen said to Charlie as he took the bendy cup from her. 'It's not the questions that caused his collapse.'

Charlie raised his eyes. She had seen them angry, dazed with drink or lust, alight with humour and soft with affection, but she had never seen them like this before: great dark pools of sadness.

'Poor little tyke,' he said in a way that made her ache with pity for the child he himself had been. 'On the scene of the killing through pure accident, tries to help another boy, and now this. D'you think he's going to die?'

Karen remembered the nurse's expression and the tone of her voice and said simply, 'Looks like it.'

'Then someone out there will think he's got away with it.' Charlie looked down at the orange-coloured tea in his cup, shuddered and dumped it under his chair. 'I must get on. Can you sort yourself out?'

Karen was already feeling for her phone. 'Call me when you need me.'

Charlie nodded, gripped her wrist for an instant in the painful way he had, then strode away. Karen watched his back view for a moment, as the crowds parted, then phoned Will.

A sign for taxis beckoned and she made her way through the crowd towards it, hoping the queue wouldn't be too long.

Will's recorded voice sounded as the ringing stopped, inviting her to leave a message, and she was so surprised she cut off the call. Only then did she remember the site of her new house was a mobile blackspot. Trying to laugh at herself, trying to ignore memories of Billy with the terrible wound in his neck as he lay in his father's arms, she dialled again, preparing her message.

Another phone was ringing somewhere near, which stopped at the very moment Will's message began. Karen waited for the beep, then said she'd be getting a taxi out to the site. While her thumb was still on the red key to end the call, her phone rang and she heard Stella demanding to know where she was because the builders were waiting down the road in the blackspot she'd left to make this call, and they couldn't wait much longer without clocking up extra time and therefore extra charges.

'I'm at the hospital still,' Karen said, surprised by Stella's aggression. 'But I've just left Will a message to say I'm getting a cab. I shouldn't be much longer. He knows he's there to represent me. Take my place. He shouldn't have made you wait.'

'Will?' Stella was impatient. 'What do you mean *Will*? I haven't seen him since that day I brought the Haut Brion to your flat.'

Karen thought of the phone that had been ringing somewhere around her and she felt as though the floor was rocking beneath her feet. Cold sweat was breaking out all over her body.

'I've got to go, Stella. Don't make them wait any longer. I'll come if I can, but don't wait.' She clicked off that call and rang Will's number again.

Once more the sound of a phone trilled somewhere out in the foyer, in synch with the noise she could hear from her own. She followed the louder one, looking amongst the crowd for his face. The noise stopped and the message started again. She clicked off and dialled yet again, following the other phone as it began to ring.

A wheeled trolley, like the one that had taken Olly away from the Blazons' house was positioned by the doors to the side of the reception desk, with three doctors crowding round it, talking to the paramedics. Shock distorted their faces as they looked down at the figure on the trolley.

The sound of both phones stopped. Karen dialled again and, again, the other phone began to ring.

'Find that phone and shut it up,' one of the doctors shouted, before adding more quietly to one of his colleagues, 'Is he stable enough for a trip to the mainland?'

Karen walked forwards, just as a crowd of people came in through the front door. She felt as if she were in a nightmare as they kept her from reaching the stretcher. She fought on, pushing, bouncing off at least three separate men who would not get out of the way in time, to emerge only feet from the body on the trolley.

The face was unrecognizable. It could have belonged to a man or a woman. The whole head was secured in the grip of a yellow contraption with straps across the forehead, and there was blood all over the cheeks and nose. The eyes were closed. Blood had drenched the brighter red blanket that covered the body.

You must be able to tell if it's Will, Karen's internal voice yelled at her. You love him. You must know if it's him.

But she didn't. What she could see of the bloodied face could have belonged to anyone.

'Out of the way,' snapped one of the doctors as Karen leaned in closer.

'I think ...' she began, then felt like Billy as panic closed her throat. Coughing to clear the emotional obstruction, she started again, 'I think that's my ... my friend.'

One of the doctors looked at her, and stepped back. His head was cocked and his eyes alert. 'Why?'

'It's my phone. I've been ringing him.'

'Name?'

'Will Hawkins.' Wanting to make sure they gave him the best care of which they were capable, she added, 'He's a neurosurgeon, consultant, at Brighton Hospital. He was driving my car on the Island this morning.'

Two of the doctors were undistracted from their assessment of the body on the stretcher, but the one who'd been asking questions, a dark-haired man in his forties, glanced at the paramedics. One of them, a woman, looked at Karen with sympathy that did not detract from the speculation in her bright eyes.

'My car's a red Subaru Justy,' Karen said, and saw from the other woman's expression that this unconscious figure had to be Will. She gave the registration number of the car just in case there could have been an appalling coincidence, then added, 'What happened?'

'From what I could ascertain a tractor with a digger attachment must have swerved out of control from a turning and hit the car at the passenger side, pushing it out into the road.' The paramedic was talking gently, but not shirking anything or using pointless euphemisms. Karen appreciated that. 'Another car, travelling normally, hit it again, then the digger mechanism broke and smashed down onto the Subaru's roof and through the windscreen. The air bag inflated properly and helped a little. But he has injuries. Severe injuries.'

Karen swayed and the paramedic rushed to her side to support her. She tried to breathe normally and to ignore the sweat that was breaking out all over her body again.

'It may not look like it,' said the doctor, with a deliberately cheering smile, 'but he's been lucky. If my colleagues judge him stable enough we'll be getting the helicopter to take him over to Southampton.'

No amount of careful breathing or self-discipline could stop Karen's dizziness. She fought to get back the sensation of solid ground beneath her feet.

'What's your name?' said the doctor, who guided her to a chair.

'Taylor. Karen Taylor.' She found the inside of her mouth had dried out so much it felt as though it had been lined with sandpaper. She tried to manufacture some saliva to put that right, then feared she might throw up as her mouth flooded with liquid.

'The police are here. They want to talk to you,' said the doctor.

Karen kept staring at her knees, thinking: if this is Eve Clarke, I'm not strong enough to deal with her. Please, don't let it be Eve.

Turning her head, she saw two very young uniformed constables, a man and a woman, both wearing cumbersome jackets of shiny bright-yellow material, decorated with silver stripes and all kinds of badges and logos. Her lips widened a little into a weak smile.

'Do you feel OK to talk?' asked the woman in a strong Island accent, which made Karen's smile stretch into a more natural version.

She nodded. 'But I wasn't in the car, so I can't help much. I've only just …' Karen wiped her forehead with the palm of her right hand, bringing it down over her eyes, and was surprised to feel tears on her cheeks. 'How did you get involved?'

'The driver of the oncoming car that hit the Subaru phoned us. He did everything he could including an emergency stop so he only slid into your car. No real impact. Then he got out and set up warning triangles he keeps in his boot, then phoned us.'

'And the tractor?' Karen asked, surprised to find that she had taken in anything the paramedics had said.

The male traffic officer nodded, as though Karen had answered a question rather than asked one. 'That's right. It'd been reported stolen first thing this morning, from a farm nearby. No sign of any driver. Probably boys taking it for a laugh and getting into trouble because they didn't know how to drive it. Whoever was driving legged it before anyone saw him. Bad luck, miss. Just very bad luck your mate was there.'

Or not, Karen thought, as her sluggish brain started to move more quickly. I should have been in the car. It should've been me lying here on the stretcher.

'Is Charlie Trench still here?' she said, looking wildly around the crowded foyer and seeing no one she recognized.

The two officers looked at each other, worried. Karen wondered if they were so new to the job that they'd arrived only after Charlie had left for the mainland.

'He was here just now,' she explained, wiping her forehead again. Her head was aching and itching, as though small rodents were inside her skull and burrowing to get out. 'DCI Trench. We were interviewing Billy … Billy … the boy who was shot. Charlie left. But he needs to know …'

Her body burned with heat, then grew so cold she shivered. The lurching floor rushed up to hit her between the eyes. As she lost consciousness she heard Charlie's familiar voice saying, as though from miles and miles away, 'What the hell's happened?' She tried to reach out to him, but something had taken away her power to move.

When Karen came round, a uniformed nurse was squatting on the floor in front of her, saying gently, 'You fainted. It's nothing serious. You're back with us now. How do you feel?'

'Wobbly.' Karen blinked twice and looked round.

The two traffic officers in their high-viz jackets were standing in front of Charlie, listening to him. There was no sign of Will's trolley or any of the three doctors.

'Will?' Karen said.

'They're taking him to the helicopter now,' said the nurse. 'DCI Trench says he'll get you back to the mainland himself so you can follow your friend to the hospital in Southampton. Better that way than a helicopter flight when you've lost consciousness like this.'

'I need to get up,' Karen said and pushed herself to her feet.

The nurse held her arm, which was lucky, because Karen was still shaky, and something had happened to her vision: she kept losing focus. One moment everything in front of her had sharp outlines; the next, they were so fuzzy that a face melted into a pillar and the floor was full of circles, like flattened balloons, which turned out to have been caused by a single child's ball made of blue and red plastic.

Moving carefully, she sat down again and assured the nurse
that she would be fine. When the woman had left, Karen let
her head fall forwards and her eyes close.

It's different this time, she told herself. Will's in hospital. It's
different. It is.

But she could no longer stop the memories of her husband's
death filling her brain.

She and Peter had had a terrible row that night, after she
had threatened to expose his dishonesty and exploitation of
the clients who had come to him for financial advice. He'd
flung himself out of the house and driven off in his Ferrari,
only to crash it into a tree just outside the gates of their house.
The bang had been like a bomb going off and she'd rushed out
in her thin nightdress to see what had happened, only to hear
him moaning her name over and over again from inside the
wreckage of his car. The police had told her to hold his hand
and stay talking to him to keep him alive until the ambulance
arrived. He had died minutes later, surrounded by the smells
of petrol and blood and fear. She had still been holding his
hand when he stopped breathing.

'That wasn't your fault,' she muttered aloud, as she so often
had before. 'It wasn't you who made Peter a crook, or put him
in a car he'd never paid for and sent it crashing into a tree.
You didn't kill him.'

Would she ever be able to forget?

She'd have found it easier to forgive herself for his death if
she hadn't spent much of her marriage longing to get the news
that something or someone had killed him, and then later
fantasizing about how she might do it herself.

'You've never wanted any harm to come to Will,' she

whispered to the accusing voices in her head, still wanting them to forgive her for the old death.

'It won't,' Charlie said, sitting down beside her and taking her hand. 'He'll be OK.'

'You can't know that.' Karen let him hold her hand but she kept staring at the floor. At least now it was still again and all the same colour. Her eyes were working properly, even if her brain was all over the place.

'I've talked to the medic in charge.' Charlie sounded confident now, as far as possible from the needy troubled man who'd fallen asleep in her lap. 'The main damage is to his abdomen, where a piece of metal has pierced his side. Otherwise, it's broken ribs, maybe a punctured lung, and a broken leg. They don't know whether the metal has ruptured his spleen. But, Karen, his head's OK. He didn't get a blow to the head. So his brain's untouched. Whatever else has happened, he's still himself. And his hands too. His surgeon's hands are not badly damaged.'

Karen let herself slide sideways until she was leaning against Charlie's arm. He let it slip out from under her weight so that he could put it round her back and hug her.

Lying against him, she said, 'Thanks for that. I dreaded brain damage. More than anything else, I think. Even . . .'

'I know.' Charlie gave her a comforting squeeze. 'Thank God you weren't in the car with him.'

'I should've been,' she said. 'It was only because you rang and got me here at the last minute that I wasn't.' She frowned as an idea loomed at her. She turned to look into his face. 'Could it have been deliberate? The crash, I mean.'

'I . . .'

Karen couldn't wait for his comment. 'It would make sense. I can see that. Fits the pattern, too: people who know something about Suzie's killing, or might know something, or are asking the wrong questions, are having ... accidents.'

'You mean Billy.'

'And Mrs Henty,' Karen said. 'Lucy.'

Charlie squeezed her again. 'Only one of them can have been the target. If Billy got in the way of the bullet, like I first thought, then the intended victim was Lucy. Or else it was Billy and her presence beside him was only an accident. You can't have it both ways.'

'And James's wife.' Karen felt her eyes widening as she thought of the way the pregnant woman had kept her nerve when Olly had held the blooded knife inches from the head of the child she was carrying.

'It can't have been Olly driving the digger today.' Charlie was fighting to keep his voice kind, which Karen appreciated, even though she could tell it was a losing fight. 'He's still under section. I've checked with the unit. He hasn't absconded.'

Karen shook her head, feeling her hair catch in one of the studs in his leather jacket. 'I'm glad it wasn't Olly.'

Charlie said nothing, but even through his clothes Karen could feel his growing tension. She pulled herself out of his arms.

'I'm going to get a Red Jet back to Southampton,' she said. 'That's where they're taking Will. I've got to be there with him.'

'I'll—' Charlie began, but Karen cut him off.

'I'll go on my own. I can manage. You need to stay here and get this sorted. Whoever's doing all this must be losing it, if he thinks arranging fatal "accidents" is going to protect him. God knows what he'll do next if you don't stop him.'

'We're working on it, Karen, but you mustn't get paranoid and think you're at risk.'

'Have you found Olly's dealer yet?' Karen felt immensely tired, as though she had been pushing a ten-ton lorry up a one-in-ten hill for hours. Her joints ached and all she wanted was to lie down and let the truck roll backwards over her. 'The one who sold him the coke?'

'Not yet.'

'You should. Haul them all in, all the dealers you know of and grill them till one of them tells you where he used to get his skunk and whether he got anything else as well.' She licked her dry lips again and realized she must have been biting them because they were swollen now, as well as itchy. 'Was there anything in the second lot of blood and urine tests?'

'Definitely cocaine,' Charlie said. 'Which is why talking to the known dealers is in hand. We just haven't found the one who supplied Olly yet. Come on, pet, up with you.'

Karen let him lift her out of the chair and help her out of the hospital itself. He'd never called her 'pet' before.

'The least you can do is let me drive you to Fountain Quay,' he said.

'What'll happen to my car?'

'You'll need to talk to your insurance company,' he said. 'I haven't seen it yet, but they say it's a write-off. We'll get it to the pound, and have it photographed for evidence in any trial, but . . .'

'If you ever catch the man who stole the digger,' she said nastily and realized she must sound exactly like the spiky and

difficult Caroline, who had so neatly escaped the embarrassment
of her brother's violence by disappearing to Innsbruck.

'In you get,' Charlie said, without responding to her irri-
tability. He'd unlocked the doors of his grey Audi and she
almost fell into the front passenger seat.

The short drive to the quay passed in a blur. Karen felt that
somewhere hidden behind her fear, and the bad temper that
cloaked it, was a fact, a crucial fact, that would bring them the
answers they needed.

'Who knew you were headed for the chalet this morning?'
Charlie asked in a quiet voice as he pulled up the handbrake.

'Stella and the builders.' Karen thought a little, then added,
'Will. Me. You. Anyone else any of us might have been
chatting to between yesterday morning and today. It wasn't a
secret, but it was all arranged at the last minute, so there can't
be all that many people who were aware of it.'

Her phone was somewhere at the bottom of her saggy
shoulder bag. She scuffled around until she found it, pulled it
out and wheeled through the few stored messages until she
came to Stella's text. She handed the phone to Charlie, saying,
'I got this yesterday morning, just after I'd seen Lucy safely
home. It was the first I'd heard about the ceremonial breaking
of the ground. So whoever it was didn't have much time to set
up the accident. Like I said, he's panicking.'

'If there is someone,' Charlie said, 'he'll do something even
more stupid next and we'll get him.'

'But another one of us will ...' Karen's voice seized up
again. She shook her head to free it, licked her lips, and turned
in her seat to face him. 'Somebody will die, Charlie. You've
got to stop this before anybody else is killed.'

Chapter 18

Day Seven: Tuesday 12 Noon

Will was under anaesthetic by the time Karen reached the big hospital in Southampton and she was told there would be no news about the operation for hours. When they'd finished removing the piece of metal from his side, they had all the internal repairs to do, then the broken leg to set, and they might turn up more damage. He would take some time to come round after such prolonged anaesthesia.

Karen couldn't see the point of sitting in amongst all these impatient, worried families in the hospital's waiting area, with nothing to do and no way of distracting herself from running over and over what might be happening within Will's crunched and broken body. She left her name and contact details with the A&E receptionist and slowly made her way home. She felt now as though she might soon be crawling out from under the ten-ton lorry, but she couldn't envisage herself ever having the strength to push anything anywhere again.

Up in her flat, she ripped off her clothes and stood under the hot pounding water of her shower, letting it rinse through her loosened hair and flood over her skin. Nothing could take away her fear, or the guilt for not being in the driving seat of her own car when it was smashed, but the sensation of being rinsed clean helped a little.

When she'd drained the tank of hot water, she turned off the taps before she froze, and wrapped a huge mushroom-coloured towel around her body, with a smaller one like a turban containing her wet hair. Next to a hot shower, food usually helped her deal with the unbearable. Drink too. And somehow the early morning had turned into lunchtime, so both food and drink were legitimate. She padded in bare feet to the kitchen.

The fridge didn't yield much, but there was a packet of bacon, a half-used jar of Hellman's mayonnaise, and some withered cherry tomatoes. They didn't have any mould on them yet, so she ran them under the cold tap and decided they would do. In the freezer there was always plenty of wholemeal bread. She put four slices in the big toaster, and laid the whole packet of bacon – all ten rashers – into a frying pan, then opened a bottle of rich, blackcurranty Australian Shiraz. It might not be Haut Brion at five pounds a sip, but it would give her everything she needed now.

With no car to drive, it wouldn't matter if she sank two large glasses, even of this 14.5 per cent proof wine. And it did help. While the bacon crisped and the tomatoes softened in its salty, flavoursome fat, and the toast popped out of the toaster, she drank, revelling in the fruitiness – and the hefty kick of alcohol.

She dolloped a big splurge of mayonnaise on the toast, scooped the tomatoes out of the pan and smeared them over the top, then added four slices of the hot crusty bacon, wiped another piece of toast around in the remaining bacon fat and laid it on top of the rashers. Looking at the depth of the resulting sandwich, she knew she'd need both hands for it.

The first mouthful was so delicious, she bolted it down and took another bite. Melting mayonnaise, bacon fat, and tomato pulp oozed out from between the slices and down her chin. She didn't want to waste any time getting the food inside her, so she wiped the mess away with her fingers, licked them, and then picked up her glass, leaving smeary fingerprints on it. She didn't care.

By the time the first sandwich was eaten, and two extra strips of crispy bacon, she'd forgotten how it had felt to be hungry. Her anxieties were all still there but they felt a little further away, and more than a little muffled. She looked at the wine bottle, now less than half full, and considered another glass, then thought she'd better keep the remnants of sobriety to get her safely back to the hospital when they called to say Will was out of theatre.

Aware at last that she was still dressed in nothing but the huge towel, she fumbled her way to her bedroom and pulled on underwear, jeans and a loose sweater. She took time to wash her hands and face then blow-dried her hair before wandering back into the sitting room.

She pressed 'play' on the hi-fi, without looking to see which CD was in it, and soon heard Mozart's watery wonderful clarinet concerto pour out around her.

A grey cashmere rug Will had given her was folded at the end of the long sofa, so she flapped that open and used it as a blanket. With its softness warming her bare feet, music rinsing her mind as effectively as the shower had cleaned her body, and a yielding cushion behind her head, she lay back and stared through the wide high windows at the blue and grey and silver sky.

A shrill sound ripped through her peace. Blinking, she saw the colour of the sky had changed and darkened. There was no more Mozart; only the ringing of her landline. Kicking away the blanket, tripping as she tried to stand, she eventually made her way to the phone, cursing herself for being so stupid, so self-indulgent, to drink so much. Will would be horrified at such a childish response to anxiety – if he ever got to hear of it.

'Yes?' she said into the phone, without even giving her name. She rang her tongue around her mouth and tried to lick the furry sensation off her teeth. 'Hello?'

'Karen?' Stella's voice was completely different from this morning's angry version. 'Karen, I've just heard what happened. Trying to track you down, I even phoned the Island police. They told me. No wonder you weren't at the site this morning. How ...? I mean, is there any news yet of Will? And how are *you*?'

'The hospital haven't got back to me yet,' Karen said, checking the answering machine with a powerful stab of guilt, which was relieved when she saw the red light was steady. No messages. At least she hadn't failed to pick up a call from the hospital.

'But you, Karen: how are you?' Stella said again.

'Hanging on. Trying not to think too much. But ...' Karen's voice dwindled, then strengthened again as some thoughts fought their way through the vinous fog that still filled her brain. 'Stella, did the contractors say why they suddenly decided to start work today?'

'It wasn't that sudden, in fact.' Stella produced a short cough of embarrassed laughter. 'The first digging was always supposed to be yesterday, but I didn't tell you because there are nearly always delays in the building trade and I didn't want you disappointed. Only when I was certain did I suggest you should be there to see it happen.'

'So who else would've known about it?'

'Everyone at head office,' Stella said. 'The men at the site, too. Why? What does it matter?'

Karen waited for her to get the point. It didn't take long.

'You don't mean you think this was deliberate? That someone was trying to ... to damage *you* with that stolen digger, do you?' Stella sounded as though she thought Karen was completely mad.

Maybe she was. Maybe mixing with James and Olly and even Giles Henty had infected her with their various kinds of paranoia.

'It would be irresponsible not to consider it,' Karen said and knew she must sound stiff and critical. 'Sorry. Stella, I've got to go. The hospital haven't rung, so I need to get in touch with them. I can't ... Sorry.'

'Don't be. You have nothing to apologize for. Give Will my love, won't you?'

If he can hear me, Karen said to herself.

'Thanks, Stella,' she said aloud. 'When I can get back to the Island, I'll go and talk to them at the site, make up for not being there when they started work.'

'Don't worry. I'll deal with them.' Stella laughed again, this time more comfortably. 'I need to earn my right to the book, after all.'

And so they said good bye as friends again. Karen was glad of that much as she went to clean her teeth and find some socks and boots.

Her retreat to the flat seemed unbelievably cowardly now, for which the alcohol-induced headache behind her eyes was fair punishment.

She reached the hospital at eight o'clock and made her way to the lifts, her mind full of the repeating pictures of the unrecognizable face she'd seen this morning, surrounded by the yellow plastic of the head-bracing contraption. Her own failure to know whether or not it was Will's seemed even worse than her resort to disgustingly fatty food and 14.5 per cent alcohol wine.

As she waited for the lift to arrive she wondered whether she would know him this time or whether there had been disfiguring wounds under the blood, which might make him unrecognizable still. She wondered about the pain, too, and the difficulty for a man as controlled as he – and as powerful within another hospital's hierarchy – in being reduced to the status of a patient, dependent on other people for everything.

The lift jerked its way upwards, stopping at every floor to disgorge some doctors and take in others. On the fifth floor a porter tried to fit an empty bed in amongst them and seemed insulted that they didn't get out of the way for him. But at last the doors opened at the eighth floor and Karen emerged to try to find the right bay.

No staff appeared, and the desk was empty, so she went from one bed to the next until she found Will.

His face, even with the closed eyes and the dressings on two cuts on the left side, was instantly recognizable. He looked impossibly young, with his long neck emerging from some striped pyjamas that must have belonged to the hospital. The cotton looked coarse and scratchy, and the horrible mixture of purple and yellow stripes made his facial pallor even worse than it was. Karen made a mental note to buy some better ones first thing in the morning.

Almost as many tubes were stuck into him as Billy had had, and Will looked quite as fragile. The torn white cellular blanket that covered him showed clearly where the cast on his broken leg lay, fat and rigid, stretching more or less from ankle to thigh. It must have been a bad break, or even several breaks, Karen thought, completely sober now.

As she stood at the foot of the bed, hoping he would wake and recognize her but well aware that sleep was probably the best thing for him, she made more mental notes of all the things she should do. The first was phone his hospital in Brighton, where he would be expected to operate tomorrow. She should have done that hours ago. Ashamed of her self-indulgence all over again, she checked that Will was still asleep, then walked out of the bay and back to the desk.

This time a nurse was there, tapping something into the computer. Karen waited for a moment, then said, 'Excuse me.'

The nurse looked up, obviously exhausted but politely smiling. Karen explained who she was and what she needed to do and asked the nurse if she could find the number for Brighton Hospital.

Two minutes later, Karen was listening to sympathy from the late-duty administrator there and promising to keep him fully up to date with Will's progress. That task complete, she shoved the phone back into her pocket.

'How is he really?' she asked the nurse. 'Has he spoken since he came round after the operation?'

'Yes,' said the nurse, checking the time on the watch pinned to her chest. 'He made sense, confirmed he wasn't in pain and didn't need anything. It's time for his next obs. You can come with me, if you like.'

Karen followed her, noticing the ugly snags in her tights and the VPL that showed with each thrust of her broad buttocks.

Both were forgivable, Karen thought, in anyone as efficient as this woman. She stepped quietly and confidently around her patient, writing up the results of her various checks. He slept through them all until she slotted the chart back into the rack at the end of his bed. Then his eyelids fluttered.

Karen waited, barely able to breathe. The nurse stood to one side, out of his direct line of sight, to give her room. Will's flickering eyelids steadied and opened fully. Karen loosened her grip on the end rail of his bed and smiled, trying to force confidence into her expression: confidence in the hospital, in Will's powers of recovery, and in her own ability to trust herself with him.

He stared at her, as though trying to decode a cypher, then slowly his lips relaxed, parted and widened.

'Karen?' he whispered. Then said it again a little more loudly.

Her whole body felt as if it were melting, now that she no longer had to brace herself. She moved round the bed, past the nurse, and stood as close as possible to the side of his bed, brushing the back of his hand with her fingertips. A drip was fixed to a cannula inserted into one of the veins in his hand, so she took care not to dislodge anything, but she needed to touch his skin with hers.

'Hello, Will,' she said. She wanted to ask all sorts of stupid questions, like: How does it feel?

'How bad is the pain?' she said at last, hoping she sounded cool and professional enough.

He licked his lips, still smiling.

'I'll cope,' he said.

'Good.' Karen stroked his face. 'I'm sorry; so, so sorry.'

'Not your fault,' Will said, as his eyebrows twitched together. 'There was a digger. Runaway. Out of control. I didn't see it in time.'

'I should've been driving. My car. My project. My ... enemies, maybe.'

'Drama queen,' he said, closing his eyes again.

Karen felt a reassuring twinge of the old crossness. She took away her hand, telling herself: This is a real drama. I'm not making it up. I'm not wallowing in it. He could have died.

His eyelids rose once more, and his lips parted in a sort of smile. 'Don't fret. All OK soon.'

'You're very tired, aren't you?' she said, running her finger across his hand again. 'Shall I leave you to sleep, or would you like me to stay? Either's fine by me. Just say. I'm all yours.'

He looked at her as though questioning the statement. If it hadn't been for the nurse waiting watchful at her side, Karen might have said more.

'Not much ... energy,' he said, forcing out the words. 'Better t'morrow.'

She kissed her fingers, then laid them on his lips and felt a small answering movement from him. Without another word, she left him to the care of the professionals and made her way slowly home, feeling that something momentous had happened.

Back in the flat, with another glass of wine beside her, she opened up her laptop and re-read the case notes she'd been composing in the Goose Inn.

As she read and expanded the existing text, adding more questions whenever anything occurred to her, she began to wish she hadn't been so dismissive of Giles's conviction that everything that had happened had been directed at him. At the time she'd thought it had been vanity. Now she wondered.

Echoes of the information Charlie's boss had given about Giles's City career came back to her. He had been a market maker, which could have brought him in contact with people like her dead husband: determined and dishonest people, who would do almost anything to guard their profits. Money – the chance of accumulating vast sums – could make all sorts of people mad enough to break any law that stood between them and the rewards they saw as rightfully theirs. Did Giles have dangerous information about someone like Peter, who had amassed a fortune by fraud? Were these attacks, one so very close to Giles's yacht and another actually on his land, part of a campaign of intimidation to ensure he kept his mouth shut?

Was Olly's devil – the truly guilty person Karen was still sure must have agitated him or perhaps drugged him into a state in which he was capable of killing Suzie – someone who felt threatened by knowledge Giles had taken with him when he left the City?

Peter had died after Karen had said she would expose his crimes, but she had seen in his face so much rage, so much violence, that she'd always thought she'd come close to being killed herself that night.

She laid her fingers on her keyboard, opened up the Google home page and typed Giles's name in the search box.

Hundreds of entries appeared. She discovered he was a major donor to several Island charities, and sat on the boards of a variety of companies there and on the mainland. But there was nothing about his past career in London. Frustration made her try different spellings of his name. Nothing came up.

Maybe she shouldn't have been surprised. Along with rich, powerful and possibly threatened and threatening investors, the City was rife with secrecy. In any other trade, publicity on the web was helpful and plentiful. But a lot of big players in the investment world liked to keep their names and client lists well away from public eyes.

Karen looked up from the screen for a second and caught sight of the pile of bills awaiting her attention. On top was her Mastercard statement and she saw the payment date: tomorrow.

'Oh, shit!' she shouted aloud. The last thing she needed now was to waste money paying huge interest and penalties for being late.

She dug into her files for all the codes and passwords and pins she kept – carefully scattered about in random places to prevent any wandering burglar finding them all together – and clicked her way into her bank's website and the page with her current account so she could pay on line.

The process was so familiar she could carry it out almost

mindlessly now, except for having to check all the passwords, clicking the button for 'pay in full'. There were so many cheaper ways to borrow money than on a credit card that she could never bear to leave anything for longer than the free credit lasted.

Only when she had confirmation that the payment had gone through did she go to her balance to double-check that there would be enough to pay the next batch of bills she was expecting.

The numbers looked wrong. Completely wrong. She came right out of her account, then logged on again. Still the weird numbers showed on her screen. She had to look three times before she believed them. Even then she felt as though someone had pulled away her chair just as she was sitting down, making her crash on to the floor.

Shuffling her bottom on it to make sure she was secure, she looked at the figures for a fourth time, before checking the account name and number to make absolutely certain she was on her own page. Everything else was right, but this balance was ludicrous. There was no way she had more than a quarter of a million pounds sitting in her account.

Chapter 19

Clicking on the 'request full statement' button, she saw that the money had been paid into her account in dollars from a bank in Boston, Massachusetts.

Aidan.

Karen's hand was on the phone before she was aware of wanting to move it, but she didn't put in his number. Instead she held the receiver, looking down at it, and practised what she might say. She checked the time. With the East Coast of the States five hours behind England, Aidan should still be in the office. She didn't know that number by heart and had to look it up on the Rolodex he had sent her for a birthday present years ago, soon after they had resumed contact after Peter's death.

A recorded message answered her, explaining that Aidan Taylor was away and that if the matter was urgent the caller should speak to his secretary or one of his partners. Karen put down the receiver before she had to listen to their names or phone numbers.

His mobile was no more productive. She got a message from that, too. But at least this one invited her to leave her details so he could call back.

'Hi, Aidan. It's me, Karen. I need to talk to you. Urgently.' She paused for a second, wondering how best to put her question, then merely added: 'I've had a bank statement.'

He had all her numbers so there was no point stretching out the expensive call to leave those. Knowing he would have his BlackBerry, wherever he was, she opened her email and quickly typed a second message.

Dear Aidan
What have you done? There's a vast amount of money in
my current account sent from your bank. Please phone me.
Will's in hospital, so I may be there and unable to answer,
but if you leave a message I'll get back to you right away. I
need to know what's happening.
When are you likely to get here?
Love, Karen

As she was typing the last question, she felt as though someone had her right wrist in both hands and was twisting in opposite directions. A Chinese burn Aidan had called it when they were children.

He was supposed to be coming here in only a few days' time. Why would he have sent all this money to her account in advance? Could he be planning to move back to England permanently and be using her account to transfer some of his funds?

Her phone rang and she picked it up. Aidan's name was on

the screen. It was a long time since he had rung her. Nearly always she was the one to initiate contact. She pressed the green phone icon.

'Hi.' She knew her voice was as hoarse as Billy's had been.

'Karen.' Aidan sounded so cold – angry even – that she had one answer without even having to ask the question.

'You're not coming, are you?' she said, her throat hurting with the effort of controlling her voice.

'No,' he agreed. 'I'm having a quick break skiing in Colorado. Just the long weekend. Listen, Karen, Christmas isn't such a big deal over here, and I've got clients screaming at me from all directions. I simply haven't time to get over to the UK.'

'And the money?' she said, her voice now as frigid as his while she tried to decode all the unspoken messages she could feel hovering in the harsh atmosphere. 'What's that about?'

'You said in an email that the contractors are starting work on the house and you're worried about paying them.' Aidan sounded injured at the very idea that she could be questioning his motives. 'This way you don't have to worry.'

She couldn't speak.

'It's enough isn't it?' He sounded even more hurt.

'More than. As you know. You're only supposed to pay half anyway.'

'Put the rest against the mortgage.' Aidan's voice had never seemed so American before, so foreign, so unlike the hero of her childhood.

'Why?' she whispered. 'What's going on? Aren't you *ever* coming back?'

This time it was he who was silent.

'You're not, are you?' Karen said, squeezing out each difficult word as though it were the last smear of toothpaste from a mashed-up tube. 'So why did you agree to buy the house with me in the first place if you knew you'd never use it? Never even come over here to see it.'

'I don't know.' He laughed and the sound made her skin feel as though insects were crawling all over it. 'You're a shrink these days. You should understand how I thought I wanted to come back until it was a reality, then found I hated the idea.'

'But *why*?' Karen thought about all her research into siblings. Often the younger would adore the elder and have no idea how much the first-born resented the supplanter. Some of them would grow out of it, but not all.

Aidan didn't answer.

'It's me, isn't it?' Karen tried to think of herself interviewing a research subject. 'Can you put it into words? Tell me what it was I did to you.'

'You were in my way.' The words she'd asked for popped with unexpected vigour, like the guns at Giles's pheasant shoot.

Karen's fingers whitened as she gripped the phone. She stared at her feet, recognizing a long-known but never-faced truth.

'"Look after your sister. Don't hit her. Read to her. Help her with her homework. Be a little gentleman. Boys shouldn't do this that or the other."' Aidan had reverted to his English accent as he repeated the instructions from long ago, but his voice switched to something much more American when he added, 'But little Karen can do anything she likes because she's the youngest and a girl. She's a smart and pretty blonde and everybody loves her. Unlike clumsy Aidan, who's a dunce and ornery with it.'

'You hate me,' she whispered, remembering the Chinese burns.

'Not now.' He produced a harsh crack of humourless laughter. 'Don't be silly. But I did. Boy, how I did. As an adult, I'm sorry for it, of course. I guess I need to atone. I have plenty of money these days, so I ...'

'You think you're buying me off?' Karen disliked the spikiness of her voice more than she could have explained to anyone.

Money was power. She'd known for a long time. And lack of it – even her kind of only comparative lack – was humiliating.

'That's right. You get your new house, Karen – all the legal papers are on their way to you; I'm signing my share over to you. You deserve it.'

Karen cut him off. Her head was ringing and she felt sick with fury that she'd conned herself all these years into believing Aidan was her champion against their neglectful parents and anyone else who might ever give her trouble. No wonder he hadn't answered any of her letters after she'd announced her engagement to Peter. Aidan must have thought he'd been let off his loathed duties at last.

She'd heard how Billy had resented being told to watch over his sisters and she'd even laid out for Charlie all the reasons why an elder sibling could turn on a younger one. She just hadn't seen the link with Aidan and herself.

What else hadn't she seen? What other obvious truths had

been lining themselves up in front of her, waving and yelling and trying to make her notice them?

Karen knew she should be thinking about the case, or about Will, lying in pain only a few hundred yards away, or even Billy, probably dying over on the Island. But she couldn't. All she could think about was the self-deception she'd practised for the past thirty-six years. Talk about cognitive dissonance, she thought in disgust at herself.

The idea of Aidan's money in her bank account was like an indigestible lump of meat in her stomach: fundamentally nourishing but so painful she would have done anything to get rid of it.

Mozart, she thought, and walked across the big room to swap the CD for the Flute and Harp concerto.

As the cheerful dialogue between the two instruments, the breathy flute and the plucked-piano sound of the harp, filled her room, she slowly made herself think like an adult again – and a professional – instead of a child sick and breathless with shock.

Aidan had also been a child when he'd conceived his loathing of the intruder she had been, she reminded herself in her role as a psychologist. And he had clearly worried over his feelings for years. She remembered how only last summer he had told her that he'd always felt guilty about the way he'd abandoned her when he'd fled to the States. That was the point at which he'd said he would come back to England for this Christmas, obviously planning to re-establish affectionate relations with her. Or – more realistically – establish them for the first time.

The poor man had probably terrified himself with the prospect of seeing and hating her all over again, she thought.

Money was not the only route to power.

Tension had been gripping Karen's neck and shoulders ever since she'd seen the figures on her bank statement. Now it eased a little. Aidan might have dealt with his panic by buying himself out of the need to see her again, but there were better ways.

She sat at her computer again, laid her fingers on the keys and, without letting her conscious mind get in the way, typed:

Dear Aidan

I'm sorry about putting the phone down on you just now.
It was an emotional moment. Thank you for the money.
You suggest you can afford it easily and on that basis I will
use it to pay the contractors who are rebuilding Granny's
house. When I can afford to, I'll pay you back. You mustn't
think you have ever owed me anything. You were a child,
too, and fighting for self-preservation. I hope your skiing
trip goes well. Take care of yourself.
    K

She knew she'd been right to do it when the ringing in her head quietened the moment she pressed 'send'.

The wine glass beside the computer was still full. Glad of the evidence that she wasn't an alcoholic even after this afternoon's excesses, she carried the glass to the sofa and lay back to sip it slowly and listen to the music, letting her mind go where it wanted without conscious direction.

Back in control once more, she slept again.

This time she woke naturally, knowing she'd been out only for a few minutes. The flute and harp were still playing, now just embarking on the rondeau. As the sounds danced and coiled around each other, Karen saw the obvious answer to the mystery that had been staring her in the face all along.

Giles. The link to everything that had happened could indeed be Giles. But not as the victim of any kind of intimidation.

Karen slid out from beneath the light cashmere rug and moved so easily to her desk that she felt as though her joints had been oiled. At the computer, she went back to the list of Giles's non-executive directorships on the Island. One of them was for the building company that was working on her new house.

Clicking and scrolling, she looked for more evidence, eventually making her way to the Land Registry site. Only one house in Paultons Square had been sold in 2008, when Charlie claimed Giles had got rid of his. He had indeed made three and a half million pounds on the deal. That would leave quite a lot of change. Enough to fund the kind of life Giles was living?

Hoping it wasn't, Karen checked further, and soon found that the rest of Charlie's information had not been quite so accurate. Two million of the sale price had been owed on the mortgage Giles had had outstanding. That didn't leave much change to fund the purchase and refurbishment of the *Dasher*, or the renovation and subsequent upkeep of his Island house, land, gardens and woods. Two top of the range cars, too. No, three. Giles's brother-in-law had said something about his 'mainland car' on the day when Karen and Charlie had gone to meet Suzie's parents.

Karen clicked some more, astonished all over again at how

easy the internet had made it to find out whatever you needed to know about virtually anyone. Only moments later, she had the prices for Giles's Jaguars and his wife's BMW: well over £200,000 for the cars alone. She also discovered that he owned a whole lot of flats over shops in Cowes. Clicking and checking, she worked out that he must be landlord to the self-absorbed composer, who hadn't noticed anything except an irritating scream when Suzie was dying.

Once Karen had an idea of all Giles's capital expenses and income, she made an assessment of the running costs of boat, house, cars and staff. Then there were Suzie's school fees and the costs of her riding, and paying off her parents' mortgage.

Karen scribbled the figures she had and added them up, goggling at the total, before picking up her phone. She took it back to the sofa, pressing in 9 for the speed dial to Charlie's mobile.

'Hi,' she said when he answered.

'Karen. How's Will?'

'Out of surgery. In pain and very tired. Charlie, I need to talk to you. Where are you?'

'At home, after a bruising meeting with my boss. I could do with some TLC. Shall I come round?'

'That'd be great.'

'Sure, Karen? You couldn't get rid of me quickly enough last time, and Will's ...'

'This is about work. I could come to you, but I'm ... I'm pretty knackered.' Karen waited for him to remind her he'd been working twenty-two hours out of every twenty-four. But he didn't.

'I'll be round in minutes. With my own beer,' Charlie said

with grim humour. She remembered how much he'd disliked the icy pilsner she kept for Will.

Karen put her boots back on and brewed a pot of coffee, before turning on all the lights and tidying the sitting room. She wanted to make it clear that this was a place for work and not an attempted seduction scene.

Charlie took in the message as soon as he came through the door. Karen could see it in his face right away.

'Fine. Let's get down to it,' he said, handing her a bottle of Black Knight bitter from the Downton Brewery. 'You still got your opener?'

She was relieved to see his dark eyes watching her with amusement and went to the kitchen for the bottle opener and a plain tall glass. He inspected the glass suspiciously but must have decided it would do because he flipped the crown cap off the bottle and poured out a stream of dark beer. Even from where she was standing, Karen could smell highly roasted malt and something citrus.

'It's the brewery's winter special,' he said. 'Good enough to keep me going while I listen. Now, what have you got for me?'

'Giles Henty,' she said. 'I think he's up to his neck in all this. He must be Olly's devil. I still can't be sure Olly didn't kill Suzie, but I'm convinced it was Giles he was trying to protect her from.'

Charlie took a deep draught of beer, then subsided on to the sofa. He didn't mock Karen, but she could see he would need a lot of persuading.

'It's like a sum, Charlie.' She got up to fetch her thick pad of lined paper and a fine felt-tipped pen, ready to write it all out for him. 'If you do each small calculation, there's only one final result you can possibly reach. And it makes sense of everything.'

'I'm listening,' he said, making it more than clear that he wasn't believing. He put his beer glass down on the floor by his feet.

'One: Giles presents himself as a very rich man with a brilliant record of investment and yet your boss, who apparently knows, says he's no such thing.'

'Right,' Charlie said when she paused for a comment, adding, 'I already told you: he's living off the equity from his London house.'

'I don't think so.' Karen handed him the printout of the information about Giles's mortgage. 'Now, I've added up a rough total, including the cost of his boat and renovating that house and the estate round it and maintaining the whole lot like an old-fashioned landed gentleman ... However good his investments are – and no one else's have done much this year – Giles is getting money from somewhere else.'

'But ...'

'The most obvious way is drugs, and drugs in serious quantity. I think he's bringing them in on that boat of his.'

'Fuck's sake, Karen! Evidence?'

'Circumstantial.' She willed confidence into her voice. 'But it makes sense: drugs are the most obvious way to make a lot of money without leaving any kind of trail. You need to search his boat, and wherever he garages his mainland car, and ...'

'As if I'd get a warrant on the basis of this kind of guesswork!'

'At least you could ask him some pertinent questions. In any case, it's not guesswork: it's analysis of a subject's behaviour and extrapolation from that analysis. As much evidence as any kind of physical marks. Can't you at least ask Giles where he took the *Dasher* when Billy first went missing? Giles was away for more than twenty-four hours.'

'How do you know that?'

'I can't remember who told me. Someone did. Yes, Dan. Billy's father. Now, Charlie, concentrate: why would you go cruising for so long in the middle of the worst winter we've known in decades if you weren't expecting substantial profit from the voyage? On the day Suzie was killed, Giles was due to meet "some mates" further along the coast. It's worth finding out if they're his distributors.'

Charlie got off the sofa and prowled about the long room, exuding so much impatience she could almost see it, like ectoplasm. At last he stopped in front of her. Karen tipped back her head so that she could look up him. She had a sudden vision of Suzie's face and hair being deposited behind her head during the post-mortem and felt sick.

'How would a man like him get involved in something like that?' he demanded.

'Giles was a market-maker in the City,' she explained, making herself forget the post-mortem. 'What's to stop him using his old skills to make a whole new market for cocaine on the Island, among all sorts of people who wouldn't otherwise touch it?'

'Nothing. But there's no evidence to say he did either. This is a pointless waste of time.'

'People like Olly,' she insisted. 'Maybe Giles didn't know that coke was likely to trigger a florid episode in someone with schizophrenia.'

Charlie got off the sofa and came to stand in front of her, looming over her. She looked up at him, refusing to be intimidated.

'Just his bad luck the effect was to make Olly kill his best-beloved niece,' she said.

'You . . .' he started, bending down so he could take her by the shoulders. For a moment she thought he was going to shake her, but all he did was press her hard into the sofa back.

'What?' she said.

'Listen. And keep your mouth shut for a minute. Just one single minute. OK?'

Karen shrugged and his hands tightened on her shoulders.

'If Giles was bringing in wholesale quantities of drugs on his boat, the last – the very last – thing he'd do is feed an unstable boy some of the product.' Charlie took his hands away and shifted backwards, as though touching her any longer might contaminate him. 'Even a psychologist like you should be able to see that. He'd know he could never trust Olly not to tell where he'd got his drugs. Giles wouldn't take a risk like that.'

Karen waited, watching the disgust playing around Charlie's face and thinking how much of it she shared.

'Finished?' she said at last, pleased with the way she was keeping her temper. 'Great. Now *you* listen to me. Giles isn't stupid, and—'

'Unlike some people.' Charlie turned away. Karen didn't care. She could talk to his black-leather back as easily as to his furious face.

'All along he's been claiming Suzie's death and Billy's were his fault, while, at the same time, making everybody understand how the real blame must lie elsewhere. Have you never heard of misdirection, Charlie? Never seen a conjurer distracting you with one hand while he hid the rabbits in his hat with the other?'

'I haven't the time to listen to this shit.' He strode towards the door, his exit only slightly spoiled by tripping over his glass. The sticky dark beer spread out over Karen's beautiful wood floor and seeped into the edge of the cream-coloured rug. 'Fuck!'

She overtook him as he was righting himself and shaking the beer off his foot.

'Have you got the DNA results from the knife yet?' she asked and watched his face darken as the blood rushed into his unshaven cheeks. Pinning the sweetest, most girlish smile on her lips, she added, 'Don't tell me, Giles's is on there.'

'So?' Never had Charlie's shoulders looked so broad or his face so menacing. 'Oliver's is too.'

'So it's interesting,' she said, glad of the confirmation that Giles had more of a connection with Olly than he'd admitted.

'No, it fucking well isn't. Giles gave a stack of money to Suzie when he told her to buy her deckies, so his DNA would have been on the notes and then transferred on to her hands as she held the money. She had defence wounds all over her hands, so the DNA could've been transferred again on to the knife.'

'That's just as speculative as anything I've said.' Now it was Karen who wanted to shake Charlie. 'Yes, Giles's DNA could have got there like that. But it could have got there because he transferred it to Olly earlier in the day. Someone filled Olly up with cocaine, and—'

'Out of my way. I've got work to do. Billy's dead.'

Karen stood aside at once. 'Why didn't you tell me?'

'What could you have done? Let me go.'

'I'm sorry, Charlie. I know how much you liked him. And ...' She quickly censored what she'd been going to say about the way Billy and his misdemeanours must have plugged into Charlie's memories of his own troubled childhood. 'I can imagine how this will change your investigation. But please, at least ask Giles about his mates and talk to them. Find out about the drugs. And get someone to look into his financial affairs. *Please*, Charlie.'

'There's no point. He'd never take risks like that,' Charlie said as he stepped across the threshold. 'Man like him? On a place as small as the Island?'

He slammed the door shut and Karen listened to his footsteps clanging on the hard floor outside, slowly diminishing as he ran downstairs.

'But Giles *is* a risk taker,' Karen said aloud to the empty space all round her as she went back to deal with the spilled beer.

When it was all mopped up and the rug and cleaning cloths rinsed out, she wondered if she'd ever get rid of the smell. Delicious at the moment when Charlie had opened the bottle, it wasn't going to be nearly so good as the days passed.

The boiler had reheated her tank, so she gave herself another shower, but not for nearly as long as this time, and went to bed. But her mind was firing too fast to allow her to sleep. After half an hour's uncomfortable pillow-beating and duvet-kicking, she gave in and got up again, to write lists of information she wanted Charlie to find, and other lists of all the questions she herself could legitimately ask.

Driving her was a cold hard anger that reminded her of the last days of her marriage, when Peter's full dishonesty had become clear at last. If Giles was doing what she suspected, then the cost of his greed had been immense already: Suzie's life; Billy's life; Will's terrible injuries.

She thought of the way Billy had been recovering, regaining the power to speak, getting stronger every day and then dying. What if Will . . .?

Karen could not complete the question, even in her mind. But it left her with the terror that after shilly-shallying for so long, not trusting him or herself, she might now have talked to him for the last time.

Chapter 20

Day Eight: Wednesday 10 a.m.

Billy's mother looked as though she had been crying for days. Karen sat at the kitchen table, understanding her desperation and holding her hands.

'I'm so sorry,' Karen said.

'You tried to help.' Sandra's voice dragged and squelched. 'If it hadn't been for you and that cop being there and taking Billy to hospital that day, he might never have come round at all, and I . . . At least he knew I . . . I was there when he died, so he wasn't alone. Oh, God.'

She bowed over their clasped hands, clinging to Karen's, squeezing her fingers until she wanted to protest.

'Where's Dan?' Karen asked, feeling like a fraud. She had arrived at the house ten minutes ago, to be greeted by Sandra as though she had come especially to help after the news of Billy's death.

'He's taken the girls out to give me time to cry in peace.' At last Sandra let go of Karen's hands and she pulled them off the table so she could stretch the cramped fingers. 'He can control himself. I can't. They mustn't see me like this. It's bad enough them knowing he's dead, without me breaking up. And just before Christmas, too.'

'Can I make you some more tea?' Karen said, knowing that a concrete suggestion was the only way to help at all, even if it were just the offer of a hot drink.

'If you want,' said Sandra in a dreary voice, which made it clear that nothing could help her. She sniffed loudly. 'Sorry.'

Filling the kettle and plugging it in, allowed Karen to turn her back and give the other woman some emotional space.

'When Mr Henty brought Billy back that day,' Karen began, when she'd silenced the gushing tap.

'Yes?'

'What did Billy have with him?'

Sandra said nothing, but the silence was so heavy it suggested she had something to tell. Karen found a teapot, warmed it, threw out the water – just as Granny had taught her – then added two teabags, waited for the kettle to boil again and filled the pot.

'He'd left his backpack and books behind in the squat,' Karen added, bringing the pot to the table and allowing her free hand to rest on Sandra's shoulder for an instant. 'But what else did he have with him?'

'Oh, what's it matter now?' Sandra wiped her dripping nose on a tissue so well used it couldn't absorb any more liquid. Karen tore a sheet of kitchen paper off the roll and handed it to her. 'He had a sweater.'

Sandra blew her nose and shoved the snotty paper up her sleeve. She placed both her palms flat on the table and heaved herself up from the chair, with as much effort as though she weighed twenty stone instead of half that. She crossed the small cluttered kitchen to where a plastic basket of clean washing lay, neatly folded and awaiting ironing.

'This.' She held it out to Karen, a soft mass of blue wool, deeper than sky but nowhere near as dark as navy.

Karen took it and felt the springy softness of the light wool and allowed her fingers to trace its elegant cabling. She looked up to meet Sandra's eyes, waiting for an explanation.

'It's cashmere,' Sandra said, sounding like someone pronouncing a death sentence.

'I know. I can feel it,' Karen said. 'Do you know where he got it?'

Sandra looked away. 'I asked and he said he'd been given it. He didn't want me to wash it, but it was all messy. Brown and stiff.' She sobbed once, then put her hand over her mouth. After a moment, she added, 'I thought he'd got chocolate all over it.'

'Wasn't it chocolate?'

Holding the sweater right up under her chin, moving her head from side to side as though she were stroking her skin on the fine wool, Sandra plumped down into a free chair.

'So I did wash it,' she said. 'The day Billy went to Mr Henty's shoot. I had to do it by hand because you can't put cashmere in the machine. And . . .'

Karen waited until she couldn't bear the suspense. 'What happened?'

Sandra shuddered and rolled the sweater into a tight ball, which she crammed into a drawer, slamming it shut. With her back to Karen, she said, 'The water ran red.'

'Was it Suzie's sweater?' Karen asked, easily able to imagine what a shock the blood must have given her.

'No. His. Oliver's.'

'How do you know?' Karen was on her feet before she realized she'd moved and quickly sat down again, moderating her voice too. 'Sandra, how do you know? Had you ever seen Oliver wear it? Did you *know* him?'

Sandra turned, pushing her long straight brown fringe out of her swollen eyes and sat down at the table again, propping her chin on her hands.

'At school one day,' she said. 'Beginning of term. Last term. I was waiting for Billy, and the big boys came out first. Oliver was lagging behind one group, on his own – he was too strange, Billy told me afterwards, to have friends, to be one of any of the gangs. This lot turned back just outside the school gates. A couple of big louts. And they grabbed his bag and ripped it open and flung everything in the road. The sweater fell out.'

'Are you sure it was the same sweater?' Karen asked, amazed anyone could remember something so clearly. 'How do you know?'

Sandra took it out of the drawer and laid it flat on the table, slightly stretching the sleeves and hem to make it lie flat after the way she'd mangled it. She pointed to a small darn at the back of the neck, where the ribbing must once have come away from the rest.

'The darn isn't cashmere, which is why the colour's different. It's ordinary wool. I remember seeing it that day. I went to help him pick up his stuff from the gutter and put it all back in the bag. He was lovely, smiled like the sweetest boy and thanked me. He seemed quite normal to me.'

'How do you know it was Oliver? Did you know him already?'

Sandra reached for the teapot and poured out two mugsful. But they'd waited too long and its colour was now like liquefied iron.

'Not at first,' she said. 'But Billy came out then and told me off for talking to Oliver, said it wouldn't do him any good if his mum was seen with the school loonie.'

More tears leaked out of her eyes.

'I told him he mustn't talk like that. He should be decent to Oliver, make a friend of him. No one deserves bullying like that. "Oliver might be bigger than you, but he needs protection," I said. "If you see anyone tormenting him, you need to tell one of the teachers." It's my fault, you see. I made Billy think he had to look after Oliver.' Sandra looked up at Karen again. 'I think that's why he ... I think Oliver gave him the sweater that afternoon, like a bribe, when he asked Billy to hide the knife he used on that girl. That's why I couldn't tell. Billy's been in so much trouble with the police for years now. I couldn't ... But now he's ... Nothing's going to hurt Billy, is it? Not now. It's not going to matter now if the police hear about the sweater.'

Sandra gulped some of the bitter, black tea, not even noticing the taste. Karen ignored her own mug. The scummy liquid in it looked revolting.

'Have the police searched his room?' Karen asked.

Sandra's head shook slightly, as though the effort of making any larger movement was more than she could manage.

'Could I have a look?'

'If you want.' Sandra made it obvious that nothing mattered to her. What she was going through was far more important than any violation of her home. 'It's the middle one at the top of the stairs, facing out the back.'

'Don't you want to be there while I look, Sandra?'

'Why would I?'

'OK,' Karen said. 'I won't be long.'

As she climbed the shallow stairs, she dreaded being faced with fitted carpet, but as she pushed open the door of Billy's room, she saw bare boards and a loose rag rug, obviously home-made from ruched strips of red and blue cotton. The sight of it made Karen admire Sandra even more.

Walking carefully, Karen tested the firmness of the boards' fixing, pressing down until at last she found one that creaked.

'Sandra!' she called out. 'Sandra!'

'What?'

'Could you come up here?' Karen said, leaning over the banisters. 'I think you need to be here for a second.'

'Why?' Sandra's voice was full of terror. 'What've you found?'

'Nothing yet,' Karen said. 'But I want to look under the floor. And I don't want to lift the board without you here.'

She waited at the top of the stairs, watching Sandra climb the treads with painful effort. At last she reached the top and Karen urged her to lead the way into Billy's room. Karen pushed aside his light metal bed to get better access to the loose board and pressed down at one end of it. The other end jumped up, as though it was operated by a spring. Karen glanced over her shoulder.

'The police search team found things under a board in his hiding place near the marina,' she said. 'I thought it was worth having a look here. Shall I see what's under it? Or do you want to?'

Sandra stepped backwards. 'Not me. Not me. They found

the knife, didn't they? I don't want to look. I don't want to. You shouldn't have made me ...'

'It's all right,' Karen said, knowing it wasn't.

She felt around under the boards and came up with nothing. It didn't seem possible that this hiding place was completely empty, so she lay down and reached her arm right into the void beneath the boards, feeling around and at last touched something with her outstretched fingertips.

'There's something here. It feels like a book. A paperback.'

'I don't want ...'

'Don't worry about it, Sandra.' Karen leaned further into the gap, feeling the pressure of the board's edge in her armpit. At last she got her hand around the small rectangle and pulled it out: money. A small neat slab of twenty-pound notes, about an inch thick. She held them between finger and thumb. Sandra just stared.

'How much is it?' she asked at last, dazed.

'We'd better not count it now,' Karen said, laying the pile carefully on Billy's bed. 'The police will need to check for fingerprints, DNA too maybe. The less we touch it, the better.'

'But how would he ...? Do you think Oliver gave it to him?'

'I don't know,' Karen said. 'But the police will need to see it. Will you phone?'

Sandra shook her head. 'I don't want to talk to them.'

'They're trying to find out who shot Billy. They need to know everything that could help find the killer.'

'They'll make out he was thieving again. They'll say it was his fault. I can't bear it.'

'They won't.' Karen tried to keep her voice soothing and

firm at the same time. The last thing they needed now was for Sandra to get rid of the money in an attempt to protect her son's reputation. 'Shall I call for you?'

Sandra shrugged her shoulders, making the prominent collar bones even more visible in the deep scoop of her black sweater.

Karen kept her gaze on Sandra, while feeling for the phone in her pocket and dialling Charlie.

'Hi,' she said as soon as he answered. 'I'm at the Jenkins'. With Billy's mum. She's found a lot of money under the floorboards in his room: new notes; very crisp. I think you should . . .'

'She found them, or you?' he demanded.

'Does it matter? You need to . . .'

'Forensicate them,' he said. 'I'll be there. Don't let her touch them.'

Forensicate? Karen thought as she put the phone away. What a ludicrous and illogical mangling of a perfectly good word! But the sight of Sandra's face, crumpling as another battery of grief hit her, put every other thought out of Karen's mind.

The two women retreated to the kitchen, leaving the board open, the bed askew, and the money still lying on the red, white and blue patchwork bed cover.

Charlie did not make them wait long, ringing the doorbell only twelve minutes later. He was already shaking out an evidence bag, even before Sandra dragged herself back up the stairs ahead of him. Karen waited in the kitchen, hearing both their voices but not able to distinguish what either of them said. At last they came back to the kitchen.

'Sandra says she has no idea where Billy could have got this kind of money,' he said to Karen, who was standing beside the empty stove. 'Have you?'

'None at all,' Karen said. 'How could I? The first time I ever met Billy was when you and I drove him to hospital that day, and the only other time was when we were all together at his bedside.'

'He didn't thieve it,' Sandra said. 'I *know* he didn't.'

Charlie glanced at Karen.

'I'm sure he didn't,' she said, earning a grateful smile from Sandra. 'No one could have lost that amount and not reported it. We didn't count it, but there must be – what? – fifty twenties there. No one loses a grand without calling you lot in.'

'Fair enough,' Charlie said. 'You going to be here long?'

Karen looked at Sandra, who wouldn't meet her eyes.

'I only came to see Billy's mum,' Karen said. 'If there's nothing I can do for you ...'

'Dan and the girls'll be back soon,' Sandra said, staring round at the kitchen, the neat piles of clean clothes, the horrible brown liquid in the dirty mugs, the bare worktops. 'I'll have to get them something for their dinner.'

Her eyes filled with tears. 'And I'll have to think of some way to give them a proper Christmas, and with Billy ... I can't.'

'We'll leave you to it, then,' Charlie said with less than usual sensitivity, taking Karen by the elbow and pulling her towards the door.

Outside, he hurried her up the pavement towards the police station. Only when they were a good hundred metres from the house did he say anything.

'What do you think you're up to?'

'Ever since you told me the news about Billy last night,' she said honestly, 'I've been thinking what I would feel if it ... if he were my son. And I came ...'

'Yeah. Maybe. Then you take advantage of her bereavement and start searching her home. How insensitive is that? And irresponsible. You could've screwed the evidence and ...'

'Then why hadn't you searched it?' Karen wasn't going to back down. 'Wasn't it the obvious thing to do, once you'd found the knife? Again at *my* suggestion. I wish you'd listen to me, Charlie. I know how people ... In any case, it doesn't take a psychologist to see that if a boy secretes something under one floorboard, he's likely to use the same kind of hiding place wherever he is.'

Charlie's eyes were narrow as he stared at her, and his nostrils flared. 'I wouldn't put it past you to have dumped the money there yourself to support your theories and con us into wasting a year's budget getting the Financial Investigation Unit to trawl through Giles's books.'

Karen turned away and walked fast in the direction of the quay.

'Don't fucking run away from me,' Charlie shouted and ran after her, grabbing her shoulder and spinning her round to face him.

'Why not? You're not going to listen to me, are you? I give you a perfectly rational explanation for everything that's going on, using the expertise for which you are paying me, and you dismiss it out of hand. Then you accuse me of planting evidence. What the hell has got into you, Charlie?'

'I'm fed up with your yammering,' he said, letting her go.

She didn't wait for anything else. Swinging her arm like a club she smashed her open hand into the side of his face.

The flash in his eyes terrified her and she backed off at once. Her palm was stinging, which brought her back to her senses – and to the knowledge of what her unprecedented violence could have triggered in a man who had seen and suffered what Charlie had as a child.

'I'm sorry,' she said, bending her head in submission. 'But I've ... I'm in a state about Will. And it frustrates me when you won't *listen*.'

'Listen to what?' he said, sounding distant and formal.

'I can't tell ... I haven't the energy to explain it all now. I need to get ... Just talk to the head of Billy's school, which is also Olly's school. You'll find that they once took a rock of crack off Billy. Doesn't that make you think?'

'Not much.'

Karen sighed and felt an old, long-buried rage surfacing in her mind. She had to hold on to it, not let it out. Trying to sound patient, she went on, 'And Billy had "worked" for Giles. His father had a story about a one-off scrubbing of the *Dasher*'s decks, but that's hardly enough, is it? Don't you think Billy could have been Giles's runner, while he was trying to make a market for drugs among the juniors at the school?'

'I've no time for this.'

A gust of wind whipped Karen's face and made her eyes stream. She didn't want Charlie to think she was crying, so she strode away, ignoring the way he called her name. At least this time he didn't follow or manhandle her.

A Red Jet was waiting at the quay. She got on and huddled herself in the seat furthest from the entrance, pulling her thick parka more tightly around her body and reknotting the yellow scarf around her neck.

Her phone bleeped to warn her a text was coming through. She ignored it, wishing the hovercraft would get going. She wanted to be right away from the Island as soon as possible and sitting at Will's bedside.

But she could never suppress her curiosity for long and so, when the hovercraft still hadn't left ten minutes later, she cracked and took out the phone. Not much to her surprise it had Charlie's name on the screen. Karen clicked on the envelope icon and read:

Sorry. He'll be OK. I'm sure of it. Hang on in there. C

This time it wasn't the wind that made her eyes water.

She disembarked, checked that she could use her ticket later in the day, and found a corner out of the wind, where she could phone the hospital.

'No change,' they said when she asked about Will. 'Nothing to worry about but no change. He's sleeping most of the time. It'll be fine if you come later.'

Karen flipped her phone shut and hailed a cab.

'Can you take me to FitzGerald and Matkens, the solicitors in the High Street?

'Right away,' said the driver.

He watched her as she settled herself on the back seat. She could see his eyes in the mirror, so she smiled and said politely that she didn't have much time. He put the car in gear and sped off into the town.

The journey didn't take long and the fare wouldn't have

troubled her even before Aidan's money had landed in her
bank account. Not that she was going to let herself live in debt
to him. His fantastic payment might have got her off the hook
with the builders, but somehow she was going to have to earn
enough to pay him back.

If she didn't do it – and quickly – she would feel even more
like Aidan's victim than she had in the moment when she'd
first understood how much he had once hated her.

A tidily dressed receptionist sat behind a high desk,
decorated with a vaguely Eastern flower arrangement. She
looked up as Karen came towards her and smiled.

'Can I help you?'

'I was hoping to talk to Philip Matken,' Karen said, pulling
out one of her cards. 'He knows me.'

The receptionist took the card, frowning, then looked up.
'He doesn't usually see anyone without an appointment.'

'Could you try? It's about his son. I'm working with the
police.'

'Have a seat,' said the young woman, waving to a bank of
six leather-covered bench-like seats.

Karen turned away, picking up one of the firm's brochures
to read while she waited. She soon discovered that FitzGerald
and Matken specialized in property, wills and trusts, and matri-
monial finance. A photograph of Philip, even better-looking
than in the flesh, decorated page one. The senior partner. So
why had he taken time off to garden on the very day that his
son knifed a friend to death?

Karen got the chance to ask the question direct, eight
minutes later. Philip was sitting behind an imposing antique
mahogany desk, with neat bookshelves laden with all

the classic legal texts and directories behind his handsome head.

He pushed back his chair and crossed his legs, now clad in the fine worsted of a traditional grey suit.

'My daughter was due back from university that day. I wanted to be at home to welcome her.'

'When she'd been away for – what? – a couple of months. And you took off the whole day. Why?'

'I told you: to welcome her.' Philip's voice was severe.

'I'm not sure many juries would believe that. A child back from a first term at boarding school, maybe. Or a traveller who'd been away a year. But a successful undergraduate at a university barely two hours' drive away, when you must have so many responsibilities here as senior partner?' Karen thought back to the tense atmosphere that had surrounded the super-confident young woman as she hectored her vulnerable mother.

'Have you always had to be a buffer between Caroline and your wife?' Karen asked, putting her head on one side and smiling, in an effort to look less judgmental.

Philip caught her eye, then looked away, coughing to clear his throat. 'For a few years, yes,' he admitted.

'Just between your wife and daughter?'

Philip did not answer.

'Because I've been thinking. Caroline is clearly a powerful personality, who didn't seem to have much tolerance for her brother, and ...'

'Oliver's behaviour has been enough to try the patience of a saint,' Philip said, his voice snapping like a leather tawse whipping the palm of a hand. 'Caroline's whole life has been affected by it. You can't be surprised she's not always as ... as tolerant as one might wish.'

'No,' Karen said, sympathy for them all welling up again. 'But, you see, I've been wondering how their relationship was before he was ill.'

'Like most girls she matured a lot earlier than any boy. She was impatient with her brother. Four years younger in any case.' Philip's voice was as clipped as an old-fashioned army officer's. 'They never shared any interests.'

'I really meant earlier than that,' Karen said. 'At four, she would have been in a powerful position when he was born, and then, say, three or four years later, when he was three or four and she was six or ...'

'You're going to tell me his condition is her fault now, aren't you?' Philip's voice had not softened in any way.

'Why would you think that, unless the idea had been in your mind already?'

'The words you used ...'

'It has been in your mind, hasn't it?' Karen said, speaking even more gently but without giving him any escape route. 'Wasn't that actually why you wanted to be at home on the day when Caroline was due back? So that if she started in on Olly again, you could step in and deflect her.'

Philip looked straight at Karen. Once more there were tears in his eyes. He knew she could see them. Maybe it was that knowledge that made him surrender at last.

'She couldn't see ... She doesn't know her own emotional strength. Never has been able to. She hasn't much imagination, and if something wouldn't upset her, she can't understand why it would bother anyone else. And she's so quick, so impatient.'

'What did she do to him? When they were little, I mean.' Karen waited. She had the feeling that Philip had been waiting a long time to talk about this. The toughness he had shown at home, the air of being at the end of his tether in the police station, everything about him suggested a man who was holding his family life together single-handedly and in the only way he knew – by self-control.

'At first I thought it was just high spirits,' he said, speaking with obvious pain. 'Teasing him, you know, suggesting there were monsters waiting to leap out of the dark at him. Then it got worse. I didn't realize how bad until one night I was late back. Very late. I'd had a client dinner and we'd gone on ... to a bar. You know.'

'I know,' Karen said, picking up guilt and regret as well as the hints of confessional relief in his expression.

'So I let myself into the house as quietly as I knew how. And there they were. In their pyjamas. Oliver was sitting shivering on one of the hall chairs, with his hands bound together with a long stocking. And Caroline was standing over him, holding his shoulder. He had bruises later, little bruises from the pressure of her fingers.' He stopped, as though the full story was too horrible to reveal.

'What was her excuse for getting him there?' Karen asked.

Philip looked at her. Now his big brown eyes were full of despair.

'She was telling him the police would be here soon, that she'd held them off for as long as she could, but he was too bad, had committed too many crimes.' Philip rubbed his hands over his face in the way Karen had seen in the police station. 'I can hear her voice now: so young, so cold, so certain. Convincing. She said he'd be locked up in a dark cell, that he'd be fed only once a week but beaten four times a day.'

'But ...' Karen suppressed her protest.

'She sounded so convincing I wasn't surprised he believed her,' Philip went on. 'He was shivering and looking as if he might throw up. I went crashing in there, yelled at her, pulled that bloody stocking from around his wrists, and just hugged him, telling him it was nonsense. That Caroline had made it up. No one was coming for him.'

Philip was staring at Karen, but she knew he wasn't seeing her, only two small figures out of the past.

'He seemed to believe me. And Caroline insisted it was only a game, promised she understood she mustn't play those sort of tricks on a younger child – or on anyone. She behaved sweetly to him whenever I was around after that. But ...' He covered his eyes again. 'I couldn't be there all the time. We couldn't sit up with them at night. He had the most terrible nightmares and ...'

'How long did it go on?' Karen asked, when it was clear he wasn't going to finish his last sentence.

Philip shrugged, but he looked anything but casual. He cared.

'I don't know. I've wondered ever since. Could that have been enough to cause the schizophrenia? I've never been able to ask before.'

'No one will ever be able to say for certain,' Karen said truthfully. 'But there are theories that say great fear can have a triggering effect on a susceptible individual. It's possible. Now, I know Olly was out for the afternoon of the day when Suzie was killed, that he'd gone out on his moped. Do you think that was because of something Caroline said to him?'

Philip shook his head. 'He went out before she got home. I thought ... When I phoned home and my wife told me he'd gone out, I thought he was taking care to avoid Caroline, and I was relieved at his ... well, his maturity. I thought it was a sign James's bizarre treatment might actually be making a difference.' He snorted. 'Ironic, isn't it?'

'What was he wearing that day?'

'What the hell difference does that make?'

'I'm not sure,' Karen said. 'But at the moment I need all the information there is so I can sift it for anything that matters. Can you remember?'

Philip looked away.

'Did you notice?' Karen asked, thinking that she might have stumbled on one of those apparently irrelevant details that had real significance.

'I did.' He rubbed his face in the familiar style. 'And I wondered ... It was a cashmere jersey Caroline gave him for his birthday a year ago last September. Very luxurious. I ... I couldn't understand why she'd spend so much. I mean, I give her a decent allowance, but she likes clothes herself and this must've eaten up a whole lot of the month's money.'

'Guilt, maybe?' Karen said, her own mind still bruised from Aidan's stupendous gesture.

'Perhaps. Anyway, he loved it. Wore it whenever he could. Took it with him in his schoolbag. Like a kind of talisman.' His eyes focused. 'I haven't seen it since ... It must be in the wash or something.'

Karen didn't think it was her job to enlighten him.

'Could they have met? I mean, could Olly have gone on the moped to pick Caroline up off the ferry?'

'Why would he?' Philip asked. 'She had her car.'

'Fine. I see.' A memory teased Karen, but she couldn't pin it down. 'Then have you any idea of where he could have gone in his lovely sweater? Who he might have ...? He seems to have been quite friendly with young Billy Jenkins. Could Oliver have had some kind of secret rendezvous set up with Billy?'

'That's absurd. They weren't friends. There's three years at least between them. More. They're at the same school, but in wildly different worlds. What are you suggesting now? That Oliver shot the Jenkins boy, too? Is that what all this is about? You come here, to my office, and show all kinds of sympathy, and it's just to trick me into ...'

'No. No,' Karen said loudly enough to break into his gathering rage. 'I am not suggesting any such thing. I am trying to find out who could have terrorized your son that day. Because I think he was terrorized ... that's why he kept saying he was protecting Suzie from the devil.'

She didn't add that she was now more or less convinced the so-called protection had included killing Suzie so the devil couldn't get at her.

Philip was beginning to relax. At least he wasn't shouting any longer.

'Olly sometimes went to Ryde,' he said. 'He's got friends there. Well, the nearest thing the poor boy has to friends. They used to meet near one of the hotels there.'

'The Star?' Karen suggested.

'Yes.' Philip looked surprised. 'Why? What do you know about it?'

'Nothing much,' Karen said quickly. 'But I know Suzie liked it. Maybe they met there that afternoon and something ...'

Her phone rang. She wasn't going to answer it. But the knowledge that it could be the hospital stopped her being able to think about anything else. She got to her feet and thanked Philip for seeing her. 'You've been very helpful.'

'Betrayed my daughter,' he said. His face was like a mask, hiding everything except pain. 'But when your son's killed someone, none of the things that once mattered so much are worth a damn. I wish to God it was all over. I can't think why the police won't just charge him and get on with it.'

'I'm sure,' Karen said, seeing at last how conflicted Philip must have been for years as he tried to feel the right things for his difficult son and to contain his emotionally brutal but beloved daughter. 'But they have to get it right. I should go.'

He opened the door of his office for her and stood, watching as Karen walked down the long corridor to the stairs. She could feel the fierceness of his attention. When she reached the stairs, she looked back to where Philip was standing in the doorway of his office. Karen thought she'd never seen anyone lonelier.

She also thought of something else she needed to ask and quickly retraced her steps. He waited for her, looking as though he expected a blow.

'Are you by any chance a member of Giles Henty's investment syndicate?' she asked and watched his face quiver in relief. 'I know you used to shoot with him, so I thought maybe you were in this too.'

'No.' He gave a quick bark of laughter. 'I'm far too cautious for that lot. They pride themselves on laughing at fear, while I'm what the trade calls "risk-averse".'

'Me too,' Karen said with warmth. 'In that case, do you know any of them? I need to talk to someone.'

Philip looked at her with so much speculation that she had to rustle up an excuse.

'He was waiting to get under way to see them when Suzie was killed,' she said. 'I just need to get the whole picture of everything that happened that afternoon, what he said when he told them he couldn't make it. That kind of thing.'

Now Philip was staring at her as though she was a lunatic, but he gave her three names, all of men, and all living, he told her, between Lymington and Chichester. Unfortunately he had neither phone numbers nor addresses.

'Thanks,' she said. 'Just one more thing: what happened on the morning when I . . . when I met Olly at the Blazons' house?'

Philip sank his head into his hands again. From behind their protection he grunted, then straightened up to say firmly, 'You can't pin this on Caroline, whatever she did or didn't do when they were children. She wasn't up by the time I left for work that morning, but Olly was. I could see from his face that he . . . Oh God! He said he was fine, but I could see . . . I put it down to more nightmares, but maybe it was worse. I should have . . . Thank God he didn't hurt anyone that day. Not seriously anyway.'

Karen thanked him once more and left him to his own nightmares. Outside his office building, she listened to her voicemail. The message hadn't come from the hospital. It had been dictated by her mother, prattling on in a much friendlier voice than any she'd used recently. Now, it seemed she wanted contact details for Karen's publisher to see whether they would buy in the services of her advertising agency.

Karen switched off the phone before the end of the message, muttering 'over my dead body'. Soon she'd have to tell her mother Aidan wasn't coming to England at all this year, and probably never again. But that would have to wait. She hailed a taxi, asking to be taken to the Star in Ryde.

The taxi pulled up outside the hotel. From out in the street, Karen could see the welcoming flicker of a big log fire. She pushed open the door and was greeted by a gush of wood smoke, freshly drawn beer and strong cheese.

A group of three men in suits were leaning against the bar, which had been stylishly decorated with garlands of evergreen shrubs lightened with an occasional matte-gold bauble. The drinkers looked so much at home that they had to be regular customers.

Jerry Eagle showed no sign of recognition when he came to serve Karen. She asked for a glass of the house red wine, then consulted the bar menu and settled on a toasted ham and cheese sandwich with salad. The fire was burning in a huge brick-lined hearth at the far end of the room, and there were brown leather sofas and chairs grouped round it. A low table, well stocked with newspapers, stood between them.

'Can I have it there?' she asked, pointing.

Jerry nodded. 'I'll bring it over.'

Karen read the Island's local paper while she waited, sipping her wine.

'This isn't bad,' she said, when Jerry brought her sandwich. 'Have you got a minute?'

'Why?' His narrow face was full of suspicion and his dark eyes glinting in the fire's flickering light.

'Do you remember me?'

'You're the police psychologist.'

'Great,' Karen said, trying the effect of a smile. It didn't lessen his wariness. 'When I was last here, you told me Suzie had to keep all knowledge of your ...' She hesitated then said, 'your relationship from her family.'

'So?'

'But especially, you said, you had to keep it from her uncle. Why was that?'

Jerry turned away.

'Why was he more important than her mother, say?'

'Keep your voice down,' Jerry hissed. 'OK, so I worked for him sometimes. Freelancing. In my free time. It's my time, so why shouldn't I?'

'But your boss doesn't like it?' Karen suggested and received a nod in return. 'OK. I'll keep that quiet. And it was in his house you met Suzie, wasn't it? What did you do there?'

Jerry shrugged, untying and then retying the neat strings of his stylish black apron. 'Bar stuff when they had parties. I met her at one of the bigger thrashes.'

'At home or on the boat?'

Jerry shied, like a horse spooked by a sudden unexpected movement.

'You have been on his boat, haven't you?' Karen had come to think he could be the weakest link in Giles's chain and she was going to break it if she could.

He came closer to her, keeping his back to the three drinkers at the bar. 'Yeah, I have. But I never did anything to hurt Suzie, so I don't know why you're asking.'

'It wasn't just bar duties, though, was it?' Karen kept her

voice quiet and warm but tried to infuse it with authority. 'You sold ... well, you sold the stuff for him, too, didn't you?'

'How do you ...?' Jerry's hands clenched.

'It's obvious. He wanted you to build up a customer base for him here, didn't he?

Jerry looked round, as though to check that there were no spies within earshot.

'Not here in the bar,' Karen said. 'He'd never have done anything so obvious. He wanted you to sell to some of the kids at your old school, didn't he?'

Jerry's head drooped.

'There's CCTV there.' Karen knew she must sound remorseless and was glad of it. Like anyone else who sold drugs, he was a wrecker of lives: not just those of his customers, but of their families too, and everyone else they hurt or short-changed in their pursuit of a temporary high.

Karen thought of the agony she'd seen in Philip's eyes, and of Suzie's mutilated body. Jerry might be only a small player, but that didn't let him off the responsibility.

'Even if there's nothing actually showing you taking money,' she added, keeping her eyes steadily staring into Jerry's, 'and handing out little packages in return, there'll be enough to show which pupils the police need to talk to. One of them will talk, you know. Someone always does, once the right questions are asked.'

'For fuck's sake, shut up,' Jerry whispered. 'If anyone knew ... If he thinks I ... He'll kill me. You too.'

Karen got to her feet. 'You've got to talk to the police,' she said. 'They can—'

'Don't tell me they'll protect me.' Jerry looked at her with a kind of pity. In the circumstances it made her detest him even more. 'They can't. He can go anywhere, do anything. Haven't you worked that one out yet?'

'What about Oliver?' Karen asked, not bothering to answer his question. 'Did you sell to him, too, Jerry?'

'Never. I never. Not after the first time. Too dangerous. I told him I wouldn't.'

'What happened to make you so careful?' Karen asked, holding onto her temper with difficulty.

'Olly had a bit, right at the start. I didn't sell him that. The old man wanted free samples given out. Billy did it, handed them out to all the known big users at the school and told them to come to me if they wanted more. Olly came and I sold him more, and he went ape, completely wild. I thought he was going to kill me. So I said to the old man he mustn't have any more. Too dangerous. People would start asking questions and we'd be right in the shit. That was when he said he'd kill me if I ever . . .'

Karen thought of the old Tom Lehrer song about the drug dealer and his free gifts. Giles was nearly the right age to have heard it the first time around. Her hatred of him made her hands curl into claws.

'You have to talk to the police,' she said again. 'I'll take you in. When does your relief come on duty?'

'Three. I told you last time you were here.' Jerry sounded pettish now. 'But I'm not talking to the cops. If you say any of this, I'll tell them you made it up.'

Could he really be as weak as he seemed?

'Call up your relief and get him over here now,' Karen said, hoping she could push Jerry over the line. 'No need to tell your boss why. Say you're ill, diarrhoea or something that makes it unhygienic for you to work at the bar. You'll probably be able to do a deal with the police so they give you anonymity and you get to save your skin. Oh, and before I forget . . .'

'Yeah?' He didn't look cooperative.

'When you're phoning your relief, ask him if Olly was here the day you were off duty with Suzie . . . Before she was killed.' Karen picked up her plate and glass, then added, 'I'll come and eat this at the bar, then as soon as your relief arrives we can go. Have you got your car?'

Jerry nodded. He had picked up her napkin and his hands twisted the fabric round and round, tighter and tighter, until it looked like a rope.

'Are you really so scared of him?' she asked a little more kindly. 'Why?'

'I told you, he'll kill me if he thinks I grassed him up.' Jerry's voice was still very quiet but that didn't destroy its conviction. 'Look what happened to Billy.'

'Hey!' shouted one of the men at the bar. 'Anyone working here today?'

Jerry rolled his eyes at Karen and hurried off to do his job. She followed him, much more slowly, carrying her plate and glass in one hand, with her laptop bag slung over the other wrist.

Jerry had already taken the money for the drinker's refill by the time she reached the bar.

'Go on,' she said. 'Phone.'

'I can't.'

'Then I'll have to get the police to come here for you.'

Karen thought Charlie would happily race over from the incident room, unless he'd forgotten his first dislike of Jerry. Charlie had always been certain Jerry knew more about Suzie's killing than he'd pretended. 'And you must have had a bellyful of them already. They've searched your car, haven't they?'

He nodded and the dark hair flopped across his narrow pale forehead.

'You're lucky they didn't find any traces of the stuff there. How's it packed?'

He said nothing, but he shivered.

'Are you a user? Is that the hold Giles has over you?'

'Don't be stupid.'

'Then what is it that makes you do everything he tells you?'

'I told you,' Jerry said, sulky now and turning away from her. 'He'll kill me if I don't. And I've got, like, debts, see.'

Karen slipped off the bar stool, leaving her half-eaten food and untouched drink on the bar. Outside, she phoned Charlie to tell him everything she had asked and Jerry had told her, adding at the end, 'I'll wait for you here. I won't be able to stop him physically if he decides to run, but he doesn't strike me as the active type. And he's scared shitless.'

'Frightened men do dangerous things,' Charlie said. 'Don't do anything stupid yourself, will you?'

'I . . .'

'Anything else stupid, I mean,' he added. She could hear in the way the pitch of his voice bounced that he was on the move. 'You know what he'll be doing now, don't you? Phoning Giles. Telling him you've been sniffing around asking dangerous questions. Which will give Giles all the time he needs to destroy any evidence.'

'But ...'

'Get away from there now, Karen.'

'I can't until I know you've got him,' she said, not prepared to see this chance ignored. 'And that you'll listen to him. And search Giles's boat.'

'Get the hell away from there as fast as you fucking well can and leave this to the pros.' Beneath the anger roughening Charlie's voice, she thought she could hear fear. 'You've exceeded your brief by miles. Go and sit by Will's bed, where you'll be safe. I'll phone you.'

I bloody won't, she thought, and looked at the poster in the pub's window, promising Wi-Fi. She went back in, unzipping her laptop bag.

'Hi,' she said to Jerry, casually smiling as though they were strangers. 'I need to use the Wi-Fi.'

He gave her the code, glaring at her with pointless hatred, and started to wash glasses vigorously enough to risk a whole sinkful of breakages.

Karen went back to the table in front of the fire, almost able to enjoy the smell of the wood smoke still, and kept half an eye on what Jerry was doing, while she Googled the names of the three members of Giles's investment club Philip had given her. She found addresses and phone numbers for them all, but – again – nothing about their financial prowess.

The screen also provided her with the number for her car insurance. She should have called them as soon as she'd learned of the crash, but other things had been more important. Now she needed a car. She rang the company and was quickly put through to the claims department. Having explained where the car was and what had happened to it, she added that it might form part of the evidence in a criminal trial and that she would need a courtesy car while everything was sorted out.

'No problem,' said the voice at the other end of the line. 'Just one moment and I'll give you the details.' After a short pause, the voice went on, 'Would you like it delivered to your address in Southampton, or would you prefer to pick it up?'

'Delivered, please,' Karen said, amazed that anything could be so simple. She'd never had an accident and had paid out thousands in insurance with an irrational feeling that the inconvenient hugeness of the payments would guarantee her safety.

'Fine,' said the helpful voice at the company's call centre. 'The car will be with you tomorrow morning before ten. Is there anything else I can help you with?'

Karen thanked her, still astonished, and packed up her laptop and phone. A flashing blue light caught her eye through the window and she looked down the room. Jerry had seen the light too and was standing with both hands pressed down on the bar, an expression on his face that surprised her. There was no fear in it, only a kind of resigned determination.

Annie walked into the pub with two uniformed constables following her. She ignored Karen and went straight up to the bar.

'Hi, Jerry. Time to come with us.'

'Are you arresting me?' he said, now showing a hint of smugness, which worried Karen.

Jerry should have sounded as frightened now as he had when he'd been telling her of Giles's threats.

'Not just now,' Annie said. 'But we do need to talk. And the nick is the best place for it.'

'I'm not coming with you,' he said, flicking a derisive glance at Karen. 'I don't have to unless you're arresting me.'

Annie heaved a sigh. 'Have it your own way. Jerry Eagles, I am arresting you on suspicion of the sale of a controlled drug. You do not have to say anything but it may harm your defence if you do not mention when questioned something you later rely on in court. Anything you do say may be given in evidence.'

The three suited men looked as though she or Jerry had thrown something disgusting at them. All of them reached for their briefcases and pushed their way past the police and out of the bar, the last one eyeing Karen's still figure in surprise.

Jerry waited till they'd gone, then said he'd have to lock up because there was no one else on the premises and he couldn't leave the bar unattended.

Karen picked up her own bag and set off to follow the men. As she passed Jerry, he looked at her with such threatening eyes that she shivered.

'Come on Jerry.' Annie's voice was brisk. 'I haven't got all day.'

He stripped off his apron and dried his hands on it, saying over his shoulder, 'You'll have to wait, won't you? My brief's a busy bloke. You could do worse than phone him now, cos you won't be able to ask me anything till he's there.'

So much, Karen thought, for the innocent boy seduced by a manipulative young woman she had imagined the first time she had come here to the Star in Ryde. Now she knew there was nothing innocent about Jerry.

His voice caught her attention. 'Hey, you, the shrink.'

She turned back to face the threat. This time the clearest emotion in his expression was malice.

'I did phone the other barman,' he said. 'He never saw Olly on the day Suzie died.'

Chapter 21

Will's breathing was heavy and sounded painful, but all the nurses on the ward had assured Karen it was normal for someone recovering from a punctured lung. Full recovery was going to take a long time, but it would come. He was no longer in danger.

He woke sometimes, they said, and still made sense, so there was no problem about the fact that he kept drifting in and out of consciousness. All his organs were working as they should. The loss of his spleen would be inconvenient in the future – making him prone to infection, probably – but it was not life-threatening.

He still looked terrible, though; much worse than when he'd come round and spoken to Karen just after the operations. His face, which had always been spare, was now cadaverous. His stubble was golden, like his hair, but his skin was the colour of dust, and his cheeks were sunken. His hands, scraped and bandaged, never stopped moving as they lay on the blanket over his body. One hand would clasp the other, then let go, even while he was unconscious, then the fingers would lace together. Sometimes his lips moved, too, as though he were trying to speak.

Whatever was happening in his brain was troubling him. Was he afraid? Or was there something he was trying to tell her?

Karen sat, hating her powerlessness, longing to help and not being able to do anything. She couldn't keep her mind from taunting her with a scene from Hemingway's *Farewell to Arms*, when the nurses have promised the hero his lover won't die after the stillbirth of their baby and yet she does die.

Watching Will's troubled hands, trying not to let her nightmares become too real, Karen felt as though an iron band were being tightened around her head.

'Karen!' Max's familiar gravelly voice was muted, and his hand came down on her shoulder with a gentle warmth she had never felt from him before.

She brought up one of her own hands to lay it on top of his and tipped her head sideways so that her cheek lay on that.

'I came the instant I heard,' he said. 'What happened?'

'Thanks,' she whispered, determined not to wake Will until his body signalled that it would be safe.

Max let her go and came back a few moments later, carrying another of the visitors' chairs, which he placed at an angle to hers so that he could see her face.

'Now, Karen. Tell me.'

Without intending to, she poured out the whole story, as she saw it, just managing to hang on to enough professional discretion to withhold the names of all the players in the Island drama. When she'd laid it all out for Max, she added the nightmare possibility that someone might have been trying to stop her questions there by crunching her car with a stolen digger, only to get the wrong driver so that Will was lying in her place, broken and in danger. At the end, she wiped her eyes and looked directly at Max:

'It happened just after I ...' She broke off, unable to put it into words.

'What, Karen? Come on, tell me.' Max waited, and then, when she couldn't speak, he prompted her, 'You'd said you would marry him. That it?'

Karen nodded, then corrected herself, 'More or less. I didn't actually say those words. But he knew what I meant.'

Max hitched his chair closer to hers so that their knees were touching.

'And now you're blaming yourself for his near death in a car accident for which you feel responsible. Karen, use your brain. You know what this is about. You've always felt guilty over the way your shit of a husband killed himself in his car. You haven't been able to trust yourself with Will because your subconscious has continually made you believe that you have only to love someone to become a mortal danger to them.'

Karen's eyelids closed, as though she were rejecting the analysis. But Max wouldn't let her off.

'You know it. I know it. Probably Will knows it, too. That's why I told him to make you angry days ago, to invade your personal space, take you for granted, treat you badly. You have to understand that no thought of yours – however violent – could do him any harm at all, let alone actually kill him.'

Karen looked at Will's body and had an instant, flashing vision of it on the mortuary slab, with the pathologist peeling back his face.

She covered her own with both hands, silently begging her mind to stop messing about with her. Brace up, she told herself. Brace up and you'll be fine.

'What?' Max said, as though she'd been talking to him. 'I can't hear.'

She looked at him again. 'You're right, of course. But it doesn't help, because here he is, like this. If I hadn't agreed to become involved in the Island investigation ... if I hadn't made Will swap his list so that he could come to the site with me ... if ... if ... if ...'

Max pushed back his chair and stood up. 'Up with you. We can't talk here. And we need to talk. Come on.'

Karen obeyed and let him take her out to the nurses' station, where he made her wait while he asked for Will's prognosis. She listened to the reassurance and the medical explanations she had already heard and tried to believe Will would one day be himself again. When the nurse stopped talking, Max thanked him and then towed Karen towards the lifts and on down to the ground floor.

'Now, we are going to have dinner and you are going to eat and drink,' he said. 'And you are going to talk about Will and let yourself believe in the future and you are going to get all this ...'

'Out of my system?' Karen suggested, with a flicker of her old humour. 'Max, it's kind of you to—'

'It's not kind. You're my friend and so is Will.' Max had sounded completely unsentimental, as though he were stating an obvious fact. 'Come on.'

'I can't,' Karen said. 'I've got too much to do. Listen, Max, can you get me in to see a patient who's under section in the adolescent secure unit?'

'Of course not. I have no authority there.'

'You must know someone. I need to talk to the boy.'

'The boy who killed your fifteen-year-old victim? Don't be absurd. Of course you can't get in to see him. Not unless the police ask you to.'

'Suit yourself.' She was angry that he wouldn't help when there was so much to sort out. 'I've got lots of other people to see. They may help.'

'Karen, stop! Talk to your policeman before you do anything else.'

She laughed in his face, a mirthless cruel sound she hated.

'*You?*' she said. 'Wanting me to talk to Charlie, while your friend Will is fighting for his life? Don't be silly.'

Max grabbed her by both arms. 'You're irrational. Calm down. And come and eat with me. You need carbs to . . .'

'Tranquillize me?'

'Stop second-guessing me and finishing my sentences, woman. You need carbs to stop your mind roaring pointlessly round and round like this. For the moment at least, your judgment's gone. Which means you *are* dangerous.'

He took her by the wrist and towed her out of the hospital and towards Millbrook Road, where they should be able to pick up a cab to take them to Mario's restaurant in the Old Town.

Karen gave up fighting before the first taxi responded to Max's wave. He let go of her wrist at once. They didn't talk on the way. Karen stared out of the window, towards the dark heavy sky, noticing the garish Christmas decorations all round and hating them all. At moments she could see out towards the Island, but even that familiar view did nothing to lift her mood.

When the driver stopped outside the door of the restaurant, she took out her phone.

'I will talk to Charlie now,' she said and was glad to hear her voice sounding normal again. Max's intervention had cut off the hysteria. 'Thanks for the rescue.'

He turned aside to pay the driver, then moved out of earshot but not out of sight, and leaned against a handy wall with his arms crossed, watching her carefully. The taxi performed a U-turn and clanked away.

'Charlie,' Karen said the instant he answered, 'I'm sorry about this morning. I shouldn't have done it, but I was so frustrated. Is Jerry talking?'

'Jerry Eagles?' Charlie said in a voice that told her he was even more angry than she had yet seen him. 'Why would he? He has the toughest brief on the Island and he's saying "no comment" to most questions, occasionally varying the pace with "Why are you asking me all this? You're as mad as the shrink who barged into the bar this lunchtime accusing me of all sorts." You've made me look like an arsehole, Karen.'

'How's Jerry able to afford a solicitor like that on a bartender's salary? Is someone else paying him?'

'He's doing it pro bono.'

'Bollocks,' said Karen, without a moment's thought.

'You better hope it's not bollocks.' A certain grim humour warmed Charlie's voice.

'It sounds as if you think there *is* another client.' Something sparked in Karen's mind. 'Who?'

'You think either Eagles or his solicitor is going to tell us?'

'Then you have to get a warrant to search the *Dasher*.' Karen wanted to bang her head on the restaurant window she felt so frustrated. 'You have to, Charlie.'

'No point. Giles Henty invited me to send the CSI on board to search it. He'd never have done that if there was anything there.' Now there was the faintest trace of pity in Charlie's voice. It didn't help Karen's mood. 'Days ago, when we were looking for the knife.'

'What?' Fury could bubble up like magma, she discovered, even breaking through the crust of guilt. 'Why the hell didn't you tell me when I first said you should search the boat?'

'Because I was pissed off, and it's nothing to do with you. Giles thought someone could've taken the knife on board and hidden it when he was off running up the marina to look for Suzie.'

'Why would anyone believe anything so absurd? Charlie, this is more misdirection. You've got to . . .'

'Shut up and listen. There's a shadow on the CCTV,' Charlie said. 'You can't see much, but it shows movement that could have been made by someone running, bent double probably, towards the *Dasher*, just after the body was discovered, moments after Giles ran up the marina, looking for Suzie. He's clear as clear on it. We had him in and showed him the shadow and asked if he could identify it. He said he couldn't but insisted that we search the boat; said it was

obvious the killer was trying to stash the knife there ...
Which was crap.'

'Of course,' Karen said. 'You'd drop it in the sea, not break
into a boat and hide it there. So ...'

'So we didn't do a full search,' Charlie agreed. 'But to
pacify Henty, we did get the CSI to take a look. Nothing had
been disturbed. No blood stains.'

Karen shut off the call without saying anything else. Max
pushed himself off the wall with one bent foot, looking almost
like the lone judgment-bringer from an arty Western.

'Food,' he said, when he reached her side. 'You look as if
you're about to lose it again.'

Back in her flat two and a half hours later, full of soothing
spaghetti puttanesca, Karen trawled through the internet,
looking for any site that could give clues to the most likely
hiding places in an antique yacht like the *Dasher*. A modern
yawl could, Karen soon discovered, have taken a huge
amount of drugs hidden inside the mast, but that would work
only with a new aluminium rig, and her memories of the
Dasher told her Giles had stuck with the classic, traditional
wooden version.

The more she looked, the more she found. There were all
kinds of places where Giles could have installed a false floor or
ceiling – or whatever shipbuilders might call them. Bearing in
mind Charlie's stubborn refusal to take her seriously, she dug
around for the correct terms, which might help persuade him
she wasn't going off on a mad frolic. It wasn't difficult. The
ceiling was a 'deckhead'.

Right up in the bows was something called a forepeak,

where the anchor chain was stowed. Under the chain was a huge space. Presumably anything kept there would get very wet, but proper waterproof wrappings could seal almost anything. Other spaces revealed themselves as she tracked through the websites. Many yachts had big gaps under the forward berths, too, where storm sails were usually stowed. But if the sails were left behind, you could get a lot in their place.

One internal shot of the cabins in a big wooden yawl under restoration showed beams just like the ones in the floor of a house, lateral beams with long teak strips running fore and aft on top. Wires and what looked like ducting had been fitted in the spaces, and some panels had already been placed to conceal the wires, leaving the beams themselves exposed. What was to stop you fitting a deckhead right across the whole lot? You could store any amount of well-packed contraband up there.

Karen wished she knew more about sailing. Presumably the extra weight of an illicit cargo would make the boat hard to handle. And the load would have to be tightly packed to stop it shifting from side to side and exaggerating any rolling. You'd have a real risk of capsize if you got that one wrong. Even she could see that. But if the *Dasher* had a full deckhead concealing the beams, it had to be worth Charlie's while to see what else was hidden there.

She copied the web page showing the boat's restoration. This wasn't exactly the same kind of yacht as Giles's *Dasher*, but they'd both been built at the start of the twentieth century and she couldn't believe there would be that much difference in their forepeaks or deckheads.

With her fingers lying on the keyboard for a moment, she considered the best way of persuading Charlie to take her seriously. At last she opened her email and typed fast.

You have to make a proper search of the boat. Giles has
been misdirecting you throughout. Look at the attached to
see the kind of spaces he could have on board. If there's
any sign of false decks or deckheads, or hidden catches,
then you'll have leverage to make him talk. And
justification for a forensic accountant. K

Next morning, when she found no answering email, she reached for her phone and called Annie.

'Karen.' Annie's voice was as brisk as it had been in the Star. 'What now?'

'I want your help to get Charlie the result he needs,' she began, remembering what Annie had said in the mortuary right at the start of all this, when she'd hoped he would make a success of the investigation.

'You've been winding him round your little finger throughout this case. Why bother with me now? Has he said no to you at last?'

'Have you been talking to Eve Clarke at the Cowes nick?' Karen asked, almost in despair. Knowing what had to be done and being forbidden to do it was like being stuck in a nightmare and seeing her means of escape from some appalling threat but never able to reach it.

'As little as possible,' Annie said, sounding more human. 'But I get the point. What do you want?'

'I have to talk to Oliver again, and I can't go into the secure unit without authorization. Charlie doesn't believe where I'm going with this, and ...'

'And he's so angry after yesterday,' Annie finished for her, 'that you know he wouldn't agree.'

'But I think I can get what we need from Olly now. Please, Annie. Can't you come with me?'

'Charlie would kill me if he found me gone and something kicked off here with Jerry.'

'You're not still interviewing him, are you?' Karen said in surprise.

'Not me. But we are holding him.'

So maybe I haven't screwed up quite as badly as Charlie thinks I did, Karen told herself, and waited.

'Sorry, Karen. It's more than my job's worth. Bye.'

Annie had gone.

Karen wanted to hit something. Suddenly the lingering aftertaste of last night's garlic, anchovies and Parmesan felt horrible in her mouth and she ran to the bathroom to scrub her teeth over and over again until the coldness of the water and the crispness of the peppermint toothpaste had banished all traces of everything else.

Reaching for her phone, she tried Philip's number. This might piss off Charlie even more, but it was the only way Karen could envisage of getting to the truth.

Philip's secretary held Karen off for a full minute, and his voice was cold and wary when he eventually came on the line.

'What now?' he said.

'I need to talk to Oliver,' Karen said, without any pretence. 'I won't disturb him, but ...'

'You couldn't promise that. Anything can disturb him. What do you want to know?'

'I need to find out about the sweater, the blue cashmere sweater: what he did with it; to whom he gave it and when.' She paused for a second, but Philip didn't comment. 'And I want you to ask him to write down a description of the devil's face.'

'Oh for God's sake! Karen, you must know as well as I – sod it – better than I, that hallucinations and delusions of religious figures are highly common in schizophrenia.'

'Philip,' she said, touched that he'd used her name, as though they were friends and he trusted her, 'I still believe there was a real live human being who terrified Olly that afternoon. I think he did stab Suzie, but I believe now that he was deliberately provoked into doing – if not precisely that – then something violent and dangerous. I did once ask him to draw me a picture ...'

'That wouldn't have done you any good. He panics when asked to draw. We've never understood why.'

'I know that now, but I didn't at the time. But I've been told that words are his thing.'

'True enough.'

'So I need him to describe the devil in words.' Karen waited, knowing this was her only chance, short of disguising herself as a member of staff in the secure unit and blagging her way in to see him. She definitely could not do that and keep her professional credibility – or Charlie's friendship.

'I may not be a criminal lawyer,' Philip said, 'but I know enough to be absolutely certain it would do you no good in court.'

Karen couldn't tell him that she was far more concerned to make Charlie see the truth at the moment than to get a conviction.

'Are you in touch with the staff in charge of Olly?' she asked, realizing far too late that she could have sorted all this out days ago.

'Of course. Both my wife and I visit when we can.'

'Then could you ask the doctor to ask Olly to do this? Even better, get Olly's solicitor to ask the doctor to do it. That way there could be no accusation of either you or me influencing what Olly writes.'

'Why?' Now Philip sounded sharp. 'Do you suspect someone in particular?'

'Don't you?'

'No,' Philip said with the determination of a martyr prepared to put up with flames of an *auto-da-fe* rather than recant.

He cut her off. She stared at the phone then out of the window towards the Island. Why would a civilized, experienced man like Philip Matken bang down the phone without a word?

Her email pinged. Bracing herself for a blast of fury from Charlie, she looked and saw her mother's name in the inbox.

With nothing more to do until one of her fishing expeditions produced a catch, she opened her mother's message.

What have you done now? I've just heard from Aidan that he's not coming back after all. When I asked why he said you'd tell me. Have you quarrelled? Put him off? *Why*, Karen? I've been waiting for him to come home for years.

Dillie
PS He told me your boyfriend's in hospital. Sorry about
that. I hope he recovers soon.

'So do I,' Karen said aloud, staring at a great flock of black
birds that were swirling around the big windows of her flat,
blocking the view. 'Oh God! So do I.'

Chapter 22

Day Nine: Thursday 10.30 a.m.

The black birds had gone half an hour later, and glimmers of sunlight quivered between the gaps in the clouds. The rain had stopped too.

Karen felt years younger than she had when she'd woken, and she found herself singing a tuneless version of one of her grandmother's favourite folk songs as she plugged in the kettle and thought about what sort of coffee she was going to brew.

> 'Early one morning, just as the sun was rising,
> I heard a maid sing in the valley below:
> "Oh, don't deceive me, oh, never leave me!
> How could you use a poor maiden so?"'

She had forgotten until she reached the last two lines that the song was a complaint rather than a paean to the rising sun and laughed at herself. Leaving the coffee to drip, she picked up the phone to find out how Will had weathered the night.

The nurse who answered her call told her that he'd slept, eaten a reasonable meal at breakfast and was now awaiting the consultant's rounds. Even though formal visiting was not allowed until after the post-lunch quiet hour, Karen was told she would be welcome any time after twelve.

She put down the phone and looked out of the window again. The sun was brighter than ever. Even though there were still some dark clouds, they didn't look too threatening. She hadn't had any exercise for days and thought she might walk to the hospital. That would take up nearly all the fifty minutes until twelve, and the steady pacing might help her brain produce some more useful ideas about how to prove Giles was Olly's devil.

Out in the small hall was the cupboard where she kept the various bits of sports equipment she had bought since Will came into her life and tried to make her share the kind of fitness he cherished in himself. There were some sturdy but amazingly comfortable boots and a padded down jacket that could see off the bitterest of winds.

Wrapped in that, she added a beanie over her straight blonde hair and some leather gloves, before grabbing her keys. On the point of double-locking the front door behind her, she thought of her last plea to Philip and went back inside to unplug her laptop, stow it in its bag and attach the shoulder strap. She would be eaten alive with frustration if she came home to find that Olly had produced something useful and she'd cut herself off from all contact.

Outside, the wind hit her in the face. Luckily it was coming up from the south and she was heading almost due west. She shoved her gloved hands in the pockets of the down jacket, set her shoulders forward and her face down and headed off towards the hospital, calling in at a newsagent's on the way for a Kit-Kat to keep her going.

By the time she reached the big, low, brick-and-glass building, the sun was blazing, as though it had been tricked into believing this was mid-summer. Karen had to unzip the jacket and felt almost as hot as if she'd been in a sauna. But it was all worthwhile when she reached Will's ward and saw him sitting up against his pillows, looking himself again in the high-quality blue cotton pyjamas she had bought him. His hair was longer than he usually kept it, but he had brushed it and shaved and was wearing his glasses and reading *The Times*. He was his own man again.

'Wow!' Karen said from the doorway.

Will looked up, took off his glasses and looked again, smiling as though his face would crack open.

Karen crossed the pristine highly polished vinyl floor to kiss him. He grabbed her hand and held on.

'I've always known when you were here,' he said, 'even when I couldn't drag myself out of the morass to answer you.'

'And I knew today was the day,' she said. 'I ate with Max yesterday and felt dreadful. First thing this morning was awful too. Then something happened, just over an hour ago. I felt as if I'd been carrying a load of manure someone had suddenly lifted off me.'

'Must have been when I insisted they let me shave and change into the glamorous pyjamas you left for me,' he said, pulling at her hand so that she bent down again and was kissed. 'You look a bit haunted though.'

He really is all right, she thought, if he can see and comment on something like that.

'This case has been a bit of a pig,' she said.

'"Has been"?' he quoted. 'It's over then?'

'Not quite.' Karen swung the laptop bag off her shoulder and laid it carefully on the floor. 'I'm awaiting the result of my latest drive for the truth. That's what's haunting me. I know – I'm sure I know – what happened, but can anyone get the evidence?'

'Can they, buggery!' Will supplied, which was one of their catchphrases. 'How's Charlie bearing up?'

'He's not. We're barely speaking at the moment.'

'Does that bother you?'

'In a way.' Karen stroked Will's head, then remembered the night Charlie had first come to her flat and stopped. 'I'll get a chair.'

When she came back with the orange plastic chair dangling from her hand, Will had his glasses back on his nose. He examined her over the top of them.

'Charlie,' he said, like a stage prompter.

'He needs to get this case right if his career is to go anywhere,' Karen said, looking at Will without any shadows left in her mind. 'And I need to help him do it if I'm to pay off my debt to him.'

Will frowned. 'I don't understand. What debt?'

'I owe him for introducing me to police work and getting me accredited,' she said, suppressing the knowledge that she'd also used him as a way of stalling while her subconscious got to grips with the idea that she was going to spend her life with Will. 'I always like to pay my debts. Now it's the only way I can move on.'

'To where?'

She clasped her hands on her knees, then moved them to the edge of his bed.

'You may have changed your mind,' she started, 'but if . . .'

His hand came down over hers, warm and secure but not, surprisingly enough, confining.

'I haven't.'

'Great.' She thought of all kinds of romantic ways of saying what had to be said, then settled for the most downbeat of them all, 'Because, as I think you already know, I'm on for it.'

'"It" being?' he said, his glistening eyes telling her he appreciated the lack of drama.

'The whole shebang.' Karen was determined to keep it casual, but she couldn't prevent a smile so wide it was making her face ache. 'Wedding, family if we can, shared house. The lot.'

Will brushed back his hair and nodded. 'Good. That's settled then. So, tell me about the case.'

'Could I just check my email?' Karen said, hearing in her mind all the things neither of them needed to put into words. 'The answer's still out there, but I . . .'

'Go ahead. There's Wi-Fi in the café downstairs. Good luck. I'll be here when you get back.'

She laughed on her way out. Downstairs, the laptop took its usual time loading all the pre-installed programs she had never used and probably never would, but eventually the email inbox flowered on the screen. She had six messages: four could be ignored, but one was from Charlie and one from Philip. There was no attachment icon. Disappointed, Karen opened the message.

Karen, Oliver says he lost the sweater the day Suzie died.
He thinks he may have left it on the *Dasher*. When our
solicitor asked what he was doing there, he said he
wanted to talk to Giles, who invited him on board, where
it was so hot he took off both sweater and fleece. But he
wouldn't say anything else about who else was there or
what they did. When Richard asked Olly to write out a
description of the face of the devil, he said he didn't know
what Richard was talking about. And he professed to
remember nothing at all about how Suzie came to die.
Sorry. P

'Not much help,' Karen muttered to herself. Having no
more reason to delay, she clicked on Charlie's email. The
message, unsigned, read simply:

Consider yourself highly commended

Karen fought her pocket to get out her phone and pressed
9.

'Karen,' Charlie said, sounding more cheerful than he had
for days. 'Got my email?'

'What've you found?'

'The rifle.'

'*What?*' That was the last thing she expected. 'Where?
Why? Who? Come on, Charlie, tell me.'

He laughed. 'I could if you'd stop talking for a minute. We
found it in a false compartment in the forepeak of the *Dasher*.
Well-wrapped and sealed in plastic, under the anchor chain.
It's been wiped of all prints, unfortunately. But secreted in

Giles's boat, not just dumped but actively hidden. Has to help swing the CPS. The rifle's with the lab now. Oh, and you're right about the deckhead: room for kilos and kilos of drugs up there. No evidence of anything, except a tiny scrap of thick polythene caught on the edge of a protruding screw. The plastic's gone to the lab. Pray for drug traces. But it's enough already to persuade my guv'nor we need to get on to the so-called investment club like you said.'

Karen was biting down so hard on all the 'I told you so' comments that she could feel a pain starting up in her head.

'And the dosh you found under Billy's bedroom floor?' Charlie said. His voice couldn't have been more different from yesterday's cold anger.

'Yes?' Karen said, beginning to smile. 'What's the lab found on that?'

'Billy's DNA. Traces of cocaine.'

'And? Come on, Charlie. Don't string me out.'

'And Giles's DNA. All over the package of notes. So you've won, Karen: the forensic accountant from FIU is due to start later today.'

'Meanwhile Giles is denying everything,' Karen said, making a statement of it because she had no doubts whatsoever.

'Right. And I want you ...'

'Go for his wife,' she said, remembering the hatred in Lucy's eyes. 'If she knows anything you should be able to get it now. Specially now you've found the gun that nearly killed her on his boat, and—'

'It's in hand.'

Another memory crashed through her satisfaction.

'And the digger?' she said. 'Have you got anything linking Giles to the digger?'

'Not yet. If we can we will. But the gun and the money should be enough to get him sent down for a long time.'

'Oliver,' Karen said. 'What'll happen to Oliver now? He's claiming he remembers nothing about Suzie's death.'

'He killed her, Karen.' Modified pity had edged into Charlie's voice, but none of the original passionate partisanship. 'Whether Giles had a hand in winding him up or not we'll probably never know, but you have to face the fact that it was Olly who wielded the knife that took her life.'

'When a man sent his pit bull after someone he wanted to punish and the dog killed the victim, it was the owner who was found guilty,' she protested. 'Not the dog. Can I be there when you interview Giles?'

'I'll have to see. Got to go now. Bye, Karen. Oh, and ...?'

'Yes?'

'Thanks.'

Trailing back upstairs to Will's ward, gloomier than she should have been, Karen thought about how much Charlie had once wanted Oliver to be innocent and yet how little he cared now that Olly was under section.

The stairs seemed steeper than before and her legs were aching before she had reached Will's floor. She paused at the turn of the stairs, looking out over the tops of the buildings towards the sea and the Island, and she began to understand.

At first, Charlie must have seen Olly as a victim of his father's loathing, guilty because he'd failed to protect a woman from 'the devil' and vulnerable beneath the veneer of toughness. Sympathizing because of his own childhood experience, perhaps seeing himself in Oliver, Charlie's instincts had all been protective. Later, faced with the evidence outside the Blazons' house that Oliver really was violent after all, Charlie must have visited all his own self-loathing on the boy.

Karen could not let it lie like that, neither for Oliver nor for Charlie himself. And she still had one more idea nagging at the back of her brain.

'It's coming,' she said to Will, who put down the paper at her approach. 'We've nearly got to the end of the case, but I need to help wind it up. D'you mind if I go over to the Island now?'

'You do what you have to do, Karen. I'm not going anywhere. You'll find me here when you're ready.'

She blew him a kiss and ran.

An hour later she was sitting in a corner of the incident room on the Island in front of a blank screen waiting for Annie to bring the CCTV tapes from the marina camera. First she wanted to see the shadow no one had yet identified near the *Dasher*'s gangway, then she wanted the tapes covering the previous four hours. She'd been afraid Charlie would refuse her access, but he had sanctioned this, and Annie had recovered most of her old affectionate support for Karen.

When she came back with the pile of discs, she also had a cardboard cup of coffee.

'Here,' Annie said. 'I know you drink it black without sugar.'

'Thanks.' Karen forced a smile. Coffee connoisseur that she

was, she would never swallow this kind of vending-machine drink with any kind of pleasure, but she didn't want to look graceless. 'Can I see the one with the shadow first?'

Annie slotted it into the computer and then fast-forwarded until she found the part that showed Giles rushing up the marina towards Captain Joe's shop, obviously shouting. Karen leaned forwards, peering into the grainy shadows he'd left behind him.

'There.' Annie's finger with the blunt-cut nail rested on the screen, making a sizzling noise. 'There's the shadow. Can you make out anything we can use?'

She took away her hand and Karen squinted, longing for any hint that could identify Billy. At last she straightened up, her whole face squeezed in disappointment.

'Sod it!'

'We have looked pretty damn carefully,' Annie said in a cool voice, which suggested a judgment withheld. 'I'd have been surprised if you had seen something.'

'I'm sure. Sorry. I just hoped . . . Never mind. Have you got film showing Suzie getting on to the boat?'

'Embarking?' Annie said, with a short laugh. 'Yeah. Hang on.' She shuffled through the hard plastic cases, then opened one. 'Here. It's half an hour, roughly, before Giles runs down after her. And she doesn't actually embark, just puts her foot on the gangplank.'

'OK. And Giles arriving?'

There was no answer. Karen looked up, caught Annie's eye and watched her shrug and colour.

'We haven't had time to look through the rest. Why would we? Nothing to say the *Dasher* was relevant to anything that happened. Not till today anyway, and there's been too much else ...'

'I'll look now.' Karen knew enough about the pressure on the whole team to add, 'You don't have to stay. I can manage.'

'Shout if you need anything,' Annie said, waving to the far end of the big room. 'Unless Charlie calls me, I'll be over there.'

Karen settled down to watch the dreary footage of the marina she now knew so well. Seagulls flew around and landed on the concrete, a few pedestrians wandered into shot and out again. Once a thin black cat slinked across the screen. She blinked to moisten her eyes and hoped she would not have to have recourse to the thin coffee.

Her hand jerked as she recognized a figure heading towards the camera, and warm coffee spilled over her fingers. Hastily putting the film on pause, she mopped up the coffee, hoping none had leaked into the keyboard or any of the unwatched discs, then set the screen moving again.

Oliver scuttled into the picture only about half an hour before Suzie was to arrive. The boy was rushing away from the gangplank, looking over his shoulder, away from the camera. He was wearing jeans and a T-shirt with a slogan on it showing between the unzipped sides of his fleece. When he straightened his head, he was already past the camera so all she could see was the back of his hair and the flopping hood that hung down over his shoulders. With no idea what his face might have told her, she still thought his body and the way he ran looked as though he was terrified – and being chased.

Karen noted the time and then substituted the next earliest disc, looking for his arrival. It came, only ten minutes before his departure. Now, as he walked toward the camera, he looked determined and surprisingly powerful. She could see that the wind was making the sides of his dark fleece flap. Between them was the unmistakable cabled front of the beautiful cashmere sweater. The film was black and white, so she couldn't tell whether the sweater was cornflower blue, but the cable stitching was clear and very familiar. She watched him put one trainer on the gangplank, then the other, then he walked up it and out of shot.

Now all she needed was Giles.

She drained the rest of the tepid liquid in the cup and settled to watch. Another hour crawled by. She dared not fast-forward for fear of missing Giles's figure coming or going. At last she saw him, sauntering along the marina and talking on his phone, not trying to conceal anything, and getting on to his boat sixty-seven minutes before Olly's arrival.

Waving to Annie, Karen put the film on pause.

'Hi,' she said when Annie arrived. 'Can you mark these? I've got the crucial scenes: Giles coming on board. Olly coming on board just over an hour later, looking tough and in control – and wearing his characteristic cashmere sweater – then running away without it, obviously scared, ten minutes after that and about half an hour before Suzie's arrival. I wonder if Giles told him she was due so that he hung about, waiting for her? Shit!'

'What?' Annie asked.

'It's so frustrating! I want to know what Giles told him and why he looks as if he's running away from something terrifying and whether Giles *was* his devil.'

'You'd better hope we get a confession from Giles,' Annie

said, not sounding too hopeful. 'Anything we get out of Olly will be rubbished by the lawyers. You can be sure of that, Karen.'

'Do you know where Charlie is?'

'I can probably find him,' Annie said. 'If you really need him.'

Chapter 23

Day Ten: Friday

Giles was pissed off. Bad enough to be summoned to the police station as though he were some lowlife from the streets but to be questioned in front of the sexy shrink was hell. He'd tried to get Morag Chitterne, his solicitor, to have the Taylor cow barred from the interview, but Morag had told him to chill out and keep his powder dry, so he was doing his best.

Still, he couldn't help glaring at the Taylor cow. She took absolutely no notice. You'd have thought any tall slim blonde with a face like a china doll would be a pushover, even if she was in her thirties and getting a bit stringy. But this one had a mind like a cross between a sewer and a steel trap and wasn't going to let anything go. She'd been banging on about something she called cognitive dissidents and what she thought it had made him do for what felt like hours. Giles couldn't understand why the Geordie cop wasn't reining her in.

She had an OK voice, though: lowish and nice round vowels. She'd have made quite a good receptionist if she hadn't got ideas above her station. Morag kicked him, so he must have been showing too clearly where he thought the shrink should come in the pecking order. He put on an exaggerated smile and waited.

'So, Mr Henty,' the shrink said, as though she expected an answer, 'here you were out of a job and needing to keep up your image of yourself as a rich man.'

Giles didn't see the need to say anything.

'The sale of your London house brought in a bit, but not nearly enough. So you had to find another source of income.' She paused. Giles wasn't going to help. It didn't silence her, though. She pushed him. 'That's right, isn't it?'

He shrugged and smiled again.

'Yah,' he said at last. 'I got together with some mates and we made a few shrewd investments. It was soon hunky-dory.'

This time it was the shrink who smiled a snooty smile. If Cruella de Ville had had a small round face with big blue eyes, long black eyelashes and a rosebud mouth, she'd have looked just like this. Though probably not as tanned.

'But not in the stock market,' she said with a casual air even he could tell was put on.

Giles watched her turn towards the cop, as though she wanted approval, or permission to carry on or something. Instead, he'd obviously had enough of her banging on about her cognitty disowners too, so he shut her up and dumped a small plastic evidence bag on the table. Morag peered at it, then had a good look at Giles himself. He shrugged at her, slightly shaking his head. Hadn't a clue what he was supposed to be looking at.

'What?' he asked the cop when no one said anything. 'Looks like a bit of litter from the beach. What's your problem?'

'It's a piece of waterproof wrapping we found in the concealed compartment above the deckhead in the *Dasher*.' The cop had obviously done a lot of this kind of thing and had no expression in his Geordie voice or on his dark face, but the shrink was silly enough to look excited. Giles wouldn't have minded slapping her pretty little face.

'And the lab has found traces of cocaine on it,' said the cop.

Giles could feel Morag stiffen.

'So?' Giles sent his lawyer a smile as reassuring as any he'd ever given Lucy. 'One of the blokes refitting the *Dasher* probably had a habit and dropped a bit of charlie about the place. It happens. Shouldn't but does. Nothing to do with me.'

'Nothing to do with the way you earned the money you needed to keep up appearances here on the Island?' said the shrink, sounding smug now as well as looking it. 'Nothing to do with the market for coke and crack you were trying to make here by handing out little packages to the school kids?'

'No idea what you're talking about,' Giles said, with a light laugh. He crossed his legs, surprised at how much she knew but certain he could ride this one out.

'You used young Billy Jenkins, didn't you?' she added, as if she really did know all about it.

Giles felt Morag twitch again. She ought to have more self-discipline. He was paying her a fortune to watch his back, not to give out encouraging signals to the plods and their side-kicks.

'Who was it who told you Billy was talking about those free samples?' The shrink didn't sound nearly as much like a good receptionist now; more like the HR bitch who'd explained his severance package. 'Or did you just decide he was too much of a risk, running away like that and so inviting the police into his life – and maybe yours, too? What exactly was it that made you think he had to die to protect your life here as the biggest and richest wheel on the Island?'

'I have – quite literally – no idea what she's talking about.' Giles decided he wouldn't deign to address the shrink directly any more. He'd talk to the cop, but no one else.

'We found the rifle,' the cop said, all man-to-man now. 'You know that. When we searched the *Dasher*, we found the rifle that killed Billy, hidden in the forepeak. No prints, though.'

The Geordie cop glanced at the shrink as if he thought her capable of finding a way to a confession. No chance! If they scared members of the investment club into giving evidence against him, the drug-dealing charges might stick. But they weren't going to get him for anything else.

'Where the police did find your prints, as well as more traces of cocaine, was on the thousand pounds hidden under Billy's bedroom floor at home,' the shrink went on. 'And your DNA on the knife that killed Suzie, which Billy had also hidden under some floorboards.'

'The boy was a notorious thief,' Giles said, pretending to be full of regret. 'I've always carried a fair amount of cash on the boat – you never know when you're going to need it – and I haven't looked at the stash for ages, but I bet he nipped on board and nicked it. Probably took the knife too and gave it to that psychopathic boy to use on my Suzie. I'm glad to hear you've got him behind bars at last. Should've been there long ago.'

'He's in a secure unit,' the shrink said, now sounding like the most repressive of the matrons at his prep school. 'That's not the same thing at all. You did see Oliver that afternoon, didn't you?'

She paused but only for a second, then looked towards the solicitor. 'We have CCTV film that shows him arriving after Mr Henty went on board and leaving ten minutes later, looking distressed. What happened between you that afternoon?'

Giles clenched his eyebrows together across the top of his nose to show how puzzled he was. 'D'you know, I've no idea? The boy arrived at the *Dasher* and asked quite politely if he could come aboard. Son of old friends, I couldn't turn him away, so I let him. He was OK to start with, interested in the boat like any boy would be, then he lost it, like he sometimes did and started shrieking. I couldn't make head nor tail of what he was banging on about. Did my best for a bit; told him to bugger off in the end. I was bored with him by then. Last I saw of him till I went running down the marina to search for Suzie.' Giles paused, then said heavily, 'And you know where he was then and what he was doing.'

'But why did he come?' the shrink said, sounding properly puzzled. 'What was it he wanted to say?'

'God knows. But he's a freak. Didn't have to have a reason for anything he did.'

'Did he talk about Suzie at all?'

'Nope,' Giles said, pleased to be able to tell the truth.

Karen admired the way he met her gaze, without a blink. But something in the quality of his stare made her certain that he was lying. The very steadiness of his eyes showed how much effort he was putting into holding her attention.

There was something else going on; some other player

involved. Karen understood that now. Snippets of conversations she'd had and facts that had been offered to her, only to be filed away in her mind because they didn't fit, came back now, linking together and leading her on.

'Your girlfriend,' she said suddenly. 'The one who so troubled your wife. Who is she?'

'Doctor Taylor, I need a word,' Charlie said, pushing back his chair with a rasp.

As Karen obediently followed him, he told the tape they were leaving. Outside the interview room, he rounded on her, grabbing her wrist in the unintentionally savage way he had.

'*Girlfriend?*' His voice was full of disbelief. 'What d'you mean, girlfriend? You're supposed to be breaking through his emotional defences about the drug dealing and the rifle so he confesses to—'

'It's Caroline Matken,' Karen said, interrupting without any doubt whatsoever. 'She's the one who wound up Olly to kill. I can explain it all, but I don't think there's time now. You said she's due back from Innsbruck today, Friday, didn't you? She'll have heard that Olly's in the secure unit and must be worrying how he might talk – and be believed – if he's been stabilized. You've got to get someone there before she has a chance to get to him. What time is she due back? There can't be many flights into Southampton International. Find out when.'

For all his rages and angst, Charlie might still trust her. If he did, then she had a chance to nudge Caroline into betraying herself. Karen saw him testing his confidence in her, then come to a decision, nodding. While he got someone to check out flight times and went back to put a temporary stop on the interview with Giles, Karen dialled the number of the Matkens' house.

'Hi,' Karen said, when Angela answered. 'It's Karen Taylor. I am sorry to bother you, but I need to ask you how much you know about Caroline's affair with Giles Henty.'

The silence at the other end of the phone was promising. At least there was no denial or accusation. After what felt like hours but can only have been moments, Angela said, 'It wasn't an affair. Not a proper affair. More like a flirtation. Neither of them took it seriously.'

'Are you sure? Did Caroline tell you that?'

'Caroline would never tell me anything.' Now Angela's voice had settled and deepened. It had an edge too. 'But I saw how much better things were recently between Lucy and Giles, and how that irritated Caroline. I added two and two.'

'Does Philip know about it?' Karen asked. Angela laughed.

'Of course not. He'd never notice anything like that. Or believe it if anyone told him. He idolizes her.'

No he doesn't, Karen thought, but she kept it to herself.

'I know she's due back today from Innsbruck. Do you know what time her flight gets into Southampton?'

'It doesn't.'

Karen's whole body tensed.

'There aren't any direct flights. It would've meant two changes. She's coming back via Heathrow. She should've landed at . . . Hang on. I've got it here, I think. Yes, she should have landed a couple of hours ago. Little bit more. And she's got her car, so I'm expecting her back fairly soon. Do you need her? Shall I tell her . . .?'

'No, it's fine. Thanks,' Karen said and turned to see Charlie talking earnestly to Annie.

'There is a flight,' he said to Karen, 'but Caroline's not listed on it.'

She told him why not, adding, 'She must have booked her car on one of the ferries or hovercraft. Can you find out which one – to make sure you get an officer over to the unit to watch Olly?'

'Annie's dealing with it,' he said. 'While we wait, you can tell me the whole thing.'

Karen listed all the links for him, all the half-noticed facts and apparently trivial comments of the past days that made sense of everything else: the unidentified and unclaimed pay-as-you-go phone found at the Matkens' house; the shagging couple the young composer had heard in the flat next to his, the flat that Giles owned; Lucy's saying Giles had been on 'his old phone' before lapsing into a catatonic state at breakfast last Monday, when Olly went rampaging round to see James Blazon; her own conversation with Angela just before she left to meet James Blazon; the small grey hatchback Jerry had noticed parked by the roadside when he dropped Suzie at the top of the marina ...

'It's all circumstantial,' Charlie said, before Karen had reached anything like the end of her list.

'I know,' she said, keeping the details of her plans to herself. 'Which is why you need a confession. It won't be enough on its own, but it'll be a start.'

Karen waited while the car passengers left their vehicles for the short trip back to the Island. At last she saw the slight attractive figure with the Siamese cat's elegance glance into the fuggy cabin, then shiver in distaste and instead lean against the rail outside.

'Caroline!' Karen called, strolling towards her, glad the sea was reasonably calm.

She saw Caroline recognize her and watched the pretty face freeze into an expression of weary distaste.

'What's that stupid dangerous boy done now?' she asked as Karen reached her.

'Nothing,' Karen said, smiling. 'That's not why I came. I wanted to talk to you, warn you what's going on with the police.'

'What do you mean?' Caroline pulled up the fur-lined hood of her elegant cream parka and stuffed her gloved hands into the pockets. She made an alluring picture posed against the green sea and the dull-grey sky. 'You're working with them, aren't you?'

'You probably don't know, but they've arrested Giles Henty.' Karen watched with interest as Caroline's face hardened just a little, then relaxed into a smile that held surprisingly open satisfaction.

'Poor Giles,' she said. 'But what's that got to do with me?'

Karen smiled sympathetically. 'Don't you see how it puts you at risk? Once they've started to unravel it all, he'll talk, and then you're going to be implicated.'

'Don't be ridiculous.'

'They know you and he had a relationship and that he told you it was all off a while before you came back from university on the day Suzie was killed.'

Caroline shrugged her neat little shoulders.

'What they don't know – yet – is that you were so pissed off that you told your volatile, vulnerable brother that Giles was the devil he was always talking about.'

Karen waited for a response, but there was nothing. She ploughed on.

'They will find out that you arranged to meet Olly in Cowes before you went home that day, and that you fed him a large quantity of cocaine and sent him to the *Dasher*.' Karen gave her a chance to protest, but she held her peace. Karen changed her tone to something warmer, and more personal, angrier too. 'What did you hope, Caroline? Were you expecting Olly to kill Giles when you told him that Giles was the devil who'd hurt you so badly? Or did you just want Olly to attack him, give him a few bruises and a fright?'

'You've lost it,' Caroline didn't sound worried, but her brilliant eyes were like a pair of calculators. 'Gone completely tonto.' Her right hand moved in the pocket of her parka.

Karen hoped she didn't share the family habit of carrying a Swiss army knife.

'What I don't understand,' Karen went on, reverting to her formal mode, 'is why you thought Olly would never tell anyone about all those things you said to him before he killed Suzie, or about the cocaine you fed him. Or why you were so sure no one would believe him if he ever did tell. You see, he *is* talking now.'

'That fucking cunt of a boy.' Caroline's pretty face was unchanged, which made the hoarse obscenity shocking. 'He's so thick on top of everything else. I mean, he couldn't even go for someone he hated. He had to go and kill a girl he liked, who'd never hurt anybody.'

She turned away from Karen, facing towards the sea.

'Just like Billy?' Karen said, fighting to keep her voice confident and steady. She knew she might have to try one story after another until she hit exactly the right one. 'He'd never hurt anyone either, but you decided he had to die, too. Why? Did he see you with Olly that day and hear you telling him how Giles was the devil? Was that why you told Giles to have Billy silenced?'

Still Caroline didn't move.

'I'm sure, you see, that you did tell Giles to get rid of Billy. What was it that Billy saw?'

Caroline's left knee twitched suddenly, knocking into the side of the ferry. No other part of her neat body registered any shock at all, but that involuntary tic told Karen she had to be right.

'Did he look up and catch you at the window of the flat, as you waited for confirmation that Olly had attacked Giles? Were you standing there in the room where you and Giles had always had sex, hoping for a double-whammy: Giles dead and Olly in prison for life?'

This time Caroline jammed her left kneecap hard against the ferry's side, as though she too had noticed how its twitching betrayed her and wanted to control it.

'You must have watched Olly going towards the *Dasher*, just like you'd told him to. You must have thought he'd done what you wanted when you saw him come rushing back, looking terrified. Haunted. I've seen the CCTV tapes, so I know what it was like.'

Caroline stood like a stone, staring out to sea, straight into the wind.

'But then before you could leave your vantage point safely,' Karen added even more confidently, 'you saw Jerry Eagles dropping Suzie at the top of the marina. You couldn't leave the flat and go to your car then, could you? You'd have risked being identified by a girl who'd known you all her life. So you waited until Jerry had driven off and Suzie had run down the marina.'

'So?' Caroline's voice was so cold that Karen stared at her in shock. At the very least Caroline must have expected the fifteen-year-old girl to find her uncle beaten and bleeding on his boat. Was she completely callous? Or just unimaginative, as her father had once suggested? 'So what?'

'Were you still there in the flat when she screamed?' Karen said, when she could speak again. 'Did you even think of going to help her? Or were you having too much fun enjoying the drama you'd set up?'

Caroline's hand tightened into a fist in her pocket, making the fabric bulge.

'Was that when you saw Billy? Did you leave the flat and come face to face with him? How did you recognize each other?'

Caroline's parka-covered shoulders shrugged again. Karen felt as though she were trying to split an iceberg with a toothpick.

'Had you met at some school function with your brother? Is that it?'

This time there was no reaction at all. Karen herself shrugged, even though Caroline couldn't have seen the gesture because she was still staring out to sea.

'Not that it matters,' Karen added. 'Maybe you didn't recognize Billy, just put two and two together later, when you heard on the Island grapevine that Giles had found him and returned him to his parents. Either way, you said something to

Giles before the shoot, didn't you? You phoned him and told him Billy was a threat. What did you use to scare Giles? Did you tell him Billy had been gossiping about the free crack he'd handed out for Giles at school? How did you know about that anyway? Had Olly told you? Or had you worked out that Giles must be getting money from somewhere and done your own investigation?'

'This is all nonsense.' Caroline's voice was as sharp as ever, but much higher pitched and tight with the stress she was putting on her larynx. 'What on earth has Giles to do with crack? It's ridiculous.'

Karen laughed. 'You'll never get me to believe you hadn't worked it all out, clever little thing like you. But I can't see why you didn't just shop Giles – anonymously – to the police as a drug smuggler.'

Caroline glanced at Karen over her shoulder with such contempt that Karen's hold on her temper slipped a little.

'Oh, that would have been too easy, would it? A court case, lawyers, at worst a few years in prison. Not like having him physically hurt, to punish him for what he'd done to you.'

Again Karen waited. Again she got no response.

'And then there was me,' she added in a voice that shocked her with its harshness. For a moment she almost wanted Caroline to attack her physically so that she could hit back. Taller and heavier than Caroline, she could have done a lot of damage. But the only weapons she could use were her ideas and her voice.

'Once you'd persuaded Giles to have Billy shot,' she went on more quietly, 'you knew you could make him do anything else you wanted. So when Olly screwed up again and went after Georgie Blazon instead of me, you turned to Giles again. You warned him I was getting too near the truth about his drug business, didn't you?'

Karen paused but Caroline had herself well in control now.

'This is stupid,' she said, but she sounded even less convincing. Karen began to hope.

'So Giles had to organize another "accident", believing it was to protect himself but really to ensure that no one would ever know the part you were playing behind the scenes.' Karen's fight to keep calm was getting harder. 'It might have worked. Just your bad luck I wasn't driving on the day he chose for my accident. Honestly, you should have known that if you want something doing you have to do it yourself.'

The hooter sounded, then the recorded voice telling drivers to return to their cars. Caroline turned and pushed past Karen, who called after her, 'And you nearly killed one of the best, most altruistic, human beings in the world.'

Caroline hesitated for a second, so Karen added, 'All because of what you set in motion to punish Giles and free your life from your schizophrenic brother.'

'I didn't do anything,' Caroline said, turning to face her accuser again. Now Caroline's voice was normal again, relaxed and easy. 'It was Giles Henty who wanted you dead. I had nothing to do with the digger that smashed into your car.'

As near an admission as I'm ever going to get, Karen thought. But good enough for me. I hope she takes the bait.

Postscript

Charlie was carefully helping Will into his favourite chair in Karen's flat. The tall Christmas tree she had decorated in scarlet and gold glowed in the corner. Mozart's Dona Nobis Pacem from the *Missa Brevis* poured out of the speakers. And the smells of turkey and roasting potatoes and spices from the pudding evoked Christmases past for all of them.

Max, who had extracted himself from his obligation to his sister after all, leaned down to pull the cork from the magnum of claret he had gripped between his feet. The cork yielded with a wonderful slow pop and Max raised the great bottle so that he could sniff the contents.

'Aaaah,' he said. 'Should be perfect in about half an hour. Got a glass, Karen?'

She brought him one and watched him pour half an inch of the rich, dark-red wine into it.

'If it won't be ready for a while,' Charlie said, 'I've got some cold champagne in my bag. Thought we ought to toast Karen's success.'

'I'm on for that,' said Will, shifting in his chair. Karen forgot everything else as she recognized pain in his eyes. She moved forwards quickly, but he held her off. 'I'll be OK.'

'Success?' Max said, his voice as gravelly as ever. 'Who's going to fill me in?'

'She should've told you,' Charlie said. He bent down to unzip an insulated backpack and brought out two bottles of Pol Roger. 'Thanks to her, we got a more or less full confession from Giles Henty: the drugs and the fear that Billy was going to talk about them. Ownership of the rifle. Confession about how he slipped away from the last drive before lunch, and took a shot at Billy. It all fits. The CPS are happy. His lawyer's bitten the bullet. He'll be going down for a long time.'

'And Caroline?' Karen asked. She hadn't been able to take part in the formal questioning because of the unconventional part she'd played on the ferry. 'Has she confessed yet?'

Charlie's face registered a familiar frustration.

'Nope,' he said. 'In all the interviews she's played a blinder. Doesn't know what we're talking about. Certainly had a brief affair with Giles but it was over by mutual consent months ago. Had no idea he was involved in any kind of smuggling or making a market in coke on the Island. Terribly shocked. How could a man like that ...? Etc.'

'What about the phones?' Karen asked. 'The unregistered pay-as-you-go phones you found in both her place and Giles's?'

'We've got Giles's, but it's no good without hers, which has gone,' Charlie said. 'And Giles won't implicate her.'

'In spite of all temptation,' Max suggested, singing the line from Gilbert and Sullivan's 'He is an Englishman' in a rich tenor that surprised them all.

'Bummer,' Karen said, sharing all Charlie's frustration. 'And presumably Caroline herself hasn't said ...?'

'Far too clever to implicate herself on any usable recording,' Charlie said. 'If we could get her for committing murder by proxy I'd do it. You know that. But we can't. No such crime yet.'

'Maybe not,' Max said. He'd been looking from one of them to the other, like the geese at Peg's pub on the Island. 'But there *is* conspiracy to murder.'

'Impossible to make it stick,' Karen said, looking sadly back at everything she'd learned about the Matken family, and everything she had worked out about Caroline's manipulations.

'More or less,' Charlie agreed. Something in his voice, some unusual bounciness, made Karen look more carefully at him. 'But we do have a witness to her and Giles rowing in one of his flats in the High Street, and him telling her he was dumping her, and ...' Charlie paused and looked first at Max and then at Karen, with an expression that made her think of someone about to give his child a particularly generous present.

'What?' she said, knowing her eyes must be alight with excitement.

'We have a statement from Olly about how his sister gave him a large amount of cocaine both on the day he killed Suzie and again on the day he went for Blazon's wife. He's lucid and rational on that score.' Charlie grinned, then added casually, 'We've found the dealer who sold it to her, too. In Bristol. She'd been planning this for a while.'

'Anything about how she told Olly that Giles was the

devil?' Karen asked, hugely relieved that her judgement had been so accurate.

'Something,' Charlie said, in a less bouncy tone.

'Well?' Will said, taking part at last. Karen was glad to see his eyes were clearer. The painkillers he'd taken just before the others had arrived must be working now. 'What did the poor boy tell you she said?'

'Olly isn't always as clear as that about the things she did and said to him,' Charlie said, 'but he did tell us the devil had hurt her, and that he knew the devil should be killed before he hurt anyone else. Olly must have thought Suzie was next in line for whatever Giles had done to Caroline. Especially when he saw her running away from the *Dasher* that day. Trouble is, he got muddled and killed her to keep her safe.'

'Another trouble is,' Will said in his familiar measured way, 'that you'd need a witness to make any jury believe it.'

Charlie acknowledged the truth of that with a sharp nod. 'Definitely. And we won't get one. Caroline was far too clever to do anything to Olly in front of witnesses that day.'

'But her buying the coke and giving it to him must go some way ...' Karen's voice died as she thought of the trials in which she'd been an expert witness and the way the barristers demolished anything that wasn't backed up by granite-hard evidence.

'It's probably enough to make everyone involved accept the part she played,' Charlie said. 'Her dad certainly does, and some of it may come out in court. Olly's lawyers will use everything they can to show that he was provoked. I doubt if we'll ever be able to charge her, but they'll call her as a witness.' Charlie laughed.

'What?' Will asked. 'None of this sounds *funny*.'

'I was just thinking how much I hate lawyers,' Charlie said, 'and the way they mess around with evidence and winkle doubt out of witnesses who looked solid at the start. But this time I hope they get the cleverest, most manipulative to have a crack at Caroline.'

Karen began to feel a little sorry for her, in spite of what she'd done to her brother.

'*Did* she go to see Olly after our session on the ferry?'

Charlie's dark face lit again and Karen felt an answering smile warming her own.

'She did. And she found a way to get my officer out of the way – charm and pleading and all that – unaware of the camera in the ceiling.'

'What does it show?' Will asked, looking from Charlie to Karen and back again. She loved the way his voice had taken on a new vigour and his eyes were clear of pain and frustration at last.

'Audio and visual evidence have him cowering in front of her and her telling him the devil will get him if he talks.' Charlie glanced at Will, looking at his sticks as though trying to decide whether he could take a full account. 'And a lot more of the same. Straight cruelty. He was cringing and chittering long before she'd finished.'

'So will you charge her?' Will didn't look at Charlie as he asked his question, concentrating on sending Karen a silent message of total approval.

'Don't know yet,' Charlie said, his voice dragging a little. 'They're looking at everything from conspiracy to murder all the way down to supplying a controlled drug. She's definitely a person of interest now. She should go down for something.'

'With luck,' Karen said, her sympathy disappearing into a longing for justice.

'Yup.' Charlie rumpled her neat blonde hair and nodded to Will again, broadening his voice into the full accent of his childhood. 'Your hinny here got the whole thing right. I'm beginning to think there might be something in this shrinky crap after all.'

Will laughed and held out a hand to her. She saw that his skin was still very thin-looking, but his hand didn't tremble. He was mending.

'I know there is,' he said, in a way that made Karen want to roll over there and then. In spite of the frustration over Caroline, life was looking wonderful.

Charlie pushed up the champagne cork with one hand, catching it in the other before it shot off across the room. The wine frothed up over the top of the bottle and he grabbed a glass to contain it, but missed so it fell into a puddle on the floor.

'Sorry. It's the beer all over again.'

'Don't worry about it, Charlie. I'll get a cloth.'

Karen hurried to the kitchen and rinsed out a J-cloth at the sink. As she was squeezing it she realized one of them had followed her and turned to see Max, looking at his most cynical. She waited, even though the champagne was probably lifting the varnish off her wooden floor.

'What?' she said.

'It's the eternal triangle.' He blew her a kiss. 'You know: you and those two. Rick and Victor Laszlo from *Casablanca*. Dark and light reflections of each other. Good friends except when they're fighting over the same woman. Arthur and Lancelot, too.'

Karen, bursting with satisfaction over Will's return from hospital and the ending of all her doubts about their future, laughed.

'And that makes you Merlin, I suppose,' she said, and kissed him.

N. J. Cooper
No Escape

'A fascinating, splendidly atmospheric read' *Guardian*

Spike Falconer is in prison on the Isle of Wight –
convicted of murder. What made him choose four
innocent strangers, a family picnicking, as
his victims? Why did he need to kill?

Forensic psychologist Karen Taylor come to probe
the mind of his psychopath. Trying to recover from the
death of her husband and the dark memories surrounding
it, Karen is drawn into life on the Island. She becomes
involved with DCI Charlie Trench, cool and abrasive,
the opposite in every way from her partner Will Hawkins.
And she has to get to know Spike's adoptive family,
the rich and influential Falconers, who are
tight-lipped and closing ranks.

Someone on the Island doesn't want Karen getting too
close to Spike. The more she learns, the more afraid she
becomes of those who are threatened by her discoveries.
And then they start to act . . .

'Informative and entertaining' *Daily Telegraph*

ISBN 978-1-84739-422-4

N. J. Cooper
Lifeblood

'If you ever talk about this, if you ever identify me to anyone, I'll find you and kill you. Wherever you are, I'll find you. And I will kill you.'

Five years ago Randall Gyre was convicted of the brutal rape of a young student, Lizzie Fane, on the Isle of Wight. Handsome, rich, slick-talking, Gyre had avoided prison for years before that, despite a string of accusations from other young women, who had been sadistically raped.

Forensic psychologist Karen Taylor is sure Gyre will attack again, and this time he will probably kill. She's prepared to stake everything – her career, her reputation – to protect Lizzie and any future victims. But Lizzie has vanished. Karen believes everyone involved in putting Gyre away could be at risk. She must warn DCI Charlie Trench – her friend, and the detective responsible for Gyre's arrest.

Soon people who gave evidence at the trial are murdered. Has Gyre started to kill, as Karen predicted? Has Lizzie herself turned avenging angel? Or is there someone else here, pulling the strings?

ISBN 978-1-84739-423-1

Natasha Cooper
A Poisoned Mind

How many people must suffer?

When a chemical explosion rips through quiet fields in
the north of England, it destroys much more than the
innocent life of the man who farmed them. In her grief
his widow, Angie, turns on the company responsible.
Enter hotshot barrister Trish Maguire, who finds herself
in turmoil when she is called on to defend not the ruined
and heartbroken Angie, but the multinational company
instead. Soon Trish comes to believe the explosion
can't possibly have been an accident, but who stood
to gain from such a dangerous act of sabotage?

Meanwhile, Trish faces trouble at home. Her adopted
son, David, has a new school friend in the damaged
and volatile Jay. When Jay's mother is found brutally
beaten, Trish finds herself embroiled in two major
battles – one for everything she has worked for,
and one for everything she believes is right.

'A smart, complex entertainment that rewards the
reader on every page. Intricate in plotting, deft in
characterisation, it is one of the best legal thrillers
I have ever read' Laura Lippman

ISBN 978-1-41652-682-7

Natasha Cooper
A Greater Evil

Everyone has something to hide.
Everyone has something to fear.

Abandoned as a baby and brutalised in care, sculptor Sam
Foundling is the obvious suspect when his wife Cecilia is
found beaten to death in his studio.

Trish Maguire, who acted for him when he was a child,
hopes he didn't do it. Her campaign for him brings her
up against DCI Caro Lyalt, the senior investigating
officer . . . and her own best friend.

Evidence against Sam mounts up. Cecilia's powerful
mother is pressing for his arrest. The police hierarchy
want him charged. If Trish is to save his sanity, she must
find out exactly what happened in the studio that
morning, and time is running out . . .

ISBN 978-0-74749-532-5

Natasha Cooper
Gagged & Bound

Knowing too much is dangerous. Telling can be fatal.

London is awash with secret information and vicious
rumour. A politician fights for his reputation. Gangs of
organized criminals poison the streets with their lesson
that greed and violence pay. Some of those who hunt
them bend the rules; others take their money.
A whistleblower goes in fear of her life.

Trish Maguire and her close friend, DI Caro Lyalt of
the Met, will have to disentangle fact from fiction if they
are to protect the innocent and pin down the guilty. but
their actions bring danger horrifyingly close to home . . .

ISBN 978-0-74349-533-2

This book and other titles by N. J. Cooper
are available from your local bookshop or can
be ordered direct from the publisher.

978-1-84739-423-1	**Lifeblood**	£7.99
978-1-84739-422-4	**No Escape**	£6.99
978-1-41652-682-7	**A Poisoned Mind**	£6.99
978-0-74349-532-5	**A Greater Evil**	£6.99
978-0-74349-533-2	**Gagged & Bound**	£6.99

Free post and packing within the UK
Overseas customers please add £2 per paperback.
Telephone Simon & Schuster Cash Sales at Bookpost
on 01624 677237 with your credit or debit card number,
or send a cheque payable to Simon & Schuster Cash Sales to:
PO Box 29, Douglas, Isle of Man, IM99 1BQ
Fax: 01624 670923
Email: bookshop@enterprise.net
www.bookpost.co.uk

Please allow 14 days for delivery. Prices and availability
are subject to change without notice.